INTRIGUE

Seek thrills. Solve crimes. Justice served.

Danger In Dade
Caridad Piñeiro

Holiday Under Wraps
Katie Mettner

MILLS & BOON

DANGER IN DADE
© 2024 by Caridad Piñeiro
Philippine Copyright 2024
Australian Copyright 2024
New Zealand Copyright 2024

First Published 2024
First Australian Paperback Edition 2024
ISBN 978 1 038 93899 2

HOLIDAY UNDER WRAPS
© 2024 by Katie Mettner
Philippine Copyright 2024
Australian Copyright 2024
New Zealand Copyright 2024

First Published 2024
First Australian Paperback Edition 2024
ISBN 978 1 038 93899 2

MIX
Paper | Supporting
responsible forestry
FSC® C001695

Published by
Harlequin Mills & Boon
An imprint of Harlequin Enterprises (Australia) Pty Limited
(ABN 47 001 180 918), a subsidiary of HarperCollins
Publishers Australia Pty Limited
(ABN 36 009 913 517)
Level 19, 201 Elizabeth Street
SYDNEY NSW 2000 AUSTRALIA

Cover art used by arrangement with Harlequin Books S.A.. All rights reserved.

Printed and bound in Australia by McPherson's Printing Group

Danger In Dade

Caridad Piñeiro

MILLS & BOON

New York Times and *USA TODAY* bestselling author **Caridad Piñeiro** is a Jersey girl who just wants to write and is the author of nearly fifty novels and novellas. She loves romance novels, superheroes, TV and cooking. For more information on Caridad and her dark, sexy romantic suspense and paranormal romances, please visit www.caridad.com.

Books by Caridad Piñeiro

Harlequin Intrigue

South Beach Security: K-9 Division

Sabotage Operation
Escape the Everglades
Killer in the Kennel
Danger in Dade

South Beach Security

Lost in Little Havana
Brickell Avenue Ambush
Biscayne Bay Breach

Cold Case Reopened
Trapping a Terrorist
Decoy Training

Visit the Author Profile page at
millsandboon.com.au.

To my amazing daughter and son-in-law, Sam and Dan.
Wishing you all the best on the addition of Axel Scott!
May he bring you immense joy!

CAST OF CHARACTERS

Brett Madison—Brett Madison loved his time as a military policeman and small-town local policeman, but when his old friend Trey Gonzalez calls and offers him a position in a new K-9 security division, Brett jumps at the chance to work with South Beach Security and build a new life in Miami. He never expected his first assignment will reunite him with the woman who has haunted him for years.

Anita Reyes—Anita has worked hard to establish her restaurant on Miami's hot Ocean Drive in South Beach. Anita is dedicated to her business but also longs for time with her family and a second chance at love after a marine ghosted her years earlier and broke her heart.

Mango—Four-year-old pit bull Mango is a new addition to the South Beach Security K-9 division.

Ramon Gonzalez III (Trey)—Marine Trey Gonzalez once served Miami Beach as an undercover detective. Trey has since retired and is now the acting head of the SBS Agency and hoping to expand it with the addition of a K-9 division.

Mia Gonzalez—Trey's younger sister Mia runs a successful lifestyle and gossip blog and is invited to every important event in Miami.

Josefina (Sophie) and Robert Whitaker Jr.—Trey's cousins Sophie and Robert are genius tech gurus who work at SBS.

Ricardo Gonzalez (Ricky)—A trained psychologist, Ricky helps SBS with their domestic abuse cases and other civil kinds of assignments.

Chapter One

The pit bull nearly yanked Brett Madison's arm out of its socket as the dog jerked its head back and forth, thrashing forcefully, the pressure on his forearm punishing.

"*Pust*, Mango. *Pust*," Sara Hernandez commanded, and the dog instantly released his arm and sat, staring at him as if ready to attack again.

Sara strolled over and bent to rub Mango's head affectionately, ruffling her short, glossy white-and-tan fur. "Good girl, Mango. Good girl," she said and fed Mango a treat as Brett slipped off his baseball cap and wiped sweat from his forehead. Despite the mid-December weather that had brought a cooling breeze through the doors of the training ring building, the dog bite suit was hot thanks to its weight and padding.

"Do you think she's ready?" he asked Sara, the K-9 trainer who South Beach Security had hired nearly seven months earlier to run their new K-9 training center just outside Miami.

Sara smiled and chuckled. "Mango's ready. What about you?" she asked and shot him a look from the corner of her eye.

Brett dragged a hand through the short, damp strands of his high-and-tight cut and shook his head. "Possibly. It's only been three weeks that we've been working together."

"A solid three weeks and you've had a K-9 partner before," Sara said and skimmed a hand down his arm to reassure him.

"I worked with a K-9 during my time in the Marines, but

it's been a while," he said and rubbed Mango's head as well to reward the dog for her good behavior. It was while working as a military policeman that he'd met SBS acting chief Trey Gonzalez and then served with him during a second tour in Iraq. A tour that they'd both survived, although the scars remained.

"I think you and Mango will be happy together," Sara said and slipped the muscular dog another treat.

Brett unzipped the suit and slipped out of it. The cooler air bathed his sweat-drenched clothes, rousing goose bumps on his overheated skin. He rubbed his arms to wipe them away and then accepted Mango's leash as Sara handed it to him.

"You're ready," Sara said, reassuring him yet again.

"I am," he said and glanced down at Mango, who cocked her head to the side and peered at him with joyful cinnamon-brown eyes and a friendly grin, her tongue lolling out of her mouth.

"You are, too, Mango," he said, almost as if to convince himself. It had only been three weeks since Sara had paired him up with the pit bull and while the dog had performed amazingly well during their training, it would take more work and time together for him to feel as if he and Mango would be up for anything Trey Gonzalez might assign.

His friend Trey had reached out to him months earlier while he'd been working as a police officer in a sleepy North Carolina town. He'd liked the quiet at first after the trauma from his tour of duty but had been feeling lost and dissatisfied after several years.

When Trey had called with the opportunity to join him in Miami, he'd jumped on it. The fact that Trey now trusted him with one of the coveted positions in their new K-9 training program spoke to the fact that Trey was pleased with what Brett had done so far with South Beach Security.

As Sara and he walked away from the training ring, he noticed Trey's cousin and Sara's new fiancé, Jose Gonzalez, leaning against the doorframe of the building, a broad smile erupting on his face as it settled on Sara.

She hurried to Jose's side and kissed him as he wrapped an arm around her waist.

When Brett approached, he held his hand out and said, "Congratulations on the engagement, Pepe."

"*Gracias.* Congrats to you as well on the promotion to the K-9 division," Jose said as he shook Brett's hand.

"Thanks. I hope I don't disappoint. I know Trey is keen on the K-9s taking off for the agency," Brett said. He owed Trey for believing in him after what had happened in Iraq.

"It was a rocky start what with the serial killer here at the kennels, but I'm sure you and the other agents Sara trains will be up to the challenge," Jose said and playfully squeezed Sara closer.

"I know Brett and Mango will be up for anything," Sara said, no indecision in her voice.

Brett smiled and dipped his head in appreciation for her trust in him and his new K-9 partner's capabilities, which were a testament to her training skills.

As they walked toward the former kennel owner's home where Sara was living with Jose, Brett bid them goodbye and peeled off to head to his car, Mango loping at his side. He buckled the pittie into the front seat and rubbed her head affectionately. The dog responded with a happy lick of his face and a doggy grin.

He was grateful for the dog's love since he knew the pit bull's powerful jaws and muscular body could inflict quite a lot of punishment if necessary. His forearm still ached from the earlier bite, and he was sure he'd have a bruise by the next day even with the padding in the suit. In a real-world situation, extensive thrashing combined with the bite could cause considerable damage.

"You're my girl, Mango," he said and massaged her head

and shoulders again to reinforce the relationship with his partner so that when the time came on assignment, he could trust
her to do as commanded.

He just hoped he would have a little more opportunity to
train with Mango before that time came. More than anyone,
he understood the dangers of not being prepared and what the
cost would be, he thought as he rubbed a spot by his collar-
bone. Beneath his fingers, the ridges of scars were a painful
reminder of the price of failure.

But not now. He would be ready when the time came.

THE NIGHT HAD been a killer.

Two of her line chefs had called in sick and a delivery of
her porterhouse steaks had gone missing, prompting a last-
minute menu change.

Her sous-chef, Melinda, pressed a glass of wine into her
hand. "Here, Chef. You need it."

Anita Reyes accepted the glass and peered around her restaurant's kitchen.

All the dinner tickets had been cleared off the rail, and despite being down the two chefs, the others had still been able
to clean as they cooked, leaving the kitchen relatively in order.

"Things look pretty good, Chef," she said.

Melinda nodded and gestured toward the back door. "They
do, and the butcher promised to get us those porterhouse steaks
for tomorrow. Why don't you get some air and enjoy that wine
while we finish up."

Anita had been running around all night filling in for the
missing line chefs while still doing her own job of making
sure that the orders were perfect and ready to go out to diners.
Her feet and back ached and sweat dripped down between her
shoulder blades from the heat in the kitchen.

A breath of fresh air and sip of a fine wine sounded like
heaven.

She pushed through the back door and onto the small landing in the narrow alley between her restaurant and the hotel behind her.

The late-fall night wrapped her in nippy air, making her shiver as it chased away the warmth of the kitchen. The street noises from busy Ocean Drive and Collins Avenue were almost nonexistent in the alley thanks to the buildings sheltering it on either side.

She sat on the stoop, leaned against the brick of the building and sipped the wine, a tasty cabernet franc they'd been lucky to find at a local distributor. The floral vintage pleasantly slipped down her throat, and she breathed a sigh of relief that her killer night was almost over.

Long minutes passed as she relaxed but soon responsibility called her to return to her kitchen and make sure everything was in order so they could start all over again for tomorrow's lunch and dinner crowds. As tired as she was, she reminded herself how lucky she was to have attained her dream of owning her own restaurant, and a successful one at that.

Varadero, her Cubano-Latino fusion restaurant, rarely had an empty seat and dinner reservations were fully booked for the rest of December and into the new year, pulling a smile from her.

But that meant lots of arduous work, and as she slowly rose to return to the kitchen, the door of the hotel across the way burst open as a man flew out and tumbled onto the rough ground in the alley. The man scrambled to his feet, as if ready to run, but a second later a masked man rushed through the door, grabbed him and wrapped an arm around the man's neck.

She recognized the unmasked man as one of the hotel's owners, Manny Ramirez.

Anita froze in place, shocked by the scene playing out before her as the two men grappled in the darkness of the alley.

She had no doubt it was a fight to the death as light suddenly gleamed on a knife blade in the masked man's hand.

He punched the knife into Manny's side and, in a growly voice, said, "You know what we want."

Manny grunted and abruptly bent over from the pain of the knifing. That seemed to break his attacker's hold for a hot second.

A mistake, since Manny was able to take a swipe at his attacker's head. His hand connected and ripped off the mask. Exposed and clearly annoyed, the man tossed Manny away, pulled a gun from beneath his black denim jacket and fired.

A perfect circle marked Manny's forehead as he stood there for a shaky second, surprised by death before he collapsed.

Shock stole Anita's breath, and the sharp sound drew the killer's attention.

He whipped around to stare straight at her, as shocked as she was.

A heartbeat later, he pointed the gun and fired.

She ducked as the bullet whizzed by her head and bit into the brick. A chip flew off and grazed her cheek, propelling her to flee as the warmth of blood trickled down her face.

The man aimed at her again and she tossed her glass of wine at his head.

A perfect strike.

It stunned him long enough for her to dash into her kitchen. Locking the door behind her, she screamed, "Call 911!"

Chapter Two

The police detective standing across from her seemed better suited for a modeling gig than a cop's life.

Detective Williams was over six feet tall with a lean, muscular physique, ice-blue eyes, boyish dimples and chestnut-colored hair with thick, rumpled waves that fell onto his forehead.

"Do you think you could identify the man who shot at you?" Williams asked, pen poised over a small notepad.

In her mind's eye, the scene she had witnessed barely an hour earlier replayed itself like a movie, pausing at the spot where the mask had come off and then again when the killer had turned his attention to her. She rewound and replayed that section and nodded.

"I'm sure I can."

"Are you sure? I mean, you only saw him for what, a few seconds?" Williams pressed, his gaze narrowed as he scrutinized her.

Her answer was immediate. "Without a doubt. I'll never forget what I just saw."

With a nod, Williams looked toward the two police officers who had been the first ones on the scene in response to her 911 call. He waved a hand in their direction, and when they approached, he said, "Detective Gonzalez has arranged for a sketch artist to work with Ms. Reyes. Please take her to headquarters while I coordinate with the CSI team."

"Yes, sir," said Officer March, a petite young Latina, before turning to her. "If you wouldn't mind following us to our cruiser?"

"Of course," she said, even though the thought of leaving the safe space of her restaurant had her gut clenching with fear.

"I'll lead the way," said Officer Garrett, a strapping Anglo six-footer with shoulders as wide as the doorway and gingery blond hair.

Anita stood and followed the policeman outside, where several other officers kept back a crowd of bystanders who packed the sidewalk and spilled onto the street. It created a traffic backlog of the cars that normally cruised up and down Ocean Drive, wanting to be seen as well as to see what was happening along the popular strip.

There were just so many people, she thought, searching the crowd for the face she had seen in the alley. She had watched one too many crime dramas and knew the suspect often hung back to watch what the police were doing at the crime scene.

For a second, she thought she saw him, and stopped short, heart pounding so hard it felt like it was climbing up her throat.

Officer March immediately came to her side, partially shielding Anita's body with hers. "Do you see something?" she asked.

Peering around again quickly, Anita shook her head. "No, I guess not," she said and continued to the cruiser, where Officer Garrett had opened the door.

She slipped into the back seat, expelling a relieved breath, comforted by the protection of the police cruiser.

But as the car pulled away from the curb, she kept a sharp eye on the crowd, feeling the continued presence of the killer chasing her until they were blocks away and almost at Miami Beach police headquarters on Washington Avenue.

Breathing easier, she settled back into the seat and closed her eyes, but as soon as she did, that night's images flashed through her brain again. The fight. The knife. The perfect little circle in Manny's forehead before he became a lifeless heap on the ground.

She shuddered, wrapped her arms around herself and rocked back and forth, shocked yet again that she'd watched a man die that night.

That she'd almost died.

The cruiser came to a stop in front of the police station, and a second later Officer March slipped from the car to open her door. But as the young Latina stepped onto the sidewalk, a sedan screeched to a halt beside them and the windows on the cruiser's driver side exploded, sending glass flying everywhere.

Officer March hauled Anita down behind the protective barrier of the police cruiser.

"Shots fired. We need backup," she shouted into her radio and returned fire on their attacker.

The sharp retort of the gun had Anita covering her ears and hunkering against the vehicle body for protection.

Officer March cursed beneath her breath. "Officer down. Officer down," she screamed into the radio as, with another angry squeal of tires, their assailant's vehicle peeled away.

Anita shot to her feet in time to watch the late-model Mercedes fishtailing as it sped off.

Officer March raced around to the driver's side of the vehicle, and Anita followed, helping the young officer move her wounded partner to the ground.

"I'm okay," he said with a grimace even though he clearly wasn't. Blood leaked from his shoulder and the many cuts and scratches on his face.

Officer March bent to apply pressure to the wound, but a

mob of other officers and EMTs rushed in to take over. "We've got this," an EMT said as he went to work on Officer Garrett.

"Let's get you inside," Officer March said, and a phalanx of officers surrounded her as they rushed across the plaza in front of the station and into the modern-looking building.

When they burst into the lobby and the officers spread out to take defensive positions at the door, a very pregnant woman walked up to her.

"Ms. Reyes, I'm Detective Gonzalez. Please follow me," she said, but as Anita took a step, her knees suddenly buckled, too weak to support her.

Detective Gonzalez and Officer March were immediately at her side, slipping their arms through hers to offer stability.

"I'm sorry. I feel so stupid," she said.

But Detective Gonzalez reassured her. "It's okay. *You're* okay. We've got you now. It's not every day someone tries to kill you."

No, it wasn't every day someone tried to kill you. Twice.

But she wasn't ready to die.

She drew on every ounce of courage she possessed, straightened her spine and walked with the officers to an interview room.

MIDNIGHT PHONE CALLS were generally not good.

Tonight's call had been no different, Brett thought as Trey and he pulled up in front of the Miami Beach police station.

Crime scene tape surrounded a police cruiser with bullet holes in the doors and shot-out windows. Glass littered the street along with gun shell casings that a CSI team had marked for collection.

A small splotch of blood also stained the pavement and Brett hoped the size of it said the officer had survived the shooting.

Inside the station, they quickly cleared security and went

to meet Trey's wife, Detective Roni Gonzalez. Because of her pregnancy and a bout of bed rest a month earlier, Roni was on desk duty but still working cases.

Roni was waiting for them by her office door along with a cover-model-handsome thirty-something man Brett assumed was her partner.

"Good to see you again, Trey," the man said and shook his boss's hand before turning to him and saying, "Detective Heath Williams."

Brett shook his hand. "SBS K-9 Agent Brett Madison. This is Mango," he said and gestured to the pit bull sitting obediently at his feet.

"Nice to meet you," Williams said as Roni waved them into her office.

"What's up? You need our help?" Trey said and stood by the side of Roni's desk as she sat and rubbed a hand across her baby belly.

"There was a murder tonight in South Beach. We have a witness who the killer tried to take out right in front of the station," Roni said and handed Trey a piece of paper.

"This is the guy?" his boss said, and when Roni nodded, he handed Brett a police sketch of their suspect. A thirty-something man, either Caucasian or Latino, with a strong jaw, sharp, thin nose and small scar beneath one eye. Short-cropped dark hair in a precise fade made Brett think ex-military.

"Pretty bold to try to take someone out right in front of the station," Brett said and handed the sketch back to Roni.

"We feel the same way. That's why we're working on finding the right safe house for our witness, because we think this guy won't stop until she's dead," Williams said and leaned his hands on the top rung of a chair in front of Roni's desk.

"I guess you want to use the penthouse," Trey said, referring to the space that Brett had heard was reserved for the

Gonzalez family when they worked late nights or clients who were either visiting or needed extra security.

Roni nodded. "Just for tonight. If this guy knows I'm on the case and knows the Gonzalez family—"

"Hard not to know them in Miami," Williams said with a shrug of wide shoulders and a touch of facetiousness.

Roni ignored her partner and continued. "He'll probably assume that's what we'll do and might try to go there. We're worried he'll do that while civilians may be present. That's why we're working on finding another safe house. But we can't get that done for another few hours."

"Say no more. Since I figured this was very urgent, Brett and Mango are also here to help protect your witness," Trey said and gestured in their direction.

Mango's ears perked up at the mention of her name and Brett reached down to rub her head. "Mango and I are ready," he said and hoped it didn't sound like he was also trying to convince himself.

"Great. We have an initial witness statement and the sketch. By early morning, we'll be able to move the witness to a safe house. With your help, if that's okay?" Roni said.

Trey nodded. "Whatever you need, SBS is here for you and Miami Beach PD."

"It's appreciated, Trey. This is going to be a high-profile case. Reporters are already leading with this on the local news because the victim is well-known and we had a very public shoot-out in front of the station," Williams said.

Roni lumbered to her feet, her pregnancy belly making her slightly unbalanced, which made Trey slip an arm around her waist.

"You feeling okay?" he asked, clearly still in protective mode considering Roni's issues a month earlier.

"Feeling like a beached whale," she said with a carefree laugh and swept her hand across the large mound of her belly.

With his concerns relieved, Trey motioned for them to head out the door. Once Roni and he were in the lead, Williams, Mango and Brett followed them to an interview room at the far end of the hall.

Roni knocked to announce herself and at the "Come in," they entered.

A shocked gasp filled the air as he stepped inside.

"Brett?" the woman said and as he met her gaze, her surprise transferred to him.

"Anita?" he said and muttered a curse.

Chapter Three

"You two know each other?" Roni asked, her narrowed gaze skipping from Anita to Brett and back to Anita.

Intimately, Anita thought, and heat rose to her face, but her embarrassment was quickly replaced by anger at seeing the man who had ghosted her so many years earlier. A man she'd loved with all her heart.

Body tight with tension, she gestured to Brett and, in what she hoped was a neutral voice, said, "I was a cook at a place not far from where Brett was stationed in North Carolina."

"Anita made the best chicken and rice I've ever tasted," Brett said with a forced smile that was bright against his dark, well-trimmed beard but didn't quite reach up into his chocolate-colored eyes.

"It's on the menu at my restaurant," she said, trying to keep the conversation sounding friendly, although with a quick look at Roni, she thought the other woman had caught on that things were anything but friendly between her and Brett.

"Maybe when this is all over, I can get a plate of it," Brett said, sounding chill as well.

"I'd like that," escaped her before she could bite it back. The last thing she wanted was to spend any more time than was necessary with the marine who had broken her heart.

"Hopefully this will be over quickly," Trey said and clapped Brett on the back.

"I'd like that also," she said, wishing for the same thing.

"We're arranging for a safe house, but in the meantime South Beach Security will help in safeguarding you tonight," Roni explained.

"We're taking you to our offices on Brickell Avenue. We have a secure penthouse there. Brett and his K-9 partner, Mango, will stay with you until you move into the police safe house," Trey said.

Brett and her alone together tonight. Luckily not much was left of the night, since Brett and she had never been able to keep their hands off each other. But she'd learned the painful lesson that passion alone wasn't enough to keep a relationship going.

Hopefully the dog, a thick-bodied, medium-sized tan-and-white pit bull, would play chaperone and provide a buffer to keep them from making a mistake they would regret in the morning.

"If you're ready, Trey and Brett will run you over to the SBS offices," Roni said and gestured to the door.

"Ready as I'll ever be, but before I go, I wanted to know how Officer Garrett is doing," she said, mindful of the officer who had been injured earlier.

Roni smiled in appreciation of her concern. "He'll be fine. Bullet went through his shoulder without doing much damage."

"Good to hear. Please thank him for me."

"I will," Roni said and motioned for her to follow the two men and the dog out of the room. They made their way through the labyrinthian halls of the police station to a more secure back exit to the building.

A big, black unmarked SUV sat at the curb, ready to transport her to SBS's secure space.

She prayed Brett and his boss could keep her safe so she could get back to the restaurant that was her life. She'd toiled and worked too hard to let what had happened tonight keep her from her dream.

Brett helped her into the back seat and then harnessed Mango into the seat next to her, issuing the dog a command. The pittie instantly obeyed and sat, obviously well trained and obedient.

They pulled away from the station and were quickly traveling down Washington toward the causeway that would take them up and over Biscayne Bay to Downtown Miami where SBS apparently had their offices. As they drove, she kept a keen eye on the vehicles in and around them, but so did Trey and Brett.

It was clear both were on the lookout, their gazes constantly darting around to take in everything going on as they pulled onto Brickell Avenue. She caught a glimpse of a plant-filled courtyard decorated with Christmas lights and a nativity scene in anticipation of the upcoming holiday. The courtyard was in front of a large glass-and-stone structure, and they drove into an underground lot for the office building.

After parking, Trey and Brett hesitated, making her wonder until Brett said, "We need to make sure we weren't followed."

Long minutes passed until the two men were seemingly satisfied that it was safe to exit the vehicle.

"Wait for us," Brett said, not that she planned on going anywhere without them.

He and Trey immediately charged into action, exiting the vehicle and removing Mango from the dog's seat. Trey checked the area to make sure it was secure before Brett swung around to her side and opened the door.

He stood by her car door, hand close to the holstered gun at his belt while the other held Mango's leash as the pittie stood tucked tight to Brett's leg, as ready for action as her partner.

She stepped from the car and was straightaway sandwiched between Trey and Brett, who provided protection until they slipped inside the building's stairwell and hurried up the staircase to the lobby. Brett opened the door and delayed for a moment, making sure the area was clear before they hurried across the lobby and to the security area.

Trey paused to say something to the two guards there, and they did a quick look in her direction and nodded.

As they walked to the elevator bank, she heard the click and static of radios as one of the guards relayed instructions to other security people in the building.

Inside the elevator, Trey used a badge to grant access to the penthouse floor, reached into his guayabera shirt pocket and handed Brett a badge. "This will clear you to enter."

"Thanks," Brett said and slipped the badge into his shirt pocket.

In what seemed like only seconds, they soared to the penthouse, which Anita guessed was about twenty stories up from the vista visible outside the windows that made up two of the walls of the immense open space. The downtown buildings jutting up into the night sky seemed harsh against the delicate palm tree fronds dancing on a night breeze and the shifting, crystalline waters of Biscayne Bay. Bright moonlight kissed the bay, making the water glitter like diamonds in the dark. Here and there, Christmas lights were visible inside offices in the buildings and on the buildings themselves. A few of the offices even boasted Christmas trees with gifts beneath. Maybe Secret Santas like they did in her restaurant, she thought.

Inside the penthouse, elegant modern furniture somehow created a comfortable atmosphere, making her almost feel at home, especially as she took in the high-end kitchen at one side of the large area. It had everything a chef would need to make a gourmet meal, not that she would be staying there long enough to cook.

Trey gestured toward the kitchen area and said, "The fridge is fully stocked in case you're hungry. I imagine you didn't have time to eat tonight. There are clean clothes in the second bedroom if you want to shower and change into something more comfortable and get some rest."

"I'd like that," she said and offered him a weak smile in thanks.

Trey nodded and clapped Brett on the back. "I'll let you get to work. The guards are on alert down below and as soon as Roni has the address for the safe house, we'll move Anita there."

"Mango and I will make sure she's safe," Brett said and shot a quick look in Anita's direction.

She had wrapped her arms around herself tightly, and even though it had been way too many years since he'd last seen her, he had no doubt she was barely holding it together. Her face was pale, the lines as tight as her body, which vibrated from the tension.

He didn't blame her. Most people rarely witnessed a murder and were almost killed themselves, especially twice in one night.

Reaching out, he trailed his fingers down her upper arm and said, "Why don't you take a hot shower. It'll help you relax."

She opened her eyes wide and shook her head. "I'm not sure how I'll ever relax."

He understood. He'd felt the same way after his first battle as a soldier. He'd never killed a man, much less almost been killed. It was something that you never forgot. That settled in your soul, staying with you no matter how hard you tried to shake it loose.

As her gaze connected with his, she seemed to also understand and took a step closer, as if seeking solace, but then abruptly jumped away.

He got it. Being close would bring back too many memories. Remind him of how her body fit naturally to his, like they were two pieces of a puzzle meant to be together. It would feel like a homecoming, but that was the last thing she probably wanted after the way things had ended between them.

Instead, he said, "It's going to be all right. The police and SBS will keep you safe until we catch this guy."

She bit her lower lip, nodded and flipped her hand in the direction of the far side of the room. "Trey mentioned a second bedroom. Is it that way?"

He shrugged. "I've never been up here, but I'm guessing that's the way," he said and followed her to the far side of the space where three doors were visible. When they reached the second door, he stepped ahead to check the area, not wanting to take any chances, although he trusted that the building had been well secured even in advance of their arrival.

Sure enough, they had nothing to fear, and with that he left Anita to shower and returned to the large open space, Mango tucked against his leg.

He unleashed the pittie, rubbed her head and rewarded her with a treat for her good behavior. Searching through the kitchen cabinets, he located a bowl, filled it with water and set it out. Mango eagerly lapped up a drink.

Since he could also use a pick-me-up, he made a pot of coffee, and thinking that a full belly might help Anita relax, he gathered what he needed from the fridge for a Western omelet and started cooking.

He had just finished flipping the omelet when Anita strolled out in University of Miami sweats that were way too big for her. She'd had to roll up both the sleeves and legs of the sweats. The loose folds of the fabric hid the curves he knew were beneath the fleece, and that was a good thing. He'd loved to explore those curves way too much when they'd been together.

Her hair was damp, making it the color of rich cocoa. The darkness of her hair made her amazing green eyes pop against creamy skin. An angry two-inch-long scrape on one cheek marred her otherwise flawless face.

He was about to skim a finger across that wound, but pulled back, certain that was too intimate a touch. Much like this moment was becoming a painful reminder of other mornings spent with her when they'd been a couple.

To break that too-personal feeling, he busied himself with getting plates and cutlery as she sat at the kitchen island.

"THAT SMELLS GREAT," Anita said, watching Brett putter around the kitchen and return with place settings he set on the counter.

He went back to the stove, grabbed the frying pan and came over to scoop out pieces of the omelet onto the plates. After he did that, he said, "Coffee?"

She shook her head. "I don't think I could sleep if I had coffee," she said and then added with a harsh laugh, "Although I don't even know how I can think about sleep with someone trying to kill me."

He laid a hand on hers and squeezed in reassurance. "We'll keep you safe."

She acknowledged his statement with a quick dip of her head, unable to muster the optimism he possessed. But the aromas from the omelet, sweet pepper and onion mingling with the creamy eggs made her stomach grumble with hunger.

"It looks and smells great. You always made a good omelet," she said and immediately wished she could take the words back because they reminded her of what they had once been to each other.

"Thanks. I had a good teacher," he said, and his words elicited the happy but unwanted memory of her showing him how to flip the eggs restaurant-style. There had been lots of runny eggs on the stove and floor, but also a lot of laughter and love.

When he had gone, she had missed that laughter almost more than the sex, although the sex had been...

Fighting that recollection because it created an ache deep inside her, she asked, "How did you end up in Miami?"

He shrugged those wide, almost impossibly broad and muscular shoulders. "I wasn't up for another tour and got a job at a local police force. I was working there when Trey reached out to me about joining SBS."

Motion from the corner of her eye caught her attention. The pit bull moved away from a water bowl and settled herself close to Brett's feet with what sounded like a happy sigh. "And ended up with a K-9 partner."

Brett smiled, bent and rubbed the dog's head and shoulders, which prompted Mango to roll over and present her belly to him, tongue flopping out of her mouth. Her tail wagged enthusiastically, smacking loudly against the wood floor. He rubbed her belly, laughing at the dog's antics.

"Mango's a good dog. Smart. We've only been paired for about three weeks, but she'd been well trained before that," he said with a final rub and returned to finish the last of his omelet.

She dug into the food as well since the fuller her belly got, the drowsier she was getting despite her earlier comments about sleep eluding her.

Brett, apparently picking up on how she was battling to keep her eyes open, said, "Go get some rest. I'll clean up."

In the old days, they'd had a rule that whoever didn't cook had to clean, but those were the old days and now they were in new and uncharted waters. Still, there was comfort in remembering those old patterns even if they were breaking them and even though she didn't want a repeat of those yesterdays.

"Thanks for cleaning and thank you for the omelet. It hit the spot," she said, rose and was about to head to the bedroom when Brett's cell phone rang.

He answered, listening intently. Nodding, he said, "Got it. I'll bring her down."

Swiping to end the call, he said, "The safe house is ready faster than expected. We're good to go if you are."

"I'm good to go," she said although she wasn't sure she was. Despite how things had ended between them years earlier, there was a sense of security and comfort with him there. Going to the safe house felt like taking a step off a cliff. But if that was what she needed to do to have this whole ugly episode finished so she could get on with her life, she was ready to do it.

But was she ready to deal with Brett's sudden return to her life?

Chapter Four

Brett leashed Mango and led the way from the penthouse to where Trey waited for them in the lobby.

"Miami Beach PD has chosen a safe house in Aventura. Small condo in a complex on Marcos Drive," Trey said and handed Brett a printout with the details of the location.

Brett flipped through the pages, wincing at the photo of the ground-level windows, making it easy for anyone to take a shot into the condo. "Doesn't seem all that secure, and I thought they were worried about civilians?" he said and handed the papers back to Trey.

"Killer doesn't know where we're headed and apparently this was the best choice available on short notice. Aventura police are already guarding the location."

With a reluctant nod and quick glance back at Anita, he said, "I'll feel better once we check it out."

"Agreed. Let's get going," Trey said and pushed off to lead them across the lobby and to the parking garage. At the entrance to the stairs, he paused to make sure the area was safe and did the same once they entered the garage.

The men became human shields to protect Anita, surrounding her until they had her out of harm's way in the SUV with Mango sitting beside her.

Trey was at the wheel, alert for any movement out of the ordinary as they pulled onto Brickell Avenue. He turned in the direction of I-95 for the short fifteen-minute-or-so trip to North Miami Beach and the condo in Aventura. In no time they were moving along the expressway. Traffic was light in the very early morning hours, and like Trey, Brett kept an eye out for a possible attack, but all was calm.

As they exited for North Miami Beach and the hospital, a car quickly raced up behind them on a side street.

"Watch your six," Brett warned Trey, who nodded and confirmed, "Roger that."

Trey pulled to the right and slowed, cautious until the car whipped around them and sped off.

"Just someone in a rush," Brett said and relaxed a little as Trey made the last few turns and finally pulled up in front of the complex for the safe house.

It was a nice-looking building with condos that boasted good-sized patios. Unlucky owners faced the parking lot, but those on the opposite side of the building had gorgeous views of the condo's pool and the waters of Maule Lake, Eastern Shores to the left, Greynolds Park to the right and, in the far distance, Oleta River State Park.

It was those views that worried him since they'd be hard to protect against anyone with a rifle who wanted to shoot into the safe house, although he had noticed heavy metal hurricane shutters in one of the photos Trey had given him earlier.

As they neared the entrance to the building, he noticed the Aventura police car parked in front, but instinct had him reaching out to grasp Trey's arm and say, "Let's wait for them to approach."

Trey nodded and slowly inched up behind the police car but with enough space to maneuver around it in the event of an emergency. *Never let yourself get boxed in*, he remembered from his time in the military.

No activity from the cruiser greeted them when Trey

stopped the car, making Brett's gut tighten with worry. Turning slightly in the seat, he said, "Keep your head down, Anita."

She slinked down in the back seat and Brett said, "I'll go check with them."

He hopped out of the car and walked the few feet to the police car. The window didn't open as he approached, heightening his fear that something was horribly wrong.

He was a foot from the driver's door when he realized both officers were slumped over, clearly injured. Possibly dead.

Backpedaling, he had barely reached the SBS SUV when a shot rang out and pinged loudly against the hood of the vehicle. Exposed, he crouched down, raced to his door and hopped back in as another bullet tore into a wooden column by the front entrance of the condo building.

Trey whipped away from the parking lot and raced back onto the street to escape the shooter, who managed another shot against a side window and then the rear window, but luckily the SUV's bulletproof glass held.

Speed-dialing Roni, Trey said, "We were attacked at the safe house. Two officers are down. Send the EMTs."

Roni muttered a curse. "Sending help immediately. Williams will head there to see what he can find out. Where are you taking Anita?"

Brett jumped in with, "We could go back to the penthouse, but it would expose too many civilians to whoever is desperate enough to do something like this."

"Agreed. I'm taking her to one of our safe houses, only... How did he know where the safe house was?" Trey pressed.

A troubled silence followed until Roni said, "We'll see who had access to that info here and in Aventura."

"*Gracias.* I'll see you later," Trey said and ended the call.

Brett was worried about how the leak had happened, but before he could say anything, Anita spoke up.

"Do you really think someone at the police station leaked the location?"

Trey shrugged as he quickly backtracked to I-95. Once he was on the highway, he said, "This shooter—or whoever hired them if it's not the guy you saw—may have the connections to get that info."

"Where are we going?" Brett asked, concerned that whoever it was might also be able to find the location of this new safe house.

"We have a place in Homestead, not far from the air force base. We'll keep Anita there until we figure out what's going on," Trey said and pushed the vehicle's speed on the highway while also staying vigilant to see if anyone was following them.

Brett did the same, watching for anyone or anything that seemed suspicious. Thinking that whoever had shot at them had done it from a distance and probably would not have had time to get into a car to chase them.

But he didn't like such uncertainty because the two officers had been shot at close range, which meant someone else might have been nearby as well.

"I think there are two shooters. One who attacked the officers and another one who shot at us."

Trey dipped his head from side to side as he considered Brett's question. "I agree. It would explain the injured officers and how someone was also taking potshots at us from a distance."

"Great. Two people trying to kill me," Anita said from the back seat, and Mango must have sensed her distress since the dog did a little whine and laid a paw on Anita's thigh.

"Thank you, Mango," Anita said with the barest hint of a smile.

"Whatever is happening, we will protect you," Trey said and shot a quick look at Brett, who reluctantly nodded.

While he'd signed up to work on any assignment South

Beach Security would give him, he'd never expected that it would involve Anita. They had a history, and that history might make things difficult. It could even open a world of hurt if old emotions rekindled between them.

But he bit his tongue, thinking about what would be necessary to safeguard the house until they could figure out who was after Anita and end the threat.

The drive to the SBS safe house in Homestead was nearly an hour, which gave him way too much time to think about the danger Anita was in and how he and Mango were going to protect her, especially if there were two people working together now.

Those thoughts were still whirling through his head as Trey pulled off the highway and navigated the streets leading to a smallish one-story, coral-colored cinder block home. It was a street with well-kept homes, many of which boasted Christmas lights and decorations for the upcoming holiday. The safe house did as well, making it look just like any other home in the neighborhood.

Once Trey had slipped into the driveway and parked, his boss took a moment to peer all around before he said, "I'll open up and make sure it's clear."

"Mango and I will hang back until you give us the go-ahead," Brett said and went into action, opening the back door and freeing Mango so she could hop onto the concrete pad of the driveway.

Trying to act naturally, he walked Mango along the edge of the drive, letting her relieve herself while he waited for Trey to return. All the time he was on high alert, vigilant for anything that seemed out of the ordinary.

When Trey hurried out a few minutes later, he came to Brett's side and handed him the keys to the house.

"Everything is good inside. You're going to need some groceries and other supplies. While you get Anita settled,

I'm going to make a quick run to the store. They'll be open at seven," Trey said and gestured toward the car, where Anita patiently waited.

"Do you think my guarding her is a good idea?" Brett asked in low tones so only Trey could hear, still worried about the complications of spending time with Anita.

"I understand your concerns, but you obviously know her better than anyone else and that's a good thing. It can't be easy for her and if I'm not reading the signals wrong, you care for her," Trey said, clearly determined that Brett stay on this assignment.

"And that's the issue. Emotion clouds your judgment. We both know where that could lead," Brett replied, worried that feelings could get in the way of his decision-making as they had once with disastrous results.

"I know you still blame yourself, but it wasn't your fault, Brett," Trey said and laid a hand on Brett's shoulder, offering reassurance.

"It was my fault. I dropped my guard—"

"Like any of us would in that situation. I trust your judgment," Trey said and peered back toward Anita. "I think she trusts you, too," he quickly added.

Brett tracked his gaze to where Anita sat, staring out the window at the two of them. "I'm not sure that's true, not that it matters."

"It does matter, but I need to get you those supplies," Trey said and jangled the car keys in his face to signal it was time to get going.

With a reluctant nod, Brett clicked his tongue to command Mango, who had been patiently sitting at his feet, to walk with him to the car. After a quick glance around, satisfied everything was still safe, he helped Anita from the SUV.

"Thanks. It was getting a little warm in there," she said as he led her into the home, locking the door behind them.

Once inside, she stood in the living room and did a quick twirl to peer around the space. "This is home for now?"

"For now. Trey went to get some supplies, but hopefully you'll be able to go home soon," Brett said, understanding her concerns.

"I hope so. I can't be away from the restaurant for that long. I need to call my sous-chef and explain. Give her instructions on what to do. I also need to call my parents so they won't worry," Anita said and pulled her phone from her pocket, but Brett quickly laid a hand on hers to stop her.

"I'm pretty sure the police asked you to shut it off and not use it," Brett said.

Anita nodded. "They did, but I really need to let my people know what's happening."

Brett stroked his hand across hers to calm her, but she jerked her hand away, clearly uncomfortable with his touch. "Wait until Trey comes back. He may have a burner phone you can use. We don't want someone tracking your phone to this location."

ANITA NODDED, understanding the why of it even as she started to pace worriedly across the length of the living room.

Her sous-chef could handle things for a day or two, maybe more, if the two line chefs showed up for work. But if not, they'd have to make arrangements for temps and she'd have to change the daily menus. Order supplies.

Brett's hand at the small of her back stopped the whirlwind of worries that had been circling around her brain.

She faced him, shaking her head in apology. "I'm sorry. I have a lot on my mind."

He offered her a sympathetic smile and said, "I could smell the wood burning from way over there. I understand, but it'll be okay."

"The restaurant is my life, Brett. I've worked so hard and

now…" Emotion tightened her throat hard, making it almost impossible to breathe, much less talk.

"It'll be okay," he repeated and went to stroke a hand down her arm but then yanked it back, clearly remembering how she had shunned his touch earlier.

A bump by her leg had her looking down to where Mango was rubbing her head against Anita's calf, also trying to comfort her.

Their care lightened the weight of worry in her soul. Wiping away tears, she smiled feebly and, in a choked voice, said, "It's going to be just fine."

"It is. How about we get the lay of the land and see the rest of the house?"

She nodded and together they did a slow stroll around the one-story building to learn the layout, locating the primary bedroom with its private bathroom. Two other bedrooms shared a Jack and Jill bathroom. A nice-sized eat-in kitchen was right off the living room in the open-concept space. Glass sliding doors by the kitchen table opened onto a patio and nicely landscaped backyard. A white vinyl fence secured the yard and they stepped out into the early-morning light to scope out the backyard.

In all the rooms and the yard, Brett took his time to let Mango nose around, and at Anita's questioning look, he said, "I want her to be familiar with the scents here."

Although he didn't say it, she got it. *In case someone came here who didn't belong.*

They had just returned to the living room when Mango's head shot up and the dog hurried toward the front door and stood there, vigilant. A low, vibrating growl erupted from her at the sound of a car pulling up.

Brett walked to the window closest to the door and drew aside the curtain to reveal the SBS SUV sitting in the driveway. The driver's door opened, and the rear hatch lifted. Trey went to the back and then walked to the front door, carting several large bags.

Brett commanded Mango to heel and opened the door for Trey, who jerked his head in the direction of the car and said, "There are a few more bags in the back."

Brett and Mango flew into action, heading outside to bring in the rest of the purchases as Trey took his haul into the kitchen.

As Trey unpacked, Anita helped him stow the food in the cabinets and fridge, her mind already racing with what she could cook with the various ingredients. Cooking might help keep her from worrying about all that was happening.

"I see Roni has trained you well," she teased since he'd managed to buy a perfect assortment of fresh foods and staples to complement the pantry items she found as she stored things away.

"Very chauvinist of you. I'm actually the cook in the family," Trey teased back with a boyish grin on his handsome face.

"Then Roni is a lucky woman," Anita said.

Trey smiled and quickly added, "The stuff in the cabinets is fresh. We change it out regularly since we never know when we'll need to use this safe house."

A couple of minutes later, Brett and Mango returned with the rest of the supplies. She laughed as she realized Mango was carrying a bag in her powerful jaws.

"She wanted to help," Brett said with a chuckle and toss of his broad shoulders.

As Brett unpacked, she realized those bags held food for Mango as well as toiletries and clothing.

"I thought you might want to change and guessed at the sizes," Trey said as Brett held up T-shirts and jeans.

"Thank you, but I'm hoping I'll be home and in my own clothes soon," she said. That only earned worried looks on both men's faces.

"I hope so, too," Brett said as he opened the refrigerator to stow the milk and cream Trey had purchased. Of course, just the fact that Trey had laid in enough food for a week warned her that going home soon would be unlikely, which reminded her that she had to call her sous-chef and make arrangements for her restaurant and staff and call her parents to tell them she was okay.

"Brett said you might have a phone I could use to call my people and my parents and let them know what's happening," she said.

"I do. I'll get it for you," he said and left her and Brett alone in the kitchen to finish unpacking.

As they put away the last of the groceries, Brett said, "You'll be back at work before you know it. Don't worry."

She gritted her teeth and nodded. What was the sense of arguing when she knew it wouldn't change a thing about her current situation.

Trey returned to the kitchen and handed her a cheap-looking cell phone. "You can use this."

Taking the phone from him, she hurried from the room to have some privacy for the call.

Chapter Five

Brett watched Anita go, understanding her worries about her business, but he had his own concerns, namely keeping her alive.

"I get the feeling you think this might take some time," Brett said.

Trey nodded and leaned close. "Roni called. No leads on this guy. They're running his police sketch against all the databases, but so far nothing. I have Sophie, Robbie and John Wilson working on it as well."

Trey's tech guru cousins worked miracles for SBS and Wilson, Trey's new brother-in-law, had a supercomputer and programs that had helped the police and SBS on various occasions. If they couldn't make something happen quickly, he didn't know who could.

"That's great. What can I do to help?" he asked.

With a shrug, Trey replied, "Besides keeping Anita safe? Once I leave here, I'm going to find out why someone would want Ramirez dead. You're welcome to help me with that."

"If there's a computer here—"

"There's a laptop on the desk in the second bedroom. You can access our network with your own credentials. If you find anything—"

"I'll keep you posted," Brett said just as Anita returned to the kitchen.

"What do we do now?" she asked.

"Brett and I, as well as the rest of the SBS team, are working on identifying the suspect you saw. For now, just get some rest and stay alert," Trey said and hastily added, "I should go back to the office to oversee things."

"I'm not sure I could sleep, but I'll try," she said.

"Take the first bedroom with the bathroom. I need to use the computer in the second room," Brett said with a flip of his hand in the direction of the far side of the house.

Anita nodded, snatched up the clothing that Trey had bought and hurried from the room again. At the sound of the bedroom door closing, Brett said, "She's barely holding it together."

Trey nodded. "Understandable, but luckily she has you. You know her and what she'll need to face this."

Face this? Brett thought. Even he felt the weight of the uncertainty, but he would help her in any way he could.

"I'll take care of her."

Trey nodded and bro-hugged him. "As soon as we have anything, you'll be the first to know."

Brett dipped his head in acknowledgment and said, "I'll start searching for any dirt on Manny Ramirez."

With that, he walked Trey to the front door. Once his friend had left, Brett locked the door and returned to the kitchen to feed Mango before he started researching the hotel owner.

The pit bull greedily gobbled down the kibble, making Brett laugh.

He bent and rubbed the dog's sides after she finished and teased, "How you don't choke is beyond me."

The dog answered him with an almost knowing grin and a kibble-scented lick of his face.

"Let's get to work," he said and issued a hand command for the dog to follow him to the second bedroom, where, as promised, a laptop sat on a small desk.

He tried to make himself comfortable on the wooden chair,

but his holster kept on banging on the furniture's side, forcing him to remove it and place it on the desktop. Powering up the laptop, he started with simple searches on the internet to get a sense of who Manny Ramirez had been.

Luckily, a local magazine had done a piece on Ramirez as part of a Latino Heritage Month celebration. The article was a glowing tribute to how Ramirez had escaped Cuba as a young boy during the Mariel boatlift in 1980 and earned scholarships to a local university known for its hospitality management program. After graduating with honors, Ramirez had launched his career by laboring in low-level positions until he'd worked his way up to management roles in a variety of boutique hotels. He'd used those as a launching pad for jobs with a large luxury chain until somehow finally purchasing a run-down South Beach hotel with a business partner. Together, the men had turned the location around and made it one of the most well-known properties in the area.

It seemed like a success story on its face, but something niggled Brett's consciousness. Mainly, how the two men had managed to find the money to buy the building, which even in its shabby state had to have been worth a great deal of money.

Searching the web, he found a website that listed similar properties for sale and whistled as he discovered a hotel in the area that was on the market for well over twenty million dollars. A lot of money for two men who hadn't owned any property before that.

Unless, of course, they had partners who had bankrolled the purchase, he thought, mulling over that possibility and who might be involved.

That had him returning to his research until Mango raised her head from where she had been sitting at his feet.

"What is it, Mango?" he asked, then rose and grabbed his holster, slipping it back on his belt.

Mango immediately raced toward the door of the primary

bedroom, where she pawed at the bottom of the door, clearly sensing that something was wrong.

Hand on his gun, Brett listened at the door. A strangled cry rent the air, worrying him. He knocked on the door. "Everything okay in there?"

ANITA WIPED AWAY the last tears of the crying jag she'd allowed herself. Straightening from the bedspread, she hurried to the door, all the while hoping Brett wouldn't take note of the tears.

He hated tears. Hated to see women cry. He'd let that slip once when they'd been lying together after making love. Not long before he was supposed to ship out to Iraq, which had been the reason for her tears that night.

Sucking in a deep breath, she forced a smile and opened the door.

Brett's gaze swept over her features, apparently seeing too much since he reached out and drew her into his arms, offering solace.

She didn't fight him this time since the warmth and feel of his body supplied a sense of security and homecoming she'd been lacking for way too long.

The long hours at the restaurant had left her little room for a personal life, and the few times she'd tried, the relationships just hadn't felt right.

Right, like what she was feeling at that moment, held in his powerful arms. No matter how it had ended between them, Brett had always been the one man who had made her feel like she'd found home.

"I'm okay," she finally mumbled into his broad chest when prompted by Mango butting her head against her leg.

She absentmindedly reached down to pet the pit bull, but then yanked her hand back, remembering that Mango was a service animal.

"I know I'm not supposed to treat her like a pet, only she's just so friendly," she said.

Brett inched away slightly and peered down at Mango. "She isn't a pet, but she's taken a liking to you, and she is here to protect you. Right, girl?" he said and bent to affectionately rub the dog's ears.

What looked like a grin spread across Mango's mouth and she bumped her head against Brett's leg, as if confirming what he'd said.

"She's really special," Anita said, tempted again to pet the animal, and at Brett's nod, she did, earning a doggy kiss on her hand.

"She is. Like I told you, I haven't had her long, but she's smart and fearless. When I took her through the obstacle course, she didn't hesitate to do things like the tunnel, which freaks out a lot of dogs."

"I'm glad to hear you're happy with her," she said, especially since she supposed Brett and Mango intended to work together for several years.

"I am," he said and wavered, focusing on her face intently. "Are you sure you're okay?"

Her smile came freely this time and she nodded. "I am. What were you doing?"

"Research into Manny Ramirez to figure out why someone would want to take him out," he said and rose to his six-feet-plus height, reminding her once again of his physical power and presence.

Why someone would want to kill Manny had been on her brain for hours. With a shrug, she said, "He seemed like a nice guy. He was very welcoming and helpful when I first opened the restaurant."

"What about his partner?" Brett asked.

Anita gestured toward the kitchen. "Why don't I make us some tea while we discuss him."

She always found tea calming, unlike coffee, which made her hyper.

Brett nodded and flipped his hand in the direction of the second bedroom. "Let me grab my laptop in case we want to look up something."

"Great," she said and hurried to the kitchen, where she located a kettle and a tea box filled with an assortment of brews.

She filled the kettle and set it on the heat, pulled mugs from the cabinets and laid them out on the table.

When her stomach did a little growl, she remembered that Trey had bought cookies, possibly because he knew his friend Brett had a wicked sweet tooth. Going to another cabinet, she found the package and placed several cookies on a plate she set in the center of the round table in the eat-in section of the kitchen.

The house was actually a great starter home with a kitchen that had her itching to cook. Then again, most kitchens had her itching to cook, and since it seemed they'd be there at least for the night, she intended to make dinner later.

Brett entered the room, placed his laptop on the kitchen table and flipped the lid open on the tea box. "Earl Grey for you, right?"

She nodded and smiled, comforted that he had remembered her favorite. In turn, she pulled out two black tea bags and handed them to him. "I know you think tea is dirty brown water—"

"And I like it as dark as I can get it," he said, then accepted the tea bags and placed them in the mug.

"I could make you coffee if you'd like," she said, but he waved her off.

"Dirty brown water is fine. I know tea calms you," he said with a chuckle.

She sat next to him to wait for the kettle to whistle and said, "You were investigating Ramirez?"

He nodded, swung the laptop around and powered it up again. "I am. We're trying to figure out why someone would want him dead. Did you know him at all?"

Anita tried to recall what she remembered about the man. "He and his partner bought the hotel about six months before I signed the lease for the restaurant. I understand most people in the area were happy about it because it would mean more tourists and possibly more business."

Brett nodded and asked, "Do you know how he got the money to buy it?"

Anita delayed, feeling awful about speaking ill of a dead man. But then again, wouldn't it be worse to let his death go unavenged? With a shrug and bobble of her head, she said, "Rumors said it was more than just Ramirez and his partner in the business."

"Meaning?" Brett asked as he typed something into the laptop, possibly his password.

"I heard from another hotel owner that there was dirty money behind the purchase."

Brett digested what she'd said. "Could be just bad blood because that owner was afraid of losing business to a new place."

She nodded. "Could be, but I heard it from more than one person who didn't have an ax to grind."

"And where there's smoke, there's fire," Brett said and typed something else into the computer.

"What are you doing?" she asked, leaning over to read what was popping up on the screen.

"Checking the property records to see if any mortgages are listed. If they are, that might dispel any rumors about the dirty money," he said and turned the laptop slightly so she could see the results more clearly.

"There's a mortgage listed. They got a loan from a bank," she said, but shook her head. "What about all the renovations? That loan barely covered the cost of the hotel."

"Are you sure?"

With a certain bop of her head, she said, "I remember the listing price because I saw it when I was searching for a restaurant space I could lease. Unless they got a huge deal, that mortgage was only for part of the purchase and none of the renovations."

"That confirms some of the info I found before. I'll send this to Roni and Trey and see what they can do with it," he said and tapped away on the computer to email his colleagues.

The whistle of the teakettle made her pop up, grab a pot holder and shut off the stove. She picked up the kettle and poured the hot water into the mugs with their tea bags.

While Brett wrote his email, she grabbed some cream and sweeteners for herself, since he took his dirty brown water as black as he could, and prepped her tea.

"What else do you know about Ramirez and his partner? Anyone they work with?" Brett asked.

Cradling the mug in her hands, Anita found the warmth was comforting, as was the citrusy fragrance of the bergamot. She dipped her head from side to side as she considered everything she'd heard about the hotel or the two men who owned it. There had been the rumors about the purchase, of course, but not much else, except...

"I think Ramirez liked to bet on the horses and sports games."

Chapter Six

"Gambling? Did he do a lot of it?" Brett asked, imagining the kind of trouble Ramirez could have gotten into if his luck hadn't been good.

She nodded. "He invited me to go with him to some big racing event. At Waterside Park, I think. He said he had friends with connections and a VIP suite."

Brett hopped online and went to the website for the racetrack. A number of events were listed, and he read them off to her. "International Derby. Hibiscus Invitational Meet. Paloma Challenge—"

She jabbed her index finger in his direction to stop him. "That's the one. The Paloma Challenge. It's some fancy racing, music and food event. Ramirez even hinted that if I went, he would make the connections for me to be one of the featured chefs for next year."

"Makes me wonder how much one of those VIP suites might cost," he said and whistled after a quick search on the internet revealed the price. "Luxury suites can run over fifty thousand plus catering and liquor."

"Ouch. His connections obviously had big bucks."

"Possibly dirty big bucks, you said, right? I'll send that info, too, and see if they can get the names of who rented those VIP suites," Brett said and drafted another email to Roni and Trey so they could do additional research.

He got an email back almost instantly.

Video meeting tonight. Twenty hundred.

Confirming he'd be available, he let Anita know about the meeting.

"I hope they've made some progress," she said, shoulders drooping.

"I know you're worried about the restaurant, but we need to keep you safe," he said and stroked a hand across her shoulders, offering comfort.

Her lips thinned into a tight slash, and she nodded. "I know. I'm just not used to being away and cooped up like this."

He remembered how she had been quite active, often jogging or hiking when she wasn't working at the restaurant where he had first met her.

Deciding that he'd already made some headway in their investigations and that he had to keep Anita sane for the moment, he jerked a thumb toward the rear of the house. "Mango could use some exercise. A walk isn't a good idea, but there is that backyard out there. We could let her have some fun."

Anita peered at the pit bull, who gazed up at her adoringly. "I'd like that."

He shut down the laptop, rose and grabbed some treats from a bag that Trey had bought.

"*Kemne*, Mango," he said and reinforced the command with a hand signal, moving his palm toward himself.

Mango immediately hopped to her feet and followed the two of them out the sliding glass doors to the small square of fenced-in yard behind the home. There were well-tended flowers planted around the edges, adding bright spots of color against the white vinyl fence and emerald of the tropical plants in the beds. By the back door was a mesh bag with an assortment of sports balls, and Brett took out a tennis ball.

He tossed it toward the back of the yard and before he could even utter the command, Mango was chasing after the ball and returning to drop it at his feet. "Good girl," he said and rubbed the dog's ears.

He offered the ball to Anita, who tossed it and laughed as Mango shot off to retrieve the object and eagerly bring it back to her. She bent to rub Mango's head and chuckled as the dog hopped up to lick her face.

"*Lehni*, Mango. *Lehni*," he said and pointed to the ground to reinforce his down command.

Mango swiftly obeyed, but Brett could swear the dog seemed unhappy that he'd instructed her away from Anita. To reward her for obeying, he fed her a treat and rubbed her head. "Good girl. I know you love Anita, but you have to listen to me."

Grabbing the ball, he tossed it again and they continued playing the game with him and Anita alternating the throws. It seemed to do Anita well to escape her thoughts about what was happening. Her face lost some of its paleness and a healthy pink glow spread across her cheeks. Her smile was bright and reached up into her green eyes, making them sparkle like a finely cut emerald.

She could distract him from what he had to do, and more than once he had to force himself to keep his mind on the area around them, vigilant for any signs of danger. Luckily the hour passed pleasantly with them playing with Mango and him reinforcing some of the commands they'd been working on together at the new SBS K-9 training facilities.

More importantly, the hour passed without a threat, and he hoped that would continue.

"We should probably head back in," he said, keen eyes surveying the area around the backyard to make sure everything was secure.

At the door to the kitchen, he held out his arm to block Anita's entry, and at her questioning gaze, he said, "Just want to make sure it's safe."

Especially after what had happened just hours earlier at their supposedly secure safe house.

He opened the door and, with a hand command, confirmed the "go check" instruction with "*Revir*, Mango. *Revir.*"

Mango raced into the house. The patter of her nails on the floor sounded loudly as she did a loop around the primary areas of the home. Quiet told him she had hit the bedrooms, which were carpeted, before the sound of her approaching again on the hard wooden floors indicated that it was safe inside.

The pit bull sat just inside the door, head tilted slightly as if to say, "Why aren't you coming in?"

"Good girl, Mango." He rubbed the dog's head and fed her a treat as Anita and he entered the house.

"I didn't realize you could train a dog to search a home like that," Anita said while walking toward the fridge.

"It takes some training, but it's useful. Psychiatric service dogs are trained to do that so they can reassure patients who are fearful of people being in their space," he said and leaned on the counter beside her as she started taking things out of the fridge.

At his questioning glance, she said, "I figured I'd start prepping some things for dinner. Cooking relaxes me."

He nodded and flipped a hand in the direction of the computer. "I'll get to work while you cook." He wanted to say that it would relax him to know they were making some progress on the case, but he bit it back, knowing it would kill the happy mood she was in.

With that in mind, he sat at the kitchen table, opened his laptop and logged in to the SBS network to continue his research.

THERE WAS SOMETHING calming about the way the knife cut through the carrots. The sharpness of the blade easily broke the flesh, creating nice sticks she chopped into smaller pieces for the stew she'd decided to make. Stew was comfort food and boy did she need comfort, although having Brett nearby, as complicated as that was, helped, as did Mango's presence.

She'd heard stories about the kind of damage that pit bulls could do. Luckily Mango seemed to like her, she thought with a quick look at the dog, who had settled herself at Brett's feet as he worked.

Armed with that sense of safety, Anita tossed the carrots into the pot, where she already had onions, celery and beef cooking in the fat from the bacon she had rendered to start the meal. Bacon always added welcome smokiness and salt.

She stirred the mixture, careful to cook it slowly, building a nice caramelization of the beef and vegetables in the pot. The brown bits would add a ton of flavor to the sauce for the stew.

When she was satisfied the mixture was ready, she deglazed the pot with some red wine, also courtesy of Trey's shopping. Roni was a lucky woman if Trey was this conscientious at home.

Scraping the bottom and sides of the pan, she got all the brown bits off, added stock and then her grandmother's mix of spices for her *carne con papas* stew. Oregano, pepper and bay leaves would add more flavor to the sauce. She'd add the potatoes later.

"Smells great," Brett said from beside her, startling her and making her jump. She had been so focused she hadn't heard him approach.

"Just me," he said, then laid a hand on her shoulder and gently squeezed to calm her.

Heart pounding, she splayed her hand over her chest and said, "A little jumpy."

"Understandable," he said, so close, the warmth of his breath spilled across her forehead. The smell of him, so familiar, both restored calm and unsettled her.

It was difficult to have him so close. The hard feel of his

arm next to hers. And his hand, so strong and possibly deadly, yet incredibly gentle as well.

It roused memories of the way it had once been between them, and as she looked up and met his gaze, it was clear he was thinking much the same thing.

She gestured with an index finger, pointing between the two of them. "This doesn't make any sense considering how things ended."

His lips tightened into a line as sharp as her knife. "I never meant for it to end that way."

She raised an eyebrow in both question and challenge. "With you ghosting me?"

Looking away, he abruptly shook his head and released a long, rough exhale peppered with an awkward rush of words. "I didn't mean to, only...the deployment wasn't going well and...you had mentioned a new job in another town. I didn't want to do anything that might hold you back."

It took a long moment for her to take in all that he'd said, but then she blurted out, "I'm sorry the deployment didn't go well for you but maybe talking to someone about it might have helped."

And she'd taken the new job mainly to get away from Brett and any memories of him.

BRETT WASN'T SURE that anything at that time could have helped him deal with what he'd experienced on the battlefield and the lingering effects of it.

"Maybe. It's not the kind of thing you share, especially with...civilians," he reluctantly admitted and quickly tacked on, "I wanted to look for you when I got back, but I couldn't. I wasn't the same man and wouldn't have been good for you. But I'm sorry I hurt you. I never meant to do that."

"And here we are now. What do they say? Fate works in mysterious ways?" she said with a shrug, then turned her attention back to dinner and covered the pot to let the stew simmer.

"It does, only...this isn't quite how I pictured a reunion and..."

His long hesitation had her glancing back up at him. "We can't trust anything we're feeling?"

He nodded. "You can say that. We've got a past and now this unpredictable present."

"But definitely not a future?" she pressed, narrowing her gaze to try to read what he was thinking.

The last thing Brett wanted to do was to hurt her, but developing feelings for her again could make him hesitate when he had to act or take unacceptable risks. That had cost him once dearly. It was the reason he wasn't the same happy-go-lucky guy she'd once loved. For those reasons, he gave a final squeeze to her shoulder and whispered, "I'm not sure this is the best time to think about a reunion."

The muscles in her jaw clenched and her lips flattened into a slash of displeasure. Her eyes, those gorgeous emerald-colored eyes, lost any luster and grew cold and distant.

"You're right. It isn't," she said and pointed toward the kitchen table, where his laptop and papers sat, waiting for him.

"I'm going to get back to work." He didn't wait for her reply before returning to the table and settling in to do more research on Manny Ramirez, his partner and any of the people he associated with at the races or his hotel.

In more than one photo he noticed the same few faces. He saved those photos to a file on his laptop and made a list of their names.

One name popped out at him: Anthony Delgado.

Brett hadn't been directly involved with the SBS case involving a possible serial killer at the location of the new SBS K-9 training center. He'd been working on another assignment, but he'd heard Delgado's name mentioned in connection with the kennel investigation.

He had no doubt Trey would immediately zero in on that name as well since it was way too much coincidence that a real estate developer with shady connections would also be tied to Ramirez.

Occam's razor. The simplest explanation is often the most likely answer.

Except that seemed a little too simple and obvious and stupid.

Why would Delgado do something to draw attention to himself?

Setting aside Delgado, Matt researched the other names on the list. Many of them were connected to horse racing and another name caught his attention: Tony Hollywood.

The mobster's name had been tossed around during another investigation a few months ago involving sabotage at a local racehorse stable.

SBS K-9 Agent Matt Perez was now engaged to the owner of the stable. He made a note in the file to have someone at SBS chat with Matt and his fiancée, Teresa Rodriguez, about the names on his list.

As he worked, the sound of Anita toiling in the kitchen and the smell of dinner accompanied him, creating a very homey and comforting environment. For a moment he could almost forget that they were dealing with a life-and-death situation... until he reminded himself that it was Anita's life at stake.

Anita, who I still care about more than I should.

He glanced in her direction. She was busy stirring something on the stove, slight frown lines across her forehead as she focused.

She had slipped into the cotton shorts and T-shirt that Trey had bought for her. They were slightly large but did nothing to hide her generous Cuban curves. Curves he was well familiar with and created an unwanted reaction that had him shifting uncomfortably in the chair.

He muttered a curse beneath his breath, but it had apparently been loud enough to draw her attention.

She stopped stirring and glanced in his direction. "Did you find something interesting?"

Chapter Seven

Yes, you.

He bit it back and instead said, "I'm wondering what you're so busy stirring."

The barest hint of a smile slipped across her face. "I remembered you liked cheesy polenta and thought that might be fun with the stew instead of rice."

"Totally fun," he said while reminding himself that nothing about what was happening was fun. But faking it made it easier to deal, especially for Anita.

Because of that, he shot to his feet and said, "I'll set the table so we can eat before the meeting."

The meeting.

Anita had gotten so involved with prepping dinner that she'd almost forgotten about the meeting. And about Brett. *Almost* being the operative word.

It was impossible to forget that the man she'd loved with all her heart was now just feet away. When he'd stopped writing or video calling her so many years earlier, she'd feared that he'd been killed, but after asking around, she'd learned that he was alive and well. Physically well anyway.

She'd gotten the sense from his earlier awkward response that the aftereffects of his deployment still possibly lingered. She told herself not to care. Not to wonder how he liked being in Miami and working with his old friend Trey Gonzalez.

She forced herself to do what she did best, ladling spoonfuls of the polenta into large bowls and topping it with the beef stew, hoping it would soothe their nerves. To finish the dish, she sprinkled fragrant chopped parsley for a bit of freshness and frizzled onions she'd fried for texture.

She picked up the bowls and took them over to the table. After, she returned to the kitchen, grabbed the bottle of wine she had opened to cook and went to pour some for Brett.

He waved her away and said, "No, thanks. I need to stay clear."

She did a small pour for herself, more to savor it with the meal she'd prepared than to calm herself. She didn't think there was much that would help ease both her fear and the conflicting emotions about Brett.

Returning the wine bottle to the kitchen counter, she poured water for Brett and brought it to the table, where he was waiting for her to eat.

"Go ahead, please. Don't let it get cold," she said as she sat, but he held off until she was in her chair to fork up some of the polenta and stew.

As soon as it was in his mouth, he hummed in appreciation and said, "This is delicious. Thank you."

"You're welcome. I figured we needed some comfort food with all that's happening."

Brett nodded and forked up another big helping that he ate before he said, "I'm sorry this is happening, but we'll get you home as soon as we can."

"That would be great. I worry about being away from the restaurant," she confessed.

He hesitated for a second, ate another healthy portion and then said, "You always wanted your own place. When did you open it?"

"About three years ago. I started with a food truck and that did well. At one of the food and wine festivals in South Beach

I made some connections that landed me on a few television cooking competitions. I was lucky enough to win," she said, then picked up her glass and took a sip of the wine.

"It wasn't just luck. You worked hard and you're a great chef," he said and fixed his gaze on her, as if he wanted her to see the sincerity in his words.

She smiled, appreciating his support. "Thank you. The competitions let me build a nest egg to open the restaurant, and once I did I got some nice reviews and more television appearances. It was demanding but worth it."

"Wow, I'm with a celebrity chef," he said, a note of playful awe in his voice.

Laughing and shaking her head, she said, "Not much of a celebrity but it is fun to be on television."

DEFINITELY MORE FUN than the way she might be plastered all over television now because of the murder, he thought, but didn't say, wanting to keep the discussion upbeat and casual. She'd had enough of death and destruction for the moment and would have more of it once they had their meeting later.

"I've never been on television. What's it like?" he asked and ate as she described the chaotic atmosphere of the televised cooking competitions, the pressure to win as well as the hectic moments as they filmed the segments.

He finished his bowl well before she did, rose and got himself another helping because the food was too delicious not to have seconds. But seeing she still had way too much on her plate because she'd been telling him about her television appearances, he said, "I'm sorry. I didn't mean to keep you from eating."

"It's not that. I'm a mindful eater. I guess it's a downside of being a chef. I'm always analyzing everything I eat. The mouth feel. If it's lush. The textures and taste," she said and finally scooped up a larger forkful.

He got it. He was always on the lookout for things that were out of place or could be dangerous to whomever he was protecting, he thought but didn't say.

Keep it casual, he reminded himself.

"You always could pick out all kinds of different flavors and textures when we went out for dinner," he said and winced, hoping his words wouldn't rouse unhappy memories.

A wistful smile drifted across her face. "We used to have fun…" she began, then shook her head and quickly switched gears. "How did you end up in Miami?"

With a shrug, he said, "It's a long story."

She wiggled her fingers in front of her in a come-and-share way. "I think we have all night at least."

He laughed harshly since he couldn't disagree with that. "I met Trey when we were Stateside, and I was working as an MP. When I deployed, I ended up working alongside him during our tour."

"You were both in Iraq at the same time?" Anita asked to confirm and resumed eating.

Brett nodded. "We were. It was hot, dusty and dangerous but we survived. When we came back, Trey headed home to Miami, and I stayed near the base. Found a job as a K-9 officer with a small local police force and did college part-time until I got my degree."

"I guess you didn't like being a cop?" she said, picking up his vibes.

With a dip of his head, he said, "It's much harder now, but I loved the job. Loved helping people. I just missed being near a big city. Small-town life wasn't for me."

"Why not go back to your family on Long Island?" she asked as she finally finished her bowl of polenta and stew.

He shrugged and said, "I was thinking about doing that when Trey reached out to me. He'd taken over the reins at SBS and was starting a new division. He remembered my work with the K-9s and wondered if I would be interested in working with him."

"And the rest is history," she said with a laugh and shake of her head.

"The rest is history," he repeated and chuckled.

"And here we are," she said and held her hands palms up, as if to say, "What now?"

He wished he knew what would come next for them, but for now his sole focus had to be on keeping Anita safe. He couldn't allow any distractions that would keep him from that, including Anita.

"I'll help you clean up so I can get ready for the meeting," he said and jumped up.

"You mean so *we* can get ready for the meeting. I don't plan on just waiting around while someone tries to kill me."

She also stood, picked up their bowls and took them to the kitchen sink.

Admiring her determination, he said, "*We* will get ready."

He joined her at the sink and together they rinsed and loaded the dishes into the dishwasher, the actions a familiar pattern since they had done it so many times when they had been dating. As it always had, it calmed and brought a sense of peace he'd often lacked while serving in the Marines.

It was with that peace that they sat together at the table for the video meeting with his colleagues at SBS.

When the image snapped to life on his laptop screen, he transferred it to a nearby television, so they'd have a larger image. Trey, Mia, Roni, Robbie and Sophie sat at the conference room table in the SBS offices.

"Good evening," Trey said, beginning the meeting.

"Is it a good evening?" Brett said, hoping his boss and friend might have good news.

The grim look on Trey's face immediately provided the answer. "Unfortunately, we're not any closer to finding out how the safe house was compromised. Because of that, we're going to be keeping Anita at our location for the time being."

Brett nodded. "Understood."

"Good," Trey said and pushed on with the meeting. "We looked at the info you sent over. We uncovered much of the same information. Delgado came to our attention during the kennel investigations."

Brett knew there was possibly more and said, "What about Hollywood?"

Trey nodded. "When we helped Teresa Rodriguez with the attacks at her stable, we also learned about Tony Hollywood. He's a mobster the FBI believes is involved in some illegal activities at the racetrack. I put my money—no pun intended—on Hollywood having a connection to this murder given Ramirez's possible gambling."

"I think we should focus on Hollywood," Brett said and everyone at the SBS table nodded in agreement.

"Good. Because of that, we've reached out to the FBI agents who were investigating Hollywood to see if they can add anything to the mix," Trey said.

"We also have John running Hollywood through his program to see if it confirms our suspicions," Mia said, referring to her newlywed husband and the software he had created that could predict the possibilities of almost anything.

At Anita's questioning look, Brett leaned close and whispered, "I'll explain later."

With a quick bob of her head, the meeting continued with Roni joining in. "The FBI believes Hollywood runs some kind of gambling ring. Fixing races, loan-sharking, illegal betting. It's possible Ramirez was involved or owed Hollywood money and our suspect was sent to clean things up."

"I'm sorry to say this, Roni, but it seems possible that if a police officer owed someone money, they could be pressured to supply information to Hollywood or his associates. Like the safe house location," Brett said.

Roni's face hardened and she frowned at his suggestion, but with the slightest nod, she reluctantly said, "It's possible. My partner, Detective Williams, is investigating that angle."

"Thank you, Detective. I know that can't be easy," Anita said, clearly reading the other woman's upset.

"It isn't, but we'll check every possible angle to make sure you're safe, Anita. Believe that," Roni said, then winced and rubbed a hand across her baby belly. "Sorry, the baby kicked. Sometimes I wonder if she wants to come out early and in time for Christmas," she said with a laugh.

Christmas, Brett thought. It was barely three weeks away, but the holiday was the last thing on his mind.

"Hopefully we'll all be home for Christmas," Anita said and shot Brett an encouraging glance.

"Hopefully," he echoed and wondered if he might somehow be spending Christmas with her as he often had in the past. He'd even taken her home to Long Island one Christmas, making his family wonder if she was "the one."

And she had been until everything that had happened in Iraq, he thought, and shook those thoughts from his head to focus on the meeting.

"In the meantime, Robbie and I are searching various sources for more information on Hollywood and his associates. We're also using facial recognition software to see if we get any hits against the artist's sketch of our suspect," Sophie said.

Robbie seconded that with, "We'll find something. I'm sure of it."

Brett didn't doubt that. Trey's tech guru cousins and fellow SBS agents were NSA-level smart. Together with Mia's tech genius husband, he was sure they'd find out more before the FBI or police would. They were just that good.

"I don't doubt it. I'll keep working at my end as well," he

said, hoping he could also help to bring this investigation to a quick close.

Once that happened…

He didn't want to think about what that would mean for him and Anita now that they'd been thrown together again.

"Great," Trey said and clapped his hands as if to signal that they were done. His next words confirmed it. "Let's all get to work on these various leads, but also get some rest. We need to be sharp if we're going to break this case and get Anita home safe and sound for the holidays."

After everyone echoed his sentiments, Trey ended the video call, leaving Brett and Anita at the table, peering at each other.

"Are you okay with all that?" he asked, wondering what she might be thinking about their actions and how they impacted her life.

ANITA SUPPOSED SHE'D have to be okay with all that they were doing to keep her safe.

"What choice do I have? You said you'd explain about Mia's husband," she said, puzzlement on her face as she recalled Mia's mention of him during the meeting.

Brett nodded. "She married John Wilson, the tech billionaire, a couple of months ago."

"And he has some kind of magic program?" she asked, still confused by the connection to the well-known and eccentric billionaire.

"You could call it that. His program sucks in data from all over and analyzes it to predict the actions that might occur, the likelihood that suspects are involved in a crime. Even victims before they become victims. All kinds of things like that," Brett explained.

It seemed a little woo-woo to her, and while she wasn't a Luddite, she preferred things she could touch and feel, which was likely why she was a chef. She loved the hands-on aspect of cooking. It grounded her.

"It sounds almost sci-fi to me, but if it works…"

"It works. I've seen it in action, but it's still hard to believe although AI can do a lot of amazing—"

"And scary things," Anita jumped in. She'd seen deep fakes and other worrisome AI-generated elements.

Brett nodded. "Definitely scary so it's good Wilson is on our side. He lets SBS use his supercomputers for a lot of our work and that gives us a huge advantage over the authorities."

"I'm glad also. I'd love for this nightmare to be over quickly," she said and gestured toward the bedrooms. "I'm going to watch some television in my room. I don't want to bother you when you work."

"You can watch out here. When I'm concentrating, nothing bothers me," he said and jerked his head in the direction of the large TV mounted on the wall and the very comfy-looking couch with its soft, deep cushions.

She tracked his gaze to the couch and large TV. "Thanks, I will."

It wasn't because of Brett that she'd stay there, she told herself. No, it wasn't, she argued internally but at the same time she couldn't deny that having him nearby brought a maelstrom of emotions. Peace, comfort and that something else she didn't want to acknowledge yet. She was still working through the hurt caused by his ghosting her and reminding herself that she had her own life now. One she'd fought hard to achieve, and which didn't have time for any kind of relationship. Especially one as complicated as it would be with Brett.

Even with all those misgivings, she snuggled into the welcoming couch cushions and flipped on the television, surfing through the channels until she found one of those treacly sweet movies that drew her into the forgetfulness of happily-ever-afters. This one was about two chefs, their nieces and an unexpected cooking competition.

Perfect, she thought as she gave herself over to the entertainment and grew drowsy.

As her eyes drifted closed, the actors on the screen melded into her and Brett, bringing visions of a happy, carefree life. But as she closed her eyes, a sudden abrupt movement roused her.

Chapter Eight

Brett had been deep into the info on the screen when Mango's head shot up.

The pit bull stood and stared toward the sliding doors that led into the backyard and growled.

A shadow shifted across the darkness.

Brett shot to his feet as one of the glass doors shattered, sending shards flying into the room.

"Get down, Anita," he shouted and whipped out his gun, but before he could shoot, Mango launched herself at the intruder and clamped down on the man's arm.

He dropped his gun and it clattered onto the floor.

Brett issued the attack command to reaffirm Mango's actions. "*Útok*, Mango. *Útok*."

The man was screaming and beating on Mango's head with his free hand.

Brett took a step in the intruder's direction but suddenly a second man burst through the broken door, forcing him to confront the new attacker.

"Hold or I'll shoot," he said, pointing his weapon at the man, who didn't seem to care, maybe because he was wearing armor on his upper body.

Brett didn't have that advantage and raced behind the kitchen island for protection, drawing him away from Anita as she huddled behind the couch.

Bullets slammed into the wood and quartz of the island, sending bits and chips of wood and countertop flying.

At a pause in the shooting, Brett surged to his feet and returned fire, striking the man mid-chest.

The man grunted from the force of the blow, stunned for a heartbeat, while a few feet away, his partner was still battling Mango, evening the odds.

The armored attacker fired once more, driving Brett to duck beneath the kitchen island again, but he couldn't stay there, leaving Anita unprotected.

He jumped up and fired at the second intruder's exposed legs. One of the bullets struck home.

The intruder muttered a curse in Spanish and grabbed at the wound.

In the distance, sirens rent the night air, growing louder as they sped closer.

"Vamanos," the wounded man shouted at his partner and trained his gun on Mango to free him from her powerful hold.

Fearing Mango would be hurt, Brett instructed the pit bull to release the man and come to him. *"Pust*, Mango, *Pust. K noze."*

In a blur of white and tan, his dog raced to his side and behind the protective barrier of the island.

The two men, realizing their mission had failed, scurried back out through the broken remains of the door.

Brett zoomed toward the couch to make sure Anita hadn't been injured.

She cowered close to the floor, clutching the burner phone. She gazed up at him, eyes wide, her face white with fear. In a stuttering whisper, she said, "I—I—I c-c-called 911."

"You did good," he said, holstering his weapon, and held out a hand to help her up.

She grasped his hand and, once on her feet, launched herself into his arms. "You're okay," she said, hugging him hard.

"I am and so are you, thanks to Mango," he said, and at the

mention of her name, the dog, who had followed him over, bumped their legs with her head.

He released Anita and bent to examine Mango, worried about the blows the intruder had inflicted. "You okay, girl?" he asked as he examined the pittie.

Mango sat and licked his hand as he ran it across her head.

Pounding on the front door had him back on his feet.

"Police. Open the door," someone shouted.

He hurried to the front door and peered through the peephole. Satisfied that it was the police, he opened the door and stepped back, hands raised as if in surrender so that they would see he was not reaching for the gun he had holstered at his side.

The cops rushed in, guns drawn. "Hands up. Keep them up there where we can see them," the one cop shouted. He planted a hand in the middle of Brett's chest and forced him back against the wall while his partner reached over and removed Brett's gun from the holster and tucked it into his waistband at the small of his back.

Mango, who had moved with him to the door, growled at the cop, forcing Brett to command the dog to sit. "*Sedni*, Mango. *Sedni*."

Anita shouted from across the width of the living room, "Stop. They're the good guys."

"I'm SBS K-9 Agent Brett Madison and this is my partner, Mango. If you let me put my hands down, I'll get my ID out of my wallet," Brett said calmly, trying to de-escalate the situation.

"Don't move," the cop said, training his gun from Brett's head to Mango's as the dog sat beside him, growling. Ready to attack.

The other officer walked over to Anita. "Are you the one who called?"

ANITA NODDED, fearing for Brett and Mango. "They are agents for South Beach Security. Brett is my bodyguard and Mango, the dog, is his partner," she said, gesturing to the pit bull.

The officer narrowed his gaze, peered at her intently and, seemingly satisfied, turned to his partner and said, "You can stand down."

His partner hesitated, still eyeballing Brett, who was several inches taller and broader, as well as Mango. Both dangers if his partner was mistaken. But then the officer reluctantly complied and holstered his weapon.

"I'm guarding Ms. Reyes because she's an eyewitness to a murder. You can call Detectives Gonzalez and Williams at Miami Beach PD to confirm," Brett said.

Turning, he slowly reached for the wallet in his back pocket with one hand, the other still held up in surrender. Once he had the wallet, he finally removed a card that he handed the cop. "Or you can call Trey Gonzalez, who runs SBS," he added.

The officer took only a quick look at the card and glanced over to where his partner stood with her. "It looks legit, Sam."

Sam—Officer Monteiro, his badge read—nodded. "Can you tell us what happened?"

"Two men shot their way into the house," Anita said and pointed toward the shattered glass of the ruined sliding door.

"Mango was able to restrain one intruder, who dropped his gun," Brett said and gestured to the weapon sitting on the wooden floor. Anita noticed that there seemed to be some blood there as well.

"What about the blood?" the officer asked, also noticing it as he walked over to examine the scene, careful not to step on any possible evidence.

"The second intruder had on body armor. I had to shoot at his leg to take him down," Brett advised, then supplied physical descriptions of the two men and pressed on. "They ran once they heard the sirens, but they had to have left a trail to their transportation. Maybe our video cams or those of the neighbors might have more info."

"We'll secure the scene until the detectives arrive," Officer Monteiro said, then walked toward Brett and returned his weapon.

Brett had no sooner holstered it when his phone started ringing. "It's Trey," he said and walked over to Anita while placing the call on speaker. Despite his calm tone, his body vibrated with tension, and he raked his fingers through the short strands of his hair almost angrily.

"What's the sitch? Are you safe?" Trey asked.

"This is a soup sandwich," Brett said, words clipped and harsh.

At her puzzled gaze, he said, "Mission has gone all ways of wrong, but we're both okay. How did they know we were here?"

"We don't know. We're still working on the first leak," Trey said, the frustration obvious in his voice and the heavy sigh that drifted across the line.

"We're moving from here, Trey. Pronto."

"Detectives won't be happy if you run. They'll want to interview you," he said.

Brett shook his head sharply. "We've got to go before these guys can regroup. I know a place that should be safe, but I need wheels," he said and scrubbed his beard with one hand, his agitation clear.

"SBS K-9 Agents Perez and Rodriguez are closest to you. They can get there in less than fifteen minutes. Roni and Williams are also on their way to work with the local PD detectives," Trey advised.

Brett met her gaze, his brown gaze filled with steely determination. "Sorry, boss, but we're not going to wait around for them. Anita is not going to get killed on my watch."

A tense silence filled the air. "We're not going to let that happen. But we need to work with the police."

"Working with people we can't trust? I won't make that mistake again," Brett replied and shook his head, lips pursed. Every line of his body radiated fury that had nothing to do with what had just happened, Anita thought.

"You wait but get ready to go to your new location. There are burner phones in the desk drawer in the bedroom. Use them for all future communications. There's a pouch there also. Take it with you and use the cash inside for all purchases," Trey instructed.

Brett relaxed, but only a little. "Roger that, Trey."

He ended the call and slipped the phone into his jeans pocket. "Pack up your things so we can head to the new location once we're done with the detectives."

"Will that do any good?" Anita asked, worried that the new place wouldn't be any safer than where they had already been.

Brett laid a hand on her shoulder and squeezed. "Do you trust me, Anita?"

Trust him? The man who had broken her heart? But the image of him putting himself in harm's way to keep her safe just moments earlier immediately replaced those thoughts.

"I trust you," she said, and he shifted his hand, wrapped his arm around her shoulders and drew her in to his strong and very capable embrace.

She wavered at first, but then relented, needing the security of his arms, fighting the rise of old emotions while at the same time telling herself he wasn't the same man she had once loved. He was harder now, not as easygoing as he had once been.

Whatever had happened before, what he clearly didn't want to happen again, had changed him.

When he shifted away slightly and met her gaze, his was dark, the melty chocolaty brown almost black. Troubled. "We need to get ready to run again."

She nodded. "I'll go pack."

BRETT WATCHED HER GO, muttered a curse and dragged a hand through his hair.

If not for Mango... I won't go there. I won't let that darkness claim me again.

He bent and rubbed the dog's ears and body, confirming yet again that the dog hadn't been seriously injured by the intruder's blows. "You're a good girl," he said, earning some doggy kisses in response.

But he had to get moving and grab what he needed to keep Anita safe.

Rushing back to his bedroom, he found the burner phones and pouch in the desk and a large empty duffel in the closet. He tucked one phone into his back pocket. The pouch and the rest of the phones went into the duffel along with the clothes Trey had bought for him.

Back in the kitchen area, he packed the laptop and filled a couple of reusable grocery bags with food, including Mango's kibble. They wouldn't be able to risk leaving the new location for supplies until he was confident they hadn't been followed.

Anita walked to meet him at the kitchen table, her things tossed into a plastic bag.

"You can put them in that duffel. There's plenty of room," he said, and she packed them as instructed.

"You've got company," the officer guarding the front door called out.

He peered past the cop to where his fellow K-9 agents Matt Perez and Natalie Rodriguez stood with their dogs, Butter, a Belgian Malinois, and Missy, a Labrador retriever.

Brett walked to the door to coordinate with his fellow agents while he waited for the detectives to arrive. As he reached them, Matt held up car keys, but as Brett went for them, Matt shifted the keys away and reminded, "Trey wants you to wait for the detectives. Full police cooperation."

"I know. I don't like it, but that's what the boss wants," Brett confirmed.

"Trey needs to keep things chill with the LEOs," Natalie said.

Brett understood. SBS often worked in connection with

local law enforcement, and they had to keep a good working relationship with them. But that didn't change one very important thing on this assignment.

"I'm sure it's a cop who's leaking our safe house info."

Matt and Natalie shared a look, and then nodded in unison.

"We agree, but we cooperate for now while we work on this case," Natalie said, basically echoing what Matt and Trey had said earlier.

Brett looked away and shook his head. Blowing out an exasperated breath, he said, "We cooperate, but as soon as we're done, Anita and I are out of here."

"Agreed. You'll let Trey know where you're going?" Matt asked, gaze narrowed as he peered at Brett.

He nodded. "Trey and only Trey."

Natalie gestured to the driveway. "We'll secure this area, but after the detectives arrive, we'll see if they'll let us track your attacker's trail to where they had their getaway car."

"That sounds like a plan. Thanks," he said and went back inside to wait.

Wait and worry. Wait and fume about the leaks that were threatening Anita's life.

He more than most knew the danger of not knowing whom to trust. In Iraq his indecision had cost his squad two good soldiers and a young child's life as well. The memories of their deaths still haunted him. He wouldn't repeat that mistake again. Especially since it was Anita's life at stake. He gazed over to where she sat on the couch, waiting for the detectives to arrive.

Chapter Nine

He reminded her of a caged tiger at the zoo, pacing back and forth across the narrow width of the kitchen. It was as if he was trying to burn up the angry energy sizzling through him.

The two officers gave him plenty of room, as if sensing that he was on the knife's edge of keeping control, and it once again struck her just how different he was from the man she'd once loved.

That man was still there. She'd seen glimpses of him in the gentle way he'd been caring for her, from making an omelet to the way he'd held her, as if she was something precious.

But now a hard veneer made of danger and anger had slipped over him, two emotions she'd rarely seen from him before.

It made her wonder again what had caused the change and if it was for the better. Or maybe that facade was what he needed to work for SBS. She'd seen something similar in his boss. Hard and in control but also caring and protective, especially around his wife, Roni.

Brett met her gaze for the briefest moment, and she glimpsed the caring there, but also fear.

He hadn't wanted to wait, worried that every second they lingered at the no-longer safe house presented danger.

Luckily, the detectives for the local police force arrived and peppered first Brett and then her with questions about the attack. Sometimes they asked the same thing in different ways, as if trying to trip them up, but they remained consistent even as she could feel Brett's rising anger, like lava getting ready to spew out of a volcano.

When he scrubbed his fingers across his hair for like the tenth time in the last ten minutes, she laid a hand on his arm to hopefully ratchet down his growing exasperation.

"I think that's about all the information we can provide, detectives. I'm sure Detectives Gonzalez and Williams can give you more details about this case once they arrive, so if you don't mind, we'll be going," she said in that sweet and very polite way her Miami mother had taught her.

And she didn't wait for their approval, knowing it was unlikely to come.

She just marched to where they had made a pile of their clothing and supplies, grabbed as many bags as she could and made a beeline for the front door.

Brett chuckled beneath his breath and followed her lead.

As they bolted past the officer stationed at the front door and rushed to where Natalie and Matt stood guard by their SUVs, he murmured, "That took *guts*, Anita."

"Why, thank you, Brett," she said with a laugh.

"You two good?" Matt asked, bewilderment on his features as Brett opened the back hatch and began loading the bags.

"Could be better, but we'll survive. Thanks for all your help," Brett said and shook his hand and Natalie's.

"Anytime. We kept the perimeter clear of any lookie-loos. Hopefully no one got any info they could use to track you," Natalie replied and quickly added, "As soon as Roni and her partner get here, we'll try to follow the blood trail to see what we can get on your attackers."

"Roger. Send that info when you can," Brett said and held the passenger door open for Anita to hop into the SUV.

He harnessed Mango into the back seat, got behind the wheel and plugged an address into the GPS.

"Where are we going?" she asked as he drove out of the development.

"A marine buddy has a place down in Key Largo. He's a skier so he's normally up north at this time of year and lets me use the place if I want to get away," he said and shot a quick look at her. "It should be safer than any police or SBS locations."

"Should be?" she repeated, not liking the uncertainty of those words.

His hands tightened on the wheel, knuckles white from the pressure he was exerting.

"Only Trey will have the address, so I know it won't get leaked."

"You don't think he'll tell Roni?" They were married after all, she thought.

BRETT PURSED HIS LIPS, giving it some consideration before he said, "I think they can separate business from the personal."

Or at least I hope so.

In the months he'd been working for Trey, he'd realized that SBS wasn't just a business, it was family as well. From the top down, the employees were all either family or an extended part of the Gonzalez clan. Even some recent clients had become relations by virtue of becoming involved with the SBS K-9 agents or Gonzalez family members.

That realization had him shooting a quick glance at Anita and wondering if somehow that would be possible for them.

Until he reminded himself that he had to keep this all business and avoid any distractions that could jeopardize her life.

He dragged his gaze away from her, giving his full attention to the road and keeping an eye out for anything out of the ordinary. Much as it had on the morning drive to the safe house, everything seemed in order. No one tailing them.

At least not physically.

With today's technologies, that was no longer necessary. Cell phones and tracking devices provided a digital trove of location information to those who knew how to collect that data.

SBS was always cautious about sweeping their vehicles to make sure they were clean. The burner phones also worked, although Trey, Anita and he had used their personal phones until their arrival at the Homestead location.

He was confident Sophie and Robbie, the tech geniuses at SBS, could easily use that phone data to know where they had been.

Could the bad guys be that sophisticated or was it a simple case of someone at the police department overhearing and leaking the information?

The simplest explanation, he reminded himself, only twice in one day?

The Aventura location could have been gleaned from discussions at the stationhouse, but Trey hadn't provided the Homestead address to anyone at the department, as far as he knew. Even if he had told Roni, Brett was sure she would have safeguarded it considering what had happened.

"What are you thinking?" Anita asked, and as he glanced over at her, she added, "I'm climbing the walls wondering why this is happening."

"Why is easy. You can ID a murderer, but like you, I'm also worried about how they could get the address for the SBS safe house."

Anita frowned and her head bobbled from side to side as she considered his question. "You don't think it's a leak at the police department?" she asked, clearly picking up his vibes.

"I don't. Roni wouldn't share that with anyone," he said with a nod.

She firmed her lips and looked upward, thoughtful, and asked, "What about a tracker, like an AirTag or something like that?"

"SBS sweeps for trackers on their transportation. AirTag is possible, only we didn't bring anything with us where they could have slipped it and I think we would have noticed something in a pocket."

"That leaves the cell phones, right? Is it that easy? Could someone be tracking us now?" she asked and peered out the window, searching the road.

"We've shut down our phones and they'd have to have access to telephone company data. That normally takes a warrant—"

"Unless they have someone on the inside there as well," she jumped in.

He didn't discount that someone like Tony Hollywood, if that's who was behind the attacks, was capable of that. But he didn't think even Hollywood could get that info so quickly.

"It's possible, but I'm leaning toward a leak at the police department and I'm sure Roni has taken steps to plug that leak," he said, trying to sound more confident than he was feeling.

"You were always bad at poker," she teased with a laugh and shake of her head.

He couldn't deny that. It was why he'd always avoided playing cards with his marine buddies.

"I am bad at poker, but I have to have faith that Roni and the SBS team will have our backs."

TONY HOLLYWOOD WAS more pissed than Santiago Kennedy had ever seen.

Hollywood marched back and forth across the floor of the now-empty garage of his used car dealership.

He'd cleared it out the second that Santiago had limped in with Hollywood's useless nephew beside him, cradling his arm and whining like a little girl about how the pit bull had broken it.

"Shut up, Billy," Hollywood snapped and whirled on them. "I sent the two of you to clean up this mess and you've made it even worse," he screamed, face almost blue from his rage. Veins popped out along his forehead and the sides of his thick neck, worrying Santiago that the man would stroke out.

Hollywood was a powerful man, well over six feet with thickly muscled shoulders and a massive chest barely constrained by the expensive bespoke shirts and suits he liked to wear.

"It's broke, Tony. That dog broke it," Billy whined again.

Hollywood's temper finally erupted.

He backhanded Billy across the face, nearly knocking him out of his chair. The blow left a bright red mark and an angry scrape, courtesy of the large diamond-encrusted championship football ring Hollywood wore.

Tony told everyone he'd gotten it playing on his college football team. While Tony was certainly big enough to have been a linebacker, Santiago knew he'd taken the ring in exchange for not breaking a man's legs when he didn't pay his gambling debts.

"Do you two know what the felony murder rule is?" Hollywood said, then leaned down and got nose to nose with Santiago. "Do you?" he shouted.

Tony's spittle sprayed onto Santiago's face, but he didn't flinch or say a word. That would only make Tony even madder, if that was even possible.

At his silence, Tony straightened to his full height and dragged his fingers through the hard strands of his gelled hair.

"I sent you to find out where Manny put my money, not to kill him, Santiago," Tony said.

"He saw my face, Tony. I didn't have a choice," Santiago said.

A mistake.

Tony leaned down, grabbed hold of his injured leg and dug his fingers into the wound. Pain blasted through Santiago's brain, nearly making him faint. Dark swirls danced before his vision as Tony said, "That makes me part of the murder. That gets me life in prison unless you fix this."

"I'll fix it, Tony. I swear, I'll fix it," Santiago whined, hating that he was sounding too much like Tony's gutless nephew.

"Fix it. Get rid of the girl. Find my money," Tony said with a rough dig into his leg that nearly made him vomit.

He swallowed the bile down and nodded. "I will, Tony. I just need a few more days."

"Make it right and take this little coward to the doctor. That arm looks broken," Tony said with a sneer as he glanced at his sniveling nephew. With a final annoyed huff, Tony stormed from the garage and back into the dealership showroom.

Santiago looked over at Billy's arm. Maybe it *was* at an odd angle. And he had to have someone look at his leg anyway before they went after the girl again.

Only this time he'd take out that pit bull first, so he'd have no worries while he made the man sorry for the hole in his leg.

As for the woman, he'd have some fun with her before he killed her. Payback for making his mess-up even worse.

Wrong move, wrong timing, wrong everything, Santiago thought as he slowly rose from the chair, wincing as pain shivered up his leg.

"Let's go, Billy. We've got to finish this so Tony won't finish us," he said and pounded the young man's back, part encouragement, part punishment.

Billy peered up at him, eyes wide with disbelief. "Finish me? I'm family," he whimpered and slowly got to his feet.

Santiago laughed and shook his head. "Tony's only family is money, Billy. Best you remember that," he said and limped toward the car they'd driven into the garage barely half an hour earlier after he'd called Tony to warn him about what had happened.

That's why the garage had been empty of the usual workers who'd be prepping and fixing the secondhand cars for the dealership Tony ran as a front for his assorted operations.

Operations Santiago knew a lot about. He'd made a point of learning and writing it all down. Insurance, he thought.

He might have made a mistake in taking out Ramirez, but he didn't intend to fry for it on Old Sparky.

Not alone, at least, he thought, and hopped back into the car to visit the doctor they used for situations just like this.

Once they were patched up, they'd find her, the man and his little dog, too, Santiago thought with a strangled laugh.

"What's so funny?" Billy asked.

"You. You're so funny," he said and finally drove out of the garage to finish what he'd started.

Chapter Ten

She hadn't thought it possible, but she'd fallen asleep and woken up to the views of wide-open expanses of water as Brett drove down South Dixie Highway on the way to his friend's home.

"Are we almost there?" she asked, voice husky from her short nap.

Brett smiled and shot a quick glance at her. "We're almost there. This is Barnes Sound and we'll hit Key Largo in a few miles. My friend's place is right near John Pennekamp Coral Reef State Park. Have you ever been there?"

He made it sound like he was a tour guide, and they were on vacation, but she guessed it was because he was trying not to worry her any more than she was already worried. Because of that, she said, "I've always wanted to go. I've heard there's some great snorkeling there."

"Glass-bottomed boats as well. Maybe after this is over…" His voice trailed off as even he must have realized how it sounded given their current situation.

"Maybe," she said meekly and gave her attention to the passing scenery, trying to distract herself from thoughts of the state of her life.

Water and more water. Greenery along the edges of the highway when it hit pockets of land. Every now and then she'd look back to see if anyone was following them. The highway rose over the water and then dipped down onto what she assumed was Key Largo.

More land and a highway with an assortment of businesses. Gas stations and stores catering to people who liked to scuba, snorkel or fish. The stores were fairly spread out on the road, with big patches of trees, palms and brush between them. Lots of boats, which made sense on what was a narrow spit of land surrounded by water. The Atlantic on one side and Florida Bay and the Gulf on the other.

The sign for the state park flew by and barely a few miles had passed when Brett turned off onto a small street barely wide enough for one car, much less two. A hodgepodge of houses, no two the same except for possibly the double-wide mobile homes here and there, lined the street.

Boats or boat trailers dotted the driveways of many of the homes. Front lawns struggling for life under the hot Florida sun and salt from the nearby waters were interspersed with homes where the owners had given up the fight and filled their front lawns with gravel or electric bright white shells. Overhead the fronds of palm trees swayed weakly with an offshore breeze, and holiday-loving owners had wrapped some of the trunks with Christmas lights.

She was sure that Brett, who'd grown up with snow and evergreens in New York, likely found that an incongruous picture, but having been raised in Miami, it was a familiar sight to her.

Several yards up, Brett pulled into a driveway much like many of the others, complete with an empty boat trailer. The stone crunched beneath the tires in front of the mobile home festooned with lights and a flat splash of color on the ground that she guessed might be an inflatable Santa.

"We're here," he said but held up his hand in a stop gesture. "Let me check it out first."

She waited as he exited the car and then released Mango from the back seat. Man and dog walked past a chain-link gate and approached the side door of the mobile home, where Brett punched in something on what she assumed was a digital lock.

Brett opened the door and called out, "Jake, you home?"

When there was no answer, he unclipped Mango's leash and signaled her to inspect the home.

Anita held her breath, nervous for the dog until Mango returned a few minutes later and sat at Brett's feet on the landing. Brett entered the home, hand cautiously on his holstered gun, but likewise exited a few minutes later and returned to the car.

"It's clear. Let's get settled and I'll call Trey and let him know we're good."

She wasn't sure *good* was the right word to use for their current situation. But they were alive, so she supposed that was as good as it got at that moment.

Nodding, she left the car and followed him to the back to grab their supplies. Together they entered the mobile home, which was surprisingly more spacious than she might have imagined.

The side door opened into a living room with two wing chairs, a coffee table, a couch and an entertainment center with a large-screen television. A breakfast bar with a sea-foam-colored countertop separated that area from a galley kitchen with standard stainless-steel appliances and clean white cabinets.

A glass door off to the side of the living room/kitchen led to a deck. Opposite the breakfast island were a bistro table and two chairs.

"The bedrooms are down the hall that way," Brett said with a flip of his hand to the end of the room as she laid a bag with groceries on the kitchen counter. "You can take the main bedroom at the end," he added.

She grabbed the bag with the few clothes she had and walked down the hall, pausing to peer into the guest bathroom and first bedroom, a smallish room with a window and bunk beds for kids, she supposed.

Which made her ask, "Does your friend Jake have a family?"

Brett met her at the door, his body too close to hers in the narrow space of the hallway. "No, but his sister does. She sometimes comes to visit in the summer when the kids are off from school."

She hurried from that room to the next because being so close to him had her body responding in ways she didn't want.

That room was larger with a queen bed, nightstand, dresser and small desk all in white that looked like IKEA offerings. Above the desk was artwork of a beach scene, likewise mass-produced. But the room was happy thanks to the sunlight streaming in through the window beside the desk.

"I'll take this room," Brett said, and she supposed it was partly because they'd have to go past him to get to her in the last bedroom.

The main bedroom was much like Brett's with all-white furniture that gleamed from the sunlight flooding through the window.

She tossed the plastic bag with her "clothes" onto the bed, jammed her hand on her hips and whirled to face Brett, who stood at the door, nonchalantly leaning on the doorjamb.

"What do we do now?" she asked.

IF IT HAD been years earlier, the answer would have been easy.

He would have walked over, kissed her and in no time they would have been on that comfy-looking bed, making love.

Just the thought of it had him hardening, but that was then, and this was now, and things were totally different.

He jerked a thumb in the direction of the kitchen. "I'm going to text Trey and then scope out the deck and see if Jake's boat is there. It might come in handy."

Not that he wanted to make an escape by boat, but if he

had to, he would. His dad and he would sometimes rent a boat at the Captree Boat Basin and head out to either the Great South Bay or the Atlantic. His father had always wanted to buy a boat or, as his mother had teased, a hole in the ocean you pour money into.

As Brett stepped out onto the tiny deck that somehow crammed in a small table and four chairs, he was surprised to see a very nice new Robalo 30-foot walk-around sitting on a boatlift by the dock on the canal behind the home. It had apparently replaced Jake's old fishing boat.

"Look at that, Mango," he said to the dog as she followed him out.

He whistled beneath his breath, wondering where Jake had gotten the money for such a luxury. From what he remembered of the catalogs his father always brought home, one as recently as his last Christmas trip home, a boat like this was easily over two hundred thousand dollars. Add several thousand for the power lift. It made no sense for a friend who often complained about being short on cash.

Jake's ears must have been burning since a spectral voice from the video camera by the back door said, "Dude, I thought someone broke in but then I saw it was you. Why aren't you answering your phone?"

"My phone broke. I have a new number. I'll send it to you," he replied into the speaker for the camera. He began to text Jake the number for the burner phone, but hesitated, well aware it might be a security breach. But he had trusted Jake with his life in Iraq and he still trusted him, although the expensive boat was worrying.

He texted the number and his phone rang a second later. "Hey, Jake. Sorry for not letting you know in advance that I was borrowing your place."

"No problema, dude. I'm up at Lake Placid for a snowboarding competition. Won't be back until the new year," Jake said, his voice barely audible over the noises in the background, a mix of bad bar music and boisterous shouts.

"Sounds like you're having fun," he said, keeping it chill to not tip Jake as to the actual reason for being there.

"A blast. YOLO, you know," his old friend replied.

"YOLO, *mano*. I love the new boat. When did you get that baby?" he asked, puzzled by how a friend who had only held intermittent jobs since leaving the Marines could afford it.

A long hesitation had the hackles on his neck rising. "You still there?" he pressed.

"Yeah, dude. I came into some money. That Camp Lejeune water settlement," Jake replied and for the first time ever, Brett wasn't buying it.

"I hope you and your family are okay, *mano*," he said, hoping they were all well and not suffering from the effects of the contaminated water at their old marine camp.

"We are. Nothing to worry about, dude. Enjoy yourself and have a Merry Christmas. I'll see you when I'm back in Miami," Jake said with forced merriment and hung up before Brett could ask him anything else.

For safety's sake, Brett shut off the phone to prevent anyone tracking that signal. He'd have to grab a different burner phone for future calls. He'd already texted Trey to let him know they were okay while Anita had been scoping out the bedrooms.

"Something wrong?" Anita asked as she stepped onto the deck and bent to rub Mango's head.

He could lie, but with their lives at stake, he didn't want a lie between them.

Motioning to the boat, he said, "That's a pricey toy."

"Boys with toys," Anita said with strangled laugh.

He nodded and rubbed two fingers together in a money gesture. "Yes, boys with toys, but Jake never had the cash for that kind of toy. He claims he got a Camp Lejeune settlement."

Anita narrowed her gaze and skipped it from him to the boat and back. "And you don't believe him?"

It was tough to say it about a man he'd trusted with his life on more than one occasion, but he didn't. "Jake's dad was a marine, too, and the family was stationed there when the water contamination occurred, so it's possible."

Anita digested that. "I hate to say it, but maybe SBS should check him out."

"Great minds think alike—"

"And fools seldom differ," she said, ending the quote for him.

"Better safe than sorry," he replied, dragging another rough laugh from her.

"We're just full of platitudes today, aren't we?" she said with a shake of her head, loosening a long lock of hair from the topknot she'd fashioned. It curled onto her forehead, and he reached over and tenderly tucked it back up the way he had so many times in the past.

"Thanks," she said and repeated the gesture, clearly uncomfortable with his touch.

It shouldn't have hurt, but it did. Still, he'd been the one to abandon her and couldn't blame her even as he told himself it had been for her own good.

Flipping his hand in the direction of the house, he said, "I'm going to take Mango for a walk and get the lay of the land. Please stay indoors."

THAT WOULD BE the safest thing for her to do, but Anita was tired of being cooped up in cars and houses. The inactivity provided too much time for bad thoughts to fester.

"I'd rather take the walk with you. I think I should know where to go, too, just in case."

He hesitated for a heartbeat, but then nodded. "It's a good idea."

Sweeping his hand toward the gate in the low railing that

surrounded the deck, he invited her to walk with him and Mango in that direction.

With a few short steps, Anita unlatched the gate and stepped onto the cement path that ran behind all the houses and next to the docks where boats in all sizes, shapes and colors lined a canal.

The late-afternoon sun was still strong, glaring down onto the area. She shielded her eyes with her hand as Brett asked, "Do you know how to drive a boat?"

She nodded. "My father used to take us out sometimes on weekends. Every now and then he let me be the captain."

Brett pointed eastward along the water. "At the end of the canal, take a left and head straight to Blackwater Sound and the Intracoastal Waterway."

"Good to know," she said, although she hoped that this time they wouldn't have to worry about making an escape, especially by water. Even though she'd regularly boated with her dad and sister, the vastness of the ocean oftentimes made her feel uneasy. Too alone even when surrounded by her family.

"Exit to the street is right around that corner," he said and pointed to the far side of the mobile home.

He clipped the leash on Mango, and they walked around the corner to a narrow alley that ran between the two homes. A double set of stairs ran to the side door, one leading toward the driveway and the other toward the canal and dock.

Brett opened the gate to the chain-link fence that formed a barrier between the homes in the alley and secured the side-entrance area.

Her sneakers crunched on the uneven white stone blanketing a driveway barely long enough for their large SUV.

The home was just a couple of doors down from the corner and Brett gestured with his hand in that direction and explained how to get back to the Overseas Highway in case she needed to get away.

It struck her then that he was preparing for her to go it alone, only she had no plans of doing so.

"I'm not going anywhere without you," she said.

His face hardened into a look she'd never seen before. It was a stony, impenetrable face that spoke volumes as he glanced away before slowly meeting her gaze again. She knew what he would say, and it sent a sickly chill through her body, making her stomach churn.

"You may have to."

"I'm not going anywhere without you," she repeated and laid a hand on her belly to quell the upset there.

He firmed his lips, battling to stay silent, and reluctantly nodded. Reaching out, he cradled her cheek and she leaned into that embrace, drawing comfort from his touch.

"We go together," he said and shifted his hand to wrap it around her neck and draw her into his embrace.

Less than twenty-four hours earlier she would have protested the move, but not now. Not when it was possible that they might die if they couldn't stop the attacks. That he would be willing to give up his life to keep her safe.

As she stepped out of the embrace, wiping away unexpected tears, he kept an arm around her waist and she did the same, slipping her arm around his.

Much like he'd changed emotionally, he had changed physically as well.

He'd been fit as a soldier, but much like he'd become harder emotionally, his body had become harder as well. Leaner and more dangerous, but maybe that's what he needed in this new line of work.

Well, that and Mango, she thought as the dog loped beside him, tongue dangling from her mouth until the animal looked up at her and seemed to grin. Except she had seen what that mouth could do and was happy Mango was on their side.

It was quiet on the narrow streets as they walked, the only

sounds that of the nearby oleanders and bushes rustling around them and an occasional boat engine in the distance. But as they walked the final block or two, the susurrus of passing cars intruded, warning they were close to the highway that ran from Key West all the way back up onto the mainland.

They turned and retraced their steps, stopping only to let Mango relieve herself.

It didn't take long to reach Jake's house again, but as he had before, Brett instructed her to stop by the gate while he made sure the area was still secure.

She held her breath, expectant, waiting for another attack, but seconds later Brett signaled to her that all was fine. She pushed through the gate and up the stairs into the home.

Inside the house, she flew into action, needing to stay busy to keep nasty thoughts from rooting in her brain.

Chapter Eleven

Brett watched Anita flit and flutter around the kitchen like a butterfly sampling nectar as she checked out the cupboards and fridge to see what was there.

She was already planning a menu, he could tell, and didn't interfere.

The planning would keep her busy and stop her from worrying.

What would keep him from worrying was knowing if they'd made any progress in identifying their suspect. Or maybe he should say suspects now that there were two of them working together.

Not wanting to add to Anita's worries, he walked to his bedroom and closed the door for privacy, but left it open just a gap so he could keep an ear open for any signs of trouble. When just the routine sound of pots and pans came, he called Trey.

"Good to hear from you, Brett. How's the place?" his boss asked.

"Safe. For now," Brett replied, that niggling worry about the boat ruining the peace he'd hoped to feel at Jake's place.

"What's the sitch?" Trey asked, picking up on his disquiet.

"Place is secure only… Could you do me a favor and check out something?" he said and when Trey agreed, he relayed the details about the boat, supposed settlement and Jake's real name and info. It made him feel guilty that he was doubting a friend, but he'd trusted the wrong person before with disastrous results. He refused to repeat that mistake.

"We can try to find out more," Trey confirmed.

"What about the leak? Any luck with that?"

"We've got the surveillance video from the back entrance at Miami Beach PD a short while ago. We're scanning it now," he said and quickly added, "The good news is that we think we've ID'd the initial suspect using facial recognition. I'll send you his info via email as well as several other photos for you to use in a photo lineup to show Anita."

Brett nodded. "Any connection to Hollywood?"

"Possibly. You'll see the rap sheet in the email. There's a major escalation from low-level bookmaking to assaults."

"You think he's been breaking legs for Hollywood?" Brett asked and blew out a rough breath, even more worried now that they had a more credible link to the mobster.

"Again, possibly. We may know more if the FBI ever gets back to us," Trey said, his tone filled with exasperation.

"Feds are slow-walking this. I guess they're worried the local LEOs are going to make their bust," Brett said, equally frustrated that the agents on the case would be more concerned with getting credit for the collar than keeping Anita safe.

Trey cursed the Feds and then quickly added, "We're going to get this guy. And his accomplice and Hollywood if we have to. Whatever it takes to keep you both safe."

"Agreed. Send me what you have—"

"I will. We'll have a video meeting at twenty hundred again, if that's good," Trey said.

With a shake of his head and rough laugh, Brett said, "I'll check my dance card and see if I'm free."

A troubled chuckle skipped across the phone before Trey signed off with, "Watch your six."

SANTIAGO SLOWED THE car they'd "stolen" from Hollywood's used car lot. If they got into trouble with it, they'd let Hollywood's manager know so he could report it missing to provide cover.

Police were still crawling all over the Homestead location. If Anita and the SBS agent were coming back here, it wouldn't be for some time.

"Why are we here?" Billy asked from beside him and gestured toward the house. His cast banged on the window, drawing the attention of an eagle-eyed cop at the curb, forcing Santiago to quickly drive away.

"You're a jerk," he said.

Billy glanced at him blankly and repeated his question. "Why? You think they'd be foolish enough to come back here?"

"Have you ever seen a rabbit on a trail when they're being hunted by a dog?" he asked.

Billy shook his head. "Do I look like I hunt rabbits?"

The Brooklyn was thick in his voice, picked up from his parents despite a lifetime in Miami.

Using one hand while keeping the other on the wheel, he mimicked Billy's accent as he said, "Rabbits will double back on a trail and wait for the dog to rush by, chasing the scent. As soon as the dog is far enough away, the rabbit will take off in the opposite direction."

"You think they're going to be rabbits and come back?" Billy said, eyes widening as the dim light bulb in his head went off as he finally understood.

"Maybe," Santiago said and pulled away to head back toward the Aventura location, another place they might rabbit to.

"What if they don't?" Billy pressed.

"If they don't, we'll find them some other way. Your uncle has a lot of connections," Santiago replied, thinking about the cop feeding them info as well as the many marks who owed Hollywood in one way or another.

A long silence followed, and Santiago could swear that he smelled wood burning. Flipping a quick glance in Billy's direction, the boy's troubled expression made his gut tighten with worry.

"What's up, Billy?"

Billy glanced at him and nervously plucked at a thread in a tear in his jeans. "Is it true what my uncle said? You know, about that rule thing?"

"The felony murder rule?" Santiago asked, just to make sure he was understanding Billy's concerns.

"Yeah, that thing," Billy said, sounding way younger than his twenty years.

Santiago understood his worry. Billy still had a lot of life to live and doing it behind bars was a scary thought.

Just as it was for him since he was only a decade older than Billy.

"It's true," he said, prompting Billy's immediate objection.

"But I didn't kill anyone. You shot Manny and the cops," he shouted, nervous sweat erupting on his upper lip as he pounded his uninjured hand on his thigh in agitation.

"It doesn't matter, Billy. You were there. You're as much a part of it as I am," he said steadily, trying to calm the increasingly agitated young man.

Waving his arms, his cast banging on the door and window again, Billy cried, "I won't go down for this. I won't. I didn't do it."

Billy was right that he hadn't pulled the trigger.

I did, and I'll be the one going to Old Sparky if Billy talks.

Which meant there was one more thing he had to do.

Like he'd thought before, Tony Hollywood only had one family: money.

He'd never miss a coward like Billy.

COOKING SOOTHED HER as it always did.

Since Brett had mentioned it, she busied herself making

the *arroz con pollo* that he had said he loved while he worked at the nearby breakfast bar.

Much like he'd said he'd loved you, the little voice in her head chastised.

Trey had bought chicken breasts, which could get too dry, so she browned them quickly and removed them from the pot with the onions, peppers, garlic and pepperoni. She'd had to substitute pepperoni for the chorizo she normally used and hoped it wouldn't change the flavor too drastically.

She added the rice to coat it with the oil and keep the rice from clumping as it cooked.

Tomato sauce came next along with oregano, bay leaves, salt and pepper. She covered the Dutch oven and slipped it into the preheated oven. Once the rice was further along, she'd add the chicken breasts and finish the meal.

Which meant she had at least fifteen minutes or so before she had to do anything else.

Walking over to Brett, she swept a hand across his shoulders and asked, "Anything new?"

Beneath her hand his muscles tensed. "SBS has some photos of possible suspects. Want to take a look?"

His tension transferred itself to her.

I want to look, but then I don't want to also. What if it isn't him in the photos, but then what if it is?

"Yes, I want to see," she finally said and plopped onto the stool beside Brett.

Slightly turning the laptop in her direction, he brought up an array of photos. All of the men had comparable looks and hair. Anita scoured the assorted faces, worried that they all had such similar features, but there was one man who stuck out.

She pointed to his photo and said, "That's him. I'm sure that's him."

Brett nodded and enlarged the photo from the suspect's rap sheet.

Anita narrowed her gaze, inspecting the photo more carefully. The jaw was the same, but the hair was different. Longer. Darker she supposed, although with the buzz cut he now had, hair color was hard to tell. What cinched it for her were the eyes, those dark, almost soulless eyes, and the small scar beneath the one.

"That's definitely him."

Brett nodded and zoomed in to show his name. "Santiago Kennedy. Teen records are sealed, but he was arrested at twenty for bookmaking. Pled it down from a five-year stretch to two and got off in one for good behavior."

"Isn't there legal gambling in Florida? Why do people still use bookies?" she asked, surprised by that.

"Florida still has a lot of restrictions on sports gambling and bookies don't do a credit check because gamblers know what happens if you don't pay."

Like Manny had paid.

A frisson of fear skipped down her spine. She pointed to the laptop and asked, "Is that it? Is that all he's done?"

Brett shook his head. "There are later arrests. Mostly misdemeanor assault and battery arrests. In a few cases the victims recanted, probably worried about retribution or losing the use of their bookie."

"So he just walks the streets, a free man? Free to kill Manny and me? Free to shoot all those cops," she said, frustration giving rise to anger.

"Not once we're done with him. We will wrap up this case so tight there will be no way for him to get free again," Brett said and placed an arm around her shoulders. Hugged her to him and dropped a kiss on her temple as he whispered, "We will get him."

"And his accomplice. But what about Tony Hollywood?" Anita asked, worried that there would be no safe place until they somehow had him in custody as well.

"If anyone can connect the dots to Hollywood, it's SBS." There was no hesitation in his voice, tempering her anger and frustration. Bringing some calm, especially as he said, "I smell something tasty. Is it what I think it is?"

She smiled and nodded. "It is. My way of saying thanks for everything."

Not that chicken and rice was any kind of payback for risking his life for her.

BRETT APPRECIATED THE gesture that could rouse so many memories. It had always been a special meal between them. And maybe it was time to put things to rights about what had happened so many years earlier.

"Thank you and... I know it's probably too late to say this, but I'm sorry for what happened between us. I truly am."

Her body did a little jump of surprise and then relaxed. "What did happen, Brett? Why did you ghost me?"

Thoughts whirled through his brain, so many, so quickly until he found himself blurting out, "Maybe because I felt like a ghost myself."

Her eyes opened wide with shock, and she tried to speak, her mouth opening and closing several times before she finally managed a stifled, "Why?"

Why? As if I haven't asked myself that hundreds, maybe thousands of times.

He shrugged and looked away, struggling to find the words as he had so many times before when others had asked. His commanding officer. A therapist. Trey, although he'd managed to unload some of it on his old friend because he had trusted him to understand.

She cradled his jaw and applied gentle pressure until he met her concerned gaze. "Why?" she repeated, patiently, like a parent coaxing a child to share a bad dream.

I only wish it had been a bad dream.

But like bad dreams that became less scary when you shared them, maybe it was time to let her in on what had happened.

"There was a young Muslim boy who used to hang out near our camp when we were deployed in Iraq. He was fascinated by my dog because some Muslim sects don't allow dogs as pets. They consider them unclean," he began, then paused to take a shaky breath before pressing on.

"I tried not to get involved with him, but he kept on tagging along and eventually he was a regular. He loved playing with Rin Tin Tin—"

"Rin Tin Tin? Really?" she said with a laugh.

He chuckled and shook his head. "Yeah, someone thought it would be funny for a German shepherd to be named Rin Tin Tin. Anyway, Yusef—that was the boy's name—asked to play with Rin—that's what I would call him—and I broke down and let him."

He had to stop then as the memories rose up, as powerful as the day it had happened. His chest tightened and his heart hammered so hard and fast it echoed in his ears. Sucking in a deep breath, he held it in, fighting for control.

Anita leaned toward him and laid a hand on his as it rested on the tabletop. "It's okay if you want to stop."

He released the breath in a steady, controlled stream and shook his head. "No, it's time. I want you to understand," he said and twined his fingers with hers.

"I'm here for you," she said, her gaze fixed on his face.

"Because we knew Yusef, trusted Yusef, we didn't think anything of it when he came into camp one morning."

Pausing, he looked away from her and forced himself to continue. "I should have seen something was off with him. I'm supposed to see things like that. Rin saw it. He was agitated, barking and jerking at his leash."

The images slammed into him almost as powerfully as the

blast that day, stealing his breath. Tightening the muscles in his throat, choking him into silence.

The reassuring squeeze of Anita's hand on his provided welcome comfort and support. When he met her gaze, the understanding there nearly undid him. Somehow, he finished.

"The local ISIS group knew Yusef had access to the camp. They'd rigged him with a suicide vest filled with explosives. Punishment for us and him since he'd played with Rin."

"You can't blame yourself for what happened," she urged, her gaze sheened with tears, her voice thick with her own upset.

"I can. Like I said, I should have seen it. By the time I realized Rin had picked up on the explosives, it was too late. The blast tore through the camp, killing two members of my squad and injuring another half a dozen."

Chapter Twelve

"You and Rin? Were you hurt?" Anita asked, worried Brett would downplay his own wounds, both physical and emotional.

With a quick shrug and jerk of his head, he said, "We were luckier than most. Luckier than my two friends and Yusef. He was only ten. Those savages sacrificed a child."

She let that sink in and realized that he didn't really think he'd been lucky that day. That he carried the heavy burden of not only survivor's guilt, but also doubt about his instincts. About whom he could trust.

Maybe that was the emotional hardness she sensed. The wall he'd built around himself.

"Is that why you stopped writing and calling?" she asked.

He looked away again, but she cradled his jaw and urged him to face her. "Is it?" she pressed.

"What we had was…so special. After what happened, I didn't feel I deserved something like that. Something the two soldiers who'd died that day and Yusef would never get to have because of me," he said, his voice breaking with the emotion he was barely keeping in check.

Tapping his chest, directly over his heart, he said, "I couldn't trust myself not to make wrong choices again. Choices that hurt the people I care about. Like now. I can't let feelings get in the way of what I have to do. I have to stay focused."

Anita had never been a patient person, but cooking had

taught her that very important virtue. You couldn't rush a dish if you wanted it to come out right.

Much like she couldn't rush this if she wanted him to be okay with his past. If she wanted things to be good between them.

After all, no matter his reasons, this man had left her without a word. And he wasn't the same man she'd once loved. He was different, and he was right that if they were going to get out of this situation alive, they couldn't let emotions distract them.

She dropped her hand from his face and untwined her fingers from his. "You're right. We need to keep level heads to finish this," she said, her voice as calm and supportive as she could muster.

He nodded and scrubbed his face with his hands. When he met her gaze again, the hard man was back. The stony look had returned and all emotion had been wrestled back inside.

For a moment she regretted that this man had reappeared, remembering the man she'd loved and who had emerged briefly to share his wounds.

But then the ding-ding-ding of the timer she'd set registered, calling her to action.

She shoved away from the table and back to the kitchen where she took out the Dutch oven, stirred the rice and nestled the chicken breasts in the rice to finish cooking.

At the breakfast bar, Brett had resumed work, his concentration on his laptop, although as she prepped the final toppings for the chicken and rice and an avocado salad, she caught him occasionally glancing in her direction. She told herself it wasn't longing she saw in that gaze. It was just worry about this case and their safety.

Armed with that conviction because it would protect her heart, she puttered around in the kitchen, cleaning and keeping busy until another timer warned dinner was ready.

Anita pulled the chicken and rice out of the oven and, satisfied it was finished, she called out to Brett, "I'm going to set the table."

He immediately closed the laptop and hopped up. "Let me do that. I'm sure you have things to finish."

She did and welcomed his assistance as he grabbed place mats from a nearby cabinet, cutlery from a drawer and napkins from a holder on the kitchen counter.

While he set the table, she spooned chicken and rice onto the plates and topped the servings with roasted red peppers she had made from a wrinkly pepper she had found wasting away in the fridge. Frozen sweet peas nuked in the microwave completed the dish.

She set those plates on the table, returned to the kitchen for the avocado salad and placed that on the table as well.

"There's some beer if you'd like, and it's not skunky. I used one of the bottles for the *arroz con pollo*," she said with a dip of her head in the direction of the fridge.

A BEER SOUNDS like heaven, Brett thought, and only one wouldn't affect his judgment in the event something happened tonight. Although he hoped for the first quiet night in days.

"Thanks. A beer would be great," he said and sat in front of a heaping plate of chicken and rice.

She set a beer in front of him and nervously wiped her hands on the apron she wore. "I normally would make *maduros* with this, but we didn't have any."

He loved sweet, ripe plantains, but understood their supplies were limited. "Maybe if things stay quiet, we can do some shopping tomorrow for food and clothing."

"That would be nice. I know Trey meant well, but something besides T-shirts and sweats would be good," she said with a half smile and tug at the oversize T-shirt she wore.

"I'll work it out with Trey," he said, and once she'd sat, he dug into the meal.

The flavors burst in his mouth, as delicious as he remembered. Maybe better, he thought and murmured in appreciation. "This is delicious."

"Thanks. I had to make do with what I had," she said, obviously uneasy as she picked at the meal she'd prepared.

"Well, you did good, Reyes. Real good," he teased and forked up a healthy portion of the chicken and rice.

HIS PRAISE LIGHTENED her mood, and they both must have been hungry since they ate in companionable silence. She was grateful for that because it kept away worry about the fact someone was trying to kill her as well as the conflicting emotions she had for Brett.

They finished the meal and cleaned up with little said, falling into the patterns they'd shared when they'd been together. After, he fed Mango, gave her fresh water and they took her for a quick walk.

Nightfall had come quickly in early December, but there was enough illumination on the street from the nearby homes, Christmas lights and scattered streetlamps. By the time they returned from the short walk, the puddled color that sprawled in the driveway by the mobile home had inflated. A large bare-chested Santa in board shorts, complete with a surfboard, greeted them upon their return.

"I gather Jake is quite a character," she said and chuckled.

"He is. You could always count on Jake to liven things up," he said and laughed, but then grew serious, his look severe and troubled.

She laid a hand on his arm. "I know you're bothered by that boat, but maybe there's a reasonable explanation."

"Maybe," he said and held up his hand to stay her entry as he went through the process that was becoming almost familiar by now. He entered through the side gate, opened the house and sent in Mango. Once Mango had given the "all clear," Brett signaled for Anita to follow.

Inside they each hurried to what had become their domains. Brett sat at the breakfast bar with the laptop, preparing for their upcoming meeting. She went to the kitchen to make coffee, expecting that it would be another late night.

By the time the coffee was sputtering in the espresso pot, Brett's laptop was chiming to warn it was time for their video meeting.

The television across the way from them snapped to life with the image of the SBS crew sitting around the table at their Brickell Avenue office. Roni and her partner were also there, faces solemn.

She worried whether that meant good or bad news but didn't press. They'd share when they were ready.

At the table, she set down the cups of coffee and took a spot beside Brett.

He mouthed a "thank you."

Trey began the meeting. "I'm sure Brett has shared the photo lineup with you," he said and displayed the array of photos she had seen earlier onto the screen. "Can you identify any of them as the man you saw the night Ramirez was murdered?"

Anita nodded and used the touch pad on the laptop to move the mouse until it rested on the photo she had picked out earlier.

"I'm sure that's the man," she said, and Trey returned the screen to the team. He handed Roni a piece of paper.

She nodded and said, "I hope this photo lineup will fly with the district attorney."

"Why wouldn't it?" Anita asked, puzzled.

"We would have preferred to do it ourselves, but there are exigent circumstances obviously. It would also be better if we could wait for the DNA analysis from the blood at the Homestead location," Roni said.

Williams quickly added, "Florida started collecting DNA in 2011 so Kennedy's DNA should be in the system because of his priors."

BUT DNA ANALYSIS could take time. *Time we don't have*, Brett thought.

"What about the leak? Trey mentioned earlier that you have video that might help?" he pressed.

Trey motioned for Sophie to take over, and a second later, a video popped up on the screen.

A uniformed officer, cap pulled low and his head tucked down, walked past the SBS SUV parked at the back entrance, paused and took a long look at the vehicle. He did another walk back and forth before entering the stationhouse again.

As he did so, he tipped his head down to avoid showing his face to the camera.

"We're working up his approximate size and weight so Roni and Heath can look through the database of officers at the stationhouse," Sophie said.

"How long will that take?" he pressed.

"Our end will be relatively quick thanks to John's supercomputer, but the police analysis may take a little time since we can't access their database," Robbie advised.

Brett slumped back in his chair and released a frustrated sigh. "Doesn't seem like we have much."

Roni quickly countered with, "Actually, we think that this officer memorized your license plate number in order to track you."

Anita leaned forward in interest and said, "Track us? With just the plate number?"

Roni and Williams shared an uneasy look and Williams finally explained, "PD has a number of automatic license plate readers in police cars as well as in static locations in Miami and along Route 1, which you took to reach Homestead. There's also a database of ALPRs from HOAs and other private places that feed info into a database we can access."

"And did someone access it?" Anita pushed.

"It will take time, but we're working to see who accessed the info," Roni confirmed with a tilt of her head.

Anita's rising tension coupled with his frustration seemed obvious since Trey said, "We're working this as fast as we can, Anita."

Brett believed that, but again, it was time they might not have if Hollywood and his crew had a say. Which made him ask, "What about Hollywood? Have you made a link to him?"

"Nothing yet, but we're—"

"Working on it," Anita finished, her irritation obvious.

"We are. Other than coincidence about the bookmaking and assaults, probably to secure payment of gambling debts, we don't have a direct link but we will," Trey confirmed, his tone brooking no disagreement. "If there's nothing else," he said.

Brett and Anita did a quick glance at each other and were clearly in silent agreement. "Nothing else. I'll keep working on whatever I can find out about our suspect," Brett said.

"We'll keep you advised as soon as we have more," Trey said and a second later the video feed ended.

Brett reached out and laid a hand on Anita's shoulder, squeezed lightly to offer reassurance. "I know it seems like there's not much progress, but you shouldn't worry."

She bit her lower lip and glanced away, but he didn't press. When she finally looked back, she said, "I'm worried about my business. My life." Pointing between the two of them, she said, "Us."

He wanted to say there was no "us" now, only it would be a lie. From the moment he'd laid eyes on her at the police station, all the old feelings and emotions had awoken. Denying them would be a lie and, as he'd thought before, he didn't want any lies between them.

Mimicking her gesture, he said, "This 'us' is complicated and dangerous right now, as we discussed."

She nodded, in agreement, and shifted the conversation to a safer topic. "Do you think I can call my sous-chef in the morning? My parents too?"

"As long as you use a burner phone. I'll get you one first thing tomorrow."

THE MORNING COULDN'T come fast enough as far as Anita was concerned.

Although she'd busied herself to keep distracted, with the meeting done and the evening looming large in front of her, it was impossible not to think about how her restaurant's lunch service had gone, whether the promised porterhouse steaks had arrived and how the dinner service was faring. By now it would be in full swing, and while she itched to call, waiting made sense.

She worried that even with a burner phone they'd be able to track them.

"Can you track a 'burner phone'?" she asked, using air quotes for emphasis.

Brett nodded. "You can track *any* phone. That's why we try to keep phone use to a minimum."

"And what about those APRs or whatever? Do you think they could have used that to track us to here?" she pressed.

Chapter Thirteen

"ALPRs," he corrected and jumped back on his laptop. "If they somehow grabbed Matt's license plate number, which I'm confident they didn't, they might be able to track it. There's a public site that may have more info," he said and popped up the video feed from the laptop to the television again.

Anita stood and walked closer to the television to get a better look as Brett typed in the zip code for Miami and chose a camera type. The website populated with a bunch of brown dots to show where various kinds of cameras were located. ALPRs, red light and speed cameras were all noted on the map.

"This is a crowd-sourced database so it relies on users providing this information," he said and used the mouse to move the map and display where ALPRs might have been on their route.

Relief flooded her as she realized the last location was in Homestead and the areas beyond that were clear of any readers until Big Pine Key, which she believed was quite a distance south of them.

"We're clear," she said with a happy sigh.

"Looks that way. Time for you to relax and get some rest. If things have settled down in the morning, you can make your call and we'll take that drive for supplies."

"That sounds good. I'm going to shower," she said and jerked a thumb in the direction of the bedrooms.

A shower, together with the info they'd just uncovered, would help her relax.

"WHAT DO YOU mean Billy took off?" Tony Hollywood roared, fists clenched, face mottled with angry red and sickly white.

Santiago held his hands out in pleading. "He freaked out when you mentioned the felony murder rule. Started crying like a little baby about how he was too young to go to prison for life. He said he needed a refill for that stupid vape thing he's always sucking on and went into the store but never came out."

"Find him. Check with my sister. Billy was always a mama's boy," Tony said and marched over. Jabbing a finger into Santiago's chest, so hard he was sure he'd have bruises, Tony said, "If he's a weak link, I need to know so we can deal with him."

"Deal with him? How?" Santiago asked, sure of what Tony would say, which was why he was surprised when his boss responded with, "Just find him and bring him here. I could always talk some sense into the kid. Besides, he's family."

Santiago cursed silently, hating that he'd been so wrong about what Tony would do to Billy, because if the truth came out...

"I'll find him, Tony. I'm sure he's just chilling somewhere and licking his wounds."

"What about the girl? Any news?" Tony asked, raising a hairy eyeball in a way that had Santiago sweating a bit.

"We lost them after they left Homestead, but I'm working on it," he said, hoping his connection at the police station could point them in the right direction again.

Tony grunted. "Make it happen. Yesterday, Santiago. And find Billy before he does something stupid."

He nodded and rushed from the room, a streak of curses escaping him as he realized he was in deep trouble.

Family meant something to Tony. He'd made a big mistake and there was possibly only one way to rectify that error.

Find the girl before the police found Billy. Or what was left of him anyway.

BRETT HAD GROWN frustrated at the dead ends he'd been hitting for information on Tony Hollywood.

Sure, there were a bunch of news articles and reports on the mobster, but nothing that could link him to a low-level criminal like Santiago Kennedy.

Wanting a fresh set of eyes, he'd taken a break to shower, and come out to find Anita stretched out on the couch in a fresh T-shirt and sleeping shorts.

He needed time to think about all that was happening and what they had so far in the investigation and stepped out onto the small deck, with Mango at his side. The night was peaceful, the only sounds those of the palm fronds moving overhead, a distant set of wind chimes and the canal waters lapping up against the nearby wooden dock and bulkhead.

There were lights on here and there in the homes along the canal. Some people even had Christmas lights strung along their docks and boats. The reflections of the colors created a watercolor-like kaleidoscope on the surface of the canal.

A few houses down, a bright green light in the water highlighted the shadows of snook attracted by the glow so a fisherman might snag them for a meal.

He'd caught more than one himself when Jake and he had fished from this dock.

Jake.

He hadn't asked about his friend during the video meeting, thinking it had likely been too soon for Trey to have any info. Plus, he wanted to believe for as long as possible that he could trust Jake.

Mango nudged his leg and glanced up at him, eyes almost sad, as if she sensed Brett's upset.

He knelt and rubbed the dog's head and ears, accepted the doggy kisses some people he'd met would think of as impure. In his mind, nothing connected to love was impure, but to each their own.

"Let's do a last walk," he said, even if the walk only consisted of a quick check around the house and the immediate area.

Since it would be a short stroll, he didn't bother clipping a leash on Mango. He just stuffed a fresh poop bag into his pocket and, without a word, the dog heeled to his side, breaking their connection only long enough to relieve herself. Brett cleaned up the waste and deposited it in a trash can in the side yard.

Thankfully there was nothing to see in and around the perimeter of the house.

With it all quiet, he went back inside to find Anita asleep in front of the television. A gentle snore escaped her every now and then, signaling she was in deep sleep.

He'd wake her if he shut off the television. He only turned down the volume, so he'd be able to hear any abnormal noises. Returning to his laptop, he fired it up and got back to work, intending to search for anything he could find on Tony Hollywood or Santiago Kennedy.

Jake.

He hated that he had to add his friend to the mix, but he couldn't risk any surprises.

He made a hand gesture to Mango to take a spot by the back door and the dog immediately obeyed, stretching out her tan-and-white body across the entrance. Her large, squarish head rested on her paws.

With Mango on guard, he gave his attention to the internet searches and found Kennedy on social media. More than once their suspect had bragged about his guns and connections but never mentioned Hollywood. It made him wonder why the posts with the weapons weren't flagged when so many other, less dangerous posts sometimes put a user in social media jail.

Brett took screenshots of the posts and saved the links to a list to share with Trey and the team. He suspected one of those guns could be the same make and caliber as the one used to shoot Ramirez and the police officers.

But as he was about to flip away from Kennedy's profile, something snagged his attention: a series of photos taken at a racetrack.

Checking the time stamps, he realized it was while the Paloma Challenge had been held. He screenshotted those and saved the links as well, and just to confirm, he pulled up photos of Waterside Park.

Bingo, he thought. The background in Kennedy's photo was Waterside Park, confirming that Kennedy had been at the racetrack at the same time as Ramirez.

Of course, that coincidence alone wasn't enough to say any wrongdoing had occurred at the track. Unless they could get more info, it was just coincidence.

The Feds might have more details, but clearly they didn't want to share. Keeping it to themselves could be about not having their case blown, but it could also be about not losing the collar of a high-profile criminal like Tony Hollywood to a bunch of local cops. Or SBS, for that matter.

Checking the dates on the races, he realized that a few months had gone by. Probably too long a time for anyone to be holding on to CCTV tapes, but you didn't have an event like that without plastering it all over social media to get the most bang for your buck. Not to mention local news stories as well.

Locating the page for the event, he scrolled through the photos leading up to the big occasion and then race day itself. Most of the photos were of the horses, jockeys and all the beautiful people and entertainers who would be there. Interspersed with them were a few screenshots of the crowd.

He zipped right past one crowd photo, but something called him back to it.

Was it just wishful thinking that the two people way in the

back, in the fuzzy section of the photo, looked like Ramirez and Kennedy?

As he had before, he did a screenshot and saved the link. This time he also downloaded the photo since Kennedy had made his profile public. *Clearly not a rocket scientist*, he thought.

Brett's own page was limited to family and private because you never knew who might be trying to find you. Like now.

The resolution of the picture wasn't good to begin with, but he still tried to enhance the fuzzy section with his very basic photo editing software. That served to convince him that he wasn't imagining it.

It certainly looked like Ramirez and Kennedy although they were both wearing hats, which hid their hair and could alter their overall look.

Still, it was worth sending that info to Sophie and Robbie. If anyone could work magic on that blurry photo, it would be them.

Satisfied that he had added one more dot to connect Ramirez's killer to Tony Hollywood, he did the one thing that he was dreading.

He pulled up Jake's social media and delved through all the posts and photos.

The latest ones confirmed that he wasn't lying about being in Lake Placid and a snowboarding competition. There was photo after photo of him with other snowboarders on the slopes. Some of Jake racing posted by the event organizers. Others with the groupies who tagged after a good-looking and charming guy like Jake.

He scrolled through the timeline, searching for anything about the boat.

Nothing.

That didn't make sense since most people who got their hands on a toy like that were likely to post photos of their new baby.

Unless you didn't want people to know, which seemed odd, especially for his friend.

Jake had always been someone who put everything out there. He'd never had anything to hide…until now.

He hadn't been wrong to think there had been hesitation when he'd asked Jake about the boat.

Growing suspicions curled their way around his gut, making him feel sick. Making him worry that he'd made a mistake again to trust his old friend.

It was that worry that drove him to pick up his phone to call Trey even though it was nearly midnight. But if he knew Trey, his friend and boss was probably still at work as well. Just in case, especially since Roni would likely be asleep, he texted him first.

You up?

Yes. Still at the office. Give me a minute. Roni's on my couch.

Because he also didn't want to wake Anita, he tiptoed to his bedroom and closed the door, but left it slightly ajar to listen for any issues.

"What's up?" Trey said after Brett answered.

"I may have found a connection between Ramirez and Kennedy. I emailed you a photo from the racetrack. I think it's them in the background."

"Good work. Every little piece of the puzzle helps," Trey said.

"What about the Feds? Still nothing?" Brett asked.

A rough sigh sputtered across the line. "Nada. They're not good at playing well with others."

"What about the cop in the video? Anything?" he pressed.

"Williams went back to the station with the info Sophie and Robbie provided about his physical description. Plus, Williams thought there was something familiar about the cop, so hopefully we'll know more soon," Trey advised, but Brett picked up something in his old friend's voice. Something that had nothing to do with the case.

"You good?" he asked, concerned about his friend.

"Roni isn't feeling well. It's why she didn't go back to the station with Williams," Trey replied.

Roni was the love of his life. He'd never expected to see that with a hard-ass like Trey, but Fate had apparently had other plans for his friend.

"Take care of her first, Trey. She and the baby are what's most important."

Another sigh filled the line. A tired one this time. "They are. I've got the others on double to get things moving. We'll work on that photo ASAP."

"Thanks, Trey. I'll keep on working on this, too," he said.

"I know you will," Trey replied and ended the call.

"Is everything okay?" Anita asked as she opened the door to the bedroom.

As Anita peered at him, Brett schooled his features, forcing away his fears about Roni but also about Anita and what he was feeling for her.

The devastation he'd feel if he somehow lost her after finding her once again.

Chapter Fourteen

Brett was standing in the room, his face in partial shadow from the dim light cast by a small bedside lamp. But despite that, it was impossible to miss the sorrow in his dark gaze as he said, "Trey is worried because Roni isn't feeling well."

"Is she going to be okay?" she asked, likewise worried because the woman was fairly far along in her pregnancy.

He did a quick jerk of his shoulders and ran his fingers across the short strands of his hair. "I hope so. She had some issues a few months ago but was doing better."

"Is she in the hospital?" she asked, and Brett quickly shook his head.

"Just resting at the SBS offices so maybe it's not all that serious."

"That's good news, I guess," she said and walked out of the room, Brett trailing behind her as she returned to the living room and plopped back onto the couch.

"We do have some good news," he said and explained the link he had discovered between Ramirez and Kennedy, as well as the possibility that they would soon have an ID for the cop who might be leaking information.

"That is definitely good news. I might just be able to sleep tonight," she said with a smile.

A half grin crept across Brett's full lips. A boyish grin that drove away the earlier sadness she had seen from his eyes.

"You were doing a pretty good job of sawing logs not that

long ago," he teased, and the grin erupted into a full-fledged smile.

She wagged a finger back and forth in a shaming gesture. "You were a pretty good lumberjack yourself."

He jammed his hands on his hips, let out a whoop of a laugh, but then turned serious as Mango popped to her feet, faced the deck and growled.

Brett rushed toward the door and gestured for Anita to move behind him. As he walked toward the door, hand on his weapon, he turned and said to her, "Don't move from there."

With a hand gesture to Mango, he said, "*K noze*, Mango. *K noze.*"

The dog instantly hugged Brett's side.

BRETT WENT TO the back door and peered through the glass.

A shadow on the dock. Moving slowly along the length of the boat.

There was little moonlight so Brett couldn't see his face until the person stepped toward the bow of the boat. A light on the deck shined on the man's face and Brett thought he recognized him as one of Jake's neighbors.

He opened the back door and stepped onto the deck, Mango plastered to his side.

"Is that you, Jim?" he called out, but never moved his hand away from his weapon.

"Brett?" the man responded and smiled. "I didn't know you were down. I was checking things out since I thought I saw someone here and knew Jake was away."

Brett relaxed and signaled Mango to lie down. After the dog had complied, Brett stepped down to the walkway to shake the man's hand. "Good to see you again, Jim."

"Same, Brett," he said and motioned to the boat. "She's a beauty, isn't she?"

"She is. My dad has been wishing for one for years. Jake

is a lucky man," he said and ran a hand across the metal railing on the boat.

"I'll say. Imagine winning a cool million in the lottery," Jim said with a low whistle as he admired the boat.

"Wow, a million, huh?" he said, his gut twisting as he realized his friend had lied to him and possibly to his neighbor.

Jim nodded and smiled, but the smile dimmed as his gaze skipped down to the gun at Brett's hip and then back up to his face.

"Trouble?" Jim asked.

He remembered then that the neighbor was a retired police officer, which might work in his favor.

"Just came straight from work. I'm a K-9 agent for SBS in Miami," he said.

Jim's eagle-eyed officer's gaze skipped to Mango lying nearby. "Your partner, I assume."

With a dip of his head, Brett said, "Her name is Mango. She's a good partner."

"Good to hear. Well, it's late and now that I know everything's okay here, I'll go," Jim said.

As the man turned to walk back to his home, Brett said, "Thanks for keeping an eye on things for Jake. If you see anything out of line around here—"

"I'll let you know. Stay safe," Jim said and glanced back toward Jake's house, where Anita's silhouette was visible by the back door.

"Thanks, Jim." He waited on the dock until Jim had gone into his own home to click his tongue for Mango to follow him back into Jake's house.

"You know him?" Anita asked as he entered the living room.

Nodding, he said, "Jake's neighbor Jim. Retired cop who saw something here and decided to check it out. We're lucky to have cop's eyes next door."

"Cop's eyes? Is that a thing?" she asked and sat back down on the couch.

"Yeah, it is. They don't miss a thing. That's why he was out there, inspecting," he said, but then quickly blurted out, "Jim said Jake told him he won the lottery and that's how he bought the boat."

She sat silently for a long moment but plucked at the hem of her shorts nervously. "But Jake told you something different," she finally said.

"He did, and who knows what the truth really is," Brett said and wiped his face with his hands, his beard rasping with the action.

Brett was clearly troubled by his friend's lies, his gaze dark and filled with worry.

"Maybe there's nothing there. Maybe he just doesn't want people to know his business," Anita said, trying to make him feel better.

"Maybe. Hopefully Trey will be able to find out more," he said, then crossed his arms against his chest and rocked back and forth on his heels. "It's late. You should think about sawing some more logs," he said, obviously trying to lighten the mood.

She jumped to her feet and smoothed the fleece of the shorts with her hands. "I should. We have a big day tomorrow."

"Big day?" he asked, puzzled.

She laughed and tapped his flat midsection. "Shopping, big boy. Or did you forget what you said earlier?"

A chuckle burst from him, and he shook his head. "I remember. Get some sleep."

She walked over, rose on her tiptoes and kissed him. Just a quick, butterfly-light peck. And then another.

It just seemed so natural, so familiar as she leaned into him, and he wrapped an arm around her waist to hold her close.

Dug his hand into her hair and undid the topknot she wore, letting her hair spill down.

He tangled his fingers in the strands and he almost groaned. "I always loved the feel of your hair in my hands. The smell of it. You still smell the same."

"You…do…too," she said in between kisses, savoring the masculine scent that had never left her brain. A fresh and citrusy cologne. Brett, all musky and male.

His aroma and the feel of his hard body, even harder now, tangled around her, urging her even closer. Calling her to rub her hips along his, against the obvious proof of his desire.

He groaned and cupped the back of her head, deepening his kiss. Dancing his tongue in to taste her before his body shook and he tempered the kisses and reluctantly shifted away.

"I want you, Anita. I can't deny that," he said and leaned his forehead against hers so that their gazes were eye level. "I've missed you forever, but now—"

"Isn't the right time for this. You've said that before," she reminded, and stepped away from him, arms wrapped around herself to keep it together.

She whirled on him, frustration and need fueling her anger. "I get it. You have responsibilities. You have to keep me safe, and I have a business to think about. One that consumes my entire life."

"You know that's right," he said, hands held out in pleading.

With an angry slash of her hand, she said, "Enough. I get it. But what if tonight is all the time we have left?"

She didn't wait for his reply. She bolted and raced to her bedroom, slammed the door shut. The loud thud of the door as it closed was somehow satisfying.

But the silence that followed…

She'd been alone for so long. Alone except for her business and chefs. The few men she'd given entry into her life had drifted in and out of it because she'd been too busy at work.

Too busy to have a life, but if she was honest with herself, staying busy had kept her from having time to think about the loneliness. To think about the one man whom she had never forgotten.

And now here he was because of the most unlikely of reasons.

Because someone was trying to kill her.

A frisson of fear skittered down her spine and drove away the anger, fear and need.

She wrapped her arms around herself and walked to the window. The night was still. Nothing moved outside except an occasional bubble and ripple in the waters of the canal. Fish, probably, she told herself.

Mango's growl sounded in the other room, causing Anita to pull back slightly from the window. A second later an odd-shaped silhouette came into view, and as the moonlight shone on it, she realized what it was.

A large green-and-fluorescent-orange iguana inched across the railing of the deck. With its long black-and-yellowish-banded tail, it had to be at least five feet long.

No threat. Not this time, anyway.

Luckily Mango was alert. Brett was lucky to have her. Anita was lucky to have both of them guarding her.

With that thought in mind, she told herself not to make Brett's life even harder than it was.

She'd stay away from him as he requested. For now. Maybe even for after.

He'd hurt her once before and she'd be a fool to let it happen again.

BRETT PACED BACK and forth across the narrow width of the living room, too awake after all that had happened.

Jim on the dock. The iguana.

Brett appreciated how alert Mango could be. It lifted a huge weight off his shoulders to know he had a second set of ears to help keep Anita safe.

Keeping Anita safe was the number one priority, which meant he had to stay focused.

He couldn't let their past relationship and lingering emotions take his focus off what was important.

With that in mind, he whipped out his phone to see if he had any text or email messages.

No texts but he had an email from Sophie forwarding the cleaned-up version of the photo he'd found online as well as other images that had been captured from the police station's CCTV footage.

The enhancement of the online photo confirmed that it was Ramirez and Santiago. And neither of the two men seemed happy.

If Santiago was one of Hollywood's goons and Ramirez owed the mobster money, it could explain what had happened the other night.

Which brought even greater worry. Would Hollywood keep on coming for Anita even if Santiago was caught?

He ran through all the permutations in his brain and decided Hollywood wouldn't come after Anita. It was way more likely he'd take out Santiago and his accomplice to avoid them spilling their guts to the police.

Unless Santiago and his accomplice got to Anita first. That was the real threat.

Opening the second email, he flipped through the images, scrutinizing them carefully to see if there was anything familiar about the officer. The man had hidden well, face always averted as he did Hollywood's dirty work.

Muttering a curse beneath his breath, he sat back down at the table and opened his laptop, but then shut it down. It was hours past midnight and even though he could function on only a few hours of sleep, he needed to get some rest to be alert.

The bed would be way more comfortable, but it was just too close to Anita.

And the two easiest entryways were visible from the living room and couch.

For safety's sake, he signaled Mango, walked her toward the front door and instructed her to guard the area. *"Pozor,"* he said and repeated it although the dog had so far proved to understand the command quite well.

Mango peered up at him and seemed to nod before splaying across the front door, head on her paws.

Satisfied, he returned to the living room and was about to sit when the need to see Anita was safe called him.

He walked to her door, leaned his ear close and listened. That soft snore confirmed she was asleep.

Opening the door a crack, he peered inside, worried about someone accessing the window.

All was good and he had no doubt that if Jake's neighbor Jim noticed anything, since Anita's bedroom was closest to the dock and Jim's home, he'd take action.

Satisfied that he could stand down for a few hours of sleep, he grabbed a pillow and blanket from his bedroom and settled in on the couch. Slipping his holster from his belt, he removed the gun and placed it within easy reach on the coffee table.

But as he lay there, a maelstrom of thoughts and images spun around his brain, making for an uneasy sleep.

His eyes had barely drifted shut when he noticed the lightening of the morning sky through the window. It bathed the room in shades of rosy gray and pale lavender.

A quick glance at his phone warned it was nearly seven. No new messages or texts. Regardless it was time to get up and get moving.

Shower first, he thought, rubbing his face and hair with his hand.

Mango was guarding the door, but she'd need to be walked

soon. A quick peek into Anita's room confirmed she was still asleep, and he closed the door to avoid waking her.

Snagging a fresh shirt and underwear from his room, he showered and dressed in fresh clothes and his one pair of jeans. Hopefully he could buy another pair or two today.

Anita still hadn't stirred so he leashed Mango and walked her in the front yard and then did a loop around the house, making sure all was in order.

Nothing had changed since the night before, although he did notice the curtains on Jim's house shift as he walked along the dock. The old cop keeping watch.

When he returned to the house, the strong and welcoming smell of bacon filled the small space as he opened the door.

Anita. Cooking. The kitchen had always been her refuge and that hadn't changed.

But so much else had. Maybe too much.

Armed with that reality, he pushed into the kitchen.

Chapter Fifteen

She didn't register the footsteps until she sensed a presence behind her.

Granny fork raised like a weapon, heart hammering in her chest, she whirled, ready to defend herself.

"Brett. You scared the life out of me," she said and laid a hand on her chest to calm her racing heart.

"I'm sorry. I thought you heard Mango and me come in," he said and took a step back, hands raised as he gave her some space to recover.

She waved off his apology. "No, I'm sorry. Sometimes I get lost in my head when I'm cooking."

"It's why you're so good at what you do," he said with a smile and an appreciative dip of his head.

"Thanks. Breakfast will be ready soon. Coffee is already made," she said and tilted her head in the direction of the espresso pot.

"Can I get you some?" he asked as he walked over.

"No, thanks. I've already had a cup," she said, which was maybe why she was as jittery as she was.

She shouldn't have been that surprised when Brett had returned. She'd seen him walking Mango past her window when she'd woken and knew he wouldn't leave her alone.

She blamed the jitters on the coffee as she grabbed the bagel from the toaster and split it between the two plates she'd warmed in the oven. A little Mornay sauce she'd made from the remains of a bar of cream cheese, butter and Swiss cheese slices went next. She topped the sauce with slices of crispy bacon and a little more cheese sauce.

Returning to the stove, she cracked the last two eggs from the fridge into the bacon grease and fried them, making sure the whites were tight, but the yolks stayed runny. Satisfied they were exactly right, she topped each of the towers of bagel, cheese sauce and bacon with a fried egg. She finished the dish with some salt and pepper.

"Wow. That looks and smells delicious," Brett said as she placed the plate in front of him.

"A fridge cleaner. There wasn't much in there and we've run through most of what we brought with us since we didn't take much," she said with a shrug, hoping the dish would satisfy a big man like Brett.

Brett broke into the egg and the yolk drizzled down, melding with the cheese sauce. He forked up a healthy portion, ate it and hummed in appreciation. "This is amazing. Really amazing," he said and dug into the meal.

His enjoyment of her food drove away the last of her jitters as well as misgivings about what had been a slapdash dish concocted from a hodgepodge of ingredients.

It awakened her own appetite, and she ate, pleased with the final product. "I could probably make you a real croque madame if we're able to do some shopping today."

He nodded. "I just want to check with the team. If they give the go-ahead, you can call your sous-chef and parents, and after we'll get supplies."

"Thanks for remembering about the call," she said, grateful for his understanding.

THERE WAS NOTHING he didn't remember about her, he thought, but didn't say.

"Let me clean up—"

She held her hand up to stop him. "I'll do it so you can make the call. Do anything else you have to."

"Roger that," he said and pushed away from the table, coffee cup in hand.

He dialed Trey and it rang a few times, which was unlike his friend. When he finally answered, he was out of breath, as if he'd been running.

"Sorry, but things are a little off the wall here this morning. Roni's in labor," Trey said.

"She's okay, right? Isn't it early?" he asked, worried since Trey had said she wasn't feeling well the night before.

"It's about a month early, but so far so good. Mia is taking over for me and can fill you in on what we've got so far," Trey said, barely audible over the noises in the background. Someone exhorting someone to breathe. A pained groan.

"Have to go," Trey said and ended the call.

"Is there a problem?" Anita asked and walked over, drying her hands on a kitchen towel.

"Roni's in labor. I have to call Mia for an update," he said and immediately dialed her number, then put the phone on speaker.

"*Buenos dias*, Brett," Mia said as she answered.

"Is it a good day, Mia?" he responded.

"It is. We've been able to identify the leak at the police station, but he's lawyered up," Mia advised.

"Wouldn't you? He's on the hook for those cops who were shot in Aventura," he said.

"Maybe more than that," Mia said with sigh.

"What do you mean?" Anita asked, obviously not liking what she was hearing.

He wasn't liking it, either, especially as Mia said, "Jogger saw a gator chomping on something this morning. Called the cops, who discovered the gator had an arm with a cast in its mouth."

"I'm not getting the connection to the case," Brett said, puzzled by this new development.

"When the coroner cut off the cast, he noticed there were some pretty serious bite marks, damage to the forearm muscles and a small fracture," Mia advised.

It all came together for Brett. "Damage like that which would occur if a pit bull was really holding on and shaking the man's arm. You think this is one of the people who attacked us in Homestead."

"I do and so does the coroner. He'd heard about the attack and put two and two together when he saw the injuries. He's taking DNA from the arm, but he's also taking DNA from the wound to confirm what kind of dog did the biting. If the victim has a record, we'll get a match on the DNA, and also from his fingerprints."

"Someone is tying up loose ends," Anita said in a small voice, clearly fearing she'd be next.

"He is, but we've plugged that leak. You're safe where you are," Mia said to calm her.

"But the cop isn't talking," Anita said, her confusion apparent.

"He isn't but once he hears there's a murder involved, he may want a plea deal, right?" Brett asked.

"Right. We've already reached out to our uncle in the DA's office to see how they can help get more info out of that cop with a plea deal," Mia confirmed.

"Are we safe enough for Anita to call her sous-chef and for us to get some supplies? We're running a little low," Brett said and glanced at Anita. Hopefulness filled her face, and as Mia acknowledged that it was clear for them to do that, a small smile slipped onto her features.

"Great. Keep us posted," he said.

Brett swiped to end the call and handed the phone to Anita. "Once you make this call, I'll burn this phone."

ANITA TOOK THE phone with shaky hands, almost dreading what she might hear from Melanie.

Her sous-chef answered on the first ring. "Anita?" she asked, a puzzled tone in her voice since she likely didn't recognize the number.

"Yes, it's me. I can't use my own phone. How are things?" she asked and braced herself for bad news.

"We miss you, but you trained us well. We got the steaks delivered as promised along with some extra filets to make up for it. We're all set for the next few days with the menu you left for us," Melanie advised, her voice relaxed, almost bordering on cheery.

But is it forced cheeriness?

"Are you sure, Melanie? I shouldn't be worried?" Anita urged, cell phone pressed so hard to her ear that her diamond stud dug into her flesh.

"I'm sure, Anita. Like I said, you trained us to handle things. Take care of things so you can come back quickly," Melanie said as someone called out to her.

"Chef, we need you here," one of her line chefs said.

"Don't worry, Chef," Melanie repeated and then the line went dead.

She dialed her parents next and it instantly went to voice mail. They had likely ignored the unfamiliar number. She left a detailed message and tried her best to tell them not to worry and that she was safe.

She handed the phone back to Brett, almost distractedly.

"It's all good, right?" he asked, ducking down so that he could read her face more clearly.

"It's all good," she repeated and actually believed it. Meeting his gaze, she said, "How about we do that shopping now."

TONY HOLLYWOOD'S FACE was buried in his hands, elbows braced on his desk, as Santiago limped into his office.

"What's up, boss?" he asked.

As Tony straightened, he could swear he saw the remnants of tears on his face and even though he knew the likely reason for it, he played stupid.

"Something wrong?"

"My sister called. The cops called to say Billy's dead. They found his arm—his freakin' arm—in a gator," Tony said and slammed his hands on the surface of the desk.

The sound was as loud as a gunshot, making him jump.

"I'm sorry, boss. What happened?" he said, feigning ignorance.

With speed he didn't think possible for a man of Tony's size, Tony rounded the corner, grabbed his throat and propelled him against the wall. He tightened his hold and lifted him off the ground, choking him.

"What happened to Billy?" Tony asked, nose to nose with him now that he had him half a foot in the air.

"Don't...know," he managed to squeak out with the little air he could breathe.

Tony tossed him away like a rag doll and, thanks to his injured leg, he crumpled to the ground.

Tony paced back and forth, raking a hand through his hair, muttering over and over as he did so. "He was family. My sister's heart is broken. He was her only child."

"I didn't do it," he lied, fearing that he'd underestimated Tony's love for his incompetent nephew.

Tony spun and cursed him out, veins bulging on his neck and forehead, angry red blossoming on his face.

"Liar. I should have you offed. You're nothing but a liability," he said with a toss of a hand in his direction.

"You should but you won't because you know I have insurance, don't you?" he said, pulling the ace card he had tucked up his sleeve.

Tony clenched his fists and shuffled his feet, almost like a bull getting ready to charge, but then he stopped and stepped back.

"Get out of here. Find the girl. Finish her off," he said from behind gritted teeth.

Santiago eased his hands into his pockets, turned and sashayed away, a newfound sense of power flowing through his veins. But he couldn't be overconfident.

He'd misjudged Tony's reaction to Billy's death, but he hoped that in time Tony would realize that he'd done the right thing. Billy had been nothing but a liability. The weakest link in the chain leading to him and eventually to Tony.

Yeah, Tony would thank him one day, he thought, and headed out to his car.

Anita Reyes and the SBS K-9 agent had flown the coop, but his mole at the police station had been very helpful so far. He had hoped to end the problem in Aventura, but the SBS agents had been too quick thinking. And Billy and that damn dog had totally messed things up in Homestead.

He should have handled it by himself and from now on he would.

First step: see what his mole could tell him.

Chapter Sixteen

Brett hauled the half-a-dozen bags onto the kitchen counter. They landed with a resounding and very pleasing thunk. Anita followed him in carrying the packages with their new clothing, Mango at her side. She passed by the kitchen, probably to take the bags to their bedrooms, and Mango tagged along with her, carrying a small bag.

All the purchases were courtesy of the cash in the pouch Trey had instructed him to take from the desk drawer. Cash was king to avoid anyone tracking his credit card.

But to do that they had to know who he was, and it worried him that the mole at the police force might have overheard his name and shared it with Santiago and his cronies. Luckily, he'd never been one to overly share on social media.

But can you say the same for your friends? he thought as he unpacked the bags onto the counter.

That was especially worrisome considering Jake and the changing stories about the cash for the boat.

Not that he'd let on about those fears to Anita.

For the first time in the last two days, the worry had seemed to slip from her as they'd shopped. He hadn't wanted to bring her down by sharing his concerns.

She almost skipped back into the kitchen to help him unpack. Mango walked beside her but left her to drink some fresh water Brett had set out that morning.

"I put the bag with your things on your bed," she said.

"Thanks. Do you mind finishing up so I can check in with Mia and Trey?" he said and wiggled a burner phone in the air in emphasis.

"Go ahead. I can handle this."

He signaled Mango to guard the door and walked to his bedroom, wanting some privacy for the call.

Trey didn't answer and his gut knotted with fear.

It had been a few hours since they'd spoken. But labor could take that long, he told himself and dialed Mia.

She answered on the first ring. "How's Roni?" he asked, his best friend's very pregnant wife first and foremost in his mind.

"Still in labor. I spoke to Trey about an hour ago and everything seems to be going well," she said.

"That's good news. Any new developments?" he asked.

"Our suspect cop still isn't talking, but his lawyer is negotiating with my uncle on a plea deal. I'm no legal expert, but if it avoids having the felony murder rule apply, I think he'd be wise to take it," Mia replied, confidence ringing in her voice.

"Is it too soon for the DNA results on the gator victim?" he asked, aware that it sometimes took days or weeks depending on resources and backlogs.

"The coroner has a new rapid DNA test, but he's double-checking the results," she said, some of her earlier confidence fading.

He narrowed his gaze as he considered what might be wrong and said, "Is there a problem? Contamination maybe?"

A long pause and awkward cough was followed by, "Possibly. Police have an ID on the gator victim from the fingerprints. It's William Allen. Tony's nephew."

"Wow. Do you think Hollywood killed his own nephew?" he asked, shocked and yet not shocked. Ruthless mobsters like Hollywood had rubbed out family on more than one occasion.

"It gets more complicated than that. The blood from the

suspect you shot and that from the gator victim show a familial connection," she explained.

"But the second Homestead attacker was probably Kennedy," Brett said and as his mind processed the new info, he added, "We have nothing that says he's related to Hollywood."

"You're right. If the second set of tests come back the same, we'll have to dig deeper into how that's possible," Mia said.

The sound of Anita putting things away in the kitchen ended. Her soft footfalls coming down the hall warned of her imminent arrival.

Since he didn't want to worry her, maybe it was time to wind down this conversation. But before he did so, he had one last question to ask.

"Have you been able to find out anything more about Jake and the boat?"

THE PHONE RANG and rang before going to voice mail.

It was the third time he'd tried to call his mole, but the third time hadn't been a charm.

His intuition warned that it wasn't a good thing that his cop wasn't answering.

He'd been compromised, which meant he wouldn't be getting more information from him.

But he wasn't the only mark tangled up with Hollywood. Santiago just had to pull the right strings to find someone who could give him the info he needed to find the chef and the SBS agent.

BRETT STOOD IN the middle of the room, head bent dejectedly. He scraped his hand across his short-cropped hair and said, "Yeah, I get it. I appreciate you working on that."

He ended the call and faced her with a forced smile. "No news on Roni. She's still in labor."

"What about the investigation? Anything?" she pressed.

"Cop still isn't talking, but Mia is confident they'll be able to work out a plea deal for his cooperation. They're double-checking the analysis. As for Jake, Trey and Mia's aunt, who's some hotshot lawyer, searched but couldn't find any evidence of Jake filing a Lejeune claim," he said. Every inch of his body communicated that not all was well with the case.

His upset transferred itself to her and she wrapped her arms around herself, trying to rein in fear and stay calm.

"What do we do now?" she asked.

"We keep on digging," he said and gestured toward the window in the room and the dock outside. "We start with that boat. Jake had to register it, and to do that he had to prove ownership. If we can find out who sold it to him, maybe they can tell us more about how he paid for it."

"You're still that worried about Jake?" she asked, trying to understand why he wouldn't trust an old friend, until she remembered.

"You're afraid to trust him because of what happened in Iraq," she said, then walked up to him and cradled his cheek. "It's okay to trust your friend."

He shook his head hard, dislodging her hand, and tapped his index finger against his chest. "Not when there are conflicting stories about how he bought a quarter-of-a-million-dollar boat. He told me it was a Lejeune settlement. Jim said it was a lottery win. The only likely reason to lie is because it's dirty money."

She couldn't argue with him about that. People lied when they had something to hide.

Nodding, she said, "Agreed. Where do we start?"

HER WORDS, her trust in him, relieved some of the concern that had twisted his gut into a knot during his conversation with Mia.

"We look up the address for the local DMV. They would

have to issue the boat registration," he said, then slipped his hand into hers and gently urged her from the room and back out to the breakfast bar and his laptop.

Mango raised her head and peered at them as they entered, but otherwise didn't shift from her spot guarding the door.

It took only a few minutes to get an address, and armed with that and Mango, whom he leashed to take with them, they went outside so he could find the boat registration. He lowered the lift until the boat was low enough that he could climb aboard.

"Wait here," he said and handed Mango's leash to Anita.

He hopped on and immediately noticed the glove box in the boat's console. He popped it open and pulled out a plastic envelope that held an owner's manual and the boat registration. He examined the owner's manual, hoping that it might have the seller's name on it, but no luck. Same with the boat registration, which only had Jake's name on it.

Shoving the materials back into the envelope, he took them with him as he got off the boat. He slipped his hand into Anita's and signaled Mango to heel.

"Time to hit the DMV."

SANTIAGO HAD PULLED on more strings than he thought possible.

None had turned up any information that could lead him to where the chef and SBS agent might have gone.

Frustrated, he banged his palm on the steering wheel and wracked his brains for any other names, running through them until one suddenly came to him.

It would be a big ask and he might have to sacrifice the money owed to Hollywood to get the info, but it would be worth it.

Pulling a burner phone from his jacket pocket, he made the call.

LUCKILY, THE DMV office on the Overseas Highway was a short five-minute ride from Jake's house since there was barely an hour left before it closed. It was in a strip mall that held a large supermarket, clothing outlet, public library and an assortment of other stores.

At the late hour, there was little activity inside the DMV and a young woman at a window quickly flagged them to come over.

Brett turned on the charm since honey always caught more flies than vinegar.

"I was hoping you could help us out. My friend Jake Winston—"

"I know Jake well," she said, which came as no surprise to Brett.

The young woman—pretty, blonde and athletic from what was visible through the window—was totally Jake's type. Plus, the locals were a close-knit group from what he had seen in past visits with his friend.

"Jake and I were in the Marines together and I was hoping you could help me out with something," he said and gave her his most boyish grin.

"Like what?" she asked, puzzlement on her features.

Placing the boat registration in the window slot, he tapped it and said, "Would you have helped Jake register this boat?"

Her gaze narrowed, shifted from him to Anita and then to Mango. "Is that a service dog?" she asked, her earlier friendliness dimming.

"Mango's my partner. I work with SBS. I'm not a cop, if that's what you're worried about. Jake is my best friend. I want to surprise him with something new for his boat," he said, and to prove it, he turned his left wrist over and shifted his watch so she could see the tattoo of the bulldog that he and all of his unit had gotten one drunken night.

The woman leaned forward, which gave him a clear view of her generous chest, but then she plopped back onto her high stool and smiled. "I helped Jake with the paperwork. He got the boat not far from here. Bob's Shipyard."

"Thanks. That's all I needed. I'll be sure to let Jake know you helped us," he said and gave her a little salute in thanks.

As they walked away from the window, Anita muttered under her breath, "Boy, can you turn on the charm."

He laughed and glanced in her direction. "You should know," he teased.

She stopped dead then and faced him, her gaze skipping all across his face. Pointing toward the DMV office, she said, "It was never fake with us the way it was in there."

He grew more serious and dipped his head in agreement. "It was never fake with you. Never," he said, cupped her cheek and leaned down to kiss her.

Chapter Seventeen

It was a kiss of promise and maybe possibly forgiveness for all that had gone wrong between them.

When he broke the kiss, he grinned, and it caused her heart to do a little flip-flop. She still wasn't immune to his charm. His real charm and not the act he had put on for Jake's fangirl in the DMV office.

Together, Mango comfortably at her side, they returned to their car. Brett harnessed Mango into the back seat, and once they were settled, Brett programmed the car for the ride to the boat dealer.

Bob's Shipyard was over half an hour away in Islamorada. As they passed multiple boat sale stores along the way, she said, "I wonder why he went that far to buy the boat."

Brett shrugged and it was clear he'd been wondering the same thing himself. "Maybe they were the only ones with the model he wanted."

"Or maybe Bob's Shipyard was the only place that wouldn't ask questions about how Jake was paying for it," she said.

Brett's lips tightened into a grimace, but he reluctantly nodded. "That's a very real possibility."

"But you don't want to believe there's anything criminal about how Jake got the money?" she pressed.

He bobbed his head, the movement stilted. Harsh. "I don't want to believe but it worries me. Jake didn't file a Lejeune settlement claim."

"Which leaves the lottery explanation," Anita said as Brett drove past yet another shipyard advertising boats for sale.

"Jake bought the boat a month ago. Florida keeps lottery winner names private for three months," Brett said, hands tight on the wheel.

She processed that info, trying to understand why Jake would lie about a settlement rather than tell Brett about the lottery win.

Brett must have been thinking the same thing since a second later he said, "Maybe he was worried I was going to hit him up for a loan. Some of our unit members have had a rough time. A couple are even homeless. Jake and I try to help when we can, but maybe he was worried people would come out of the woodwork once they found out about the lottery win."

"But he told Jim about it," Anita pushed.

Another shrug, followed by, "He didn't see Jim that way. As a taker."

She bit back that it meant Jake saw him as a taker because she didn't want to hurt him any more than he must be hurting.

Brett's comment created a pall in the vehicle that even Mango sensed since she sat up and whined.

Anita reached back and petted the pit bull, reassuring her that all was well. Mango licked her hand, dragging a laugh from her.

"Mango likes you," Brett said, watching the interaction in the rearview mirror.

"I'm glad," she said and rubbed the dog's ears and head again, earning another doggy kiss.

A ghost of a smile drifted across his lips. "I'm glad, too," he said and slowed the car.

She looked out the window and noticed the sign for Bob's Shipyard. Hopefully Brett would get the answers that confirmed his trust in his friend hadn't been misplaced.

SANTIAGO CURSED AS yet another online search came up blank for the SBS agent.

Brett Madison was the name that his contact at the FBI had provided.

Whoever he was, he had done an excellent job of scrubbing himself off the internet.

Either that or the SBS team had done it for him.

He pulled up the agency's website again and stared at the smiling faces of the Gonzalez family members who ran it.

Much like what had happened with Madison, there was little private info for the family members, except for Mia Gonzalez, now Mia Gonzalez Wilson.

Mia and her cousin Carolina had been top influencers before Mia had cut back on those activities to join her family's agency and marry John Wilson, a wealthy tech CEO.

There were hundreds of thousands of hits for Mia thanks to the successful business her cousin and she had run. He started reviewing them, but after scrolling through dozens of pages, he gave up on that angle because there were just too many articles, and most were about public events.

He went back to the website for the agency and tried to find out more about the acting head, Ramon Gonzalez III who was sometimes referred to as "Trey." Probably because he was the third Ramon.

Much as with the elusive Brett Madison, there was little confidential information online. But since Trey had been a detective on several high-profile cases, there were news articles galore. The only thing he could glean from them was Gonzalez's age and that he'd once been a marine.

Santiago closed his eyes, trying to remember what had happened in Homestead.

The dog attack on Billy.

Poor Billy, he thought for a fleeting moment.

The man commanding the dog in some foreign language.

A big man. Tall and broad-shouldered. Thickly muscled and hard-bodied and yet he had moved quickly. Decisively.

The way a soldier might.

That sent him down another rabbit hole, trying to locate any stories that might tie Gonzalez and Madison.

Well over an hour passed with nothing and his stomach grumbled, complaining that it was dinnertime.

He picked up his cell phone and ordered a Cubano, mango *batido* and *maduros* from a local place that had the best Cuban sandwiches and shakes.

Handheld food because he didn't intend to leave that computer until he had a clue as to where he would find the elusive Brett Madison and the chef who could send him to the electric chair.

THE NEWS CAME as they were driving back from the boat dealer.

After many long hours of labor, Roni had given birth to a baby girl they'd named Marielena after the two families' grandmothers.

"Roni and the baby are both doing well," Trey said.

Brett didn't miss the fatigue in his friend's voice. "How are you doing?"

"Exhausted," Trey admitted, but then quickly tacked on, "But I'm headed to the office now that I know Roni and the baby are fine."

He shared a look with Anita, who seemed to be totally in sync with him. "Maybe you should stay with Roni and your new daughter."

"Roni understands. Believe me. She's already been on the phone with her partner," Trey said.

Brett hated to ask, but Trey had opened the door with his statement.

"Any news on the cop or the plea deal?"

"Williams told Roni that the plea deal was in place. Williams is in the interview room with him right now. As soon as I know more, I'll let you know," Trey said as the sound of voices nearby faded into silence when he apparently stepped out of the hospital.

"I have something to share as well. You may be able to take Jake off your plate. Jake's neighbor and the dealer he bought the boat from told us Jake won a big lottery prize a month ago. That's how he got the cash for the boat."

"We'll try to confirm that, but it seems like your gut wasn't wrong about going to Jake's," Trey replied, the subtext clear.

"I'm glad, too. We'll talk to you later," he said.

"Video call twenty-two hundred. Maybe we'll have more news by then."

"Roger," Brett said and ended the call.

"SEEMS LIKE GOOD news all around," Anita said, trying to understand why Brett didn't seem more excited about all the progress and his friend's happy event.

An abrupt nod was her only answer.

Brett did a quick glance at the cell phone. "It's well past dinnertime. I don't know about you, but I'm hungry."

In response her stomach did a little growl, dragging a chuckle from her. "I'm a mite peckish," she joked and covered her noisy belly with a hand.

"I think we can risk dinner out since things seem under control for now," he said and executed a quick U-turn back toward Islamorada.

Barely five minutes later they were at a local restaurant that Anita recognized as an icon in the Keys. It had been around since the 1940s and was famous for its turtle chowder, classic Keys food and down-home dishes.

"I've heard about this place, but I've never been here," she said and shot a quick look back at Mango. "Will we able to bring Mango in?"

Brett tracked her gaze and shook his head. "I'm not sure, but probably not. Would you mind takeout and a picnic? It might be more secure to not let a lot of people see us as well."

"I'm game. Let's check out the menu online," she said, and within a few minutes they'd placed an order for conch fritters, turtle chowder and fresh-caught grilled wahoo and snapper. For Mango they added meat loaf with mashed potatoes, apparently a favorite of the pit bull.

They parked in front of the restaurant's patio with the colorful sea turtles where diners could wait for a table. Barely twenty minutes later, a server approached with a large shopping bag.

Brett stepped out to grab their order and slipped the bag into the back seat by Mango. Easing into the driver's seat again, he pulled out of the parking lot and turned onto the Old Highway. A few blocks up, another turn had them driving through a neighborhood of cinder block ranch homes on postage-stamp lots dotted with palm trees, crotons and other tropical plants and flowers.

They hadn't gone far when they reached a cul-de-sac with parking next to a beach access point.

Anita stepped out of the car and took hold of the bag with their food while Brett grabbed a blanket from the back of the car, unharnessed Mango and leashed her for the walk onto the beach. But as he did so, he peered around, clearly still vigilant despite his earlier comment that everything seemed to be under control for the moment.

"We're good to go," he said and together they walked down a path between some beachside houses and to the sand until they were several yards from the water, where Brett spread out the blanket for them to sit.

Once they were comfortably settled, Mango stretched out beside Brett on the blanket, they emptied the bag and spread the take-out dishes between them. Finding the conch fritters, they shared those first, laughing and talking as they ate.

It was easy for her mind and heart to drift back to when they used to date and how wonderful it had been between them. But every now and then, Brett would scan the area around them, reminding her that this wasn't just like it once was.

Someone was still trying to kill her, and it was only a matter of time before the peace they were feeling now would be shattered.

It dimmed her appetite, enough that Brett noticed she had stopped eating what was an absolutely wonderful grilled wahoo and started picking at it.

He offered her a smile and cradled her cheek. "It's going to be okay, Anita. Trust me."

She dropped her plastic fork onto her plate, shook her head and said, "Trust you? Seriously?"

His face hardened, confirming her shot had struck home on so many levels.

How could she trust a man who had ghosted her, but worse, trust a man who didn't trust himself?

She waited for an explosion of anger, almost welcoming it if it would clear the air around them.

But Brett only stared straight ahead, his body ramrod stiff, muscles tense. Hands taut on the plastic take-out tray with his meal.

In clipped tones, he said, "Yes, trust me. I would do anything to keep you safe."

As he finished, he slowly faced her, eyes blazing with emotion. "Anything, Anita. Don't doubt that."

She muttered a curse and looked away from that intense gaze because deep in her heart she didn't doubt him.

That almost scared her more.

"Don't die for me, Brett. Please don't," she said, aware that he wouldn't hesitate to do that. As both a soldier and SBS agent, Brett had committed to risk his life to protect others. That duty was as much a part of his DNA as the color of his hair and eyes.

Brett slipped an arm around her shoulders and drew her close. "It won't get to that, my love. It won't."

Throat tight with emotion, she said, "Promise me."

With a half smile on his face, he nodded and said, "I promise."

Mango, sensing the emotion and tension, popped away from her plate of food to stand before them, nose slathered with the remnants of meat loaf and mashed potatoes until her tongue swept out to lick them away.

It dragged laughs from them, ending the emotional moment and restoring the peace she had been feeling when they had first sat to eat.

Brett playfully bumped her shoulder with his and tossed Mango a bit of his fish that the dog snagged midair and gulped down in a single bite.

Their picnic finished with them feeding Mango the remnants of their meals. After packing their dishes and cutlery back into the bag, which Brett tossed into a nearby garbage can, they shook out the blanket, folded it and took Mango for a long walk along the beach. The dog needed the activity, but Anita did as well since she wasn't used to just sitting around.

As an executive chef, she spent her days at the market scoping out the freshest ingredients for her restaurant's menu and then on her feet in the kitchen.

She welcomed the walk and the beauty of the beach at night since it had grown dark while they were eating.

A full moon scattered playful light on the surface of the water, making it glitter happily. Lights had snapped on in the homes along the beachfront, casting a warm, welcoming glow on the sand.

The slightest breeze stirred palm trees and the nearby bushes, making them crackle and rustle and prompting Brett to peer in their direction to make sure it was only the breeze and not more.

They reluctantly returned to the car for the trip to Jake's house, aware that Trey had scheduled a meeting for later that night.

The drive back was silent at first, but it was impossible for Anita not to notice that at one point Brett was nervously checking his rearview mirror, on high alert.

As he pulled into the right lane and slowed the car, he glanced at the mirror again and muttered a curse beneath his breath.

"Something wrong?" she asked just to make sure she was reading the signals right.

"Car has been on our tail for about two miles. Windows are too tinted to see who's driving," he said, and with a quick peek at the side mirror, he pulled back into the left lane and raced ahead, so rapidly it pushed her into her seat.

She flipped down the visor and opened the vanity mirror, noted the late model Mercedes sedan that did an exaggerated shift to the left lane, mimicking what Brett had done.

"The shooter at the police station was driving a Mercedes," she said, fear gripping her.

"I know," he said calmly and increased his speed, whipping around a slow-moving car in front of him, so quickly it tossed her from side to side.

He was speeding forward, but Fate intervened as the light just several yards away turned red and an oversize truck jack-rabbited into the intersection.

Brett swore and screeched to a halt to avoid a collision.

The Mercedes that had been tailing them pulled right up next to them at the light.

As the driver's side window on the Mercedes lowered, Brett swept his arm across her body and said, "Get down."

Chapter Eighteen

As soon as Anita hunkered down in the seat, Brett freed his gun from the holster and slid down the passenger side window.

To his surprise, an elderly woman, in her eighties if he had to guess, raised an arthritis-gnarled finger and with a quaver in her voice said, "My husband wants me to let you know your left taillight is broken."

Relief slammed through him, almost violently. He dipped his head, smiled and said, "Thank you, ma'am. I appreciate you letting me know."

Anita must have overheard since she sat up in her seat, her body trembling, a response to the initial adrenaline rush. She wrapped her arms around herself, apparently trying to rein in her fear.

He laid his hand on her shoulder and stroked it back and forth, trying to calm her. "It was just a helpful senior citizen."

Anita scoffed. "Helpful nearly got them shot. I saw you reach for your gun."

He couldn't deny it as he holstered the weapon and someone honked from behind them, annoyed that the light had turned green and they weren't moving.

Driving forward, Brett traveled down the Overseas Highway until they reached the turn for the street that would take them to the almost serpentine labyrinth of roads along the man-made canals where Jake had his home.

He parked in the gravel driveway and raised his hand in

a stop gesture to warn Anita to stay put until he made sure all was safe.

As he freed Mango from the back seat, he noticed a light snap on in the front room of Jim's home. A second later the curtain was drawn slightly away.

Jim checking up on who had arrived.

He waved at the man. The curtain drifted back into place and the light snapped off.

Brett examined the area all around. Quiet along the front of the home.

Walking with Mango to the side door, he let her sniff there for anything out of the ordinary, then walked to the back dock, where everything also seemed in order.

He unlocked the entrance and released Mango to inspect the area. A short while later, Mango returned to the front door and sat, confirming that it was okay for them to enter.

With a hand signal, he commanded Mango to heel, and they returned to the car for Anita.

"All clear," he said and helped her from the car.

Arm around her waist since she still seemed shaken by what had happened earlier, they walked to the side door, where he entered first and confirmed Mango's decision that it was safe. Satisfied, he opened the side door and held out a hand to invite her to come in.

She slipped her hand into his and walked in, but as she did so, she tucked herself against him and said, "Thank you. For everything."

He wanted to say that he was just doing his job, but Anita wasn't just a job. She could never be just that.

Hugging her tight, he bent his head and tucked it to hers, needing that connection. Wishing that they weren't in this situation so that they could rekindle the magic they'd once had, only they weren't those same people anymore.

He was a man with a lot of trust issues and baggage. She was a woman with her own life and a busy one at that.

"I wish…" she whispered against his ear, but stopped, as if knowing what he was thinking and the impossibility of not only the now but also the future.

"I wish, too, but if wishes were horses, beggars would ride," he said, repeating a phrase he'd heard the nuns in his Catholic elementary school utter whenever they'd long for a snow day.

Grudgingly they separated, hopes dashed.

With close to an hour before their big meeting, Anita excused herself to go unpack and wash the clothing they'd bought earlier that day.

He was too wired after the nonincident with the elderly couple, plus pit bulls were typically very active dogs. By now he would have normally walked or exercised Mango a few times, and as good as the dog had been, harnessed into the car or guarding the door, she needed more than the few walks she'd had. Even their earlier walk on the beach probably hadn't been enough.

Because of that, he headed to his bedroom and grabbed the tug toy and hard rubber ball he'd picked up while they'd been shopping.

Anita was at the end of the hall in the small laundry room, and he let her know he was going to exercise Mango.

"I'll meet you in a few minutes," she said.

With little space on the back deck or dock, he went behind his parked car and Jake's boat trailer to the narrow sliver of driveway that remained. There he unleashed Mango and tossed the ball.

The dog took off like a rocket, gravel flying up as she dug her powerful legs into the stone. She snagged the ball as it was still bouncing, whipped around and brought it back to drop it at his feet.

"Good girl," he said and rewarded her with a hearty rub of her squarish head and short pointy ears.

When Anita came out to join them, Mango raced to her and glued herself to her side until Anita bent and stroked her hands all along the pittie's glossy fur and muscular body. "I love you, too," she said, earning a doggy kiss.

Brett handed Anita the ball and for the next half hour or so they played with Mango, having her chase the ball and run through a number of the basic commands. He explained to Anita what each one meant and that he issued the commands in Czech.

"Why Czech?" she asked as he finally instructed the dog to heel so they could return inside for their meeting.

"So the crooks won't know what they mean and so Mango won't react to a commonly used word," he said, and after they entered, he locked up and instructed Mango to guard the back door since he'd have a clean line of sight to the side door from the breakfast bar.

As he had the night before, he powered up his laptop, sent the monitor image to the larger television screen and clicked on the link to join the video meeting.

The SBS crew, except for Roni, were gathered around the table with Roni's partner, Heath Williams, and Mia's husband, John Wilson.

"CONGRATULATIONS TO YOU and Roni, Trey," Anita said.

Deep smudges under his eyes, like swipes of charcoal on a drawing, and thick stubble darkened his otherwise handsome face, but a brilliant smile lit his aqua eyes.

"*Gracias*, Anita. I'm a lucky man. Marielena is a beauty," Trey said and popped up a picture of the new baby, which earned the requisite oohs and aahs from everyone.

"She is at that, Trey. Congrats," Brett said and for a second

Anita thought she detected a wistful note in his tones, but then he was all action.

"I'm hoping for some good news."

Trey and Heath shared a look from across the table and Trey motioned for Heath to report.

"Our crooked cop agreed to a plea deal. He'll still do a good amount of time for the shootings of the two Aventura cops, but he won't get life for Billy Allen's murder," Heath advised.

"Have you found the rest of Billy in the gator?" Brett asked matter-of-factly.

Anita's stomach turned at the thought of what the gator had done to the man and Brett's seemingly uncaring tone. But then again, Billy had tried to kill them and Mango.

Heath nodded and continued. "Homestead police located his remains not far from where the jogger saw the gator with the arm. Coroner says COD was a bullet to the head," Heath said and mimicked a shot to the forehead.

Trey jumped in with, "Same caliber and make as with Ramirez and the stray bullets CSI dug out of the cabinets in Homestead. Ballistics should be able to confirm shortly if all those bullets came from the same gun."

She supposed that was some progress, not that it made her feel any more comfortable with her own situation.

"If I remember correctly, whoever shot Billy might be related to him?" Anita said, recalling something Mia had said the night before.

"Cousins, but what's more interesting is that the shooter is Tony Hollywood's son," Trey replied.

Brett shot a quick look at her, apparently as puzzled as she was since he asked, "Why is it interesting?"

"Because Tony Hollywood's one and only son is currently serving a five-year sentence for aggravated assault," Mia advised.

Anita processed that for a moment and shook her head. "Santiago Kennedy is Tony Hollywood's illegitimate child?"

"And now we have evidence also tying Kennedy to the assault on you in Homestead. Once ballistics confirms whether the bullets are the same, we've got him," Trey said.

"But not Hollywood," Anita said and pushed a stray lock of hair back from her face, feeling frustration despite all the progress that had been made.

Brett wrapped an arm around her shoulders, consoling her with a squeeze. "Once we get Kennedy, he may roll on Hollywood. But even if he doesn't, Hollywood is not going to come after you. There is nothing you know that can hurt Hollywood."

"Brett's right," Trey interjected. "The only person Hollywood should be worried about is Santiago Kennedy. He's the key in all this. He killed Ramirez and I'm sure that he killed Hollywood's nephew."

Everyone around the table nodded in agreement and then John Wilson piped in with, "I ran them through my program and the probability is almost one hundred percent that Kennedy killed both Ramirez and his cousin. But there is also a high probability that we won't get Kennedy alive."

"You think Hollywood is going to kill him?" Anita asked, thinking that the mobster had a lot to worry about with his illegitimate son.

Using his fingers, Wilson counted down the reasons. "One, Kennedy messed up with Ramirez. The program—and my gut—says he wasn't supposed to kill him, just scare him. Two, the nephew's murder. Three, the fear his wife will find out he fooled around. And finally, four, the fear Kennedy will spill his guts as part of a plea deal."

Trey had been nodding along as Wilson spoke and voiced his agreement. "I don't need the program to tell me you're one hundred percent right, John. It's why we have to find Kennedy because he knows Anita is the final nail in the coffin to charging him with Ramirez's murder."

ANITA SHOOK BENEATH his arm at Trey's words.

Brett understood. She was more worried about being in the coffin than being the nail.

He leaned close and whispered in her ear, "We will get him."

She half glanced at him, eyes wide with fear. "But when, Brett. When?"

Her whispered words cut through the air and were picked up by the laptop mic, transmitting them to those seated at the SBS offices.

"Soon. We will have Kennedy soon," Trey promised, earning a chorus of assurances from those gathered around the table.

Buoyed by his colleagues, Brett nevertheless had concerns about one front. "What about the Feds? Still not cooperating?"

"Still not cooperating," Trey said, his annoyance obvious.

Roni's partner, Heath, tacked on, "But we're working on it."

He had to be satisfied with that, Brett supposed. "What are our next steps?"

Trey and Heath glanced at each other from across the table.

"We tie together the ballistics and get a BOLO out for Kennedy. Keep on working on the Feds," Heath said.

"SBS will work on finding out what we can about Kennedy's familial connection to Hollywood. Maybe there's something there that we can use," Trey said.

"Like where he might be hiding?" Anita asked, her body still trembling and tense beneath his arm.

Trey nodded. "Yes, like that. If we find his mother, we may be able to get info from her."

"We can work on that as well," Brett offered, his mind already racing on where he could search for that information.

"How long before they release Allen's body to his family?"

Brett added, thinking that a visit to the funeral mass might also yield valuable insights.

"Not soon. They literally have to piece him together and search all those pieces for evidence. That's going to take time," Heath advised.

"Patience, Brett. I know you feel otherwise, but we've made a lot of progress," Trey shot back, testiness in his tone that made his baby sister, Mia, reach over and lay a hand on his forearm as it rested on the tabletop.

Trey shook his head and looked down, chastised. "As you can imagine, I've had a lot on my mind in the last twenty-four hours."

Although he hadn't said the words, the apology was apparent in his tone and the droop of his head. Brett accepted it and offered his own apology of sorts. "I get it. We've been kind of busy ourselves."

"Luckily, we do have some progress. I think you can rest a little easier tonight," Mia said, stepping in to be the mediator.

"Yes, we can. Maybe it's time we all got some rest," Trey said and rubbed his hands across the stubble on his face.

Brett nodded. "We'll check in tomorrow morning."

"Agreed. Ten hundred sharp," Trey said, and after a quick perusal of the table to see if anyone had anything to add, he ended the call.

"Can we rest easier tonight?" Anita asked, doubt alive in her voice.

Brett understood her concerns and they weren't just about Hollywood and Kennedy. The tension had been building between them for days and the long night loomed large.

He had to do what he could to alleviate her fears and keep from doing something they might both regret.

Chapter Nineteen

Anita swiveled in her seat, wanting to make sure she didn't miss any nuance of Brett's response.

There was the slightest hesitation and furrow of his brow before he said, "We can. It's unlikely Kennedy knows where we are right now and considering what he's done—"

"You mean killing Hollywood's nephew, who is also his cousin?" she jumped in, needing to make sure she understood exactly what was happening.

"For starters. I'd put money on it that Hollywood sent Kennedy to collect a debt, not kill Ramirez. He's probably angry now that he's unlikely to get his money."

"Unless Ramirez's partner knows something he's not talking about. I got the sense that Manny and his partner, Kevin Marino, shared a lot," she said, recalling how close they'd seemed to be the many times she'd interacted with them.

Brett mulled over her comments and nodded. "The police have probably already talked to him, but maybe he'd share more if he wasn't worried about being arrested."

"It's worth investigating, right? That and Kennedy's mother. Who was she? Does Mrs. Hollywood know? I'd be royally pissed if my husband was cheating," she said, then frowned and shook her head. "Not to mention he had a child," she added.

"Any man who cheated on you would need his head examined," he said, a dangerous gleam in his gaze as he fixed it on her and reached up to stroke the back of his hand across her cheek.

"Leaving me isn't much better," she said, then covered his hand with hers and drew it away, but she didn't let go.

He nodded. "I left you. I think I left me as well. I'm not the same man. He's long gone."

Pain colored his words and his body, which sagged from the weight of it.

Squeezing his hand, she tempered her response. "He is, but the man I see here is honorable, brave and loving."

"Does that mean there's hope for us?" he asked, lifting an eyebrow in emphasis.

"Maybe," she said, needing honesty between them.

A smile filled with longing and hopefulness drifted across his lips.

With a final squeeze of his hand, she said, "What do we do now?"

SANTIAGO KEPT TO the shadows in the alley behind Marino's condo building. It had made sense to handle this first before searching for the woman and the SBS agent. If his research was on the money, they were hours away in the Keys.

As a light snapped on a few floors above, he leaped into action, pulling down the ladder for the fire escape and silently climbing until he reached the right condo. His injured leg protested the movement and he limped onto the last landing.

Flattening against the wall, he held his breath until he confirmed he hadn't been seen by Ramirez's partner, Marino, who had just entered the apartment. Sneaking a quick look, he noticed the man had poured himself a drink and sat at the small dining table close to the window. His back was to the window and his head was buried in his hands, as if he was crying.

Santiago scoffed at the man's show of emotion. *Weakling*, he thought.

He bent and tried the window.

Locked, but there was another window at the other end of the fire escape.

He hurried there, tried the window. Unlocked.

Smiling, he grabbed the frame to lift it, but a sudden knock on the condo door had Marino's head snapping up. The man wiped away the trails of tears, and disgust filled Santiago again at the man's weakness.

Marino hurried to the door and opened it, obviously surprised by guests, especially at such a late hour.

Santiago was surprised as well as he recognized Trey Gonzalez from the photos he'd found online. A woman was with him. His sister, Mia, he guessed. She didn't look like the party girl he'd seen in the photos on her social media, but there was no denying she was a beautiful woman. He'd have no issue with doing her before he killed her, he thought, but forced his thoughts away from that to what was happening in the condo.

Whatever the SBS duo said had Marino inviting them into the room. Ever the host, he must have offered them something, but the siblings waved him off.

Santiago couldn't hear from where he was standing but as the three moved to the table where Marino had been sitting earlier, he shifted to listen to their conversation.

Even though he was closer, the sound from the nearby street and the arrival of a garbage truck in the alley behind the building made it hard for him to hear everything. Only bits and pieces of their discussion drifted out, but it was enough to know they were pressing Marino about Ramirez.

Marino, who according to his police mole hadn't said a thing, was saying more now.

"Silent partner…struggle…pandemic."

He hadn't heard Hollywood's name yet but was sure it was coming.

He couldn't let that happen.

Whipping out his gun, he centered himself at the window and opened fire.

For the briefest moment, he squinted against the shattering glass.

A mistake.

Before he could shoot at Marino again, Trey had upended the table for protection and pulled both Marino and his sister behind it.

Stunned, he delayed another dangerous second.

Trey popped up from behind the protection of the table and fired.

The bullet slammed into the body armor beneath his guayabera, stealing his breath, but he forced himself to move.

Turning, he scrambled to the fire escape ladder and raced down, cursing as pain lanced through his leg.

"Call 911," Trey called out and, at the pounding above him, Santiago knew the SBS chief was giving chase.

He fired upward wildly and stumbled down the last few steps on the ladder.

His leg crumpled beneath him as he hit the ground, a lucky thing, otherwise Trey's shot from above might have struck home again.

Cradling an arm against his bruised ribs, he raced around the corner and onto Collins, dodging cars as he hurried across the street.

He didn't look back as he heard the screech of wheels, the crunch of metal and glass, and drivers cursing. His one hope was that Gonzalez was sandwiched between those crashed cars.

As he reached the BMW he had parked by Española Way, he risked a glance back.

No one was following.

Satisfied he was in the clear, he hopped into the BMW and sped off.

Chapter Twenty

Brett had barely laid his head on the couch pillow when his phone vibrated, rattling on the coffee table.

He snatched it up, not wanting to disturb Anita and disturbed enough himself since calls at this hour were never good.

Trey, he realized with a quick glance at the caller ID. He answered the video call.

Trey looked even more tired than before and his hair was disheveled, as if he'd repeatedly run his fingers through it.

"What's up, boss?" he whispered.

"Anita was on the money about Marino. He knew more than he was sharing with the police, but he's sharing now since someone tried to take him out less than an hour ago," Trey advised.

"Kennedy?" he asked, then popped off the couch and started pacing, waking Mango, who had been dozing by the front door. The pit bull popped up her head, instantly alert to the action, but seeing it was him, she laid her head back down on her paws.

"Kennedy. I got a look at him after he fired at Marino," Trey said, but Brett could tell there was more his friend and boss wasn't saying.

"Please tell me you didn't go after him," Brett pleaded, scared that Marielena would grow up without her father.

"I'm fine but Kennedy got away. CCTV tracked him to Española Way and a black BMW. Heath ran the plates, but the car was reported stolen just like the Mercedes he was driving earlier," Trey said with a rough sigh.

"Let me guess. Stolen from one of Hollywood's car lots," he said and angrily wagged his head.

"You got it. But Marino is talking, and Hollywood is definitely involved. Turns out he was a silent partner. Gave Ramirez and Marino a few million in exchange for access to the hotel and all its facilities. Probably to run his bookmaking and sell drugs. In addition, they were supposed to repay him, a million every year, but then the pandemic hit—"

"And all the best-laid plans fell apart," Brett finished for him.

Trey nodded. "Marino admitted that Kennedy had come around a time or two, asking about the money. Apparently, Hollywood thinks they're hiding the profits that should be repaid to him."

"We have our link," Brett considered and wiped a hand across his mouth. "Are you going to share this with the Feds?"

Trey smirked and laughed. "Do you think we should?"

Brett immediately shook his head. "Not unless it's going to be quid pro quo."

"I agree. They're keeping something from us, and we need to know what that is," Trey said and then looked across the room. A second later Mia walked into view and laid a hand on her brother's shoulder.

"I apologize but I'm taking *mi hermanito* home before he falls flat on his face," she said.

"Ten hundred sharp," Trey said as Mia's finger appeared on screen a second before the call ended.

Now that's real progress, he thought, grateful that Anita and he had shared her thoughts about Marino with his SBS colleagues.

And little by little, the case against Kennedy, and Hollywood as well, was getting stronger.

Which meant they were getting closer to ending the threat to Anita's safety.

He should have been happy about that, he thought as he softly padded down to her room and peeked in.

She was sound asleep in a tangle of sheets, her beautiful legs peeking out as she lay on her back. Her dark hair was free of the topknot she normally wore, a dark spill across the electric white of the sheets. Her hand lay outspread, palm open and wide next to her.

How many times had he come to her after a late shift on the base and found her like this. Slipped his hand into hers and woken her. Made love with her.

He hardened in the confines of his jeans and sucked in a breath to control his response.

That slightest noise woke her.

Her eyes fluttered open, and she seemed startled at first, but then relaxed as she realized it was him.

"Everything okay?" she asked and sat up slightly.

The blanket slipped down, exposing her upper body. The thin white fabric of the cheap pajamas did nothing to hide the generous globes of her breasts and darker areolas.

As she realized where his gaze had gone, her nipples tightened into hard points.

He forced himself not to remember how they'd tasted. How she'd moan...

"Everything's okay," he shot out and more calmly added, "You were right about Marino. He knew more than he was saying. Kennedy tried to shut him up, but luckily Trey was there."

Anita snatched the blanket back up in a stranglehold, a reaction to both his gaze and the news. "Trey wasn't hurt, was he?"

He shook his head. "Everyone is fine. They have Kennedy on CCTV fleeing the scene in a black BMW and Marino has implicated Hollywood. The noose is tightening so this will all be over soon," he said and in a softer, sadder tone, added, "You'll be home soon."

ANITA SHOULD HAVE been happy about that.

But she wasn't.

Being home again meant saying goodbye to Brett.

Or did it? she asked herself, her body humming with need from the hungry look he'd given her before he schooled his emotions and walked out the door.

Even now her insides vibrated and dampened as she remembered making love with him. She drifted her hand up over her breast, bit back a moan at the sensitivity of her tight nipples.

He'd always done this to her. Always roused this kind of passion.

Always satisfied as a lover, but as she'd painfully discovered, that alone hadn't been enough.

But as he'd said over and over, he was no longer the same man.

But was he a better man? A man who would stay? she asked herself as she willed passion to subside in her body so she could think clearly.

The answer came immediately.

Yes.

BRETT HAD BARELY settled onto the couch when he heard a footfall in the hallway.

He half rose on the couch and reached for his weapon, but immediately recognized Anita's silhouette in the dim light.

"What's wrong?" he asked and sat up.

She padded over and sat cross-legged on the couch beside him, looking slightly girlish with her loose hair cascading down onto her breasts.

Breasts he instantly pulled his gaze from to avoid an embarrassing reaction she would surely see.

"Earlier tonight you asked if there was hope for us and I said 'maybe.'"

Hopeful emotion choked his throat, making it impossible for him to speak. He tipped his head, urging her to continue.

"I was wrong," she said, making his heart plummet until she shifted and crawled into his lap.

She cupped his jaw and ran a finger across his thick, closely cropped beard. The sound rasped loudly in the quiet of night.

"Anita?" he asked but she laid an index finger across his lips.

"The past is…the past. The last few days…you've shown me what kind of man you've become, and while you're not perfect—"

"Ouch," he muttered against her finger.

"I'm not, either," she admitted with a siren's smile.

Being this close to her, with the woman he'd loved and wanted for so long, made it impossible to curb his need any longer. Especially as she snuggled close, bringing her warm center directly above his hardness.

He swept his hands to her hips to urge her even closer and she moaned and pressed herself to him.

"Brett," she rasped.

"I want you. I want this, whatever this is," he said, afraid to say the four-letter word he suspected she wanted to hear most.

"I'm a big girl. I'll take whatever this is," Anita said, then bent her head and kissed him.

Her consent released the hunger he'd been holding in check.

He ripped the thin cotton nightshirt from her body, exposing her to his gaze. Cradling her breast, he rubbed his thumb across her hard nipple and whispered, "You are so beautiful. More beautiful than I remembered."

She followed his lead, fumbling for a second before yanking his T-shirt away.

A shocked gasp filled the air and she gently, almost reverently, skipped her fingers across the silvery and hard ridges across his upper chest.

"Do they hurt?" she asked, voice tight with emotion.

He shook his head. "Not anymore."

IT WAS IMPOSSIBLE not to think about how he must have suffered, she thought as she traced the uneven ridges scattered across his upper body. Slightly lower there was a longer, smoother but clearly man-made scar. A physician's handiwork, and she shuddered at the thought that she might have lost him permanently so many years ago.

He tucked his thumb and forefinger beneath her chin and gently urged her gaze to his. She waited for him to say something. Anything. Instead, he just tenderly brushed back a lock of stray hair and kissed her.

A whisper-light kiss. An invitation and not a demand.

She accepted, opening her mouth to his. Dancing her tongue with his as he cradled her breast and teased the tip.

She wanted his mouth on her. Wanted him buried deep inside as she shifted her hips against him, and he groaned and pushed upward.

In the dance of partners familiar with each other, he cradled her breasts together and kissed her, shifting from one tip to the other, until he suckled on one and nearly sent her over the edge.

"Please, Brett," she keened, and he shot to his feet, cradling her against his chest.

At the front door, Mango jumped to her feet and growled, misunderstanding his action.

With a hand signal, he confirmed the command with, "*Lehni,* Mango. *Lehni.*"

The dog hesitated but lay down.

"Good girl, Mango. *Pozor,*" he said, commanding her to guard the door.

Mango settled in at the entrance, head on her paws.

He pushed forward to his bedroom, laid her on the bed and

quickly stripped off his jeans. He slowed only long enough to remove his wallet and a condom he set on the nightstand.

As he climbed on the bed beside her, facing her, she once again explored his body, trailing her hand across his upper chest and down the long scar she hated seeing. She kept on going until she'd encircled him, and he sucked in a breath.

"You like?" she asked, feeling like a temptress.

He laughed and cupped her breast. Tweaked the hard nipple.

Now it was her turn to gasp as that tug ripped straight to her center.

"You like?" he teased, a boyish grin on his face before he bent and took the tip into his mouth.

When he sucked on it, she nearly lost it, but she bit her lip and cupped the back of his skull, urging him on while stroking him with her other hand.

The years of separation slipped away as they made love. Moves both familiar and yet also unexpected lifted desire to heights she hadn't experienced before until she was on the edge, barely hanging on.

He shifted inside her, driving her ever higher, and she called out his name, drawing his gaze to her face.

The words nearly slipped from her then. Nearly, but it was too soon. Too uncertain.

"It's okay, Anita. It's okay," he said as if aware of what she was keeping hidden, protected, deep in her heart.

But while the words wouldn't come, she splayed her hand over his heart and held on as he drove them ever higher until they both held their breath, poised on the precipice.

With one last stroke, he pushed them over and they fell together to the bed, joined. Wrapped in each other's arms.

Chapter Twenty-One

They woke tangled together, peaceful until Mango's growl had Brett flying from the bed naked.

He rushed to the coffee table and grabbed his gun as Mango rose and faced the front door, another low rumble coming from her throat.

Peering through the peephole, he realized it was Jake's neighbor and instructed Mango to sit down.

Tucking the gun behind him, he unlocked the door and opened it, staying behind it to hide his nudity.

"Mornin', Jim."

"Mornin', Brett. Sorry to wake you so early, but I thought you should know that I noticed a red Jeep driving by a few times. Seemed a little suspicious to me," the old man said.

Brett dipped his head in thanks, grateful for the retired cop's eagle eyes. "Any chance you have a video camera that might have picked it up?"

Jim shook his head. "Don't believe in all that new technology. I like my privacy," he said and, with a wave of his hand, turned and walked away.

Too bad, he thought.

It was also too bad that the video doorbell on Jake's house didn't face the street. At best the camera might have gotten only a sliver of anything passing by. Still, a sliver was better than nothing.

Since he'd helped Jake set up the camera and sometimes stayed there, he had access to the recorded videos.

Sure enough, the history showed that a red Jeep Wrangler had passed by the house in the early-morning hours. It had gone east, then west, then east again, toward the homes at the end of the canal. If it was just another neighbor, the car should be parked somewhere along this street or the perpendicular cul-de-sac at the end.

A quick walk with Mango would confirm that.

Anita slipped her arms around his waist, surprising him and making him jump.

He cursed and faced her. "You snuck up on me."

"You were lost in thought," she said and rose on tiptoe to brush a kiss on his lips, her naked body flush against his, rousing desire that he had to tamp down.

"Who was at the door?" she asked.

"Jim. It was nothing," he assured her and quickly tacked on, "We have a meeting in about an hour and I don't know about you, but I need some coffee and food." He rubbed his belly in emphasis.

She stroked the back of her hand across his stomach and laughed. "Man cannot live on love alone, right?"

The moment had been relatively lighthearted, but turned serious with what should have been playful words.

Stammering, he jerked his thumb in the direction of the kitchen. "How about I make some coffee while you shower—"

"And I'll cook breakfast while you clean up," she finished for him.

ANITA NODDED AND rushed off to shower. Alone. Thankfully.

Showering with Brett, which she'd done dozens of times in the past, would have been way too intimate now.

Way more intimate than what you already did all night long? the little voice in her head challenged, but she shushed it.

I won't apologize for having needs.

Needs? the voice chided but she ignored it and hurried into the shower. Washing quickly, she dried off and dashed to her bedroom to dress. She wouldn't have much time to make breakfast and clean up before the meeting with the rest of the SBS crew.

As she entered the kitchen, he handed her a mug. "I hope I got it right."

She sipped it, then nodded and smiled, pleased that he'd remembered how she took her coffee. "Perfect."

With that, he almost ran down the hall and her heart sank with the awkwardness between them this morning.

What did you expect? the annoying voice chimed in.

She ignored it, focusing on the delicious, perfectly made mug of coffee and the breakfast she had to prepare.

With the clock ticking away, she played it safe with blueberry pancakes, breakfast sausage and warm maple syrup. She normally wouldn't have bought the premade sausage, but she had remembered that Brett liked it and impulsively grabbed some while they'd been shopping.

Brett returned barely fifteen minutes later, dressed in khaki shorts and a pale yellow guayabera like those so many men wore in Miami. The pale color emphasized the cocoa brown of his beard, hair and eyes.

He went to the fridge and took out fresh food for Mango, dished it out and refilled her water bowl. He called the pit bull over, and Mango gobbled the food down so fast, Anita worried the dog might choke. But when she finished and drank deeply from the water bowl, she returned to her spot by the front door.

When Brett passed by her to grab place mats and cutlery, he laid a possessive hand at her waist and dropped a kiss on her cheek, alleviating some of the morning's earlier self-consciousness.

With a quick toss of the pan, she flipped the pancake, earning a "Show-off" from him.

She chuckled and winked. "Jealous much?"

He responded with a laugh and finished setting the bistro table as she placed a stack of pancakes on their plates and added the sausage. He took those over to the table while she poured warm maple syrup into a small jug for serving.

Because time was short, breakfast was relatively silent except for appreciative murmurs from Brett. When the plates were empty of everything but some scattered crumbs and a few drops of maple syrup, they worked together to clean and prepare for their meeting.

Barely five minutes later, they were staring at the SBS team.

"You look a little better than you did last night," Brett said. The smudges beneath his friend's eyes were not as deep and his skin had a little more color.

"Some sleep and a visit to Roni and the baby this morning worked some magic," he said and, for good measure, shared a picture of mama and baby.

Everyone around the table responded with congrats again, but then Trey quickly turned the conversation over to Sophie and Robbie's report.

"As Trey advised, CCTV picked up on Kennedy's escape after he tried to kill Marino. The police sent us the footage and we were able to trace the passage of the vehicle using an assortment of traffic cameras and ALPRs. The BMW headed south. We lost it in the Homestead area," Sophie said, worry on her engaging features, so much like Trey's and Mia's that there was no denying they were cousins.

"You think he's headed here?" Brett pressed, brows rising in question.

"Possibly," Robbie advised and continued. "An ALPR at a traffic light last picked up the BMW on Route 1. There is a BOLO out for Kennedy and the vehicle so hopefully either a sharp-eyed officer or another ALPR will see it."

"But you're sure it was a black BMW?" he asked, mindful of what Jim had seen and the footage on Jake's doorbell video.

"Positive but be mindful Kennedy may have already dumped the Bimmer and secured another vehicle," Trey warned.

"Roger that. What about Marino and the Feds? Any progress?" he pushed.

"We're waiting for a complete report from Williams, but he texted to say that Marino has implicated both Kennedy and Hollywood in various crimes. As for the Feds, it seems there's been a change in their attitude, possibly because they don't want the local LEOs to get sole credit for apprehending a high-profile target like Hollywood," Trey said.

"Sounds good. Is it okay if I send you some footage from our video doorbell?" he asked.

"Something hinky?" Trey asked, espresso-colored brows furrowing.

"Maybe or it could be nothing. Jake's neighbor is a retired cop and noticed a suspicious red Jeep Wrangler. Our doorbell picked up the vehicle, but it's at a bad angle. I was hoping Sophie and Robbie could take a look."

"Send it over," Sophie immediately said.

"Will do," he confirmed.

Trey did a quick glance around the table to see if anyone else had anything to say and when all remained silent, he said, "We'll be in touch as soon as we have more."

When he ended the call, Anita leaned close and said, "Jim saw something?"

He didn't want to worry her, so he said, "It could just be a retired cop seeing things that aren't there."

"Or his expert eyes really picked up on something," she said and splayed her fingers on the countertop, as if trying to stabilize her world.

He laid his hand on hers and squeezed. "Let me send the video to Sophie and Robbie and see what they make of it."

Chapter Twenty-Two

Anita hoped that the SBS tech gurus would be able to allay their fears, but she was too anxious to just sit and wait for a reply.

Gesturing to Mango, she asked, "Is it time to take her for a walk?"

He nodded. "Now is a good time. That red Jeep headed toward the cul-de-sac at the end of the canal. Could just be someone heading home."

She hoped he was right and trusted that he would make the right decisions to keep her safe.

They walked to the front door, where he grabbed Mango's leash and clipped it on. He opened the door but said, "Hold on while I check."

He went ahead, Mango at his side, inspected the side and front yard and then doubled back to let her know it was clear.

Outside, they strolled to the street, still as quiet as it had been the day before. He assumed the position closest to the road, Mango between them, as they leisurely walked down the block, heading for the cul-de-sac to find the red Jeep, hopefully parked in front of the owner's home.

As they reached the end of the block, she peered down the street and pointed. "There it is," she said.

BRETT HAD SEEN the vehicle also. It was on the east side of the cul-de-sac in front of a small ranch-style home. Directly opposite that home was a row of tall, thick oleanders, flush with pink flowers, forming a dense border along another home's yard.

Too dense.

Someone could easily be hiding behind those bushes.

Because of that, he shifted to the other side of the street, the one where the Jeep was stationed, and directed Anita to the inside, away from the street and those possibly dangerous bushes.

He approached the Jeep, but nothing seemed out of order. For safety's sake, he snapped off a photo of the license plate so Sophie and Robbie could check to see who owned it.

Swiveling around, he inspected the area, but all was quiet.

Gesturing to the other end of the street, he said, "Let's finish our walk and get back to the house."

SANTIAGO CLIMBED OVER the short fence and hurried down the dock, working his way toward the house where he suspected Mr. Brett Madison was guarding the chef who could ID him.

After getting the name from his FBI contact, he'd searched the internet and, although Mr. Brett Madison had done an excellent job of scrubbing himself from most places, he'd found an article that the *Marine Corps Times* had done when several marine units had helped distribute food in the Philippines after a typhoon had caused extensive devastation.

He'd recognized Madison immediately, although he'd been several years younger. The photo had shown him, SBS Chief Trey Gonzalez and fellow marine Jacob Benjamin Anderson.

Jacob, apparently known as Jake to his friends, hadn't been as careful as Gonzalez and Madison.

Social media content galore and easily found via a free online phone book.

Just a few more houses, Santiago thought, but then he caught sight of the old man sitting on a lawn chair farther down the dock that ran behind the homes.

Even though he was older, the man was still in good shape.

Whipcord lean muscles warned he'd put up quite a fight. Worse, he had that look about him. Either ex-cop or ex-military and he was directly in the way of him reaching his destination.

He could fight him or even just shoot him, but that would alert Madison to trouble.

That was the last thing he wanted to do. He needed the element of surprise if he was going to be able to overcome Madison and that powerful pit bull.

With a nonchalant wave at the man, he doubled back to where he'd parked the Jeep. He'd return later, when it was dark and easier to avoid prying eyes.

He hopped the fence again and raced across the last yard and around the thick row of oleanders.

As he slipped into the Jeep, he couldn't believe what he was seeing right in front of him.

Madison, the woman and that damn dog.

They were at the far end of the cul-de-sac and boxed in by cars on either side of the street.

Perfect, he thought, then started the car and gunned the engine.

Chapter Twenty-Three

Brett whirled around at the sound of the racing engine.

The Jeep was barreling toward them, but they were at the end of the street and cars lined either side, leaving no room for escape. But at their end of the block a wide swath of dock ran perpendicular to the street along the waters of another canal.

"Run," he said, urging Anita in the direction of the dock and scooping up Mango.

At the edge of the narrow dock, Anita hesitated.

He wrapped an arm around her and hauled her close as he jumped into the water.

SANTIAGO SCREECHED TO a stop, cursing and hitting the steering wheel in frustration as he watched the trio leap into the canal.

He raced out of the Jeep and ran to the edge of the dock, but he couldn't see them in the waters below.

That didn't stop him from opening fire into the canal.

He emptied his clip, but as people raced out of their homes, he couldn't linger.

He raced back to the Jeep, reversed down the block and, with a quick K-turn, sped away.

MANGO FOUGHT AGAINST HIM, clawing to be free of the water.

Anita started to rise, but he laid a hand on her shoulder and kept her down.

She looked at him, fearful eyes wide against the stinging seawater, and he gestured upward.

Above them bullets pierced the surface and flew downward, creating deadly trails in the water.

When the last of the bullets swam by, he pushed off the bottom and to the surface. Anita popped up next to him a second later.

He released Mango, who immediately began dog-paddling beside him as Brett searched for some way to reach the dock again.

Suddenly, Jim leaned over the edge of the dock and held out his hand. "Heard the commotion and came to help," he said.

Brett grabbed hold of Jim's hand and that of another neighbor who had also come to assist. The two men boosted him up easily and, in turn, he bent to lift Anita out of the water.

"You're not hurt, are you?" he asked, inspecting Anita as she stood beside him.

"I'm fine," she said.

Jim lifted Mango out of the water and deposited her on the dock.

The dog shook her body, sending water everywhere, and then immediately came to Brett's side and bumped his leg with her head, almost as if in apology.

Her thick nails had torn his shirt and raked deep scratches into his chest as she'd struggled against him underwater, fear gripping her.

"You're a good girl, Mango," he said and rubbed her head and ears.

The sound of approaching sirens perked up Mango's ears, and barely a minute later, a squad car came around the corner and parked.

Brett had wanted to keep a low profile but clearly that would no longer be possible.

"Neighbors probably called 911," Jim said as he looked at the cruiser.

Brett nodded. His mind raced with all the possible things he could do to protect Anita now that this location was also blown.

One immediately came to mind. Turning to the old cop, he said, "Could you do me a favor?"

Jim bowed his head and said, "Sure. What is it?"

Not wanting others to overhear, he leaned close and whispered his request to the older man.

"Got it. I'll reach out to Jake and be waiting for you," he said and pushed off, hurrying past the police officer with a quick salute.

Anita stood shivering beside him, but a fifty-something female walked over and wrapped a beach towel around her. "Th-th-thank y-y-ou," Anita said past her chattering lips.

"No worries, honey. Keep it," the woman said and handed Brett another towel to dry down.

Not that it would take long. Even though it was December, the sun was strong and the day warm. Already in the low seventies, if he had to guess.

Anita's trembling was likely more from fear than cold.

He wrapped an arm around her and rubbed his hand up and down her side, offering support and reassurance as they answered the volley of questions the officer, a young Latino man named Hernandez, was asking.

Names, addresses and their business in the area. A description of the car, which also had Brett pulling out his cell phone to provide the license plate number. Officer Hernandez jotted it all down and was about to start asking even more questions when his radio chirped to life.

"Hernandez here," he said as he answered.

"Miami PD wants your report and said to release the victims ASAP," the dispatcher advised.

"10-4. We're done here anyway," Hernandez said and faced them.

"You heard. You're free to go. Do you need a ride?" he asked.

Brett flipped a hand in the direction of the street off the cul-de-sac. "We're just a few doors down."

The officer nodded and headed to his patrol car while Anita, Mango and he rushed down the block. But the officer, obviously aware that this was an unusual and dangerous situation, followed them in his cruiser and parked in front of Jake's house.

Brett walked Anita toward the entrance of the side yard and door and said, "Wait here."

Hurrying back to the cruiser, he leaned down and said, "This guy won't hesitate to shoot, so stay vigilant."

The young officer nodded. "10-4. Do you need an escort to somewhere else?"

Brett peered toward the SUV in the driveway. He had no doubt it had already been compromised by Kennedy noting the plate number. They had no idea how many dirty cops Kennedy had in his pocket who would use the ALPRs to track their travel.

He shook his head. "We're going to stay here for now," he said, even though he had no plans to do that.

"I'll be sure to drive past here often while I'm on patrol," he said.

"That would be appreciated," Brett said and tapped his hand on the window frame to let the officer know he was good to go.

Hands on hips, he watched the officer drive away, did another quick look around the property and then walked with Mango back toward the side yard and door.

As he had so many times before, he opened the door and sent Mango ahead to scope out the house.

Not that he expected Kennedy to have lingered there after trying to run them down.

But he had no doubt Kennedy would be back, which meant they had to be on the move as soon as possible.

Inside, he turned to Anita, who stood in the dining room,

shaking even with the towel and her arms wrapped around herself.

He laid a hand on her shoulder and cupped her cheek. Leaning down so she couldn't avoid his gaze, he said, "It's going to be okay. Take a warm shower and pack up your things. We'll be on the move as soon as I talk to Trey."

She nodded and walked down the hall, and he pulled out a fresh burner phone and called Trey.

"Are you all okay?" Trey asked, clearly having been filled in by MPD.

"Pretty much," Brett said and peered at the angry scrapes on his chest that were stinging from the salt water in the canal.

Trey released a colorful stream of curses about the state of things and Brett had to agree. "Yes, it's totally messed up. We can't stay here, it's compromised."

"I agree. I'm looking for another place for you—"

"No need, Trey. I have an idea," he said and relayed the plan that had occurred to him.

"Unorthodox, but it makes sense," Trey said with a low whistle.

"How did he find us? I thought you had plugged the leak at PD," Brett pressed, angry that another location had been compromised.

"I don't know but I have my suspicions, particularly since the FBI is finally involved in this," his friend said.

"You think the leak is there?" Brett asked, not that the FBI agents were so far beyond reproach.

"Possibly. Williams, Roni and I are going to speak with the lead Fed. Alone. In the meantime, go ahead with your plan. I'll reach out to you later once we've finished," Trey said.

"Roger that," he said and ended the call.

THE SHOWER HAD helped immensely to chase away the fear of the moment and the salt water of the canal.

And as she'd shoved her meager belongings into a plastic bag, anger replaced fear. Determination replaced worry.

She marched out to the dining room where Brett had just finished his call.

"What can I do?" she asked, chin tilted up defiantly.

But as Trey turned in her direction, she gasped and walked over to him to gently brush aside the torn fabric of his shirt. "Oh my god. We need to tend to those," she said, shocked by the deep, angry scratches on his chest.

"Mango panicked underwater, but I couldn't let her stay on the dock. Kennedy would have shot her," he said in explanation.

Anita bobbed her head in agreement. "I get it. Why don't you shower, and after, I'll get those cleaned and bandaged."

"Thanks. We're leaving here. Would you mind packing up our food supplies? Nothing too perishable."

"I'll get them ready," she said and hurried to do as he asked, mentally preparing a menu from the foods they had and which would keep for a few days.

She carefully packed things away and then returned to her bathroom and searched the cabinet for disinfectant, antibiotic ointment, gauze and tape.

Brett exited his bedroom bare-chested and wearing unbuttoned jeans that hung loose on his lean hips, toweling dry his high-and-tight hair.

Lord, but he was gorgeous, even with his warrior's scars.

Her heart pounded with need, but also that fear again that she'd almost lost him forever.

Juggling the items to tend to the scratches, she said, "Why don't you sit on the couch."

When he did so, legs splayed wide, she slipped between his powerful thighs and sat opposite him on the coffee table. She laid out her first aid supplies, applied disinfectant to some gauze and swiped it across the scratches to clean them.

His muscles jumped beneath her ministrations, but he didn't move otherwise.

With fresh gauze, she applied the antibiotic ointment and then taped more gauze in place over the scratches.

"Did you pack up?" he asked when she'd finished, and he offered her a hand up from the coffee table.

She motioned to the assortment of bags on the floor by the kitchen counter. "All ready to go."

He smiled, waggled his head and said, "I'll be back."

He sauntered down the hall, popped into his bedroom and exited a second later, shrugging on a fresh guayabera, the duffel with his clothes in hand.

When he reached her, he stuffed her clothes into the duffel and slung it on his shoulder. After, he filled his hands with a number of the bags she'd packed and she did the same, grabbing as many as she could. Mango helped out as well, picking up a smaller bag with her mouth.

She followed Brett to the back door, where he paused and peered out.

Looking back at her, he said, "We're good to go."

Chapter Twenty-Four

When they stepped outside, she realized Jim was by their dock, a shotgun cradled in his arms. The boat that had previously been high up on the lift had been lowered into the water, where it bobbed gently in the canal.

"Was Jake cool with us taking the boat?" He'd asked Jim to call his friend for permission to use the boat and, if it was okay, prep it.

"He is," Jim said with a dip of his head.

"Thanks, Jim," Brett said and clapped Jim on the back.

The older man nodded and handed him the shotgun. "You might need this," he said and added, "Put a box of shells in the console glove box."

"Thanks again. I truly appreciate it," he said and shook the other man's hand. It was then he noticed the Semper Fi tattooed on the man's forearm.

"Anything for a fellow marine," he said, then turned to Anita and jabbed a finger in her direction.

"You take care of him and you," Jim said with another determined point.

"Good man," she said and watched him walk away in the direction of his house.

"Yes, he is," Brett agreed, then laid his bags on the deck and gently placed the shotgun against the nearest console on the boat. He turned, reached across for her bags and put them on the deck of the boat as well. Finished loading the bags, he asked, "Did you take Mango's food also?"

"Of course. I would never forget Mango," she said and kneeled to pet the dog, who had been patiently sitting on the dock beside her.

Smiling, he held out a hand to help her onto the boat. She stumbled a little as the boat rocked and laid a hand over her stomach, as if a little nauseous already.

"It'll be better once we move. There is a sleeping area, galley and head down below," he said and opened the cockpit door, familiar with the boat from his father's catalogs and having rented similar vessels.

"I'll get these supplies put away," she said, then grabbed some of the bags and disappeared through the opening to belowdecks.

Brett picked up the shotgun and placed it at the cockpit door, just in case. He checked the console for the shells and, satisfied they were in easy reach, stowed his gun there as well to keep it dry but easily accessible. He hopped back onto the dock and signaled Mango to heel as he returned to Jake's house and went into a pantry where he had noticed a big-box-store-sized package of bottled water.

He hoisted that in one hand, locked up the house and returned to the boat.

Mango didn't follow him down, remaining on the dock, where she paced almost nervously. Unusual for the normally fearless dog, and he wondered if she was associating the boat and nearby waters with the scary moments she had experienced not that long ago.

"Come on, Mango. *Kemne,*" he urged, instructing her to come onto the boat. She hesitated and he repeated the command. *"Kemne."*

This time she finally hopped up and over the side, her feet

skidding on the smooth surface amidships as she landed on the deck.

"Good girl," he said and stroked her head. He caught sight of a familiar package through the thin plastic bag, reached in and took out Mango's treats. He handed her one and further reinforced her behavior with another rub of her head.

"Lehni," he instructed, and she immediately lay down, sprawling in the middle of the deck. He was grateful for her quick response because he had to be able to rely on her following her commands without hesitation.

He snatched up the last of the bags and took them down to the galley, where Anita was unpacking and stowing items in the cabinets. She turned as he entered and said, "The fridge isn't working."

Nodding, he said, "It probably needs the engine running or a solar panel for power. We'll figure it out once we're underway."

He returned topside for the bottled water, brought it down to her and then went back up to untie the boat.

Anita came up then. "I'll get the bumpers," she said, reminding him that she'd sometimes gone boating with her father.

"Thanks," he said, and as he maneuvered away from the dock, she pulled up the bumpers that protected the boat from dock damage and stowed them beneath the seats at the stern.

She stepped over Mango, who hadn't moved, and joined him at the console.

Laying a hand on his shoulder, she asked, "Where are we going?"

"Jake and I used to go fishing in this area and sometimes stay overnight. There's an anchorage spot near Islamorada and Shell Key that's perfect for tonight," he said, carefully steering the boat to the end of their canal. He turned away from the spot where they'd had to jump into the water.

He cruised wide past that area slowly, keeping an eye out for anything untoward, and caught sight of a police cruiser doing a K-turn on that block.

Officer Hernandez, patrolling as he'd promised.

Brett drove ahead sluggishly, aware of the no-wake zone in the canal area, but as soon as he cleared the last bit of canal, he pushed the boat to its top speed, heading for the Atlantic Intracoastal Waterway and Cowpens Cut. That channel would let them navigate down the Intracoastal and to the familiar spot where they could anchor. Maybe even fish for dinner.

He kept an eye on the boat's radar to make sure he was avoiding any of the shallow shoals or reefs in the area.

"You seem comfortable with this," she said and slipped onto the seat opposite him. Surprisingly, Mango hopped up into her lap, dragging a laugh from her.

"You are so not a lapdog," she said as Mango insinuated herself into the tight space between Anita and the padded console in front of her.

"Mango. Get down. *Lehni*," he called out, but the dog remained in Anita's lap, worrying him, but he didn't press since it seemed to reassure Anita.

"IT'S OKAY. REALLY. She's not too heavy," Anita said and rubbed the dog's head as she sat there, tongue lolling out of her mouth. A cooling breeze bathed them as the boat moved along, and Anita raised her head to catch the air, much like Mango was doing.

If she hadn't been on the run for her life, she might have appreciated the lovely views of the bright cerulean waters, darker in spots from the reefs below, or the lush, verdant foliage and expensive homes along the shore.

It didn't take long to reach what she supposed was Cowpens Cut.

Mangrove and underbrush marked the edges of the narrow strait while channel markers warned of the depth in the center.

Blue-green waters also identified the navigable areas in the middle while white sand was visible beneath the shallow waters along the edges of the cut.

It was a short trip through the area, and once he'd cleared it, Brett increased the boat's speed, following the buoys and channel markers that identified the path for the Intracoastal Waterway.

"That's Plantation Key over there," Brett said and gestured eastward to a larger collection of homes and land along the spit of sand and highway that made up the Keys.

"Will it take long to reach Islamorada?" she asked, unfamiliar with these waters. When she'd gone out with her father, they'd stayed in Biscayne Bay.

"Not long. We should be there in about an hour. Once we get there, we'll anchor and see if there are solar panels we can set up to power the fridge, appliances and the lights for tonight," he said, his gaze constantly traveling along the route and also peering back, making sure all was good.

"What about Trey? Can we reach him out here?" she asked, worried about cell reception, not that they were all that far from land.

"We have service where we anchor even though it's not all that close to shore. I'll call as soon as we're anchored and set up for power."

As PROMISED, it wasn't long before they had reached their destination.

In one of the storage areas, Brett located solar panels and cables that connected to a battery array on the boat. In a second area along the hull of the boat, he found rods, reels and Jake's tackle box, filled with lures and other necessities.

He quickly set up the solar panels and plugged them in to power the appliances and provide light at night. Once he'd done that, he pulled out the rods, reels and tackle box and brought them to a bait station at the stern.

"I thought we might fish for our meal," he said, thinking that the task would also distract Anita from thinking about what had happened just hours earlier.

He was about to help her assemble the tackle, but she went into action without hesitation. "This is old hat to me. My *papi* didn't cut me and my sister any slack when we went fishing."

"Good to know. Since you can handle that, I'm going to call Trey," he said, then pulled out the burner phone and walked around the cockpit area to the bow of the boat. He climbed up onto the seats there and perused the area, vigilant for any danger.

There were several pleasure craft out on the waters, but none seemed to be heading in their direction. Feeling secure, he dialed Trey.

"Have you anchored?" he asked as soon as he answered.

"We have. Everything seems secure for now," Brett advised and did another slow swivel to scope out the area around Shell Key.

"Good. We spoke to the FBI agent handling the Hollywood investigation. He admitted that they'd suspected they had a leak on their team since Hollywood kept slipping through their fingers every time they got close," Trey advised.

Brett blew out a breath, shook his head and drove a hand through his hair. "Is that why they didn't want to cooperate?"

"Yes. They were afraid the leak could compromise our investigation, which had made more progress than theirs," his friend reported.

"And now? Why the change in their attitude?" Brett wondered. He hopped off the seat cushion and walked back to the stern, where Anita had their poles all set to go.

He sauntered to her and said, "I'm putting the phone on speaker."

"Great," Trey said and continued with his report. "The FBI had their suspicions on who the leak was and, with all that was happening, upped their surveillance. That caught one of their agents sending your name to what turned out to be a burner phone. The agent confessed that he had sent it to Kennedy."

"And Kennedy somehow connected me to Jake? Is that possible?" he asked.

"I doubted it, too, but I put Sophie and Robbie on it, and they instantly got a hit in a marines newsletter that's also posted online. Jake, you and me were identified in the photo and Jake's info—"

"Is readily available online," Brett finished for him.

"What do we do now?" Anita asked. He noticed the worry lines across her forehead.

An awkward silence followed until Trey said, "The accused FBI agent lawyered up, but he's willing to assist us in exchange for a lighter sentence. We're working on a plan to draw out Kennedy."

Brett didn't like the sound of that at all. "Draw out. Like in a trap?" he asked just to confirm.

That long, pregnant hesitation came again. "Yes, as in a trap."

"And we're the bait?" Anita shot out, obviously understanding exactly what they were planning.

"I'm not a fan of this, either, but it's local cops and the FBI in charge and making the decisions. But I'm not going to hang you out to dry. I'll call in Matt, Natalie and their canines, as well as several of our other agents, to safeguard you," Trey said, his conviction clear.

Brett and Anita gazed at each other, and as one they nodded, trusting Trey. "Whatever you need so we can close this case and Anita can get back to her life," Brett said.

"I'll call at 0900 with an update," Trey said before disconnecting.

Chapter Twenty-Five

Anita didn't know why the thought of returning to her old life saddened her, but she bit her lip and fought off that emotion.

When the call ended, Brett powered down the phone and laid a hand on her shoulder. "Trey will keep his promise. You'll be home soon. Back at the restaurant and with your family well before Christmas."

She forced a smile and bobbed her head up. "I know. It's just that…"

She couldn't finish. Stepping against him, she leaned into this comforting strength. He was like the proverbial oak, strong and steady, but also flexible enough to move as he'd had to with each challenge that had arisen.

He wrapped his arms around her and rocked her gently, comforting her, murmuring over and over that she would be fine. That everything would turn out okay.

She made herself believe that. Repeated it to herself as she stepped away and picked up a rod to distract herself from everything that was happening.

"We have a few hours before it gets dark. Should be enough time to catch something. We usually have luck in this area," Brett said and took hold of the second reel.

Since it seemed like he wanted to keep things chill, she asked, "What do you normally catch here?"

"Snapper, hogfish or snook. Sometimes mahi-mahi," he said.

"All good-eating fish," she said. She reeled in some line and, after releasing the bale arm, did an overhead cast that sent the lure flying out into the waters.

"Good cast. Your *papi* taught you well," he said and playfully clapped her on the back.

"He'd be happy to hear you say that," she said, not intending to return things to serious mode and yet that's where it went.

After a long moment during which Brett cast out his line, he said, "I'd like to meet your *papi* someday. Your *mami*. Maybe your *hermanita*, too. Are you the oldest?"

"I am," she said, but couldn't risk a look at him, afraid of what she might see. Instead, she reeled in her line slowly, hoping for a bite. Anything to keep from looking over at him. To keep it from getting more personal.

She was about to give up on a bite and reel the line in more quickly, but a sharp tug followed by a second stronger hit had her instinctively jerking the rod back to hopefully set the hook.

It worked.

Suddenly a fish came flying out of the water, battling against being hooked. The powerful surge of its leap nearly unbalanced her, but Brett was immediately there, his big body behind her. Hands at her waist to help steady her.

"It's a big tarpon," he said, laughter and surprise in his voice.

Tarpons were known for the fight they put up, Anita knew. Her father had snagged one many years earlier and had spent some time working the fish up to the boat, battling the many leaps and runs the fish had made.

Today was no different.

Over and over the silvery body of the tarpon shot out of the water, leaping and thrashing, its large scales flashing silver in the sunshine. A rattling noise from the fish's gills escaped with each leap.

Mango, hearing the commotion, had hopped up and placed

her front legs on the edges of the stern, watching the leaps and the two of them battling to bring in the big fish.

Anita's arms ached from fighting the jerk and tug of the line and the constant reeling. Sweat dripped down her back and her legs ached, but she had Brett's support behind her, urging her on until she was finally able to reel the tired fish close.

They leaned over to examine the tarpon as it rested on the surface behind the boat, sucking in air through its big mouth, a trait unique to the almost prehistoric fish.

"I'm guessing it's about thirty inches long," Brett said with a low whistle, then whipped out his phone, turned it on and snapped a photo.

At her puzzled look, he said, "So you can show your dad. Tarpon are catch-and-release only."

The catch-and-release made sense. A beautiful warrior like this deserved to go free, she thought.

Just like you have to let Brett go? the little voice in her head challenged.

This investigation may have hooked him into being with her, but she had no doubt that Brett was free to make his own decisions, much like she was.

Brett bent and gently worked the lure out of the tarpon's mouth. He cradled it gently in the water, letting it rest and recover in his hands after the ferocious fight. As soon as the fish seemed to have more energy, he released the tarpon and it slowly swam off, silvery body gliding along the surface for a few feet until it dived and became a dark blue blur speeding away underwater.

Body trembling from the fight, she sat down on one of the cushioned seats behind the console. "I'm beat," she said and wiped some sweat from her brow with the back of her arm.

Brett nodded and smiled. "Understandable. I guess it's up to me to catch our supper," he said and cast out his line.

Mango had remained by the stern, but seemingly bored with what was happening, the pit bull lay down by her feet.

Anita bent and stroked the dog's body, and Mango rolled over to present her belly for a rub. She did, giving her a good massage with both hands. But as she did so, it occurred to her that they had no way to walk the pit bull.

Rising, she strode to Brett's side, careful to avoid the line as he cast. Watching him from the side of her eye, she asked, "How will we walk Mango?"

Brett risked a quick glance back at the pittie, who had risen to watch them as they stood at the stern. "She's trained to go on command. I'll take her up front to relieve herself. Mind taking the rod?"

"Sure," she said and accepted the rod while Brett went below and came back with a plastic bag and some paper towels.

"*Kemne*, Mango," he said and swayed his palm toward him in command.

Mango immediately obeyed, following him toward the bow.

A tug on her line dragged Anita's attention back to fishing.

She tried to set the hook, and when she had a stronger tug and slight run on the line, she knew she had possibly snared dinner. Not a tarpon, she could tell from the way the fish stayed underwater, fighting against the line.

When Brett returned with Mango barely a few minutes later, she handed him the rod, too tired to finish hauling in the fish.

Mango and she stood at the stern and watched Brett work the line, slowly maneuvering the fish closer and closer until he finally brought it to the stern. He leaned over, hooked his fingers into the fish's gills and hauled it onboard.

"Lane snapper, luckily. We're out of season for red snapper," he said as the nice-sized fish flopped around on the floor of the boat.

"Excellent eating. Do you want to prep it or should I?" she asked, but even as she said it, the loud sound of an engine approaching had them both turning.

A Boston Whaler headed straight for them at breakneck speed.

Chapter Twenty-Six

Brett swept his arm in front of Anita and urged her behind him. "Go below," he said, unsure whether the approaching boat was friend or foe.

As Anita hurried away, he slowly backed toward the cockpit door as well to grab the shotgun.

But as he reached for it, the Boston Whaler slowed. As it did so, the bow dipped slightly, allowing him to see the khaki-clad person at the wheel, wearing a familiar drab green baseball cap and black life vest.

Trusting his gut that it really was a game warden patrol boat, he walked back toward the stern of the boat, waiting for the other vessel to pull closer.

The craft slowed and tossed out large white bumpers to protect the two boats from bashing into each other. As they did so, he caught sight of two game wardens, one at the wheel and another at the stern. A large gold star in a circle with the FWC's name sat on a large green vertical stripe on the side of the boat along with the words "Florida Wildlife Commission State Law Enforcement."

"Mind us seeing what you have there?" the officer at the stern asked.

"Feel free," Brett said and waved at the officer to come aboard.

The FWC warden did just that, agilely hopping from his boat to theirs.

"Nice-looking snapper," the warden said, hands on his hips.

"A keeper from what I can see," Brett said with a bob of his head.

The officer nodded in agreement. "It is. You have your license with you?"

Brett reached into the back pocket of his shorts, took out his wallet and eased out the colorful, credit-card-style fishing license. He handed it to the game warden, who reviewed it and said, "Looks like we're all good. You plan on anchoring here overnight?"

"We do. Just taking a few days off," he said.

The warden narrowed his gaze, peered around the boat and noticed the shotgun by the cockpit door. It had him laying a hand on the weapon on his belt as he said, "Do you have a license for that?"

Brett nodded and pulled out both his concealed carry license and an SBS business card, still damp from the unexpected swim he'd taken earlier that day. He handed them to the warden.

"SBS agent, huh? On the job?" the warden asked and returned the documents.

Shaking his head, Brett said, "Just a few days off from work. Shotgun is for protection. I know this area is pretty safe, but I don't like taking chances."

Seemingly satisfied, the other man did a little wave and said, "Enjoy the snapper. My wife makes it oreganata-style and it's delicious."

The other man hopped onto the gunwales and then across into the Boston Whaler. As his partner, a blonde warden, started up the engines and pulled away, the man hauled in the big white bumpers and waved again.

Brett breathed a sigh of relief, picked up the snapper and removed the hook.

Anita popped out from below, walked over to him and, with

a laugh, said, "His wife is right. Oreganata-style would be a good way to cook this."

With a chuckle, Brett nodded. "I'll get it scaled and clean. Do you want me to filet it?" he asked.

"If you don't mind. I'm going to cook up some sides," she said, then turned and went back below.

On the portside of the boat was a bait prep station with a freshwater hose and an assortment of knives and pliers he could use to prepare the filets. Jake had clearly spared no expense when he had equipped his boat.

As he tossed the scales, bones and scraps into the water, an assortment of fish came up to feed. At one point a small blacktip shark swam by to eat the scraps and one of the smaller fish.

The circle of life, Brett thought.

It had him looking back toward the cockpit and wondering about his life.

Anita had never responded to his less-than-subtle probing about meeting her family, but then again, what did he expect?

He wasn't the man she had fallen in love with nearly a decade earlier. The man who had ghosted her because he had lost faith in himself.

But Trey and this assignment had forced him to believe in himself. To trust his gut to do what was right.

And what was right was to finally admit that he still loved her. That he could be the man for her.

If she wanted him, that was. If she was willing to let him into her very busy life. A life she'd worked so hard to build for herself.

But he could handle that. Handle giving her the space she needed because he would need space at times as well if he was going to be a reliable SBS K-9 agent.

Armed with that, he scooped up the filets and whistled to Mango to follow him below.

IT HAD TAKEN Anita some time to familiarize herself with the galley kitchen tucked amidships in the bow, almost directly in front of the cockpit area.

There was one small electric burner and a combo toaster/microwave oven. Beneath them, the fridge was gratefully chilling now that they'd set up the solar panels. To the side was a circular sink and faucet. She'd been careful when using the water, unsure of just how much the boat stored for cooking and washing. But they also had the bottled water just in case.

In the deeper, V-shaped portion of the bow, a comfy-looking padded bench wrapped around the area with a trapezium-shaped table at the center. She hadn't seen any kind of sleeping area except for a small nook to one side. She assumed the table and cushions would do double duty later that night.

The snapper was baking, as the warden had suggested, in the oven. Brett had brought it down earlier but then gone back up to clean up and secure the fishing equipment.

The flavorful aromas of toasty breadcrumbs, garlic and lemon with the subtler sweeter scents of the snapper filled the bow as she stirred a pseudo rice pilaf, a mix of butter, garlic, onion and chicken broth. She had lacked the orzo to make it a real pilaf.

Already resting on the dining table was a plate of roasted asparagus dressed with a simple vinaigrette.

Simple being the key because of the minimal ingredients onboard and the single burner.

It was a real challenge to her normal cooking style, but maybe that was a good thing.

Sometimes she got too caught up in fancy and forgot what was really important.

Like tasty meals made from simple ingredients.

Brett poked his head through the cockpit door. "Permission to come down, Captain," he teased.

She laughed and waved him in. "Permission granted."

It was a tight squeeze past her into the table area as he came down the spiral steps from above, Mango awkwardly hopping from one step to the other. Once he was there, he lifted the cushions to check what was beneath them.

He came up with a bottle of wine that he waggled in the air. "I assume white? Jake has a nice stash in there. Sheets and pillows, too."

"White would be nice," she said, and he tucked it into the fridge.

"Hopefully it will cool down a little," he said, then came up behind her and laid a hand on her waist as he watched her cook.

It was a familiar stance. He'd done it often when they'd been together, always seemingly fascinated by how she created while at the stove.

"Smells good. Looks great," he said. He dropped a kiss on the side of her face and then worked on feeding Mango, spilling out kibble and fresh water into the bowls they'd brought with them.

After, and with nothing to do, he sat at the table and Mango settled at his feet, content now that she'd been fed.

With a side-eyed glance, Anita watched him turn on the burner phone. His fingers flew over the keys and then stilled. His gaze narrowed and his lips thinned into a knife-sharp slash. Another flurry of texting followed until he stopped and powered down the phone again.

"Nothing new?" she asked and stirred, worried about what he might say.

"Police and FBI are still working out the details of the trap. We'll know more in the morning."

The morning. Nearly a dozen hours away, she thought and peered out through the small oval window. Dusk had arrived and night would come quickly, before six at this time of year.

A lot of time for them to be alone together in that confined area.

Memories of the night before flamed to life. She couldn't deny wanting that. Wanting him, but once again she told herself that passion alone wasn't enough.

Because of that, as she stirred the pilaf, she shot him a half glance and said, "It might be nice if you met my parents and sister. *Papi* might be a little gruff. He probably still remembers how you broke my heart."

"I didn't want to," he said, his tone soft, almost pained. "I didn't think you'd want to be with me the way I was."

"I know," she said, then grabbed plates from one of the cubbyholes above the stove and spooned pilaf onto them.

She grabbed pot holders and opened the oven. Satisfied the snapper was ready, she pulled out the pan onto a trivet on the granite countertop. With a long spatula, she lifted the snapper from the pan and laid a filet on each plate beside the pilaf.

She took a few steps to the table, placed a dish before Brett and sat opposite him.

He thanked her, rose and went to the fridge, where he grabbed the wine, twisted off the cap and served it.

His pour was substantially smaller, she realized as he returned with the glasses.

At her questioning glance, he said, "I feel like celebrating, but have to stay sharp."

Smiling, she lifted her glass, and he did the same as she toasted with, "To the tarpon catch, which my dad wouldn't believe without your photo, the snapper and, more importantly, being alive."

He added, "And second chances."

She couldn't disagree. Nodding, she clinked her glass against his and said, "To second chances."

Dinner passed without much talk, both of them seemingly lost in their thoughts and the scrumptious food.

"This is absolutely delicious," he said as he forked up the

last bits of his fish and rice, leaving such a clean plate it didn't seem to need any washing.

Humbled by his praise, she said, "Or maybe you're hungry because we haven't eaten in hours."

He pointed his index finger down at the plate. "No way. This gets five out of five stars in the Madison review of restaurants," he teased.

The heat of a flush swept across her cheeks. "High praise. Thank you," she said, then rose and grabbed her plate, but he stayed her hand.

"You cooked so I'll clean. Why don't you grab another glass of wine and get some fresh air on the foredeck?" he said as he piled all the plates together.

It had been getting a little warm belowdecks. "Will you join me?" she asked, her emotions in turmoil.

She wanted to explore what was happening with him especially since no matter what Brett said, this might be the only time they'd have to be together.

She didn't want to die without experiencing his loving once again.

Chapter Twenty-Seven

Brett nodded. "I won't be long."

He waited until she climbed the tiny, twisty stairs up into the cockpit area. Seconds later he heard her footfall above him as her shadow passed by the porthole in the middle of the ceiling and she settled into the cushions above the bow.

Knowing the clock was ticking between them in so many ways, he hurried in cleaning and drying the dinnerware, pots and pans, and making sure everything was shipshape. Satisfied, he headed above deck, signaling Mango to follow him up.

Anita was lying across the cushions on one side of the foredeck, her head resting along the edge of the gunwale, her gaze focused on the stars that had flared to life with the coming of night.

They weren't all that far from civilization but remote enough that there was little light pollution, making the celestial bodies brilliant against the inky night sky since the moon hadn't risen yet.

He mimicked her posture, stretching out as best he could against the cushions, his long legs hanging over at the end of them. With a click of his tongue, he instructed Mango to lie down and she immediately settled in the middle of the deck.

Gesturing with his hand up at the night sky, he said, "That's Jupiter. The big one."

"Is that Orion over there?" Anita asked, pointing to the telltale belt of three stars that identified that constellation.

"It is," he said, but then silence reigned as they enjoyed the cooler night air and quiet.

There was little movement on the water where they had moored, the boat remaining fairly still on the surface.

He'd left only one small lamp on in the deck below to conserve their power and it cast muted light up through the porthole. But with no moonlight for hours, he had to snap on more lights to warn other boats of their position.

Returning to the cockpit area, he searched beneath the cushions and dug out an anchor light that he snapped into place at the stern and turned on. It cast a glow all around, alerting others to stay clear.

"Bright," Anita said as she came up behind him and stroked a hand down his back.

"Safety," he said and dipped his head in the direction of the cockpit door. "Why don't you head belowdecks. I'll take care of Mango and be down in a second."

She nodded and walked away.

Mango must have followed her aft and now sat at his feet, looking up at him almost accusingly.

Did Mango have a clue what he wanted to do with Anita once they were belowdecks?

"Don't give me that look," he muttered, then grabbed a fresh plastic bag and paper towels from beneath a cushion and set them up at one corner of the stern.

"Hovno," he commanded and pointed at the bag and towels.

Mango hesitated, worrying him. He needed Mango to listen to his commands without fail if they were going to protect Anita.

He repeated the instruction with more urgency, and to his relief, Mango immediately complied. Cleaning up the waste, he stuffed it into a garbage bag beneath one of the cushions and headed to the door of the cockpit.

Mango followed but he raised his hand, palm open and outward, to stop the pit bull.

"*Pozor,*" he said, and without delay, Mango settled herself across the width of the opening.

"Good girl," he said and rubbed her head and fed her a treat.

Closing the cockpit door, he carefully navigated the steps down in the near dark.

Anita had figured out how to convert the dining area for sleeping. Cushions now ran from one side of the bow to the other and she had spread out sheets and pillows on them. She had also opened the four small oval windows and the porthole above, letting the cooler night air sweep through where she lay in the middle of the makeshift bed.

But there was also a narrow sleeping nook to one side of the galley. He flipped a hand in its direction. "I can bunk there if you want."

This was the moment, Anita thought.

"I don't want. I want you here. With me," she said, then lay down on the cushions and pulled off her cotton nightshirt, baring her body to him.

He jerked his shirt over his head and tossed it aside. Then he kicked off his boat shoes and hopped around as he slipped off his shorts and briefs before crawling onto the bed with her.

The space was narrow, not that they needed space as they spooned together and made love like there had never been any hurt in the past, but also like they weren't sure of any joy for the future.

He worshipped her with his mouth and hands, exploring every inch of her until she was shaking and pleading with him to take her.

Leaving only long enough to grab a condom and roll it on, he laid a knee on the cushion and, like a big cat, prowled over and slipped between her thighs. But he hesitated and in the dim light of the cabin, it was almost impossible to see his face.

She rose on an elbow, needing to see his face. Needing to know what he was feeling at that exact moment.

She knew even before he said the words.

"I love you, Anita. I've never stopped loving you," he said and cradled her cheek.

"I love you, too, Brett. I loved the man you were, but I love the man you've become even more."

She kissed him, taking his groan of relief deep inside. Taking him deep into her body as he began the rhythm of their loving. He shifted over and over, dropping kisses on her lips and body as he moved, lifting her ever higher until she could no longer refuse giving him everything.

ANITA ARCHED BENEATH HIM, driving him ever deeper, and he lost it.

A harsh breath left him as he climaxed, but he didn't move, riding the wave of their mutual release as long as he could. Even then, he gently lowered himself to her side and laid an arm around her waist.

"I love you," he said again, just to be sure she had no doubt about it.

"I know," she teased, then ran her hand across his arm and turned to face him. The smile on her face was bright even in the murkiness of the night.

"I love you, too," she said.

A sharp breeze swept through the cabin, rousing goose bumps on her skin and making her shiver. He used that opportunity to ease a sheet over her and excuse himself to clean up in the head just off the galley.

When he returned, she had closed her eyes, but sleepily opened them and smiled again before sadness crept into her gaze, turning the green so deep it looked black.

She didn't have to say why. "Don't worry about tomorrow. No matter what, Mango and I will protect you."

"But at what cost?" she said in a strangled voice and laid a hand over his heart. Then she skimmed that hand over the bandages on his chest and the older, scattered shrapnel scars.

He covered his hand with hers and brought it back over his heart. "After what happened, I sometimes felt I didn't deserve to live. I even sometimes didn't care whether I lived or died, but I care now. A lot. There's nothing I won't do so we can be together."

She shifted closer and twined their legs together. Kissing him, she said, "That's what worries me. I want to be safe, but I want you to be safe, too."

He raked back a lock of her hair that had fallen forward. "Trust me," he said, and as she leaned forward to kiss him again, relaxed her body into his, he realized that she did.

She trusted him with her body. With her heart. With her life.

He would guard all three with everything he had no matter what tomorrow brought.

Chapter Twenty-Eight

They woke well before the sun had risen and made love again.

She cooked breakfast just as the first rays of sun, a blurry blend of pinks and purples, filtered through the windows.

They ate and since the tide was so far out, Brett slung Mango over his shoulders so they could walk to a small nearby cay and let Mango relieve herself and run loose. Brett found a piece of driftwood and played fetch with the pit for well over half an hour, exercising her after the day spent cooped up on the boat.

Soon, however, the tide started coming in and reality drifted in with it, she thought.

Brett scooped up Mango again, struggling slightly with the pit bull's weight and the deeper water. Mango seemed skittish, probably recalling what had happened the day before.

Fortunately, they were able to board Jake's boat without any problems.

But once onboard, Anita felt like a caged animal, anxiously awaiting the moment when Trey would call.

Like her, Brett nervously paced back and forth across the stern, constantly checking his watch.

The sun rose, bringing heat in the early morning.

She sat beneath the canopy protecting the console area, trying to stay cool. Telling herself the damp sweat across her body was from the ever-rising temperature and not fear.

It seemed like hours and yet it had barely been twenty minutes since they'd come onboard. Brett powered up the phone and it rang.

"Any progress?" he asked, put the phone on speaker and walked back to where she sat.

"Police and FBI have a plan. They want you to come to the Miami Beach Marina on Alton Road," Trey said, and it was obvious from his tone that he was less than happy with the plan.

"That's a busy marina," Brett said, apparently well familiar with it.

"It is, but they're making arrangements for you to come into the slips by the watersports and parasailing companies," he said.

"That's a pretty exposed area. There's the causeway and at least two parking lots nearby. Perfect spots for a shooter," Brett countered.

"It is, which is why we're working up our own plan to protect you. Do you have your laptop?" Trey asked.

"I do. I should be able to use this phone as a hot spot," he advised, worry about the plan overriding concerns about someone tracking the phone.

"Law enforcement wants you at the dock at thirteen hundred, but I think we have enough time to have a meeting," Trey responded, and from the background, someone called out to him.

"We do have time. It should only take a little over two hours to get there," Brett advised.

"Roger. Give us an hour at most," Trey said and ended the call.

She'd been staring back and forth from the phone to Brett's face, trying to read what he was thinking and feeling.

"You're really worried," she said because it was so obvious from the deep ridges across his forehead and the frown lines bracketing his mouth.

He nodded and ran a hand across the short strands of hair

at the top of his head. "Like I told Trey, that area is really exposed. We'd be close to a walkway along the edge of the marina. Anyone could take potshots at us from the causeway or parking lots and then hop into a car and speed off."

She stroked a hand across his arm, trying to reassure him. "What can *we* do?"

BRETT'S MIND HAD been running through possibilities as Trey had been speaking, imagining the area at the marina that he knew quite well.

When he had first arrived in Miami so many months earlier, he had used to rent WaveRunners there before he had reconnected with Jake and visited him down on Key Largo instead.

"Let me show you the area so you're familiar with it," he said and hopped down the stairs belowdecks to where he'd stowed his things.

He pulled out his laptop and went back on deck. He placed the computer on the free space of the passenger console, powered it up and turned on the phone's hot spot. It took a few seconds for the laptop to connect to the wireless, but as soon as it did, he pulled up a satellite view of the area to show Anita the layout of the marina and the nearby elements.

Running his fingers along the screen, he pointed out the areas he thought would be the riskiest. "If I pull in here, you'll be exposed. Anyone in these parking lots or the causeway will have a shot and easy escape."

ANITA TRACKED BRETT'S FINGER, understanding his concerns. Unless he reversed the boat into a slip, a possibly time-consuming maneuver, she'd be a sitting duck if she was above board.

"Someone can shoot at me from all these areas," she said, motioning to the locations with her index finger.

"Nothing about Kennedy says *sniper*, so I'd rule out the far parking lot. Causeway is possibly too exposed. There's nowhere to hide," Brett advised, but then quickly tacked on, "My money is on that walkway and the ground level of that parking lot."

She agreed, which made her say, "I think you're right. I could hide belowdecks, but if I do—"

"We might not draw him out. He's not likely to shoot at you once you're surrounded by the police and FBI. He wants to do it before," he said and waggled his head, obviously unsettled.

"I have to be where he can see me," she said, willing to take the risk if it would bring an end to the nightmare.

He encircled her shoulder with his hand and drew her close. "I don't want you hurt. There has to be another way."

She shook her head and laughed harshly. "I could wear a disguise. Maybe one of those fake noses with the glasses and moustache," she kidded.

Brett's eyes opened wide, and she could swear she saw the light bulb pop up over his head.

"It's not a bad idea."

IT HAD TAKEN him almost all night and multiple calls to reach his informant at the FBI.

He had worried that the man wouldn't come through for him, but he had finally answered as Santiago had been picking up a *café con leche* and Cuban toast at a small breakfast shop in a strip mall not far from Jake's home.

"*Mano*, why are you avoiding me?" he asked, trying for a friendly tone and not the worry twisting his gut into knots.

In a low whisper, the man said, "Things are moving quickly here. They plan on bringing the woman in today."

"Where?" he asked and sipped on the coffee, wincing as the heat of it burned his tongue.

His informant hesitated, making Santiago worry that the man was going to burn him as well, but then he said, "I need to know this is it. If I give you this info—"

"You're paid in full," he said, because if he didn't finish this woman and maybe Marino as well, Hollywood was going to finish him.

"They're on a boat and coming into the Miami Beach Marina," the FBI agent said and continued laying out the details of the plan for bringing in the chef and the SBS agent.

Santiago listened carefully, logging all the info into his brain while planning what he would do at the same time.

After the man hung up, he considered what he'd heard and finalized his plan.

Surprise, firepower and speed.

That would be the key to ending this disaster.

BRETT NAVIGATED PAST Key Biscayne, steering toward the Bay Bridge in the Rickenbacker Causeway. Once he cleared the bridge, he'd head toward Fisher Island and work his way into the Government Cut to reach the marina just as planned.

The boat's radio crackled, snapping to life, and Trey's voice erupted across the line. "We're in place," he said.

"Roger that. We're on schedule. Any luck with the search warrant at Kennedy's place?" Trey had mentioned in an earlier call that a judge had finally felt they had enough evidence thanks to the DNA match from the blood at the Homestead location.

"Police executed the warrant this morning. His mom wasn't surprised that the police were knocking on her door. We expect them to bring us some of his clothing in about twenty minutes so we can confirm it's him," Trey said.

Brett bit back a curse. "That's cutting it close, *mano*."

"I know, *mano*. I know," Trey said wearily.

"I'll radio as soon as I'm closer," he said and replaced the handset on the console hook.

He thrust forward, catching sight of the luxury buildings

on Fisher Island and the ferry that carried residents to the exclusive enclave.

Slowing, he made sure he was clear of any other boats or the large ocean cruise ships that also used the man-made channel. Satisfied the way was clear, he gunned the engine, aware they had a schedule to keep.

Heart pounding, hands gripping the steering wheel so tightly they cramped, he searched the area, keen eyes taking in the boats parked in the marina slips. Everything from immense multimillion-dollar cabin cruisers to small fishing boats. People walked here and there on the docks, worrying him.

Kennedy could be one of those people as well.

As he passed the last few docks for the marina, he throttled down the engine and radioed Trey. "I'm here. Heading toward the watersports dock."

"Roger. Matt and Natalie have the sample. They're searching the ground floor of that parking lot right now."

Little consolation, Brett thought. It might be way too late already.

They would be sitting ducks as he pulled into the slip, especially since the police and FBI agents would not jump into action until they had a clear view of Kennedy.

If he even decided to show up.

But Wilson's program had predicted he would, and Trey had reached out to his psychologist brother, Ricky, whose profile of Kennedy warned he was a loose cannon and probably fearless of what might happen to him. Ricky had agreed with Wilson's program.

Brett couldn't disagree. Anyone who would knowingly take out Hollywood's nephew, and his own cousin, was reckless.

But that kind of reckless came with a price.

He hoped one of the many agents supposedly stationed in and around the marina would be able to either take him down or take him into custody.

Turning to the starboard side, he navigated into the gap for the last slips next to the floating docks for the WaveRunners and other personal watercraft.

This is it. This is when it'll happen, he thought and risked a quick last glance at the console seat opposite him.

Chapter Twenty-Nine

As he turned starboard again, motion on the walkway caught his attention.

Kennedy in full body armor. Agents racing from all over, but all too far to make a difference.

Bullets sprayed across the side of the boat, shattering the windscreen and pinging against the metal railings and hull.

Brett released the wheel and hit the deck, swiping the throttle on the way down to kill the engine.

A surprising pause came in the shooting. Metal clacking was followed by a loud stream of Spanish curses.

Brett jumped to his feet, pointed at land and shouted, *"Vpred. Útok."*

Mango leaped from the boat and at Kennedy, a white-and-tan missile flying through the air.

To protect her, Brett fired at the other man, who seemed to be struggling with the magazine on the assault rifle.

The bullet struck his shoulder, and he staggered back.

Mango latched onto his right arm and thrashed her head until he dropped the weapon.

Kennedy was screaming and trying to dislodge the pit bull as Brett leaped from the boat, ran down the dock and launched himself at Kennedy, tackling him to the ground.

"Pust, Mango. *Pust,"* he said so the dog would release his hold.

Mango instantly complied and Brett flipped Kennedy onto

his stomach and placed a knee in the middle of his back to hold him down as an assortment of agents swarmed around them, including Trey and his fellow K-9 agents, Matt and Natalie.

Trey helped him to his feet, but as he looked toward the boat, he cursed. "Anita. *Dios*, Anita," he said and was about to race to the dock when Brett laid a hand on his arm.

"It's okay, Trey," he said and faced the boat where Anita slumped on the console seat.

"What do you mean it's okay?" Trey shouted, almost frantic.

"Anita, you can come out now," Brett called out and headed back onto the boat to help Anita from belowdecks.

Trey hurried over with the other SBS K-9 agents as well as several other SBS personnel, local law enforcement and some suits he assumed were the Feds.

ANITA SHAKILY CLIMBED the stairs to the deck, heart hammering and a sick feeling in her gut, especially as she looked at "herself" on the console seat.

A number of bullets had torn through the dummy they had assembled in secret.

Fake Anita had been fashioned from some boat cushions, Anita's clothes and handfuls of dry seaweed ribbons Brett had gathered that morning to make fake hair held in place by a baseball cap. Foam guts spilled from the body, a reminder of how deadly the shots might have been if she had been sitting there.

She quickly examined Brett, who had been exposed to the gunfire, shifting her hands across his chest and arms as she searched for any injuries.

He grasped her hands and held them tenderly. "I'm okay."

"Mango?" she said and peered toward the dock where the pit bull sat beside her K-9 counterparts, tongue hanging from her mouth. Not a scratch on her apparently.

Relief washed through her, making her knees weak.

As she started to crumple, Brett hugged an arm around her waist and offered support.

She glanced up at him and smiled. "Thanks."

"Ms. Reyes," said one of the suits as he dipped his head in greeting and approached the boat. "I'm Special Agent Santoro. We'd like to have a word with you."

"She's not going anywhere without me," Brett said.

The FBI agent hesitated, but recognizing that Brett was serious, he said, "If you both wouldn't mind coming with us to the police station." He gestured to the dock, inviting them to deboard and follow him.

Trey laid a hand on her shoulder. "I'll have Aunt Elena meet you there in case you need assistance."

"Thanks, Trey," Brett said and glanced at her intently. "Are you ready to go?"

Anita nodded and accepted the FBI agent's assistance onto the dock. But once she was there, she turned and examined the beautiful new boat, now pockmarked with ugly bullet holes. The windscreen lay in ruined shards on the deck. A side window had also been blown out.

She glanced at Brett and then at Trey. "I think you owe your friend a new boat."

WHEN THEY ARRIVED at the Miami Beach police station, Detective Williams was waiting there along with Roni and Trey's aunt, a respected trial attorney. Tia Elena had married Trey's father's brother. Tio Jose was a member of the Miami district attorney's office and the man who had helped them negotiate the plea deal with the crooked cop.

They greeted Roni effusively, happy to see her. "Isn't it too soon after the baby?" Brett asked, worried that she was pushing herself before she was ready.

Roni smiled, a tired smile that spoke volumes about the demands of tending to a newborn. "I'm just here for the interview and the lineup. I had to be here for that," she said.

Brett understood. It was a huge collar to not only get Kennedy but also possibly a mobster like Tony Hollywood.

Special Agent Santoro had been waiting patiently as they exchanged niceties, but clearly wasn't happy with the delay and the presence of Elena Gonzalez.

As Trey's aunt introduced herself to the FBI agent, he said, "There's really no reason for you to be here. Ms. Reyes isn't a suspect."

Elena nodded. "I know, but we want to make sure everything is done properly so that both Kennedy and Hollywood don't have any cracks to crawl through. Ms. Reyes needs closure so she can get on with her life."

Brett had been standing next to Anita, a hand on her shoulder, offering support. She jumped with Elena's words and softly said, "I need to get on with my life."

After she said that, she shot a quick look up in his direction and smiled, offering hope that her life would be one spent with him.

Agent Santoro's lips thinned into a line of displeasure. "Let's get going, then."

They walked toward one of the police interrogation rooms, but when they reached it, the FBI agent barred his entry with a beefy arm.

"You'll have to wait outside," he said and then eyeballed Roni and Williams. "I assume you two will tape this for us?"

"We'll be in the viewing room. Brett can join us there," Roni said and directed him to a door several feet away from the interrogation room.

He walked with Roni and her partner to the viewing room and was about to enter when he turned and locked his gaze with Anita's. He mouthed, "You'll be fine."

She offered him a weak smile, nodded and entered the room.

WHAT SEEMED LIKE hours dragged by as she answered questions for Santoro and his partner, who had walked into the interrogation room right after Trey's tia Elena and she had entered.

She was grateful for Elena, whose steady presence and gentle encouragement buoyed her flagging energy and patience. She wanted all this over. She wanted to get back to her restaurant. She wanted to get back to Brett.

When the interrogation finished, they took her to another room with a large two-way mirror that faced a narrow space. A lineup room, she realized from the true crime shows she watched. The far wall of that space had horizontal lines that marked off the height of the men who marched into the room.

"I'll be waiting outside," Elena said and squeezed Anita's shoulder in reassurance.

The door closed behind Elena, leaving her alone with Agent Santoro. A few seconds later, six men walked into the lineup room. They were all dressed similarly and of like height, race and weight. Once they were in the room, Santoro had them step to the left and then to the right before facing forward again.

"Can you identify the man who shot Manuel Ramirez? Take your time," he said.

Because of his admonition, Anita examined each man carefully even though she had recognized Kennedy right away. Slowly drifting her gaze over each face, she finally said, "It's the third man from the left. That's the man I saw that night."

"Are you sure?" Santoro asked.

Anita nodded. "I'm sure."

With a wave of his hand, Santoro directed her out of the room. Not only was Elena there, but she had also been joined by Roni, Williams and Brett.

She immediately went to Brett's side and slipped her hands into his. "I'm ready to go."

Turning, she looked at the FBI agent and said, "Are we done now?"

Santoro peered at her and then Roni and Williams. "We're done…for now. We may have more questions for you."

Relief swept through her until Roni asked, "What about Hollywood? When do we pull him in?"

Agent Santoro clearly didn't like being challenged by Roni. "As soon as *we* finish with Kennedy. His lawyer has already offered to flip on Hollywood to avoid the death penalty," he said, his tone as biting as a great white shark.

Roni wasn't backing down. She walked up to the much taller and broader agent and rose up on her tiptoes until she was almost nose to nose with him. "You button this up and keep Anita out of Hollywood's business. She has nothing to do with that."

She appreciated Roni's defense, worried that this wouldn't be over if Hollywood thought she was a threat to his freedom in any way.

"I got it, Detective. Your friend doesn't need to worry about Hollywood or Kennedy," Santoro said.

Brett slipped an arm around her waist and said, "We'll get going, then. I'm sure Anita wants to check in with her restaurant and her parents, and get some rest."

At Santoro's nod, she thanked Elena for her help and hugged Roni, embracing the other woman hard since she imagined it had taken a lot for her to leave her newborn to come to the station. She shook hands with Williams, Santoro and his partner, and then Brett was there again, his arm around her waist as he guided her out of the station and out to the large plaza in front of the building.

The FBI agents had driven them to the station in one of their vehicles, but it would be an easy enough walk to her restaurant and then her condo, although her things, including her pocketbook and keys, were still on the boat.

"What now?" she asked, looking around and wondering what to do about so many things.

He cradled her cheek and smiled wistfully. "What do you want to do now?"

Pushing away a lock of hair that had come loose of her top-knot, she shook her head, confused about almost everything except one thing.

"I want to be with you. I love you, Brett. I want a life with you."

His smile broadened and he wrapped his arms around her waist and drew her close for a deep kiss.

When they finally broke apart, he said, "I love you, too, Anita. I want a life with you, too, but there's one thing I want right now."

Puzzled, she narrowed her gaze, wondering what it was, especially seeing the gleam in his dark eyes, so reminiscent of the young man she had fallen in love with so many years earlier.

"What is that?" she asked.

He spread the fingers of one hand wide across his stomach and, with a broad smile on his face, said, "A nice big bowl of your famous chicken and rice. With chorizo this time. Do you think you can do that?"

She stopped, faced him and cupped his face in her hands. Rising on her tiptoes, she brushed a kiss on his lips and said, "I can do that today and forever."

He chuckled. "I might get a little tired of chicken and rice forever, but I'll never get tired of you," he said and deepened the kiss until a rough cough broke them apart.

Trey was standing there holding her pocketbook and a set of car keys, which he handed to Brett.

Eyeballing them, he said, "I guess things are good between you two?"

Brett smiled and said, "Never been better."

He tugged her hand, leading her in the direction of the SBS SUV sitting at the curb, and as she hurried there with him, eager to get to her restaurant and the after, she couldn't argue with him.

They'd faced death multiple times and now it was time to live, Brett at her side. Forever. Nothing could ever be better than that.

* * * * *

Holiday Under Wraps
Katie Mettner

MILLS & BOON

Katie Mettner wears the title of "the only person to lose her leg after falling down the bunny hill" and loves decorating her prosthetic leg to fit the season. She lives in Northern Wisconsin with her own happily-ever-after and spends the day writing romantic stories with her sweet puppy by her side. Katie has an addiction to coffee and dachshunds and a lessening aversion to Pinterest—now that she's quit trying to make the things she pins.

Books by Katie Mettner

Harlequin Intrigue

Secure One

Going Rogue in Red Rye County
The Perfect Witness
The Red River Slayer
The Silent Setup
Holiday Under Wraps

Visit the Author Profile page at millsandboon.com.au.

For the "Jameses" of the world. It takes someone
special to do what you do. Thank you.

For the supply chain managers.
You truly are unsung heroes.

CAST OF CHARACTERS

Delilah Hartman—As a former army cybersecurity officer, she knows something she shouldn't, and someone is willing to kill for it. This Christmas, she has no choice but to ask for help from the man she's been protecting for six years. He won't be happy to see her.

Lucas Porter—The former army warrant officer is now working as a security technician for Secure One with his PTSD service dog by his side. When he gets a call to pick up the ashes of the woman he once loved, he can't help but wonder what the real story is.

Haven—A former war dog turned PTSD service dog, he has one job—keep his handler calm and safe. He will go to any length to make that happen, even if it means getting in the line of fire.

Major George Burris—His side project put Delilah in danger. Will he go out on a limb for her now?

Secure One Crew—They've run a lot of missions, but going up against the people who trained them might be the one to bring them to their knees.

Chapter One

"Hey, there, Lilah," a voice said.

She smiled as she turned to him. "Luca. Where have you been?"

"Reloading our water and campfire supply. Did you find anything?"

"Sea glass," Delilah said, holding her hand out to show him a broken piece of pottery. It was worn smooth from tumbling around in the lake for years.

"Your favorite," he said, taking her hand and pulling her into a dance pose as he rocked her back and forth on the sand. "What will you do with all that sea glass, Lilah?"

"I don't know," she whispered, gazing into his eyes. "Maybe I'll make art from it to always remember the summer we turned twenty-eight."

"I hope you won't need the sea glass to remember." Luca lowered his magical lips to hers and kissed her like a man in love. While they had never said the words, they didn't need to. Their bodies did the talking. "I hope to be by your side the summer we turn sixty-eight." He spun her around in a wide arc until they toppled to the sand, where they stayed, laughing as Lake Superior lapped over them and the sun shone down to dry them.

"Luca, you're the kind of guy my daddy would have wanted me to bring home. I know it."

"You think so? I thought your daddy was strict about everything, including his little girl dating."

"Oh, he'd hate that I left the church and went to war, but he'd have loved you."

"Since he's been dead for twenty years, I guess I'll have to take your word for it."

"I've been thinking, Luca."

"Uh-oh. It's never good when a woman opens with that line."

Delilah rolled up onto her arm to look him in the eye. *"You won't think it's good, but I made a phone call yesterday while picking up groceries."*

"Who did you call?" His words dripped with defensive dread.

"The VA hospital in Minneapolis. It turns out they have a program there that helps veterans with PTSD."

"I don't need a shrink!" His growled exclamation should have made her pull back, but she was past that fear. Delilah knew he'd never hurt her, but he might hurt himself. She couldn't let that happen.

"It's not just a shrink, Luca. It's talking to other people in your situation and developing ways to channel your anxiety so you can live in the world as it is now."

"My PTSD isn't any worse than yours, Lilah." His words were soft this time, and he caressed her face as though she would drop the conversation and fall into bed with him. In the past, she might have, but with his episodes escalating, she couldn't put off the hard stuff any longer.

"But it is, Luca, and it's okay to admit that. We had

different experiences that did different things to our minds. I can't wake up to find you in the middle of Lake Superior again. Not when I know there are people who can help you."

"Will you go, too?"

"If you want me to," she agreed, even though it was a lie. "I'll do anything if it means you get help before it's too late."

"How long do I have to be there?"

"I can't answer that question, Luca. That's up to you and the doctors to decide, but from what I understand, it's usually one to three months."

He gathered handfuls of the warm September sand as he stared at the cloudless Wisconsin sky. "I don't want our time here to end, Lilah. When I'm here, I can forget what happened over there. When I'm holding you, I can forget about the men who—"

What was that music? It was familiar, and Delilah Hartman was supposed to remember what to do when she heard it. Her eyes popped open and she grabbed her glasses, slipping them on to stare at the phone screen.

You've been found.

Technically, that's not what the screen said, but she knew that's what it meant. Her gaze flicked to the time at the top of the phone. It was 2:37 a.m. Not a great time of day to tuck tail and run, but she didn't know if she had five minutes or five hours until someone started breaking down her door, so she couldn't worry about anything other than getting out undetected.

She slid out from under the covers and stayed low below the level of the windows. Her go bag was packed and easily accessible, something she made sure of every night before bed. Her only decision was how to exit the apartment. It was the start of December, cold, and the recent snow was going to make footprints easy to follow. She could walk out the front door as though everything was fine and it was any other early Wednesday morning, climb in her car and drive away, or opt for escape via the balcony. She'd rented this apartment for the balcony. Beyond it was a forest as far as the eye could see, giving her a place to disappear as soon as she made the tree line. This escape would be the eighth in six years. It was a habit she didn't like, and as she tied on a pair of boots, slid into her winter gear and slung the go bag around her shoulders, the truth settled low in her gut. She couldn't do this alone any longer, but the only man who could help her lived somewhere in the middle of northern Minnesota. The one thing she knew for sure was that she wasn't a Christmas present he'd be happy about unwrapping.

Then again, maybe he would be.

Delilah wondered how Lucas would feel about her popping back into his life unexpectedly after disappearing six years ago. He was probably angry that she'd dropped him off at the VA Medical Center and never returned. That wasn't by choice. If he wasn't angry with her, that would quickly change if she brought a passel of bad guys along with her, so she had to be thoughtful about her approach. None of that mattered if she didn't successfully escape from 679 North Bradley Street in one piece.

Her fingers found the scar on her chin and traced it while she rechecked the app. They had just broken the code and accessed her information, so there was no way they'd be here this quickly. She had time to walk down the stairs, get in her car and drive away. She'd abandon the car at the airport and hop on a plane. When she did, Lavena Hanson would cease to exist. The same way all those other names had over the years. Whether she liked it or not, it was time to be Delilah Hartman again if she ever wanted to live a normal life. Not that she could even define what a normal life was anymore. Normal ended the day she signed up for the army. What a lousy life decision that turned out to be. Not that she had many options. After her father died, her mother struggled to make ends meet, much less pay for college. Enlisting was a way to get her education paid for and come out with real-world work experience. Delilah couldn't argue with that. She'd gotten the necessary experience, but she couldn't use it if she wanted to stay alive. Not exactly what she'd had in mind as a fresh-faced army recruit.

Crouched low, she snuck out of the bedroom into the sparse main room of the apartment. The one-bedroom upper had been the perfect place for her when she'd found it nearly five months ago, but she knew better than to do anything but live in it like a hotel room. A stopover on the road of life. She'd been disappointed the first time she'd had to leave a place she'd made her home and promised herself she'd steer clear of using that word again. She patted the fridge on her way by, which held her only decorations for the holidays. Magnets in the shape of Christmas ornaments covered the front of it in holiday cheer. They'd remain there now for someone else to enjoy.

Delilah had her hand on the doorknob when she heard a commotion in the hallway. "Hey, man, you don't belong here," came her neighbor's muffled voice through the front door. She peered through the peephole, and her insides congealed with fear at the scene in the hallway. There was a man dressed in black with a gun, and behind him was the man who fueled her nightmares. He'd come again, and by the looks of the knife in his hand, he meant business this time.

She heard the *pop-pop* and was running for the balcony before she even registered that her neighbor had just been shot. *Don't die. Don't die.* She hummed to herself as she silently cut the screen and slithered down the rope tied to the balcony post for this very purpose. She hit the ground quietly, flipped her night vision goggles down, a throwback to her military days, and searched the grounds for signs of life.

Movement to her left caught her eye. The dude was in black head to toe but had his back to her as he faced the front of the building. Slowly, she turned her head to the right and saw another guy dressed the same at the opposite end of the building. Unfortunately, they were wearing night vision goggles, too, which meant she wasn't undetectable. She pulled her pistol from her holster and steeled herself. She had to make a run for it, but she had to do it right if she didn't want to be caught in the crossfire. She also didn't want more innocent people to die here tonight. Her bullets had to find their marks for multiple reasons, the least of which was this snow was going to make it easy to track her. Shooting on the run was always hard, but she had no choice. A part of her brain registered that this was the first time they'd sent more than two guys. Maybe that meant something, maybe it didn't, but she didn't have time to dwell on it if she wanted to stay alive. Her concentration could be nowhere but on getting to the trees.

A deep, steadying breath in and she ran, her movement catching their attention, as expected. The guy to her left turned first, and the pop of her gun had him on the ground before he got off a round. Unfortunately, the guy on her right heard the shot and swung his gun in an arc toward her. By the time his buddy hit the ground, she was already firing. Dude number two crumpled, and she turned tail, slid through the trees and ran like the hounds of hell were on her heels.

DEATH. NOT AN easy word to wrap a person's head around, especially when no one can escape it. At the same time, very few people live like they know that. Lucas Porter wasn't one of those people. He had intimate knowledge of how swiftly death came and held no illusions that he had any control over it. Lucas agreed with the idea that when it's your time, it's your time, but he didn't agree with the old saying that someone *cheated* death. No. No one ever *cheats* death. It simply wasn't their day to die. He'd seen it on the battlefield so many times. Days when three men rode side by side, an IED exploded and two died, but one was unscathed just inches away. That soldier didn't cheat death. He had something left to do before death took him. And it took everyone.

Lucas saw death enough times that he made the conscious decision to live every day like he was dying. He wasn't afraid of death, knowing it was inevitable, so he also made every effort not to leave anything unresolved in life. Unresolved situations only hurt the living, and Lucas never wanted to put that on anyone's shoulders. He carried some of those situations and feelings that could never be resolved as anyone does, but those memories were motivation not to create more.

He could accept those unresolved situations as casualties of the war he had been forced to fight. He went into the army thinking he could make a career, make a difference, right some wrongs—how wrong he'd been. He was sold a pack of lies, shipped off to a foreign land and given no choice but to fight for his life by taking someone else's way too many times. He understood it had to be done to protect his country, but he didn't have to like how it had to be done.

"Time to work, Haven," Lucas said, unsnapping the dog's seat belt from the SUV. "Get dressed." The German shepherd patiently waited while Lucas slipped the military-style harness over his head, fastened the buckles and then double-checked the patches to make sure they were easy to read. Six words stared back at him. PTSD Service Dog. Do Not Distract.

That was Haven's job. When they were at Secure One, the dog didn't need his harness to announce why he was there. He was an extension of Lucas, and everyone knew why. When on assignment, not a soul on the team cared about the real reason Haven stood beside Lucas. They knew he would defend any team member. Haven may have been the runt of the litter, but dressed in a black harness with his ears at attention, Lucas hadn't met anyone who would take him on.

Was he ashamed of having PTSD? No. He knew it wasn't his fault that he had it, but that didn't mean he liked announcing to the world why Haven was always with him. Despite the acceptance of PTSD throughout the country, it still carried a stigma that was difficult to see on public faces when they read the patches. He couldn't count the times he'd been told to "get over it," "just forget about it, you're home now," "just think happy thoughts" and "it will go away with time." Lucas wished even one of those things were true, but they weren't and it had taken a lot of therapy for him to trust in his coping mechanisms.

Truthfully, PTSD was a shared experience at Secure One, which Lucas had come to appreciate quickly. The team was great at pulling someone back who was falling too deeply into the past. Haven was trained to key in on Lucas and keep him steady, but he never ignored signs of anxiety from any team member. If they needed help returning to the present or decompressing from an assignment, Haven was there for them. He felt lucky that he could contribute to the team by sharing his dog that way.

"Today, you're all mine, buddy," he told the dog as he checked the SUV and glanced around the area, a habit he had picked up on the base that now came in handy working for Secure One. "If what Cal said is true, I'll need you to keep me steady."

A deep breath in and a walk up the sidewalk gave him time to focus on the perimeter of the past instead of the center of it. He reminded himself that he didn't have to think about his time over there, only the time he'd spent with Delilah on the beach six years ago. Determined to keep his breathing steady, he opened the double door and entered the funeral home. The plush carpet deadened the sound of his footsteps, as though even his footfalls were too loud for the dead.

Silence pervaded the funeral home, other than a piano rendition of "Silent Night" flowing through the speakers. Apparently, you couldn't escape Christmas music anywhere this time of year. A glance to his left revealed a small tree decorated with white lights, gold ribbon and a gold star. It was simple and understated, but felt like it belonged in the space where it sat. Recognition of the hope and peace of the season, even in a place where there was likely little of either to be found for families of lost loved ones.

He'd been told to ask for James, but first, he'd have to find a living soul in the building. Haven whined and stepped on Lucas's foot twice, a sign that his anxiety was building. He stopped and inhaled a breath, counted to three and let it out. Then he held his breath for the count of three, inhaled to the count of three and then held his breath to the count of three. He'd been taught several breathing techniques in therapy, but box breathing was the one that helped him the most. It distracted his mind and his body from the situation that was causing the anxiety. Technically, it was called the triple fours, but he'd modified it using a three count, something he'd been accustomed to using in the service and could do without thinking.

"Are you Lucas Porter?"

Lucas turned to a man dressed in a dark gray suit. His shirt was white, bright and starched, with a dark burgundy tie resting against his chest. He wore a name tag that said Edwards, Roberts and Thomas Funeral Home. James.

"I am," he answered, shaking the outstretched hand. "Nice to meet you, James."

"I'm sorry that it's under these circumstances."

Lucas suspected James said that a lot in his line of work. The man was shorter than Lucas's six feet, had a head full of blond curly hair and a baby face that was at odds with what he saw and did in a place like this.

"Me, too. It's been a long time since I've heard the name Delilah Hartman." That was a lie, for James's sake. Lucas heard that name every night in his dreams and thought of it every time he looked at Haven. "Is this situation common for you?"

"You mean having decedents arrive in the mail?" James asked, motioning him into a small room. At the front was a granite altar the size of a podium where an urn sat next to a spray of flowers. "More common than you might think. With the rise of cremation and the ability to send remains through the mail, we're often the go-between for families who live across the country to get a loved one home to a family plot."

"That makes sense, I guess," Lucas said, awkwardly shifting from foot to foot. "Not that I ever thought about it. We have a much different system in the military."

James patted his shoulder. "From what I understand, Delilah was no longer active military?"

"As of six years ago, she had been discharged. What happened after that, I can't say. I haven't seen or heard from her. That's why I was so surprised to get this call."

"I'm sure you were. I wish we could have softened the blow, but sometimes, there is no easy way to break the news to someone."

How well Lucas knew the truth of that statement. Too many times, he'd had to be the one to break the news to someone on the base that their buddy, girlfriend or boy-friend was not coming back.

"I understand that on a level that would probably sur-prise you."

James's gaze landed on Haven for a moment before he spoke. "Truthfully, not much surprises me anymore, Lucas. Did you serve with Delilah?"

"Indirectly," Lucas answered, inhaling a breath and holding it for the count of three. "Is that her?" He mo-tioned at the small altar where the urn sat. There was a laser-etched American flag on the front, the only indi-cation that the person inside had once served her coun-try on foreign soil.

"Yes. The box next to it is also for you. It came sealed and has remained sealed to maintain privacy."

"Do you know how she died?"

"I'm sorry, we don't. It all arrived in the mail with a note to ensure you got the items and Delilah's urn. We're still working to get a death certificate. The whole thing has also surprised us, but we'll try to sort it out. In the meantime, take as much time as you need. The room is yours for the day. Did you bring anyone with you?"

"Just Haven," Lucas answered, staring at the box by the altar.

"Then please, stay until you feel comfortable driving again. Would you or Haven like some water? We also have coffee and pastries."

"We're okay for now. Thank you, though."

"You betcha," James said with that classic Minnesota twang. "If you have questions, I'll be around. Don't think you're bothering me by asking them."

"Yes, sir," Lucas said with a nod. Haven stepped

down on his foot until Lucas shook his head. "Sorry. That urn is throwing me. Can we turn it so the flag isn't facing out?"

James patted Lucas's shoulder and walked to the altar, turning the urn until only the brushed steel faced them. "I'll be right outside this door." He showed Lucas where, and after he nodded, James walked through it and closed it behind him.

"Delilah, what happened?" he whispered, dropping Haven's lead and walking to the altar. He rested his hands on the cold granite and hung his head, the memories of the summer they spent together rolling through his mind and his heart. Those days had been some of the best and worst days of his life. While he hadn't talked to Delilah in years, he thought about that summer they spent together every one of the last 2,190 days apart.

Haven budged his leg with his nose, and Lucas snapped back to the room, eyeing the dog for a moment before he nodded and picked up the box. It was small and weighed almost nothing, which surprised him, though maybe it shouldn't. Delilah was never about material things. She was always about experiences. Probably because her job in the army focused on things. Things people needed and it was her job to get, and things that other people wanted and would do anything to obtain at any cost.

"Something feels smudgy about this, Haven," he whispered to the dog as he stared at the box. "Delilah was a veteran and would have been treated and buried as such, even if she had no one else."

Voicing what his brain had been saying freed him. He split open the tape on the box and moved aside the packing paper. At the bottom was an envelope that said Luca. She had always called him that, and he allowed it, but only from her. He recognized the slanting *L* immediately as her handwriting, so he gingerly lifted it from the box. Under it, taped to the bottom, was her army Distinguished Service Medal—the only possession she ever cared about in life and wanted to be buried with in death.

Chapter Two

Lucas pulled the medal from the box, tucked it into his shirt pocket and then slipped his finger under the lip of the envelope. He hesitated when he grasped the note inside. Hell, he did more than hesitate. His fingers shook, knowing that one of those situations he thought could never be resolved was about to be. He opened the note and stared at the handwriting scrawled across the page.

Hey, there,

Those two words brought everything back. Every touch. Every fear. Every moment they spent together seared his already muddled mind. The hope that the letter wasn't from her had ended when he read the greeting. That was their greeting. He always sang the words whenever he approached her from behind so she didn't get scared. He shook his head to clear it and forced himself to keep reading.

Don't show anyone this, Luca. I'm not dead, but I am in trouble, and you're the only one who can help me now. I saw in the papers that you're working for Secure One. They sound like great company to keep and just the kind of company I'm going to need if you don't want this note to be my last will and testament. Since I couldn't find their address, I had to hope the funeral home could reach you. I'm sending my medal along so you know it's really me. It's the only possession I care about other than the one I left with you long ago. I need it back now, or someone will make sure those ashes in that urn aren't fake. I'll explain everything when you catch up with me. I'm on island time now, but you can call me at the number printed below. When you come, come alone. Don't tell anyone. Don't use the internet to search for me. They have eyes everywhere. Mele Kalikimaka. *Lilah*

Lucas lowered the paper to the table and stared at the urn. What was going on? Was this a joke? He read the note over and over until Haven whined and butted his thigh with his nose. It broke his concentration, and he glanced down at the dog, who put a paw on his leg. A sign that his anxiety was too high. Lucas did another round of breathing to calm his mind. When he finished, he reread the note, this time with the trained eye of a security expert, not as a man who had once cared deeply about this woman. Hell, as a man who still cared about this woman.

I'm on island time now. Mele Kalikimaka.

Why was she wishing him Merry Christmas in Hawaiian? The penny dropped, shooting Lucas to his feet. "Boy, it's time to go."

He grabbed Haven's lead after folding the note and

tucking it into his wallet until he could return to Secure One. He was never more grateful that he'd be back on base in less than an hour, but first, he had to get out of there without raising any suspicion.

An idea came to him, and he pulled the medal from his pocket, rubbing his thumb across the gold eagle. Delilah always said after everything she did over there, the least they could do was give her a medal or two. She was kidding, of course, until she was notified that she'd be getting this one. The service had been short, but he remembered every second of it as though it were yesterday. He'd never been prouder of a human being than he was of her that day. Little did he know how quickly life would change right after.

Making a fist around the medal, he held it like a lifeline. A part of him couldn't deny that it was for the simple reason that, for the first time in too many years, he could feel Lilah in the present instead of the past. For now, he would play the part of a grieving friend, and while he knew too much about military funerals, he didn't know much about civilian ones. He stuck his head around the door and noticed James sitting at a table, working on a laptop.

The man lifted his head as though his tingly funeral senses told him someone was in need. "Everything okay?" James asked, standing and walking to the door.

"As okay as they can be when you lose a friend and fellow soldier." Lucas held out his palm. "She sent along her Distinguished Service Medal. It was the only thing she ever wanted buried with her."

"Was there a note indicating where she'd like to be buried?" James asked as they walked back into the room to face the urn. The urn Lucas now knew was, thankfully, not holding what was left of his friend.

"No, there was nothing else in the box. I know where Delilah would like to be spread, though. Am I allowed to take the urn?"

"Not yet," James answered immediately. "We're still trying to sort this out, so I can't turn it over to you until we have a death certificate in hand."

Lucas nodded solemnly, though he felt terrible that the funeral home was spending time and resources on a futile endeavor. Maybe he could fix that much, at least. "If you keep the urn, I'll move things up through the chain of command at Secure One and the military. Just sit tight and don't do any more work on it until I get back to you. There's no reason for you to dump a lot of time into it when I can get the answers much quicker and easier."

"Are you sure?" James seemed uncomfortable now, and Lucas wondered if he saw right through his words. "We're generally able to get all the information we need, but we're hitting a brick wall." So, he was uncomfortable because it looked unprofessional, not because he suspected Lucas was playing him.

"Likely because of who she was and what she did for the government. I can't say more than that, but I'm confident you understand what I'm saying." A curt nod from James was all he needed before he continued. "I appreciate the time you've put into this and for reaching out to us at Secure One. I'll find the answers you need and get back to you."

That was the truth. Lucas would get answers, hopefully, from Lilah herself.

"We're happy to help or facilitate anything we can,

once we know where to start," James said, walking along as Lucas moved toward the door with Haven following him dutifully. "Here's my card." He pulled a business card from his pocket and handed it to Lucas. "When you know something, please call. We'll go from there. Again, I'm sorry for your loss and that things are complicated."

"No need to apologize. Not when you did the hard work of tracking me down so my friend's wishes could be followed. I appreciate all your help. I'll contact you as soon as I know something."

With a final handshake, Lucas left Edwards, Roberts and Thomas Funeral Home and helped Haven into the SUV. As he pulled away from the curb, he glanced at the dog, who had settled on the seat, content that his handler was steady again. "Looks like we're going island hopping, buddy." Laughter filled the cab as he shook his head. "Too bad I'm going to need a parka instead of a bathing suit."

LUCAS WALKED INTO the cafeteria hoping to locate his boss. Whenever they weren't on assignment, the core team gathered for lunch to chat and plan for the afternoon. Today, he was both grateful and terrified that they were all there.

"Secure one, Lima," he said, releasing Haven from the lead.

"Secure two, Charlie," Cal answered, standing immediately and walking to him as a hush fell over the room. "Was it true?"

"No." The word expressed a heaviness he felt through his entire body. His feet felt like lead weights that tethered him to the ground. "It's a mess, though."

Cal held up a finger to him and turned his head. "Sadie, could you feed Haven for Lucas?"

"Oh, you know I will! Come on, boy," she called from the kitchen, giving him a whistle. "Time for lunch!"

Haven bounced on his front paws while he stared at his handler, awaiting a command. Lucas couldn't help but laugh before he pointed to the kitchen. "Rest time!"

The dog skittered off to get his lunch while Cal led him to the table to sit. Eric, Roman, Efren and Mack sat finishing their lunch. The same lunch magically appeared before Lucas as soon as he was settled. He pushed the plate away, his appetite long gone after the events at the funeral home. "Hey," he said, glancing around the table at the brotherhood he'd come to rely on over the last eighteen months. "I don't know where to start to sort out this mess."

"We're good at sorting out messes," Mina said, walking into the room with her noticeable baby bump. She was five months pregnant with a baby girl, and everyone at Secure One had pink fever. "Break it down for us." She sat next to her husband, Roman, who kissed her cheek as she got out her computer, something that rarely left her hands.

Lucas reached into his shirt pocket and pulled out Delilah's medal, lowering it to the table. It earned him four deeply inhaled breaths from the guys who had served in the army and knew it wasn't a medal just anyone received. "That medal is the only possession my friend Delilah ever wanted to be buried with her."

"This is the friend the funeral home called about?" Efren asked, eyeing the medal. "Not just anyone gets the Distinguished Service Medal."

"Yes, Delilah Hartman. We served on the same base. She was a security tech and supply chain manager. Since I was an ordnance officer, we interacted frequently. She earned that medal the hard way."

"Munitions," Roman said. "That's dangerous stuff."

"It is, but I was more on the IT side of the weapons systems. Since Lilah was also techie, we often helped each other with glitches in the field. As you know, the bases were well connected, but the tech was always at the mercy of what was flying overhead."

"Which made both of your jobs harder over there."

"It did on the satellite base. Oddly enough, our main base was in Germany, but we never ran into each other until we got on the smaller base. We had only been on that base for a month when it fell." Lucas cleared his throat and shook his head, trying to force the memories of that day down and away so he could focus on Delilah. Haven nudged his side, telling him he was back and ready to work. Lucas stroked his head several times as the dog put his paws on his lap. "We haven't seen each other in six years."

"Then, out of the blue, you get notice that she's dead and wants you to bury her?" Eric asked. "That's the military's job for veterans."

"It is," Lucas said with a nod. "That's why I was immediately suspicious. A box was sent with her remains. When I opened it, the medal was inside. I was with her when she got it, so I knew it was real. On top of the medal was a note."

"Read it," Cal said.

They all stared at him as he pulled the note from his wallet. He noticed his hand shook as he opened it. Was he afraid that, somehow, the words had changed, and she was dead? Truthfully? Yes.

"'Don't show anyone this, Luca. I'm not dead, but I am in trouble, and you're the only one who can help me.'" Lucas read the first line, and their brows all went up. "No one else ever called me Luca. I know she wrote this." Their nods told him they understood, so he finished reading the note to them.

Mina was already typing. "A 904 area code? Jacksonville doesn't make sense unless she's on Sanibel or Key West?"

Lucas shook his head and set the note down on the table. "It's not a phone number. Try 46.8135 north and 90.6913 west."

Mina typed and then glanced up at him. "Madeline Island?"

"Yep," Lucas agreed, his hand straying to Haven's head again. "After we were healed and discharged from the army, we met up unexpectedly in Duluth one night. We decided to camp on the island for the summer."

"'I'm on island time now,'" Roman repeated. "Smart."

"She knew if I got the letter, I would understand that she just transposed the numbers in the coordinates to confuse anyone else."

"What percentage of you believes she's really in trouble?" Cal asked.

Lucas reached for the medal, picked it up and ran his finger across the eagle again. "Every fiber of my being. I haven't heard from her in six years, and suddenly, out of the blue, she's sending me her ashes. No. For whatever reason, she's desperate. The way she mentions Secure One tells me that much."

"Let's talk about the elephant in the room," Efren said. "What do you have of hers that she wants back? It can't be the medal."

Lucas's fist closed around the metal eagle. "Oh, she'll want this back, but whatever she thinks I have, I don't have."

"I don't understand," Eric said, leaning forward on the table.

"I don't, either." Lucas's growl was enough for Haven to press his nose into his side again until he did his breathing while the team waited. They all understood how difficult it was when their service life crossed into their present life. "I don't have anything left from our time together. Listen, that summer we spent on Madeline Island was rough. We were both dealing with what happened on the base and its fallout. I'd been in a rehab facility for my back for almost two months and hadn't addressed anything that had happened to me, emotionally or physically. All these years later, I can admit that the PTSD was spiraling out of control, but she was the only one who could see it. Delilah dropped me off at the VA hospital in Minneapolis that September when we left the island. She promised to return the next day, but she never showed her face again. When I left the hospital almost three months later and started the training program with Haven, I tried to find her. By all accounts, Delilah Hartman had disappeared into thin air."

"We all know you have to go to her now," Mina said, typing on her computer. "Madeline Island is rather chilly in December, though. How long ago was this note written?"

"She's there," Lucas said with conviction. "Delilah

will stay on the island for as long as it takes me to find her, or until someone else finds her first. The box that her 'remains' came in," he said, using air quotes, "was dated less than a week ago from Minneapolis. That means she mailed them and went to the island."

"If she made it to the island," Roman said. Mina elbowed him, and he huffed. "Someone had to say it."

"No, you're right," Lucas agreed, shaking his head with frustration. "If she mailed the box from that far out, which I'm sure she did on purpose to confuse anyone looking for her, then she wasn't on the island yet. I still have to try. The fact that she reached out to me all these years later tells me she's desperate for whatever she thinks I have. Whether I have it or not is irrelevant. She needs help. That's something we can provide her, right?"

Cal was the first to stand up from the table. "No one left behind. This search and rescue will take some coordinating, though."

Efren stood and headed for the door. "Meet me in the conference room in ten minutes."

"Where are you going?" Cal asked, and Efren stopped in the doorway.

"If we're going to undertake a search and rescue, you'll need my future wife. Tango, out."

When Lucas turned back to the group, they were all grinning as they gathered their things. For the first time all day, he felt like he might be able to save the woman he hadn't stopped thinking about for six long years. If nothing else, bringing her back to Secure One and helping her out of this dilemma might be his one-way ticket to getting her out of his system. That, or finding her, only to lose her again, would make his soul bleed forever.

Chapter Three

Delilah crouched low in the darkness, praying the falling snow would hide her as she crossed the open expanse of the lake. She had lucked out. It was two weeks before Christmas and northern Wisconsin was in a deep freeze. That meant Lake Superior between Bayfield and Madeline Island was frozen, which didn't happen every year. The freeze allowed her to snowshoe to the island from the mainland under the shadows of darkness. She just had to be careful about where she stepped since there could be open spots she couldn't see in the dark.

She glanced down at her new white winter gear. Everything was new, from her snowsuit to her snowshoes to her backpack. Knowing she had no trackers on her didn't mean she was safe. It just meant it would take them longer to find her. And they would find her. Hopefully, it would take them even longer this far out from civilization.

Her choices were few, though. If the funeral home found Luca and gave him her "remains," she had to be on the island as promised. Were there better places to meet up with the man she'd abandoned without so much as a word? Yes, but Madeline Island would be a safe zone for Luca and his emotions. At least, she prayed it still would be. It had been enough years that she could no longer assume she knew anything about the man. She knew if he didn't show, she would have to initiate a more direct approach with him, putting both of them in undue danger.

Faking your death and sending an urn of fake ashes was dramatic, but Secure One was so off-the-grid that she couldn't find it. Considering all she needed was a computer for an hour and she could find anything, that spoke to the lengths Secure One went to remain incognito. Their business phone number was easy to find, but the address, not so much. They'd been in the news multiple times over the last few years, and Delilah had followed those cases, completely unaware that Luca was working for them. She was watching a news report on how Secure One had rescued two kidnapping victims from the Mafia, and when the news team panned out during a live report, Luca walked behind them. She had watched the clip at least two dozen times, trying to convince herself it wasn't him and trying to convince herself it was. Over the years, Delilah had kept track of him, but the last information she had put him as a guard for a state senator.

That was then, a time when she believed she'd finally outsmarted the people after her. But that time was over. Delilah glanced behind her, satisfied that the snow covered her tracks across the lake, even if it covered her head to toe, too. She had to get to base camp, set up her tent and get the stove going so she could dry out. After some tense moments searching for a way onto the island with thick enough ice to support her, Delilah finally stepped on shore. She'd made it. Before her stretched a winter wonderland that didn't hold the promise of snow-ball fights and cups of hot cocoa. It held the promise of death if Luca didn't find her.

He had seven days before she'd have to return to civilization or freeze to death. She didn't like either of those options, so she prayed Luca was willing to stick his neck out to find her despite breaking his trust years ago. She had to hope that his curiosity wouldn't let her down. He had always been a curious soul, and she had to play on that personality trait if she had any hope of convincing him to help. She just hoped popping back up in his life out of the blue would override the anger and disappointment he surely felt about how things ended between them. Once they were face-to-face again, she could explain why she ran.

A shudder went through Delilah, and it wasn't from the cold. It was from the memory that invaded her mind. She had dropped Luca at the hospital, her heart heavy as she pulled into the parking lot of her long-term-stay hotel. Barely out of the car, she was attacked by two men—one with a knife—and only managed to escape thanks to some kind older man who shouted out his window when he heard the commotion. She'd been running ever since. She had reached the finish line, though. To say she was exhausted was an understatement. Nothing was left in the tank, and she feared what would come if she didn't get the only possible thing they could want.

Concentrate on the now, not the tomorrow.

Those were his words. He would recite them whenever she tried to talk about the future with him that summer on this island. Now, they were a reminder to take things one step at a time. Getting hung up on what could hap-

pen tomorrow manifested itself frequently and unexpectedly, but Delilah chalked that up to her PTSD. She had
lied to Luca the day she told him she didn't qualify for
treatment at the VA. She had simply convinced herself
Luca needed help more than her. How wrong she'd been.

Those thoughts had to go back into the box she kept
them in if she hoped to survive alone in the wilder-
ness. She rolled her shoulders and stayed low as she
approached the campground in case someone else was
winter camping, too. She doubted it. As Christmas approached, most people were with their families inside a
loving home filled with the scent of pine trees and cin-
namon. She wasn't like most people. Never had been.
All she wanted now was a place to rest—if not her tired
mind, at least her exhausted body. Ironically, when she
got the travel stove fired up to warm the tent, the scent
of pine trees would be in the air. She would be thankful for that, too.

Campsite 61 came into sight, and she slowed as the
memories rolled through her one after the other. Delilah
lowered her pack to the ground at the ghostly sound of
Luca laughing. Luca crying. Luca screaming in terror.
The loudest of those ghostly sounds were of Luca loving her unlike anyone else ever had.

She lifted her face to send a message into the atmosphere. "Find me, Luca. I need you more than I ever
have before."

When she lowered her head, she was sure of one
thing: the countdown started now.

A WHISPER OF cold air swirled through Lucas, and he
shuddered. It had been five days since Delilah mailed

that urn, and he was running out of time to find her. If he missed her on the island tonight, he wouldn't give up. Those two words weren't in his vocabulary. Never give up, never give in. Those were the words he lived by. There had been plenty of times he could have given up, but there was an unseen force that kept him going. Death had walked alongside him, but he was still on this earth for a reason, whether he knew why yet or not. As he stared at the snowy tundra below, he was acutely aware of how unusual it was for the lake to be frozen this early in the season, so he couldn't help but wonder if this was the reason. If *Delilah* was the reason.

"You sure you want to do this alone, son?" Cal's words came over the headset he wore in the chopper as they flew toward their destination in Bayfield, Wisconsin. "I've been a ghost before. I can do it again."

"As much as I appreciate it, Cal, this bird is our ticket off that island, so I need you behind the controls. Delilah's note said to come alone. If I show up on the island and she gets a whiff that I'm not, she'll bolt. Besides, I don't know what I'm walking into. The less collateral damage, the better."

"That's the thing, kid," Roman said from where he sat next to Cal. "We'd be there to prevent the collateral damage. Think long and hard about this, Lucas. Having an unseen lookout may be the only reason you both walk out alive. You don't know why someone is after her, so for all you know, you're walking into a trap."

Lucas bit his lip as he considered what Roman had said. In the end, they were both right. It wasn't exactly smart to walk into the situation alone, but he also couldn't scare Lilah away.

"If we'd had more time to plan the mission, that would have helped," Cal said, as though driving home the point. "You barely let Selina call her contact at The Cliff Badgers Search and Rescue team to find the best way to get Haven to the island. I don't like leaping without looking."

"I know," Lucas said between clenched teeth as he stroked Haven's head. The dog sat beside him with one paw on his lap to keep him grounded. They'd worked together for so long now that Lucas never had to give the dog a command for help with anxiety. Haven knew it was coming long before he did. "I don't like it, either, but it's cold and she's probably been out there for days. If we wait too long, she'll dip and we'll be back to square one. We had to move on it and move on it in the dark."

Lucas waited, but neither of the men in the chopper said another word. Was he nervous about going out onto that island alone? Yes. But he was more nervous about seeing Lilah. He'd buried her so deep that he was afraid seeing her would dig up all those emotions he never wanted to see the light of day again. Did that make him a coward? Probably, but the truth was true, as his mom used to say.

"Let me ask you a question," he said, waiting for Cal to nod. "What would you do if you were me? Be honest."

"When I was your age, exactly what you're doing now," Cal admitted with a chuckle. "Since then, I've learned the importance of tactical strategy. I learned that strategy by almost dying more times than I want to admit."

"And he means that literally," Roman added. "I was there for several of them."

Cal reached over and punched his brother playfully while laughing. Roman and Cal were foster brothers who grew up together and joined the army. When they got injured on a mission and left the service, Cal went into private security while Roman went into the FBI. Now they were working together again, and Lucas trusted the two of them explicitly. The thought made his chest rise with surprise momentarily before he spoke.

"Are you guys familiar with the island?" Lucas asked, and they both made the so-so hand motion. "That's a no. Here's what you don't understand, guys. The island is much bigger and denser than it looks on a map. Lilah won't be near a paved road, so if you aren't standing next to me, you're impotent in an emergency. The forest is dense, which means the snow will hamper us even more. I know I need your help, but tactically, I'll be better off with you providing air support."

Lucas's mind entered planning mode. He ran through his intimate knowledge of the island, the best place to approach and all the ways he could stay hidden while doing it.

"It's impossible to be stealthy while offering air support," Cal finally said.

"That's fine, as long as you don't start this whirlybird until after I've met up with Delilah. I'll explain that I'm alone, but you're our ride out of there."

"You wear an earpiece and keep it on at all times?"

"All times?" Lucas shook his head. "No, I'll have to mute it when I approach her. I don't know what this is about, and until I do, I won't expose you guys to something that you can't deny to the authorities."

"You think it's that serious?"

"I don't know what to think," Lucas admitted. "I haven't seen her in six years, but the Delilah I used to know had never been dramatic a day in her life. She was calm, cool and calculated, so if she's scared and scattered, I'm terrified."

"Understood," Roman said.

"What's your plan?" Lucas asked, knowing they needed to be all on the same page.

"Don't you worry about what we're going to do, son," Roman answered. "Worry about what you have to do." He held up an earpiece for Lucas to see. "We'll all have one, and we can talk to each other." He held up his hand. "Yes, you can mute it so we can't hear you and Delilah talking."

"The rest of the time," Cal butted in, "mute is off so we can communicate. Understood?"

"Heard, understood and acknowledged," he said with a nod.

"Good, then let's get you out there to find this woman. My curiosity is piqued. I'm dying to know the story."

"Can we not use the phrase 'dying to know' for the next few hours?" Lucas asked, glancing out the chopper's window at the blackness below.

"Heard, understood and acknowledged," Cal said with a chuckle before he headed for solid ground.

Chapter Four

Lucas glanced at the sky as he and Haven stepped onto the island. The moon was starting to peek out from behind the clouds, which meant the temperature was about to drop again. He used hand motions to tell Haven to follow him into a wall of trees. When Lucas took the job with the senator as a security guard, he'd taught Haven hand signs he could use when situations didn't allow speech. The dog, a former K-9 in the army, had taken to the training immediately. Lucas had been grateful he'd already taught him the signs, so when he applied for the Secure One job, he could prove the dog wouldn't be a liability in a tense situation.

He paused for a moment and checked Haven over. The walk to the island had been less difficult than expected since the wind had blown them a path relatively free of snow. He'd come prepared with a sled at the recommendation of Selina's friend Kai, but it hadn't been necessary, so he abandoned it on shore for someone else to use. Now that they were on land, moving around would get more complicated. He straightened Haven's coat, checked his boots to ensure they were secure and did the same with his gear, including stowing his snowshoes on his pack. The shoes would only inhibit his ability to move quickly and efficiently through the forest and brush. If he was lucky, a path would already be made once he reached the campground.

Lucas clipped a short lead on Haven and quietly motioned him forward. They had purposely approached the island at an angle closest to the campground when he noticed a whisper of smoke through the trees as he stood on the shore. He had no doubt that the long-lost Delilah Hartman was awaiting his arrival. His mantra as he traversed the lake had been simple: *Stay neutral. Learn the facts. Act accordingly.* Something told him it would be a harder mantra to stick to once he was face-to-face with Lilah again.

"Secure one, Lima," he said into the earpiece.

"Secure two, Charlie," Cal said in his ear to tell him to go ahead and speak freely. If he ever heard a different greeting, it was an immediate signal that their teammate was in trouble.

"On the island, about half a klick from the campsite."

"Smoke in the air at your target. Proceed with caution."

"I noted that from shore. It's in the right vicinity for site 61. Will make contact in under five."

"The bird will be in the air in a few," Cal said, and Lucas could hear him flipping switches as they spoke. "I'll be waiting at the extraction point. You can hear us even if we can't hear you."

"You've got twenty minutes to convince her to leave with us, kid. Get it done," Roman said.

"Roger that," Lucas answered and then muted the microphone.

Did it annoy him that they always called him kid and son? It did initially, but now he saw it for what it was. Team members had to earn their stripes at Secure One. Until he did, he was a kid to them, but they never said it in a derogatory way. It came from a place of protection and teaching. Lucas had made sure to pay attention and learn those lessons well. If someone shared their knowledge with him, it only made sense to listen and learn so he could implement it when the time was right.

The time was finally right. He had no question in his mind as he silently approached the edge of the campground through the snow. Undoubtedly, Lilah was aware someone was nearby. That was who she was, but he couldn't worry about that as he approached. All he could do was continue to move forward, hoping she believed he'd come for her.

One last obstacle to overcome was the steep bank they had to climb. Lucas glanced at it and then at Haven, wondering if the dog could even make it, but the eye movement must have been enough because Haven plowed his way forward, forcing Lucas to follow as he held the lead. They were on top of the bank in just a few seconds. He was surprised how much easier it had been to scale that bank than it used to be. Whether that was due to the snow or the fact he took care of himself now was hard to say, but he was glad he was back on even ground.

Lucas stood in the tree line and took in campsite 61. A canvas cowboy range tent was set up with a stovepipe through the center, explaining the smoke's origin. The tent could belong to anyone. He eyed the area around it, noting a large wood berm built next to the tent the way they used to build their sandbag bunkers in the army. Lilah was here somewhere.

He had no choice but to announce his presence and wait. He unhooked Haven from the lead and pulled his Glock out from under his coat. After crouching into the shooter position, he flicked on his earpiece. "Found her campsite. I'm about to call out to her. Going dark for a few."

"Ten-four," Cal said. "Loop us back in as soon as you find her."

"Ten-four," he whispered, then put his microphone on mute.

Lucas cleared his throat and prayed his voice didn't sound like a scared twelve-year-old when he spoke. "Hey, there, Lilah." His words were firm but laced with the nervousness that filled him.

He'd been scared while running missions overseas, but hoping that Lilah was in that tent while worried she wasn't terrified him more than any of those missions had. He waited, the air crackling with tension, hope and fear. Had he missed her? Had it taken too long to get the message to him? Maybe she left information in the tent to tell him where to go next. Did he dare look? No, that didn't make sense. There was still smoke drifting from the stovepipe, which meant the fire was recent.

His gaze darted around the area, while his mind took him back to the time he had spent with Lilah here. It had been her suggestion to spend the summer on the island. After the base fell, they both ended up at the Minneapolis VA to heal, but never ran into each other. It was an unexpected meeting in a bar in Duluth that had reconnected them. That night, they'd shared a hotel room, not platonically, so he was all in when she suggested taking a summer to find themselves again before worrying about school or a job. They both had money; there was no problem in that respect, but they were both quick to realize they had no one but each other.

Lilah's parents were both dead by the time she was eighteen and Lucas never had parents to speak of. Sure, his mom was around, but she was too busy getting high to worry about what her kid was doing. By age eight, he was in foster care, so it made sense for him to join the service when he graduated. He had been led to believe it was his golden ticket in life after enduring a crappy childhood. Little did he know it would be a ticket to a house of horrors far worse than any childhood nightmare.

They'd brought only what they could carry onto the island, knowing there was access to everything else already there. That included access to nature therapy to help heal their fractured minds. Lucas glanced down at Haven and sighed. Nature therapy may have been enough for Lilah, but not for him. Still, all he could remember about his time at campsite 61 were the good memories—the memories of her touching him, loving him and protecting him from himself.

"Hey, there, Lilah," he said again, a bit louder, hoping she just hadn't heard him the first time. He doubted that was the case. Maybe she wasn't on the islan—

"Are you alone, Luca?"

The question came from his left, and he recognized the voice immediately. He fought back the wave of equal parts nostalgia and desire to focus on his pounding heart. *Stay neutral. Learn the facts. Act accordingly.* He ran the motto through his head before he answered.

"Other than my dog, yes." He had a decision to make. Keep his gun out in case she was being controlled by someone out to hurt them or put it away so he didn't scare her. "Are you alone?"

"I've never been more alone, Luca."

At the sound of her voice, he slipped his Glock into his coat pocket and stepped out of the woods with his hands up. "You're not alone, Lilah. You called, so I came."

And then, before his eyes appeared an apparition of his past. Delilah was dressed in white from head to toe. Even with most of her face covered, he knew it was her. The eyes never lied, and the gray ones hiding behind those prism lenses told him more than her words ever could. She had seen things over the last six years that haunted her and terrified her in equal measure.

Lilah pulled the balaclava down and sent him back to that summer under the Wisconsin sun. Life was complicated but simple. Love was in the air, and for the first time, Lucas was sure he'd found his family. He could still feel the softness of her skin under his hands as he ran them down her ribs to rest on her hips. Then she'd plaster her lips on his and carry him to another place where everything was simple. The only thing he needed back then was her.

Lucas hadn't agreed to get treatment for himself. He'd agreed to go for her so they could live the life they'd planned that summer. Once his treatment was over, they'd get a little apartment in Duluth and find work. They'd put down roots, learn about each other, build a life together, whatever that may look like as the months and years passed. He'd held on to that idea for the first month he was at the VA, hoping and praying that she hadn't visited because she was busy setting up their life. How naive he had been.

"*I don't want you to leave,*" Lucas said, *holding her hand at the entrance to registration.*

"*I don't want to leave, but you need to be here, Lucas. You must find a way to live with the horrors you saw over there. I don't want you to be a statistic. I want you in my life for years, okay?*"

He trailed a finger down her cheek and tucked a piece of hair behind her ear. "*You promise you'll visit?*"

"*As much as they'll let me,*" *she whispered, lifting herself on her tiptoes to kiss him.* "*In between those times, I'll find us a place and prepare it for your home-coming. I know we can do this if we do it together, Luca.*"

"*Together,*" *he whispered.*

Haven dug his nose into his thigh, leaned against him and rumbled a low growl as a reminder to return to the present. Lucas took a breath, his gloved hand stroking Haven's head as he gazed at the woman he'd been sure was lost to him forever.

"Delilah Hartman, long time no see." Lucas forced the words from his lips. His mind was having difficulty accepting that the woman who stood before him was the same woman he had shared so much with on this island.

He wanted to demand to know why she'd abandoned him. He also wanted to hug her and never let her go. She took a step toward him, and that was when he saw it. A scar ran from under the balaclava's edge to the side of her lip and another one across her chin and down her neck. The intensity of the situation was written on her face. The black bags under her eyes said she wasn't sleeping, and the fear in those globes of dusky gray told him she was scared, tired and unsure about everything. Everything but him.

"Luca. You came."

"Of course, I came. You fell off the face of the earth six years ago, and when you pop back up in my life, it's in an urn full of God knows what? I had to come."

"Sand."

"Sand?"

"That's what's in the urn. I'm sorry for the dramatics. I could find a phone number for Secure One, but no address."

"I'm just glad it wasn't you, Lilah." He took his glove off and traced the scar across her chin. "Help me understand. You dropped me off at the hospital and disappeared from my life. I waited for you for months, but you never returned. When I got out, there wasn't a trace of you. If you wanted to break things off, you should have at least said it to my face. I imagined all kinds of horrible things that may have happened to you."

"I know, I know." Her words were filled with desperation. "None of this was supposed to happen. I didn't want to break things off, but that choice was taken from me. You'll know everything soon, but we don't have much time. We have to get off the island. How did you get here?"

"I snowshoed from the mainland. How did you get here?"

"The same way. If we're going to get back before daylight, we have to go now."

She dashed into the tent, and when he pulled the side back, she was putting out the fire in the small travel stove. Once that was out, she grabbed her pack and flipped it over her shoulders.

"What's the dog's name?" she asked when leaving the tent.

"Haven." The dog immediately stood at attention next to his handler. "We went into a training program together when I left the VA hospital. He's a retired army K-9 turned trained PTSD dog. Haven is what allows me to function normally in the world we live in. He won't slow us down," he added, sure that was why she asked.

"That wasn't my concern," she assured him, holding her hand out for Haven to sniff. "If we're traveling together, he has to know I'm a friend and not a foe."

"Are you a friend, though?" he asked, the bitterness loud and clear in his words. "Or am I merely a matter of convenience for you?"

"No, Luca," she said, turning and stepping up to him so he had no choice but to meet her gaze. "I know you're hurt and you don't understand what happened. That's on me. I'll explain everything, but you're not a matter of convenience. You're the person I've been protecting all this time. I hoped it wouldn't come to this, but here we are, so first we must get somewhere safe, and then I can help you understand."

"I just don't know if I can trust you, Lilah."

"That's fair," she agreed with a nod of her head, but Lucas noticed her shoulders slump with shame. He instantly felt horrible. "I'll tell you how you can trust me." She pointed to the scars on her face and chin. "These are some of my visible scars from the last six years. There are more that damn near killed me, but they didn't—for one reason. I refused to die. If I did, they were going to come after you. Every scar on my body is a mark on the tally board of trust, Luca."

"How many scars are there?" His question was filled with anguish this time. The idea of her being tormented to protect him was too much to bear.

"We need to get out of here, Luca," Lilah whispered.

She wasn't going to answer him, leaving him with a decision. Do as she said and get them to safety so she could fill in the picture or press her here where danger lurked around any tree. Lucas held up his finger and flicked the mute button off his earpiece. "I need to let the team know we're on the move."

"Team? You said you came alone."

"I did, but two of the best army special ops police are in a chopper on the mainland. We were afraid to land on the island and draw attention, so I shoed in. We'll shoe back out and catch a ride to Secure One with Cal and Roman. You can trust them. I wouldn't be here if it weren't for them."

With her nod, he hit the button and spoke. "Secure one, Lima."

"Secure two, Charlie. Did you find her?"

"Affirmative," he answered, his gaze pinned to hers by an unseen force. "We're loading up and heading to you."

"ETA?" Roman asked.

Lucas did some calculating, considering that he would have to go at Lilah's pace and she was exhausted. "Haven will slow us down, so plan for seventy-five minutes."

"Ten-four. I'll have the blades going," Cal answered.

"Lima out," he said before clicking the mute button again.

"Haven will slow us down?" Lilah asked with her brow in the air. "You don't have to spare my feelings by lying to your team, Luca. I'm fully aware I'm a hot mess, but I want to get off this island alive, so set the pace. I'll keep up."

He should have known she would see right through his excuse, but being with Lilah again activated his protective side. There had never been a time since he first laid eyes on her that he didn't want to protect her. He would have died if it meant she lived, and he nearly did, but he forced his mind away from those thoughts. Concentrating on the past would do him no favors when trying to navigate the wildness of Lake Superior in the dark.

"We can't return to Secure One, Luca. We have to find the—"

The first pop confused him until a tree to his right exploded. Before he could react, Lilah grabbed his backpack and hauled him behind the wood berm, Haven hot on his heels. He dropped his pack and swung his automatic rifle to his shoulder, returning fire.

"What the hell have you gotten yourself involved in, Lilah?" His question was yelled over his shoulder as he tried to take out an unseen enemy. The question was rhetorical, but he swore he heard her say, "A living hell," right before the next barrage of bullets rained down.

Chapter Five

"They shouldn't be here already!" Delilah yelled as he ducked behind the wood. "I came in clean!"

"Someone forgot to tell them that!" he yelled as more wood exploded around them.

Luca had come for her, but Lilah couldn't help but think he'd brought some unwanted guests. Not that it was his fault. He couldn't have known that her every move was tracked by an unknown enemy. A bullet dug into the log fortress she'd built for this very reason. Haven pushed her back toward the woods, his experience with combat obvious as he protected her from harm. She was glad Lucas had Haven now.

There were a lot of cases of PTSD after the war. Hell, she had her own to deal with, but Luca's was by far the worst she'd ever seen. They had only been on the base a month when it came to an unexpected, barbaric end. She'd been protected from some of the horrors he'd seen, so she could only imagine what he'd witnessed before they jumped on that last Black Hawk out of hell.

Lilah noticed him touch his earpiece before he yelled. "Under fire! Need extraction! Need extraction!"

While he waited, he sent a few more bullets over the

top of the wood berm. If they didn't end this soon, even her wooden fortress wouldn't be enough to protect them.

"Negative," Lucas yelled just as more gunfire filled the air. He tucked his gun around the wood's edge and sent some bullets into the darkness. All Lilah could do was sit idly by and pray one of them would find their target. Her handgun would do no good in this firefight. "We're due east of Basswood Island. The airport is miles away!"

Lucas turned and addressed her as bullets slammed into the wood protecting them, throwing splinters into the air. "Who are these guys?" She saw him take notice of Haven, who had positioned his body to block her lower half.

"I wish I knew!"

Her words had barely died off when the report of gunfire ended. Lucas took his chance. He flipped his night vision goggles down, stood and sprayed the woods with bullets. He dropped down again and turned to her. "Two down," he said, and she wasn't sure if he was addressing her or the team in the chopper. "It seems like they'd send more than two guys." His gaze darted to her, and she shrugged.

"Hard to know," she whispered, in case others were out there. "I've always only been approached by two, but the last time there were four. This island is a bit of a needle in a haystack for two guys, so starting with the campground makes the most sense."

Lucas nodded and then spoke, but not to her. "The sat phone should have sent my coordinates." He stood cautiously, his gun aimed at the woods, as he scanned the area with his night vision goggles. "Still just the two," he said, talking to his team again. "Ope!" His rifle cracked once, and Lilah noticed a shudder go through him before he spoke. "Target down. Both targets are down." He nodded as he stood, searching the forest beyond the berm. "I don't see much choice. Yes, we can make it there in twenty minutes if we don't encounter more friends along the way." Lucas ducked back down and flipped his goggles up. "We have to move," he said to her. "Cal is bringing the chopper in to pick us up, but he can't risk landing on the ice. He'll get close, drop the basket and we'll have to climb in."

Knowing she had to help any way she could, she slung her pack off for a moment and dug in a side pocket, pulling out a handgun. "Don't ask me where I got it. Just tell me what to do."

Luca handed her a pair of night vision goggles. "Put these on and stay on your toes. The extraction point is two klicks west. We should be able to cover that in twenty minutes."

"As long as there aren't more guys waiting for us," she said, slinging her pack back on her shoulders.

"The only way out is forward," Luca said with half a lip tilt. "Haven, fall in," he said, and the dog stood and went to his handler.

"Side by side?" she asked, and he nodded once. "What about those two?" She motioned toward the forest.

"They started it?" he asked, and she heard all those same emotions in his voice that she'd heard when they were on the island so long ago. Disgust. Anger. Pain. Terror. Haven noticed, too, because he butted him with his nose three times. Luca stroked his head while he breathed in and out before he nodded. "Let's hope they're the last of it. We need to move. Cal is coming in over Big Bay for extraction."

"Ten-four," Lilah said but then held up her hand for him to pause. "Let's avoid the stairs. They could be waiting to ambush us there."

"Everything else is pretty craggy, Lilah," he said, grabbing her suit as she fixed her balaclava.

"Lucky for you, I already planned a route. You better let your team know it will only take us six minutes to get there."

"Six minutes?" he asked, dropping his hands. "That's impossible."

"Not if you trust me, Luca," she said, flipping her goggles down. "Follow me?"

Lilah stepped around the berm and prayed they were still alone and that he would trust her enough to get them to safety. Within a few steps, she heard them following and picked up her pace, jinking and jiving through the woods on a path she had memorized the first day she was here. It was one of several escape routes she had mastered because no matter what Luca thought, she would walk through fire to protect him.

"So far, so good," Luca said from behind her. "How much farther?"

"Two minutes," she answered, surprised by how easily Haven kept up with them as they ran. "I hear the chopper."

"They'll be waiting," he assured her as they ran, their heads on a swivel, waiting for a sneak attack that could end this reunion much quicker than she wanted.

As soon as the white ribbon came into sight, she threw her arm out as a sign to slow. "I marked this because the rocks here can have ice under the snow. You have to go slow, but you're also exposed, so stay vigilant."

Since she was the reason they were in this position to start with, she took the first step into the open so that Luca could follow safely in her footsteps. Funny. Up until now, they'd been equals in every way. Today, she could no longer say that about her relationship with Lucas Porter. While she'd been running for her life, he was building one. Suddenly, the wasted years without him weighed heavily on her shoulders. This situation was hers by default but not her fault. She just had to stay alive long enough to get that flash drive back from Luca and, hopefully, end this chess match for good.

Lucas and Haven met her on the ice, where she crouched low and waited. "Thirty seconds out," Luca whispered, and she nodded. "Roman will drop a basket big enough for all of us. Pile in and grab hold. Cal will take off while Roman lifts us on board."

"Ten-four," she said, fighting back the racking shudders that went through her. The scene felt too much like the last time they had to jump on a chopper and pray they made it inside before a bullet took them out. "Be careful," she whispered. "Your back."

"Is fine," he answered in her ear.

"It can't be like last time, Luca. It can't be," she said, the tone going higher with each word. "It can't be."

"Focus on three," he whispered into her ear. "Breathe in for three, hold it for three, breathe out for three. If you do that, you'll make it. I promise."

"You did always like the number three," she said with a lip tilt before she did what he'd instructed. The fact was, it did calm her and let her focus on what needed to be done to stay alive. "Maybe they only sent in the two guys."

The thumping of the chopper blades drowned out her

voice, and in seconds, it came into view. She followed Luca out into the open, praying they had time to get on board before anyone else could reach them. She wanted to believe only two guys were on the island, but she wasn't that naive. The two he took out were just their scout team, but the gunfire and chopper would now draw them like a moth to a flame.

"Go, go!" Luca yelled, pointing at the basket as it came down from the chopper. Lucas helped her in before hoisting Haven into it. The first bullet whizzed past her ear just as Luca somersaulted into the wire basket. He motioned with his arm over his head for Roman to go but quickly dropped it as more bullets came their way. "Stay down!" he yelled, covering Haven with his body while Roman returned fire.

They were going to ride this basket until they were clear of the gunfire, so all she could do was hang on for dear life and pray.

"THAT ONE GAINED purchase, eh?" Selina asked as she dropped a bullet into a pan next to him on the table. "Didn't anyone ever teach you to duck?"

Lucas meant to laugh, but it came out as a groan. "Must have been sick that day. Better me than Haven, though," he said, hissing when she stuck him with a needle and filled him with more Novocain.

"You're lucky you had that pack on your back or you'd be in a hospital. Maybe even a morgue."

"Trust me, I wish things had gone differently. We're lucky to have walked away with only minor injuries."

"Patch him up good, babe," Efren said, walking into the med bay. "They're not staying."

"They have to stay long enough for me to pump him

full of antibiotics and make sure this doesn't end up infected."

"Better talk to the boss about that. He says this is a pit stop to change tires and fuel up before they hit the track again."

Lucas glanced between them. "Cal wants us out?"

"He's waiting in the conference room to discuss it, but from what Delilah has said, if she's here, no one is safe."

"I haven't even had a chance to talk to her," Lucas said between gritted teeth as Selina started suturing the wound.

The ride back to Secure One had been short but tense. Lilah spent the ride holding pressure to his wound while all he wanted to do was hold her. Once they arrived at Secure One, Mina had whisked Lilah off while Selina tended to his leg. Thankfully, his pack had diverted the bullet and it lodged in the flesh of his thigh rather than his back or his head. In a few days, he'd be fine, but Lilah wouldn't be if Cal couldn't offer her protection.

Selina smoothed a clear bandage across the small wound, then snapped off her gloves. "That plastic coating is Tegaderm. You can shower with the stitches as long as the Tegaderm is in place. I'll give you some extra to take, but it's meant to stay on until it loosens itself. I used dissolvable stitches, so you don't have to worry about removal. They'll disappear on their own. Keep them dry."

"Thanks, Selina." He tried to stand, but she forced him back to the stretcher.

"Not so fast," she said, spinning her stool around. "You need antibiotics. If I can't give them to you via intravenous, then you'll have to take pills. We can't risk an infection. Especially if you won't be around for me to keep an eye on it."

Selina was their head medic on the team, but she was also an operative. In her prior life, she'd been a Chicago cop and search and rescue medic, so she understood the situations they often found themselves in when a case took a turn.

"Fine, give me the bottle." He held his hand out. "I need to get down to the conference room."

"I'll let them know you're on your way," Efren said before he kissed Selina on the cheek and left the room. It was only a few months ago that Selina spent her days snipping at Efren for every little thing. It turned out that forcing them together to save their own lives changed their relationship for the better. He could only be so lucky. Then again, the Delilah he picked up off that island wasn't the same Delilah he knew six years ago. She was different. Sadder. Untrusting. Harder.

"What's going on here, Lucas?" Selina asked, grabbing an empty bottle from her cabinet and counting pills from a different bottle.

"I wish I could answer that," he admitted. He climbed off the gurney, pulled up his pants and tested his leg. It was tender, but he'd had worse injuries in the field. "That's why I have to get down to the conference room. If Cal isn't going to let us stay here, I'll have to figure something else out."

"If Cal isn't going to let you stay here, then that woman is in serious trouble."

"And me by default."

"I also know that Cal isn't going to abandon you. He'll have a plan, so stay calm and listen to what he'll lay out. Twice a day for a week," she said, shaking the bottle before she handed it to him. "More a precaution than a certainty, but try."

"Got it, doc," he said, pocketing the bottle.

"Do you want me to keep Haven for you?" Selina asked, walking him and the dog to the door.

"Yes, but no. I don't want to put him in danger, but—"

"But you're going to need him," she finished, taking his hand to stop the patting to the count of three on Haven's head. "Before you leave, get his bulletproof vest. I know it's heavy, but it's smart to have the Kevlar on him in this situation."

"I agree. I should have done it when we went out there, but I wasn't expecting a full-blown war within minutes of arriving."

"I don't know anyone who would, Lucas. You got this. We're here for you, so if anything happens, you call in and we cover your back. In any way we need to, right?"

Lucas rubbed his hand down over his cargo pants, now torn from the bullet. "I feel terrible that Secure One has gotten hit with this after what happened with you and Vaccaro. I can't lose this job."

"Listen," Selina said, grasping his shoulder. It offered him a moment of solidarity in a situation he couldn't control. "You might be the newest member of Secure One, but you have saved all of our butts multiple times since joining the team. Cal knows that, and so does everyone else who will be around that table. Whatever is going on has nothing to do with you and everything to do with you, but not by your creation."

"Truer than you know," he agreed with a nod. "I'm afraid this will come to a fast end when I tell Delilah

I have nothing left from our time together. Then she'll disappear from my life forever, and I don't want that to happen. She may not be the Delilah I knew six years ago, but it's easy to see that's because of what she's lived through since we parted ways. If we force her out, I'm afraid she'll end up in an urn, for real this time."

"Then stand up and be the person she needs to help her out of this situation. We're here for backup, but we know you can do this."

"I'm glad someone has confidence in me. I barely got her off that island alive."

"But you did," she said with a wink. "You know what to do. You just have to remember how to do it."

Lucas stroked Haven's head three times and then met her gaze. "That's the problem. If I remember how to do it, I also remember everything else. Everything they taught me how to forget."

Selina leaned back on the wall and crossed her ankles. "Then the question you have to ask yourself is, if you don't help her, can you live with the consequences?"

That question had been sitting hard in his gut since they'd climbed aboard the chopper. He could give her what she came for if he had it and leave her to sort it out. But if he did that, would he be able to live with himself when she met an enemy she couldn't evade? The unequivocal answer to that was no. Knowing that he could have helped her but was too much of a coward would be worse than taking a stroll down memory lane. At least at the end of the walk, there was a chance for a happy ending.

Lucas kissed Selina on the cheek with a thank-you and left the med bay to rediscover his past.

Chapter Six

"I think this should fit," Mina said, handing Delilah a pair of black cargo pants. "They were mine before this." She patted her pregnant belly. "If they fit, I have several more pairs. You'll also need some of these." She handed her a stack of black T-shirts and sweatshirts.

"Black seems to be a theme here," Delilah said as she sat on the bed to pull on the pants.

"Makes it easy to match your clothes in the morning," Mina said with a wink before she handed her a pair of boots, also black. "Once we know the mission plan, we'll hook you up with the outerwear you need."

Delilah nodded but was only half-focused on the woman before her. The other half was focused on the man who had gone straight to the med bay to have a bullet dug out of his thigh.

"He's fine," Mina said, and Delilah glanced up. "Lucas. Selina messaged me she's already got the bullet out and the wound sutured."

"Luca took that bullet because of me. That's messed up."

"You weren't the one out there shooting up the island. Remember that."

"True, but I was the one who made a decision years ago that put him in danger. That was never my intention."

"I'm sure Lucas knows that, but you can tell him when we get to the conference room. Are you ready?"

Mina held the door for her, and then they walked down a hallway that could only be described as a fortress made of wood grain and steel. The log exterior made a person believe you were walking into a cozy log cabin, but instead, the interior housed high-tech security equipment and, from what she could gather, some rather deadly security techs.

The flight back from the island had been strained and nerve-racking. Cal was a master pilot, though, and managed to get them out of harm's way quickly. The problem? He made the point that whoever was after her now knew his chopper. Eventually, they'd show up at his door looking for her. That was not her goal. Her only goal was to get what she needed from Luca and go before anyone else got hurt. After he took a bullet on the way into the chopper, all she could do was hold pressure on it for the short ride back to Secure One. She hadn't seen him since. Delilah was desperate to tell him everything so he could promise to take care of her, but the chopper was not the time or the place. Instead, that time and place would be in front of people she didn't know.

Talking to Luca alone was preferable, but she also understood the complexities of the situation and that the team had to know the specifics. At least the specifics that she knew, which weren't many. She had suspicions, but that's all they were. She had no choice but to air her dirty laundry in front of all. Her steps faltered when she glanced up and noticed Luca walking toward them,

Haven by his side. "You're walking," she said when they neared.

"Of course," he said with a smile. "It was just a flesh wound. I suffered worse injuries on the base."

"I know, but that doesn't make me feel better. If you'd lost Haven or gotten hurt worse because of me, I couldn't go on."

"Good thing that didn't happen then. Now it's time we sort out who is after you and why."

"We?"

"We," he said, squeezing her hand. "Secure One isn't just a company. It's a family, and we take care of our own."

"I'm not one of you, though. My situation isn't your responsibility beyond giving me what I need."

"The moment you involved me in this, you became one of us. That's how it works, so there's no sense arguing with anyone here."

"Sounds like you already tried," Lilah said, holding his gaze. His brown eyes were just as bottomless as they had always been, but now they held a touch of something she couldn't name. Pain? Distrust? Or was it something else entirely?

Luca tipped his head in agreement. "They're already involved, so we may as well let them help us, right?"

With her nod, he motioned her forward into the conference room. There was a large whiteboard at the front of the room and a festively decorated Christmas tree in the corner that belied the reason they were here. A large wooden conference table sat to the left of the whiteboard with at least a dozen chairs around it. Filling those chairs were a few familiar faces and many unfamiliar ones, but they were all smiling as she walked in behind Luca and Haven.

"Welcome to Secure One, Delilah," Cal said. "I'm sure you're nervous after the situation on the island, but we're here to help, so don't feel bad about it. When one of ours is under attack, we all fight back."

"And make no mistake," Roman said, facing her. "You're one of us now."

"See?" Luca whispered in her ear, sending a shiver down her spine.

She might be one of them now, but in a few minutes, they would learn that what she brought to the table would take them back to the life they'd tried to leave behind.

"As some of you know, this is my friend Delilah Hartman. We were stationed together nine years ago in Germany before we were moved to a satellite base."

"What base?" Mack asked, taking notes on a pad.

"I wish we could tell you," Delilah said, biting her lower lip momentarily. "Unfortunately, we can't."

"You can't tell us the base you were on?" Efren asked to clarify. "What's the big secret?"

"The base," Lucas answered with a shrug. "It was classified. That's why you never heard about its fall. It was never in the news and was that way by design. I know you're all ex-military, so you'll understand that we still can't disclose the location."

Heads nodded around the table before Cal spoke. "Seems a moot point if the base no longer exists. We can work around it. Go on."

"Right, well, when we were discharged nearly eight years ago, we both had some recovering to do from injuries we sustained getting off the base. My back was broken in several places." He glanced at Lilah, who nodded. "Lilah suffered a TBI that left her with double vision, among other issues with her eyes." Everyone nodded, so he cleared his throat and went on. "When we were free of the hospitals, we ran into each other unexpectedly in Duluth. We decided we'd spend the summer on Madeline Island. The base fell in an unexpected and traumatic manner, but we had no time to decompress. We thought nature therapy might help as we considered our futures."

"It became obvious quickly," Delilah said, picking up the story, "that Luca—I'm sorry—Lucas started spiraling further and further into his episodes of PTSD. I knew we would never be able to have the life we wanted unless he got treatment as quickly as possible. While I witnessed atrocities on the base that day, they didn't hold a candle to what Lucas saw and did. I knew he would need a better way to deal with it before rejoining society."

"What Lilah's not saying is she saved my life several times that summer. She pulled me out of Lake Superior more than once," Lucas said, his spine stiff. Haven leaned into his leg, keeping him grounded in the room.

"Trust us," Mack said. "We've all been there. We understand the hard fight required to accept what we did when we had no other choice."

"It was one of those situations where I knew I needed help but didn't know how to ask for it," Lucas admitted. "Thankfully, Lilah realized it and got me into the VA hospital."

"While he was undergoing treatment, I planned to set up our new life in Duluth. That's when everything fell apart." She paused and shook her head as her gaze dropped to the floor. "I don't know how to explain what's happened since then."

"Just start at the beginning," Lucas said. "If we don't understand the beginning, we can't make this end."

"He's right," Cal agreed. "Feel free to use the whiteboard. Sometimes it helps to write things down chronologically for you and us."

Lilah walked to the board while Lucas took a seat next to Cal. He was just as anxious as the rest of them to find out what had kept her from him all these years. From the little she'd said and the scars she had, it wasn't simply because she didn't want to be with him. She had been fighting her own war these past six years. When she stepped away from the board, she had written and underlined several names.

"To start, you need to know my background," Lilah explained, pointing at the board. "I began as a supply chain manager for the army. Eventually, that morphed into cybersecurity, which is where I earned my keep. So, as a cybersecurity expert, it was my job to protect the base and to follow the intel on ops occurring off the base."

"Wait, you're a cybersecurity expert?" Cal asked, a brow raised.

"Well, I was six years ago. I may be a little rusty after being in hiding, but I've tried to keep my skills current. My commanding officer, Major Burris, knew I was also a supply chain manager. He ordered me to document historical antiquities found within the rubble and brought to the base by the locals or nervous curators. The agreement was, once the antiquity, artifact or artwork was documented, I shipped it to a museum here in the States for safekeeping."

"Were you still doing that when the base fell?" Mina asked, typing on her computer.

"I was, but over the time I was there, I backed up all the antiquity information and shipping schedules to a flash drive," Lilah explained. "When I returned stateside, I learned that Major Burris was being investigated for war crimes. Something felt off, not that I could tell you what it was other than this feeling that I needed to protect myself."

"I think we all understand that feeling," Cal said. "We all did sketchy stuff on the orders of our commanding officers."

"Then you'll understand why I told no one I had the flash drive. I didn't want anyone to know until Major Burris's case had been sorted out. I worried that I may need it to prove my innocence."

"Rightly so," Roman said. "We all know bad things roll downhill."

Lilah pointed at him with a nod. "Exactly what I was afraid of, so I was happy to keep it under my hat and go on with my life. At least until I was either called to the stand or it no longer mattered."

"How many antiquities are we talking about here? A dozen?" Efren asked from his end of the table.

"Oh, times itself and then quadruple that, at least."

"Seriously?" Mina asked. "There were that many curators worried about their collection?"

"Considering how long the war had gone on, yeah. Think about what happened in World War II with priceless artwork. Mind you, they weren't bringing one or two things, either. They brought large collections of items they didn't want to fall into the wrong hands. Keeping track of it all and organizing the shipping schedule on these items was a full-time job that I was trying to do on the side."

"Did you get the Distinguished Service Medal for your work with the antiquities?" Eric asked. "That medal is only given to soldiers who do duty to the government under great responsibility."

"That defines what Lilah did over there." Lucas's voice held respect and adoration when he spoke. "If it hadn't been for her, no one would have gotten off that base alive."

"The medal wasn't for saving the antiquities but for saving lives?" Roman asked to clarify.

"No," Lilah answered. "The medal was for what happened when the base fell. I can't say more than that, but if you're implying that the antiquities cataloging wasn't on the up-and-up, you're wrong."

Roman held his hands up in front of him. "Not what I was implying. We're just trying to get a feel for what's happening right now, considering the situation on the island tonight."

"That's fair," she said with a tip of her head.

"From the news articles, Major Burris never went to trial," Mina said, her fingers stopping on the keyboard as she read the screen before her.

"I found that same information three years ago," Delilah agreed, stepping forward. "That's when I expected everything to die down so I could get my life back."

"That's not what happened?" Cal asked.

Lilah shook her head. "No, if anything, it got worse."

"What happened after you dropped me off at the hospital?" Lucas asked, his impatience loud and clear in the room. "You said someone attacked you?"

"Several someones. After I dropped you in Minneapolis, I went to a long-term-stay hotel. I planned to stay for a week so that I could visit you. I was barely out of my car when two men attacked me. I managed to get away when someone yelled out their window about the commotion, but not before they did this," she explained, motioning at her chin. "With my face bleeding and sliced open to the bone, I tore out of the city. The men who attacked me were trying to abduct me by knifepoint. I had originally thought it was a random attack until one of them said I should stop fighting and go with them because they'd keep coming until I gave up my information."

"Gave up your information?" Mina asked with a raised brow. "You were their information?"

"That's the vibe," she agreed, crossing her arms over her chest. "At first, I thought they knew I downloaded information before the base fell."

"Probably a time stamp in the code," Mina agreed.

"Right, that's what I thought, but then I realized that wasn't true. My flash drive has information that isn't downloaded. I transferred the information for each item to the flash drive before I put it through to shipping, so there was no way for them to know I made a backup."

"Which brings me back to the fact that at some point you were feeling sketchy about that whole side of the operation," Roman said.

Her shrug said more than her words. "As someone who works in the cyber world, I was protecting myself."

"Okay, so if that's the case, and there was no way for

them to know you made that copy, then they wanted you because you had the information in here?" Cal asked, tapping his temple.

"That's been my working theory thus far," she agreed.

"I still don't understand what I have to do with this," Lucas said, standing and walking to where she stood by the board. "I haven't seen or heard from you since that day at the VA. I have nothing left from our time together. What is it that you think I have?"

"The flash drive. I tucked it in your army bag for safekeeping."

Chapter Seven

Lucas took a step back as a shudder ran through him. "What now?"

Lilah refused to make eye contact with him when she spoke. "When we stopped at the storage facility in Superior before we left for the VA, I stuck the flash drive inside the bag so I didn't lose it. Since the storage unit was in both of our names, and I was going to set up house in Duluth, I had easy access to it should I need it while you were in the hospital."

"Why didn't you put it with your things?" Lucas asked, his teeth clenched tightly to keep from yelling. "You knew better than to ever touch that bag."

"I don't think that matters six years later, son," Cal said, trying to diffuse the situation. "What matters is now we know what Delilah needs."

"It does matter," Lucas answered, spinning on his heel. "I haven't opened that bag in seven years. It's a Pandora's box that would have grave consequences for me and all of you. It means reliving everything I've tried to forget. It means nightmares, flashbacks and losing the parts of me that I've found since that time."

"No," Delilah said, stepping up until they were chest-to-chest. "We aren't going to open the bag. The flash drive is in the outside pocket. I didn't open the bag, Luca. That's your history. I respect that. It was an afterthought on the way out. I had planned to move it as soon as I got back to set up the house. Somehow, we need to get to Superior and get the bag without being traced."

"No, we don't," Lucas said, gazing into her eyes. They were still terrified, but he noticed the same heat that was always there between them. Smoke tendrils that curled across her pupils to tease him into submission. "When I started working here, I moved everything in that storage unit to one just outside of town."

"Name?" Mina asked, already typing on her computer.

"Sal's Storage," Lucas answered without taking his eyes off Delilah. "Unit 57."

"That's twelve miles northwest of our location," she answered. "Corner unit with two doors."

Lucas heard them talking and making plans around him, but he couldn't drag his attention away from the woman who held him tightly in her aura. There had been an electric draw between them since the day they met on the base most unexpectedly.

The collision rattled his teeth. The cart in front of him had stopped dead in the middle of the road, and he'd had no time to react. When he looked up, a woman was on the ground next to the cart. Lucas jumped out, running to the woman staring at the blue sky, blinking every few seconds.

"Are you okay?" Lucas asked, checking her over for injuries. "I didn't have time to react, much less stop."

The woman blinked twice more, drawing his eye to hers. They were the most unusual shade of gray but

*beautifully framed by her heart-shaped face. Her straw-
berry blond hair was shoulder-length and topped with
an army cap. She let out a puff of air, and he couldn't
help but smile at the way her Cupid's bow lips puckered
as she tried to form words.*

"I'm fine," she finally managed to say. "Just stunned.
Help me up."

"Maybe we should call for help first? Make sure you
don't have anything wrong with your head or neck?"

"I don't," she promised, pushing herself to a sitting
position. "Just got the wind knocked out of me when
we collided."

"I'm Lucas," he said, sticking his hand out to help
her. "Glad you're okay."

"Thanks," she said, taking his hand until she was
upright. She seemed hesitant to drop it, so he didn't let
her. He held it loosely while they stood on the old tarmac. "I don't know what happened, but it just came to
a grinding halt and tossed me out."

Lucas released her hand and crouched to look under
the cart. "Looks like you blew the drivetrain. That will
bring things to a halt quickly. Let me push this one out
of the way, and then I'll take you back in mine."

"That would be great," she said, starting toward her
cart. "I'm Delilah, by the way."

"Hey, there, Delilah," he said with a wink. "I bet
you've never heard that before."

"Oh, no," she agreed, helping him push the busted
cart off to the side. "Only once or ten thousand."

His laughter filled the air, and he brushed off his
hands. "Fair, but I've always loved the name. Just never
knew anyone with it before."

"Well, now you do," she said, climbing into the passenger side of his cart. "Would you drop me off at the cafeteria? I was going to grab lunch, but I guess the cart decided I needed more exercise. Too many hours sitting at the computer."

"The cafeteria it is," he agreed. "I was headed there myself." He wasn't, but it was lunchtime, and he would take any chance to share lunch with a beautiful woman. His mama didn't raise no fool. Besides, Delilah intrigued him, and he knew nothing about her other than her name. "I haven't seen you around the base before."

"Just got here a few days ago," she answered with a shrug. "Pulled me in from a unit in Duluth stationed in Germany due to my skill set."

"No kidding?" he asked, nearly swerving off the road. "Duluth, Minnesota?"

"You betcha," she said with a cheesy grin.

"Small world. I'm out of Superior, Wisconsin."

"The good old Twin Ports. Looks like we have something in common, Lucas..."

"Ammunition Warrant Officer Lucas Porter," he said to finish the sentence. "What's your skill set? Must be big if they pulled you in for it."

"Looks like we have quite a bit in common. I'm a cyber warfare officer," she answered, with a flick of her eyes toward him. "Intel on ops. Maybe I shouldn't be telling you this stuff."

"You're fine. I work in munitions. My team plans those operations, and we provide the ammunition support. Looks like we go together like peanut butter and jelly."

Her laughter filled the cart, and Lucas couldn't help but chuckle, too. The way she tossed her head to the side, allowing the sunshine to kiss her cheeks with freckles, was too adorable not to notice. There was nothing about Delilah he didn't like, but he knew better than to start an on-base relationship. That was an excellent way to get your heart broken—

"Luca?"

The name hit him and he snapped back to the present, realizing the room had gone silent. He turned toward the table where everyone sat expectantly. "Sorry, I got lost in thought for a moment there. What was the question?"

"In a nutshell?" Cal asked, and Lucas nodded. "How do you want to proceed?"

"Alone," he answered, and with one last look at Delilah, he walked out the door.

"I'll go talk to him," Cal said as he stood.

Delilah held up her hand. "Give him a few minutes to settle down. I knew he wouldn't react well to this, but unfortunately, contacting him was my only choice."

"What's the big deal about his army duffel bag?" Charlotte, Secure One's public liaison and Mack's girlfriend, asked. "Everyone around this table has one."

"True, but for Luca, it holds the reminders of what happened that day on the base," Delilah explained. "All of his medals went into it, too, because those remind him of what he didn't do instead of what he did do."

"Medals?" Cal asked in surprise. "We had no idea he had medals."

"That doesn't surprise me," Delilah said. "He doesn't tell anyone. He refused to do anything more than have them mailed to him. He never even opened the boxes, just stuffed each one in the bag and walked away. I can't remember them all, but one is the Purple Heart and the last one he got while I was with him was the Distinguished Service Cross."

Efren whistled low before he spoke. "That's not something you hear every day. I had no idea he was so decorated."

"Well—" she motioned at the door "—Luca likes it that way. That duffel bag is a time capsule that'll never be opened if he has anything to say about it. I tried to bring it with us to the VA hospital so that they could go through it with him, but he refused, adamantly so. Selfishly, I'm glad he's moved it with him over the years rather than dump it. I could never return to that part of the state to get the flash drive. I banked on the hope that, while he hated everything the bag represented, he would never get rid of it."

"I don't care what he says," Mina interrupted. "He's not doing this alone."

"She's right," Roman said. "The smart move would be for a team of us to retrieve the bag."

Delilah laughed loudly, and they all turned to stare at her. "Sorry," she said, momentarily putting her hand over her mouth. "But trust me. That will never happen. You saw his reaction to the idea that I even touched the bag to put the flash drive in the pocket. There's no way he'll let anyone else pick it up."

"You're saying Lucas is possessive of something he wants nothing to do with?" Marlise, who was Secure One's Client Coordinator and Cal's wife, often broke things down in a way that made it easy for everyone to understand.

"Everyone carries their ghosts differently, I guess.

Mine are wrapped up in the medal I sent him, and it's the only thing I carry from that time. If you knew the things he did that day, it would be easy to understand why he is the way he is. Right now, none of that matters. Top priority is convincing him to go with me to get that flash drive. I need to get out of here before all of you pay the price."

"I couldn't agree more," Cal said with a nod. "We'll prepare a plan to help you get to the storage unit and then find somewhere safe for you to go while we figure out who is after you. That somewhere will not be here."

"Understood," Delilah said with a nod. "Believe me when I say I never intended for any of this to happen or to drag all of you into this. I only wanted to get the drive and disappear again."

Mina's laughter filled the room as she shook her head. "You honestly thought you could contact Lucas the way you did and expect him to be like, 'Here's your flash drive. Bye,' as though the last six years hadn't happened?"

"You must understand that I was desperate," she said imploringly. "I didn't mean for any of this to happen or to drag Lucas back through his past. That's the last thing I wanted to do, but I was out of options."

Mina stood and walked around the table. "You have to stop apologizing, Delilah," she said, taking her elbow. "You're here now, which means you're one of us."

"We're called Secure One for a reason," Cal said from where he sat. "We are one under this roof, which means we are one for all and all for one. Right now, we are all for you, so this is what will happen. You'll help Lucas find the headspace he needs to be in while we make a plan. When he's ready, we'll be ready."

Mina walked Delilah to the door and leaned into her ear. "The only way out of this is through it, so start at the most important place. The beginning."

As Delilah walked out the conference room door, she couldn't help but think that was why they were in this spot to begin with.

Chapter Eight

Lucas sat in the dark kitchen with his head in his hands. His rhythmic breathing was second nature as Haven kept his paws on his leg and his muzzle under his handler's chin. If putting eyes on Lilah again wasn't enough of a shock, what she told him in that room pushed him past his breaking point.

"Luca," she said from the doorway, but he didn't look up. "I'm sorry. This was never supposed to happen. When I put the flash drive in the bag, it was for a week, not six years."

"It's the fact that you put it in there at all, Delilah. You knew how I felt about that bag."

"You need to get a grip, Luca," she said, and he snapped his head around to make eye contact. "Seriously. In the years since the war you've made yourself a new life here and found a brotherhood again. Yet, you continue to act like that bag is going to stand up and gun you down. I see all the work you've done to overcome everything that happened that day, and I respect the hell out of that, but you're not done. You can't have your life back until you open that bag and face the items inside."

"That's never going to happen."

"What are you so afraid of?" she asked, frustration loud and clear in her tone. "The memories? The idea that you saved lives and were commended for that?"

"I also took lives, Lilah. A whole lot of them."

"True, but they were trying to take yours and a whole lot of other Americans' lives."

"So that makes it right?"

"Luca, we both know there is nothing about war that is right to anyone with a decent moral compass. That doesn't mean we're given a choice. If you hadn't stepped up to be the hero that day—"

"Don't," he hissed from between his teeth. "Don't use that word."

"This is what I'm talking about," she said with a shake of her head. "Maybe you don't feel like one, but to me, you are. To the people you saved on that base that day, you are one. That doesn't mean you're flying through the sky with a cape. It means you stepped up when no one else would or could. That's what makes someone commendable. I understand that you're still mad all these years after you were put in that position, but it must be an awfully heavy load to carry every day."

"You don't know anything about it, Lilah."

"But I do. You always seem to forget I was also there. I live with the nightmares and the terror, too. My trauma may be different than yours, but that doesn't mean it's not there. None of this has been easy for me, either. The last thing I wanted was to be on the run for my life for six years, but here we are, aren't we? If I could go back and do things differently, I would, but I can't, so can we make a plan to get the drive? Without it, I'm a dead woman walking."

"Who are these people after you?" he asked, finally turning to face her again. If she wanted to read him the riot act about his choices in life, he could do the same. "You can't expect me to believe you have no idea who they are if this has gone on for six years."

"I honestly don't, Lucas. All I know is it has something to do with the antiquity cataloging."

"You swore you were only keeping the flash drive until Burris's trial."

"That was my plan, but again, I never returned to Superior for the flash drive. I was already on the run when the investigation ended without charges. I know you don't want to face that bag again, but it's time, don't you think?"

"You're not giving me a choice, are you, Lilah? You're just waltzing in with the demand that I do."

"There are no demands here, Luca," she said with a shake of her head. "Cal and Roman offered to go get the drive and leave the bag untouched. You're the one who said you were going alone."

"I don't want anyone around that bag but me."

"Do you keep that bag in the storage unit because you're afraid to face it or because you're afraid to live?"

He gazed at her in confusion for a moment. "What does that mean?"

"Every day that you keep that bag 'alive,'" she said, using air quotes, "is another day you can keep living in the past. From what I've seen about this place and its people, you could have a successful and fulfilling future if the past wasn't hanging around your neck like a dead albatross."

Lucas whistled while he shook his head. "Boy, you think you know a lot, don't you?"

"That's not what I think at all. The thing is, I know you, Luca. You can pretend that I don't or that the years we've been apart mean I can't possibly understand who you are now, but that's all it is—pretending. I know who you are to your core," she whispered, tapping her finger on his chest.

Lucas grabbed her finger and held it tightly. He tried to tell himself it was because she was annoying him, but the truth was, he wanted to touch her. He wanted to feel her warmth again after all these years. He wanted her to see how much he'd changed and the improvements he'd made in his life.

She can't do that if you don't show her those things. You're behaving the same way you did six years ago. Be the man she needs right now.

The thought halted his count of three, and he pulled in one breath and held it. The voice was right. He wasn't showing Delilah that he'd changed since she left. If anything, he was proving to her that he hadn't moved anywhere or learned anything about himself since they were last together. The very idea stiffened his spine. He stood, holding his hand out.

"Can I trust you, Delilah Hartman?" What he didn't ask was if he could trust her not to break his heart.

"You can, Luca. I know how much I hurt you by disappearing from your life, but know that was the last thing I wanted to happen. The choice was run and protect you, or stay and risk them trying to get to me through you. I couldn't let that happen."

"Then let's do what we've always done best."

Lilah lifted a brow, and it brought a smile to his lips.

"The one thing we did best probably shouldn't be done right now, Luca."

This time, he couldn't help but laugh when he chucked her gently under the chin. "Let me rephrase that. The second thing we did best."

"Work together?"

"That," he agreed, taking her hand. "We were always a great team. Maybe that was practice for what was to come."

"For the time when it would be imperative to know each other's strengths and weaknesses?"

"And that time is now," he finished. "Let's find out what the team has planned, get that flash drive and win your life back."

Delilah leaned into him, resting her head on his shoulder. "Thank you, Luca. I hate that I've stirred all of this up for you again."

"No," he whispered, holding her gaze for a beat. "Thank you for reminding me that I'm standing in front of the person who changed my life six years ago and the person I wanted to change my life for back then. I have changed, and now it's time to prove it."

"And I'm standing in front of the person who changed my life six years ago and the person I was protecting all this time. I don't regret losing out on those years because you were safe, but I'm glad we have this time together, even if it's fraught with danger."

"Me, too, even if it looks different than the life we planned." He led her toward the door. "Haven, forward," he called to the dog. Once they got to the doorway, he paused. "I will still do everything in my power to protect you, Lilah. That means whatever needs to be done, I'll do."

"There's the Luca I knew was in there," she said, dropping one lid down in a wink.

THE DARKNESS SWALLOWED them as they slid from the van parked southwest of the storage units. They hadn't picked up a tail as far as they could tell, and Lucas had been in constant contact with the other two cars that held Secure One teams running diversions. She and Lucas planned to slide in, get the flash drive, head back to the van and drive to a small motel an hour away from the Canadian border. Once they had the flash drive, they couldn't go back to headquarters, but Mina sent a laptop and equipment for Delilah to communicate with her once the flash drive was in their possession.

Delilah glanced over at Lucas, who was gauging the distance they had to walk without cover. Trees surrounded the storage facility on three sides, leaving the only unprotected side at the driveway approach.

"My unit is in the back corner. If we stay in the trees until we're opposite it, the only time we'll be exposed is the time it takes to unlock the door."

"All of this cloak and dagger stuff might be a bit much, Luca," she whispered as they walked, Haven glued to his handler's side, step for step. This time, the dog was wearing his bulletproof vest, too. "Lately, it has taken them four or five days to find me."

"Maybe, but that was before the island. Now they know who you're with, so I'm not taking any chances."

"Fair enough," Delilah said, but she still thought it was unnecessary. It would take that team on the island a long time to regroup and relocate her. They hadn't been at Secure One longer than three hours before the team had a plan and implemented it.

Another hundred yards farther, and Lucas pulled her to a stop. "The unit is right there," he said, pointing at the metal building in front of them. Not surprisingly, strings of Christmas lights hung from the eaves of the metal buildings. It offered a little light in the darkness, and it slowed her pounding heart. "As soon as I open the side walk-through door, you get inside. I'm not going to mess with the roll-up door. That leaves us too visible."

"Why don't I just wait here?" she asked, leaning into his ear to speak now that he had her spooked. "The flash drive is in the outside pocket—"

"I can't prevent a sneak attack if you're in the woods and I'm not. We're a team and we stay together."

"Ten-four," she whispered with a smile he couldn't see. They were a team. It hadn't taken much to remind him of that.

Lucas gestured to Haven and slid out of the woods like a ghost. It was easy to see his time at Secure One had taught him new skills that she suspected took a lot of practice. Especially since he took Haven with him everywhere. He had the door open by the time she reached him, and he practically shoved her through the small opening, followed her in with Haven and closed the door with barely a click.

Lucas flicked a flashlight on and shone it around the space. One glance was all she needed to see that the only thing in the storage unit was the bag. Rather than comment on it, she glanced up at him.

"The side pocket," she said as Lucas knelt over the

bag. She noticed him hesitate with his hand over the pocket. She crouched and put her hand on his shoulder. "You got this," she whispered. "Baby steps."

He nodded as he breathed in and waited, then blew it out and reached for the pocket just as the first bullet slammed into the metal unit.

"Dammit!" Lucas hissed, grabbing her and shoving her behind him as another bullet hit the side door. It was a steel door but wouldn't hold bullets back for long. They were trapped in a tin box and had no way out except through the steel curtain roll-up door, which was padlocked from the outside.

"Stay down," Lucas yelled, and she could tell he was running their options through his head. They didn't have many other than praying the steel door held. "Get down on your belly and get to the back of the unit. It's protected by the opposite one! When they hit that rolling door, it will give quickly. I'll get one chance to end them before they end us."

Delilah was pulling Haven down by her when the shooting stopped. "Now," Lucas hissed, moving with her to the back of the unit until a sound stopped them in their tracks.

"Secure one, Charlie," Cal called through the door.

"Secure two, Lima!" Lucas answered, scrambling to the side door and throwing it open. "Cal! Are you alone?"

"Not a chance," Roman said, stepping out of the woods.

"I thought we were screwed six ways to Sunday until you called out. You guys being here wasn't part of the plan."

"It always was, son," Cal said while they checked the

pulses on the four guys on the ground. "We didn't want you to argue about us coming along for the ride. If you didn't need us, you never had to know we were here."

"I probably would have argued, but I'm sure glad you're here."

"Four this time," Delilah said, stepping around Lucas. "They're upping the ante."

"All carrying ARs," Cal said as he got to the final guy. "Got a live one." He grabbed a pair of restraints and cuffed him.

"These three have gone on to the great hellscape beyond," Roman answered. "No IDs. No anything other than their weapons."

"Did you find the drive?" Cal asked, standing up to address Lucas.

"I was just reaching for the bag when they started shooting. They had to be hot on our heels by no more than minutes. How did they find us so quickly?" Lucas turned to her. "What did you bring from your last place?"

"Nothing," she swore, holding up her hands. "I bought everything new before I went to the island, including undergarments."

"I don't understand it," Lucas said. "They're tracking you somehow. Your glasses?"

She shook her head. "I buy new ones every time I move, and always from a different online provider."

"What are we going to do with these guys?" Roman asked, interrupting Lucas's train of thought.

"Well, we can't exactly hide this," Cal motioned around the area with his hands. "Shall we claim it was a shoot-out at Christmas corral?" Lucas grunted with laughter, something he didn't think he was capable of at the moment. His laughter brought a smile to Cal's lips, too. "I'll call the cops, and we'll say we were working security when we heard the ruckus."

"How are you going to explain the bullet holes in them?" Roman asked with a smirk.

"We've got a live one here. Since he's unconscious, we blame it on him. He can sort it out when he's awake, alert and oriented."

"I just want to know who they are and what they want with me!" Delilah exclaimed, frustration evident in her voice.

Lucas ran to her and put his arm around her shoulder while Haven moved in and propped his snout under her elbow. "It's okay. We'll figure this out," he promised, helping her over to where Cal and Roman stood. "Same plan?"

Cal nodded. "Take the van to the motel while we handle this situation. Once you're there safely, call in. Mack and Efren report that these were the only guys in the area, so your walk to the van is clear. Lucas, grab your bag."

"We only need the flash drive," he said, headed toward the doorway, but Cal grabbed his arm.

"The cops will be crawling around here in about an hour. Take the whole bag, or it will become evidence. What else is in the unit that's tied to your name?"

Delilah noticed Lucas's spine stiffen as he considered Cal's words. "Nothing. The only thing in it is the bag. I rented the unit online under a different name and a PO Box."

Cal nodded once as he glanced around the units. "It looks like Sal invested in Christmas lights instead of security cameras, so that helps. Get the bag and get out. We'll take care of everything else."

The door was open, so Delilah watched Lucas stare at the bag for a full thirty seconds before he slowly bent over and picked it up. When he stood, the expression on his face was unlike any she'd seen before. It was determination mixed with something else. Pride? Hatred? Pain? Maybe all of the above. As he strode toward her, the look intensified until he took her hand.

"We'll be in touch once we're safe. Give us three hours. I want to be sure we don't pick up a tail."

"I've got GPS on the van, so we'll keep a close eye on it. I would send a follow team, but I don't want to make your identity obvious."

"I've got this," Lucas assured his boss. "Hopefully, we can get a few hours head start before the next team is sent out."

"There will be a next team," Delilah added, glancing at Cal and Roman. "Watch yourselves."

"Haven, forward," Lucas ordered, and the dog lined up beside his leg. "Lima, out," he said as they entered the tree line.

Delilah jogged through the woods next to Lucas, but they never spoke. As he held the bag tightly, it was like watching him be reborn. The bag used to be the enemy, but now, he was ready to make peace with it.

Then he glanced at her, and the look in his eyes said that was the furthest thing from the truth.

Chapter Nine

"The dome light is disabled. Climb in while I get Haven situated," Lucas whispered to Delilah once he cleared the van of interlopers. While she settled in the front, Lucas slid open the side door and lowered the sizeable duffel bag to the floor. He struggled to unclench his fist of its prize. It wasn't that the bag was physically heavy, but emotionally, it weighed more than he could carry. This time, he hadn't been given a choice. He had to carry the weight for her. If what she said was true, she'd been fighting this war alone for the last six years. She needed a team to back her up now.

He hooked Haven into his seat, slammed the door and jumped in the driver's side. "Buckle up."

Delilah slid her seat belt over her chest while he started the van. "Did you find the flash drive?"

"Didn't look," he answered, straightening his seat belt. "It's hidden in the bag right now. We'll leave it until we get to the motel. If we get into an altercation on the road, I'd rather it wasn't on your person."

"They won't find us that fast," she said, turning in her seat to look at the bag.

"That's what you said about the guys we just took

out." Lucas was ready to put the van in Drive when something Cal said sent a zap of fear through his gut. "GPS."

Delilah's look was curious. "What about it? Cal said he was tracking the van. That can only help us if we encounter more resistance."

"What did you bring from Secure One?" he asked, leaving the van in Park and turning to her.

After glancing down at herself, she met his gaze. "Just the clothes Mina gave me and the issued equipment Cal insisted I take, like the handgun and cuffs. Mina gave me a new lip gloss and a few toiletries. The only other thing I have is my identification, which is fake, and my medal."

Disgust slithered through Lucas's belly at the thought running through his mind. "Do you keep the medal with you all the time, or do you normally leave it in a safety deposit box?"

She shook her head immediately. "It's always with me, since I'm never in the same place very long."

Lucas swallowed back the bile in his throat and held out his hand. "Can I see it?"

"Why?" she asked, digging inside her jacket pocket for a moment before she pulled it out. "It hasn't changed since you gave it back to me."

Once it was in his hand, he ran his fingers over the medal, looking for bumps or outcroppings. "That's what has been bugging me, Lilah," he explained, holding up the medal. "You carried this everywhere and they kept finding you. You sent it to me, and I showed up on the island with extra visitors. You have it in your pocket tonight and they're on us in minutes. They're using the medal to track you."

"Impossible," she whispered with a shake of her head.

"There's no way there's a tracker small enough to put in that medal. Not to mention, I've had it for six years. The battery would never last."

"Nothing is impossible if it's the military tracking you. You'd be surprised by the tech they have that no one knows about, including solar-powered trackers."

"You can't prove it, though." She motioned at the medal in his hand. "And we don't have time to take it apart."

"Don't need to, as long as it doesn't go with us."

He climbed out of the van and dug a hole with his multi-tool deep enough to lay the medal in and cover it up. He took a picture with the Secure One phone and sent it to Cal with a message before he climbed back into the van. She stared at him with her lips pulled in a thin line.

"I'm sorry, Lilah, but we can't take it with us. Just in case. I sent the information to Cal to get the medal and move it somewhere." He pulled the lever into Drive and left the curb, knowing there were still over two hours to go in this long night. "He'll keep watch on it. If another group of armed guys shows up at the location, it's a good bet the medal is to blame."

"That doesn't make sense, though, Luca," she said, leaning back in the seat with her arms crossed. "Why would the military want to track me? I've been discharged free and clear for years."

"Let me ask you. Who else knows about these antiquities being in the States?"

"Now? I don't know. Back then, only my boss, his boss and the museum curators."

"Which tells me it was a top-secret operation at the

time. That means you are one of the few people with the information in your head."

"I'm probably the only one with it in my head, but my boss and his bosses have access to that information, too," she said, throwing up her hands. "I had to transmit the information daily to the person in charge of the shipments."

"I could be dead wrong about everything," he said to appease her, but he was convinced the medal was to blame. "It's just a better-safe-than-sorry situation. If we don't have the medal with us, and the guys find us again, then we know it wasn't the medal."

"All I know is, I'm exhausted," she said, staring out the back window as though she expected headlights to pop up and mow them down. "I've been running for so many years, all over the country. It isn't conducive to having any quality of life." She turned around in the seat and slumped down into her coat.

Lucas reached over and turned up the heat. "I wish I hadn't been so angry with you and had tried harder to find you when I got out," he whispered, squeezing her shoulder. "When the information didn't come easily, I gave up. It was easier to convince myself that you didn't want me to find you, and it was better to let you go, than it was to fight against the memories of us."

"It wasn't easy staying off the internet," she admitted with a tip of her head. "It required burner phones, lots of fake identifications and some pretty shady living situations."

"But no matter what you did, they kept coming for you?"

"They always found me. Sometimes it was weeks or

months, and one time it was a year, but whoever they are, they're great at keeping me unbalanced and unhinged."

"You aren't unhinged," he corrected her as he steered the van down the two-lane highway. "You're scared and confused. After being attacked like that, it had to be difficult to trust anyone."

"I didn't trust anyone. In hindsight, I should have trusted you, Luca."

Lucas heard the slur to her words, and he turned the radio up as Frank Sinatra crooned about having a merry little Christmas. He glanced away from the road for a split second to see her sinking into sleep, comforted by the warmth of the van and the company of another person after so many years alone. They were both exhausted, so he'd let her sleep while they found their way to safety—at least for a little while—and then he'd sit her down and get the real story. The guys they'd come across screamed military to him, and that scared him more than anything else would. If the government wanted her, they'd have her. Lucas could do nothing to stop it.

LILAH WOKE WITH a start to realize the van had stopped moving. She glanced at the old blue building in front of her and then to her left, where Lucas sat in the driver's seat, grasping the steering wheel with an iron grip.

"We made it," she said, stretching in the seat. "I didn't mean to fall asleep. You should have woken me so I could keep watch."

"It wasn't a problem, Lilah," he said, his gaze firmly planted on the building beyond the windshield. "The drive was uneventful and I had some thinking to do, anyway. I need to go check in. The second I close the door, move to the driver's seat and keep the van running. If anyone approaches you, get out of here."

"I can't just leave you!" she exclaimed, turning in her seat.

"You can and you will. The van is being tracked in the control room, and we'll catch up with you."

"What about Haven?"

"He's coming with me, of course. If everything is safe, we'll return to the van once I clear the room. Ten-four?"

"Heard and acknowledged," she agreed, waiting for him to unhook Haven from his seat belt. After he checked all sides of the van, he climbed out, and Haven hopped over the console and out of the van to follow his handler.

The moment the locks engaged, fear drove Lilah to climb into the driver's seat and put her hands on the wheel. She had to stay on her toes and shut out the memories of the last time she was in a place like this with Luca. It had been a beautiful summer day, and they'd been driving up the north shore along Lake Superior. Their destination had been Thunder Bay, but they had no schedule to follow or place to be. They'd come across this little town, well, you couldn't call it a town as much as a place you passed through on the road to somewhere else. Luca had seen the blue brick building and steered the car into the parking lot—

The locks disengaged and Lilah jumped. Her attention captured by the memories, she totally missed Luca returning to the van. She was lucky no one else approached her while she was daydreaming. "All clear," he said, grabbing their bags from the back. He helped her out of the van before he propelled her into the small room. He closed the door, threw the lock, drew the curtains and dropped the bags on the floor. "I need to let the team know we made it."

"You said they were tracking the van. Aren't they already aware?"

Rather than answer her, he pushed past her and grabbed a gear bag, unzipping it and pulling out computer equipment. She left him for a moment to use the bathroom. The shower beckoned her, so she stripped from her dusty clothes and stepped under the warm spray. She forced the memories of a long-ago time in a place like this where she and Luca had shared the shower—had shared everything—and focused on the present. She couldn't help but wonder if what Luca thought about the medal was true. In hindsight, it was the only thing she always had with her when she moved from place to place. The sticking point for her was, if someone was tracking her with the medal, that could only mean one thing. They had to be military. She couldn't think of any reason why the military would track her or accost her. They didn't even know the flash drive existed.

But you exist.

The thought jarred her, and she dropped the soap bar on the floor. She stooped to pick it up and thought back to the day she'd found the secret file on the server. There was no identifying information as to who had put it there, but there was also no way anyone knew she had a copy. She'd covered her digital trail over there to avoid being picked up by the enemy, who were always looking for a way to start a cyberwar. There was no way anyone could know she'd seen that file, right?

A cold shudder went through her even as she stood under the hot water. None of this made sense. She was distracted and jumpy, which made her feel out of control and scattered. It didn't help that she was continually trapped in small spaces with the man she'd loved for years, all while knowing she could never have him. Not as long as she was being hunted. There was no way she would be the one to remind him of the things he tried to forget.

It's too late for that.

Slamming the water off, Lilah huffed at that voice. She was starting to hate it, mainly because it was always right. It was too late to protect Luca from the memories of that time. As she dried herself, part of her wondered if that was such a bad thing. He'd told her he learned how to work around the memories of what happened to him, not that he'd dealt with them head-on. She was well aware through personal experience that confronting them wasn't going to make them go away, but not being afraid of how each memory ended, because she already knew what was coming, did make it easier to let them roll over her and fall away rather than roll over her and drown her.

Lilah tucked the towel under her armpit and glanced at herself in the minuscule mirror over the sink. "That may not be the case for Luca, and you know that. The things he saw and did are incomprehensible to most people."

With a tip of her shoulder, she gathered her clothes off the floor. Maybe that was why he learned to work around them rather than face them. Talking about those things, admitting to what he did that day to ensure his fellow soldiers got off that base, might make everything worse.

When she opened the door, Lucas had finished with

the devices he'd laid out on the small desk against the bathroom wall. "Are there clean clothes in any of those bags, or should I put these back on?"

He spun as though he hadn't heard her come out but came to an abrupt halt when he saw her wrapped in only a towel. He cleared his throat before he spoke. "Enjoy your shower?"

"I did, but don't worry, I left you plenty of hot water."

"I'm not worried about the hot water. I am worried about you. You're hurt," he said, stepping forward and tracing a large bruise on her shoulder.

She glanced down at his finger on her skin. He left a trail of deep yearning that burned her skin with every inch. She deserved the pain of the bruise and to withstand his touch, knowing his hands would never be on her as a lover.

"It's fine. I must have hurt it on the island and didn't realize it. What did Secure One say?"

Luca shook his head as though the question snapped him back to reality. "The cops bought their story and took over the scene, but not before Cal snapped pictures of the guys' faces. Mina was able to use facial recognition to identify them. They're all ex-military."

Lilah's heart sank as she sucked in air. "Dammit. I've been telling myself there's no way they could be military. This doesn't make any sense, Luca."

"They aren't military. They're ex-military, but that raises the question of who they're working for now."

"Good point," Lilah agreed, sinking to the bed in the center of the room. "I'm no closer to figuring this out now than I was six years ago."

"You haven't had time to figure it out," he said, kneeling beside her. "You've been too busy trying to stay alive, right?"

"Which would have been easier if I knew who was after me and why," she admitted to the man who was much too close for her liking. All she had to do was turn her head, and she could have her lips on his. She resisted by staring straight ahead at the door.

"We'll get to the bottom of this so you can have your life back," Lucas promised. "Mina is working on things now and will keep us posted."

"What life?" she asked with a shake of her head. "I have no life, Luca. I haven't since the day I left you and ran headlong into the night. The cut on my chin turned the car into a crime scene, so I had hoped by abandoning it, they would think Delilah Hartman had died a tragic death. How wrong I'd been. Getting to the bottom of this means I'm free, but I'm thirty-four years old and have no idea how to live a normal life."

They sat in silence, their gazes locked together, and Lilah wondered if he was thinking about the last time they were together in a place like this. She couldn't force her mind away from those memories, even as they heated her cheeks and sent waves of sensation through her belly, then lower to the place she had shared with no one since she lost him. Back then, Luca had been a fast and furious lover. It was rare that they took their time, even if they tried. The heat built too quickly and drove them to touch, taste and tease each other as fast as they could until the explosive end.

"Do you remember the last time we were in this motel?" Luca's question pulled her out of her daydreams and back to reality.

"I haven't stopped thinking about it since I opened my eyes in the van. It feels like we were in a motel like this just yesterday with fewer, or maybe different, worries."

"Not a different motel. If it were daylight, you'd realize this is the same motel, on the same road, just not the same room."

"You mean, this is—"

"Yes," he answered, dropping his knee to the floor. "Mina picked it. I had no idea it was the same place until I realized it could be the only place."

Lilah's fingers traced his five o'clock shadow, and the rasp against her skin reminded her how he felt against her as they made love. "If you're uncomfortable, we can keep driving."

"I'm not uncomfortable," he promised, his hand capturing hers against his cheek. "At least not in the memory department. In the 'being trapped in a motel with an almost naked woman who I know can blow my mind the moment I put my lips on hers' department, I'm uncomfortable."

Instinctively, she tightened her grip around the towel. "I'm sorry. Let me get dressed so we can focus."

"You think we'll be able to focus just because you put clothes on, or do you think no matter what we do, being here together is a walk down memory lane we need to take?"

"Are you saying what I think you're saying?"

He tipped his head in agreement. "Once and done. Get it out of our system so we can focus on the case without this constant pull between us."

He was dead wrong if he thought falling into bed with him once would stop that pull between them. Lilah wasn't sure years of falling into bed with him would stop that pull, but she had to ask herself if she wanted to be with him one more time or if she wanted to remember who they were together before all of this happened.

Her decision made, she stood and walked into the bathroom, the memory of the days those brown eyes were hers too much to bear.

Chapter Ten

Lucas watched Lilah close the bathroom door to shut him out. He knew it was a risk to suggest they make love again, but he was scared. He was scared that the connection between them was stronger than ever and the only way for him to know for sure was to be with her in the most elemental way. If the connection was just as strong as it was six years ago, he had to rethink how he'd been living. Delilah's reappearance was going to put a crimp in his ability to live in the land of denial he'd so firmly planted himself in at that hospital when she never showed again.

He stood and glanced at Haven, who lay on a make-shift bed of blankets in the corner. The dog kept his eyes on him but didn't approach, which meant he didn't think his handler needed him. Yet. That time could come, but for now, Lucas raised his hand and knocked on the bath-room door. "Lilah? Come out and talk to me. You don't even have any clothes in there."

Her heavy sigh from the other side of the door made him smile. She always hated it when he used logic to thwart her emotions. She told him it took her out of the moment and forced her to think instead of feel. That's what he needed her to do right now. Think. Research. React. Participate. She couldn't do that if there was a constant wall between them.

The doorknob turned, and the door swung open. She held his gaze as she walked out and motioned at the bags. "Which one is mine? I'll get dressed."

"Sit," he said instead, motioning at the bed. "If we don't clear the air between us, working together as a team will be impossible." What he didn't say was working with her was tasking his emotions, and clearing the air wouldn't help that, but it would, hopefully, help her. Once she was sitting, he pulled the blanket up and wrapped it around her shoulders, then he sat next to her. "You're walking on eggshells around me. That can't continue."

"I'm trying not to upset you," she whispered, her eyes on the floor until he tipped her chin to face him.

"Stop doing that," he ordered, and her gaze snapped to his. "I'm not emotionally labile the way I was the last time we were together. I don't snap the way I used to. I've learned how to manage my emotions in a way that doesn't hurt anyone, including myself."

"I'm glad," she said with a smile. "I could tell how different you were the moment you showed up on the island. That's not why I'm being cautious."

"I don't understand then, Lilah. Explain it to me."

He watched her tighten the blanket around her chest and drop her gaze again. He let her, for now, in case it was the only way she could talk about what she was going through. "I need help, and I can't—"

"Make me angry, or I might stop helping you?" He'd interrupted her in hopes of taking her by surprise. She could say whatever she wanted and he wouldn't know if he could believe it. If he told the truth, there would be no way she could hide her reaction from him. The fact that she hadn't looked up and continued to stare at the floor told him he was right. He tipped her chin up again and cocked a smile across his lips. "You're stuck with me, kid."

"I don't want you to feel obligated, Luca," she said in a whisper. "I can take the flash drive and go. Then I'm no longer your problem."

"Not exactly true," he said, that smile faltering. "We're connected now. Whoever is after you knows that. Besides, you've been my problem for many years, so now that you're back, I can't let you walk out the door while you're in danger."

"I've been your problem?"

His stomach roiled at the question. If he answered it honestly, he would hurt her. If he lied, he hurt himself. Gazing into her eyes, he decided this one time, he could take the pain. "As I told you, I looked for you over the years, Lilah. I went from a man in love, to a man who was hurt, to a man who was worried, to a man who was numb."

"I wanted to contact you, Luca, so badly—"

"But you couldn't, or you'd put me at risk, too."

"Truthfully, I couldn't be sure of that, but I had to assume that if you were connected to me in any way, you'd be in danger. I didn't want you to live the way I had to live. Going from town to town, seedy apartment to seedy apartment. Low-wage job to day work here and there. Spending time in the forests surviving on fish and rabbits as I moved across the countryside."

"That doesn't sound like any kind of life."

"It wasn't, but I had to keep moving or risk being captured again. If you're right about the medal, they must laugh at my stupidity whenever they come after me."

"No," he said, taking her hand between his. "You knew you were being tracked, but you didn't know how, so there was no reason for you to suspect it was the medal."

"I was so careful with everything else, Luca. If I hadn't let my pride overrule my common sense, I would have put the medal in a safety deposit box and walked away. The thought never crossed my mind."

"Was it pride that made you hold on to that medal?" She didn't answer, so he pushed her a bit. "Was it, Lilah? Or was it something else?"

"That ceremony was the last time you told me you were proud of me before I dropped you at that hospital and abandoned you!" she exclaimed, tears shimmering in her eyes. "I abandoned you. For that, you should never forgive me, Lucas Porter."

"Wrong," he insisted, wiping away a stray tear that fell lazily down her cheek. "You didn't abandon me. You left me somewhere safe with every intention of returning, right?" Her nod was enough for him. "You couldn't control what happened after that to either one of us, so you have to stop carrying guilt about it. Was I upset and angry in the beginning? Yes. Have I been angry at you all of these years? No. I locked away every emotion I didn't need to live in the outside world into a box. That box was locked tight until I got called to a funeral home to collect the ashes of the woman I thought I'd love forever. That's when the box broke open again."

"I wish so many things, Luca," she whispered. "The biggest thing I wish is that I could have spared you all of that pain. That I could have gotten you a message somehow or someway, but I couldn't risk it."

"Because you didn't want me to get hurt, right?" he asked, thumbing away another tear. Her tears always broke his heart, and tonight was no different because, once again, she was crying over him.

"Yes, of course. I couldn't risk that my message would lead them to you and they'd hurt you to get to me. Can you ever forgive me, Luca? I mean, truly forgive me for all of this."

"There's nothing to forgive, Lilah. That's what you aren't grasping. You didn't start this. But what you did after it began, you did out of love. I know that, sometimes, doing something out of love is the hardest thing of all." Like pretending for the rest of his life that he no longer needed this woman to feel alive. "Carrying around anger about it only wastes energy we could be using to find the guys after you and end it so you can live again. Right here, right now, you have to let the guilt go. You've carried it too long and for no reason. The biggest thing they taught me at the VA was to let go of anything that didn't serve to improve your life. This guilt and shame you're carrying doesn't improve your life. It keeps you from staying present and being my partner as we try to navigate who's after you and why. Do you understand what I'm trying to say?"

Lilah never answered him with words. She purposefully leaned forward until their lips connected. A bright light exploded behind his eyes, and he dragged her to him. The sensation of her lips on his had been a memory for so long. Her body, soft and warm under his hands, moved against him in familiar ways as his tongue probed her lips to take the kiss back to days gone by. The moment he slipped his tongue between those sweet lips, he knew she hadn't put their past behind her, either.

"Lilah." The word fell from his lips as he kissed his way down her neck toward the towel that had slipped, teasing him with the imagery of her sweet body. "You're so beautiful."

She jerked, grasped the towel and tried to push him away all in one movement. It was more knee-jerk than intentional, so he held her still. "We can't do this," she finally gasped.

"Feels to me like we should," he answered, holding her gaze so she knew he was fully engaged with her. "We're explosive together, Lilah, and we don't want that explosion to happen at the wrong time and put us at risk. We're safe here tonight. After that, I can't promise anything."

She pushed herself off his lap and grabbed a bag off the floor. "That's where you're wrong. We aren't safe here. Those guys could surround this place as we sit here letting our hormones run away with our common sense. You're a security guy. You know I'm right. That," she said, motioning at the bed she'd just leaped from, "will never happen again." The slamming of the bathroom door punctuated her sentence, leaving him to do nothing but stare after her and wonder where he had gone wrong.

THE KEYBOARD CLACKED as Lilah finished sending her message to Mina. She wanted to know if they could track the men at the storage unit to any particular employer or if they were more of a thugs-for-hire situation. Knowing they were ex-military explained their ability to penetrate her defenses without fail, but that didn't explain who they worked for or what they wanted. She had to know who was giving the orders if she was ever going to solve this problem and move on with her life.

A quick flick of her gaze to Luca told her that may never be possible. At least not fully moving on. Having her lips on his was as explosive as it ever was until she remembered she wasn't the same woman he had made love to in this motel the last time. She wanted him to remember her body the way it was then rather than see her body now. There was nothing beautiful about her anymore—body, mind or spirit.

Unfortunately, she had hurt him by reacting the way she did without explanation. That couldn't be helped. What he didn't know was helping him move on with his life. She could only make him understand that with deeds and not words. Luca had a future, a promising future where he could help others. She didn't. She lived in the moment, knowing any moment could be her last.

He'd been standing by the window for the last hour, peering through a crack in the curtain. He had his gun out and at his side with his spine ramrod straight, or as straight as it would go since he broke it trying to defend the base all those years ago. He never talked about how he had broken multiple vertebrae in his back that day or how lucky he was that it never impinged the spinal cord. They were able to stabilize his spine, and with six months of physical therapy, he could now do most things again. It appeared he had a new health regimen that kept him in far better shape than when she left him at the VA, too.

She didn't need him to tell her that lifting weights was part of his workout routine. She liked that he cared for himself and knew he mattered to others who depended on him. That hadn't been the case for the longest time.

She pushed herself up from the desk chair and walked closer to him, still keeping a healthy distance so she didn't throw herself at him again. "We should get the flash drive while we wait."

Luca turned from the window and stuck his gun into the holster at his back. "I'll grab it for you." His steps were stilted, but he reached the bag and stuck his hand into the pocket, feeling around. "It's not here."

"What?" Her heart started racing, and she ran to him, grabbed the strap and tossed it on the bed. She didn't care if he liked it or not. If her bargaining chip was gone, she was as good as dead. She didn't know much, but she did know that. Whoever this was, they weren't hunting her for funsies. She stuck her hand into the pocket and felt around, her pent-up breath releasing when her finger entered the bag's main compartment. "There's a hole," she said, looking up at Lucas, watching her closely with his hands in fists. "It had to have fallen into the main compartment."

"There shouldn't be a hole in it. It's been untouched for years."

"Luca, you've had it in an unprotected storage unit surrounded by woods. Chances are a mouse found its way in. You should probably brace yourself for what's inside, both from the memories and the fact that some of it may now be in a mouse's nest."

She stepped away and let him be the one to unhook the strap and open the bag. It opened at the top, so he had to remove each item to get to the bottom. Soon, the bed was covered in his fatigues, dress uniform, medals and boots. He pulled a wooden box out that fell open when he set it on the bed. Inside were letters, the envelopes dirty and wrinkled.

"Letters?" she asked, glancing up at him. She knew better than to reach for them. There was little Lucas was territorial of other than the contents of this bag.

"From my mom," he agreed, running a finger across the top of one. "She died when I was at the training facility with Haven."

"Did you go to her funeral?"

"The hospice center called and told me it was time to come say my final goodbyes. The school packed up Haven and sent a trainer with me for the two-hour trip to Rochester. I was with her when she took her final breath. She asked me to wear my dress uniform to her funeral, but that was a final wish I couldn't grant."

She grasped his elbow, hoping it would keep him grounded in the room with her. "I'm sure it mattered more to her that you were there with her at the end, Luca. I'm proud of you for going to her when she needed you."

"Our relationship had always been strained," he agreed, staring at the letters. "I was always surprised when a letter would arrive from her. She could have sent an email, but she went to the trouble of writing a letter and mailing it every time."

"A mother's love is like that," Lilah said, gently rubbing his shoulder. "She wanted you to know she cared."

"Some might say a day late and a dollar short, but I tried not to look at it like that," he said, closing the box with a click. "She did her best with what she had, and that wasn't much of anything. Mom was who she was, but by the time I went into the service, she was clean again and had found stable work and an apartment."

"Then the dementia struck."

"And it struck hard," he agreed with a nod. "Mom was barely fifty-five when she died, but I always knew the years of drug abuse would come back to haunt her."

"I'm glad you got to make amends with her, or at the very least, you were together when she took her last breath as you were when you took your first."

His lips turned up in a smile, and he glanced at her for the first time since she'd pushed him away. "Now, that is truly a Delilah Hartman statement. You always had a way of summing everything up in the neatest bow."

"I don't know if that's a compliment or a knock."

"A compliment. I always appreciated your ability to eliminate all the noise so I could hear the truth." Rather than continue speaking, he eyed her as though he were challenging her to do the same now, but she couldn't. Wouldn't. Not when their lives were on the line. Once she knew he was safe, she could leave him to live the life he'd built without her. A life he had worked hard for and didn't need her screwing up more than she already had.

"I don't see any evidence of a mouse yet. Or my flash drive," she said, returning them to the business at hand.

"There's not much left in here." He pulled out his army-issued winter coat, and a black rectangle fell to the floor.

Delilah scooped it up and held it to her chest with an exhale. "We got it." She held her hand out, revealing a high-tech drive. "Now we just have to hope the information on it isn't corrupt."

"What are the numbers for?" he asked, pointing at the buttons on the outside of the flash drive.

"A passcode to open it. This drive encrypts the information as you transfer it to keep the information secure."

"Do you remember the passcode?" Lucas asked as she walked past him toward the computer.

"Of course. I used a number I could never forget." She typed in a sequence and pulled the cover off the top of it. "Your birthday."

Chapter Eleven

Lucas's gaze roved over the bed that now held his old life. The uniforms. The boots. The medals. All the things he wanted to forget but couldn't. They stared back at him in judgment. They weren't judging him, though. Only a human could pass judgment, and he was excellent at being his own judge and jury. He couldn't help but wonder if his judgment of himself had been too harsh. Truthfully, he'd played judge, jury and executioner for so long he wasn't sure how to stop.

You can't have your life back until you open that bag and face the items inside. What are you so afraid of?

The words she'd said floated through his mind. He'd done what he had always believed was the impossible. He'd opened the bag and was again face-to-face with his past. That meant only the last question remained. What was he afraid of and why? When and why did he give this bag the power over him? He wasn't even wearing these clothes or boots when the base fell. Those items were cut off him and destroyed at the hospital in Germany.

The bag was on the floor, and he picked it up, sticking his hand into the pocket to pull out his discharge papers. He read them, his unconscious mind forcing him into the triangle breathing as he did so. He read every word, letting them pulse boldly in his head before shrinking back to normal. Each word released a little bit of hold the bag had on him. Each paragraph he finished snapped a bind that had tied him to it for years. When he finished, he slid them back into the envelope, ready to put them back in the bag. Something stopped him. Instead, he slipped them into the side pocket of his cargo pants and lifted the medals from the bed.

They had arrived in the mail each time he refused to go to the ceremony, and went directly into the bag. He never even opened the boxes to look at the medals. What was the point? Pieces of metal and ribbon didn't change what he did to earn them. Earn them. How ridiculous did that sound? It was a way to pretty up the fact that he had killed for them. Bled for them. Hurt for them. He didn't want to be remembered for any of that.

It means you stepped up when no one else would or could. That's what makes someone commendable.

All of the therapy he'd gone through hadn't had the same effect that hearing her words in his head had. He allowed them to be there and change his perspective. He earned the medals for things he did that were good, not the things he did that were bad. Yes, people had died, but had he done nothing, everyone would have died. They'd lost people on the base, and he caused deaths on the enemy side doing what he did, and chances were some civilians, too, who were caught up in the fight that wasn't theirs. That didn't make it his fault.

"This is Warrant Officer Lucas Porter!" he yelled into the microphone. "The base is under attack! We need air support! Air support!" Another round of gunfire

tore through the station, and he dropped to the ground, his heart beating wildly in his chest. He looked left and right, knowing he was alone but hoping and praying he wasn't. Being alone meant being the one to make the decisions. Life and death decisions.

A firm headbutt to his thigh brought him back to the motel room. Haven was budging him, a whine low in his throat as he looked up at him with worried eyes. "I'm okay, boy," he promised, stroking his head until the dog sat back on his haunches. Haven didn't relax, but he didn't force him into the comfort position, either.

Lucas's gaze strayed to the bed again, and he lifted the fatigues, his fingers working at the Velcro on a patch that said PORTER until he could pull it off. The sound was soft but felt like ripping a bandage off an old wound. Sometimes, removing the bandage revealed a healed wound. He reached for the next patch, pulling that one off, too. Lucas held the patches in his hand, closed his eyes and did a mental search of his body for wounds. They were there. Some were healed. Some were closed over but still oozing. That told him he was getting somewhere. Slow as the healing was, he *was* healing.

The patches went into his pocket and the fatigues, dress blues and shoes were tucked into the bag. Before he put the medals away, he opened each box and ran his fingers over the object inside. "Earned for saving lives, not taking them," he uttered with each medal.

The one point they drove home at the VA in therapy was that he had to do the hard work if he wanted to be free of the guilt that plagued him. Would his mind ever heal from the horrific things he saw and participated in? No. Those scars would always remain, but if he could stop carrying some of the guilt and shame about them, his life would be better by default. He'd feel better physically and emotionally. Life still wouldn't be Skittles and rainbows, but it would be manageable again. He'd genuinely believed he'd done that, but seeing this bag again told him in no uncertain terms that he hadn't done anything at all.

His gaze strayed to the woman sitting at the desk, her concentration on the screen in front of her. She made him want to forget the guilt and shame he carried from those years long ago. Her honesty and openness about her struggles with PTSD made him feel less shame for having it, too. Her beliefs that he saved countless lives, including hers, made him want to set the guilt on a shelf somewhere and stop carrying it around in such a destructive way. There would always be triggers he'd have to work around. Those triggers were frequent and out of his control, and the reason he had Haven by his side. He had worked hard to protect himself and others by working with Haven, but now he understood the truth. He hadn't done the most demanding job of all. With his gaze pinned on Lilah's beautiful hair, he wondered if the episodes might be less frequent and less crushing each time they happened if he found a way to free himself of the shame and guilt. For the first time, he wanted to try.

Once the medals were back in the bag, he closed it and clicked the handle through the loops. The bag felt lighter when he carried it to the door and set it aside. Not just because he'd taken items out but because he did the hard work of taking back some of his power from it.

"You forgot the coat," Lilah said, and his head snapped up to meet her gaze. She was turned halfway in the chair and pointed at the bed with the field jacket spread across the end.

"I was thinking about keeping it out," he said, walking over to where she sat by the computer. "It was a new issue to me in Germany, but I never wore it but a couple of times. I noticed snowflakes earlier, and let's face it, that coat is warmer than anything we have with us. Seems smart to keep it handy, just in case."

"As long as you think you can," she said, her gaze pinned on him again.

As much as he wanted to talk to her about his feelings, he bit back the words on his tongue. They needed to concentrate on staying alive. "We have bigger problems on our hands right now, Lilah. Were you able to access the flash drive?"

After glancing at him, she turned back to the computer and clicked on the mouse pad. "I was. I've been familiarizing myself with it all again."

"These are the files that I was working on at the time of the attack," she explained, running the mouse down the screen, and he counted twelve files. She clicked the first one open. "I don't even know if these got shipped. As you can see," she explained, pointing out the different pieces of information on the screen, "I had just hit Send to get central shipping the routing information when the first missile hit." She closed her eyes with her breath held tightly in her chest. It had always been that way for her. Thinking about the first minutes of the attack. The confusion. The terror. All the things that go through your mind when you think you're about to die.

He gently massaged her back while Haven rested his

chin on her lap. "Open your eyes. You're not there any-more. You're with me again. I'll keep you safe."

Lilah opened her eyes and turned to meet his gaze. "Just like you did that day, Luca. I hate having to put you through that again. I hate that my presence here has put you in danger, but I can't change it, can I?"

"Nope," he said with a chuckle. "Embrace the suck, as they say, and remember that we did a lot of hard things as a team. We can do it again."

"Right," she said with a nod of her head and the clear-ing of her throat. "As I said, I don't know if central ship-ping got any of this."

"I thought Mina said they could see it all from a dif-ferent computer or something."

"That depends on if the email sent or was stopped by the missile attack. You know how the tech was over there. Also, I don't know if the relics were found on the base afterward."

"Wait, you mean these twelve were actually on the base? They weren't spread out across other bases?"

"That's what I'm saying. I was finishing the cata-log for a collection brought to us by a museum curator turned soldier. He wanted to protect the oldest relics of his collection."

"And then we go and lose them to history," Lucas said, whistling a low tune. "Doesn't look good on our end."

"Or his," she said, showing him the country of ori-gin. "It was his government that attacked us. The thing is, I don't know if they're lost to history or not. Those twelve are an unknown to me."

"Ha," Lucas said with a shake of his head. "Okay, I feel less bad about it now. Do you think they want this information because they found the relics? Maybe they want to get them back to the right people or need the paper trail to get them back home?"

"First, they don't know I have this drive with the information on it, so why wouldn't they simply send me official army orders to return to a base and give them whatever information I could remember? Why all the games and the attempts to take me against my will?" she asked, motioning at her chin. "It doesn't make sense."

She was right, it didn't make sense. None of it made sense. He stared at the computer screen and a folder caught his eye. He pointed at it. "What's that file?"

"That's a bit of a side project I was working on. It doesn't apply to these files." She motioned at the list before her.

"The Lost Key of Honor. It sounds important." He lifted a brow, and she sighed, bringing the cursor up but stopping before she clicked it open.

"I think it's important. Important enough that I'm not going to open this file and show you any part of it. What you don't know, you can't tell."

"I don't understand. Is it top secret or something?"

"I don't know what it is, Luca. Okay, I mean, I know what it is, but I don't know why there was so much subterfuge based around it."

"You mean they didn't assign you this file?" When she shook her head, he got a bad feeling in his gut. A feeling that said the file was TNT. "Show me."

"No," she said with another shake of her head. "The less you know about all of this, the better. It still gives you plausible deniability."

"It also makes it impossible for me to protect you,

Lilah. Plausible deniability is useless if you're dead or captured." His voice vibrated with all the fear bottled up in his gut. Haven walked over and sat next to him, leaning into his leg. Lucas found his head and stroked him, his gaze locked on the woman in the chair. Her face was drawn and drained of color, making the scars on her chin appear more prominent than ever before. Lucas traced the scar on her chin with his thumb, drawing a jagged breath from her lips. "You told me I had to trust you, so now I'm telling you the same thing. Trust me, Lilah, and we'll get through this."

Chapter Twelve

"You're sure?" she asked with a hard swallow punctuating the sentence. "Once you're involved, you're involved to the end."

"I'm already involved, Lilah," he reminded her, motioning at the room. "I've been involved since you walked out on me six years ago."

"That's not what I did, Luca! I was protecting you!" She shot up from her chair, but he grasped her upper arms to hold her in place. "I was protecting you," she whispered again, as though he hadn't heard her the first time.

"Which was honorable and, I'm sure, terribly difficult. I'm here now, and you've already involved me, so let me help you. If what you say about these guys is true, I can't go back to Secure One and carry on with my life as though the last few days didn't happen, right?" She shook her head, her lips in a thin line. "Then let me help you, really help you, end this situation so you can have your life back."

"You keep saying that, but if this ends and I'm still standing, I'm a woman with nothing. Now that's just as terrifying as facing down these guys."

"Now?" he asked, his thumb still tracing her chin.

Her heavy sigh said more as an answer than any words could have. She had relied on herself for so long that now, after finding him again, she found it difficult to walk away. He understood that sigh on a soul-deep level.

"You're sure you want to know all of this information?" she asked again, motioning at the computer. "We can't go back, so make sure you're prepared for what's to come."

"I'll be wading through what's to come with you whether I know or not, Lilah. I'm all in until you're safe. It's better to know what we're up against than fight an enemy without the knowledge needed to beat them."

Her curt nod and how she turned to the computer told him she accepted his decision. "This file refers to a trunk that a curator had brought in. It was a trunk they couldn't get open."

"He didn't bring the key along?"

"There is no key," she said, biting her lower lip. "The trunk is from ancient Iraq. It hasn't been opened for hundreds of years."

"The Lost Key of Honor," he said when the name struck him.

"Loosely translated," she agreed with a nod. "It was written in an old, dead language, but that was the best the curator could guess."

"He knew there was no key but wanted the trunk saved anyway?"

"There's a reason," she said, worrying her teeth across her lip as she clicked open the file. "It's been long believed that the trunk could hold—"

"The Holy Grail," he said with a breath as he pulled up a chair from the small table so he could sit. He took a moment to read the top paragraph of the file and let out a low whistle. "The trunk cannot be opened in any way other than with the key."

"There was little time to worry about it when it was brought in at the beginning of the war, so it was shipped to the States to be held at a museum."

"This file says they were actively looking for intel on the key. How did they expect to find a hundreds-year-old key in that kind of rubble when the country's own people couldn't find it?"

"Because it's not a key," she said, facing him. "It's a piece of a stone tablet. The museum has long had half of the tablet that fits into the top of the trunk. The word *grail* is written several times on that half of the tablet. Without the other half, they can't translate the entire tablet or open the trunk."

"Okay, but grail can just mean something sought after, too. That doesn't mean it's the Holy Grail, and why would it be in Iraq?"

"The four rivers of Eden are said to converge in southern Mesopotamia, which we know is modern-day Iraq. How it got there or why, I can't say, but as you can see, they have put together a strong argument for it being the Holy Grail. If you believe in all of that, of course."

"You don't?" Lucas asked, holding her gaze for a heartbeat before dragging it away to read the file. The information on the drive was extensive and would take more than a cursory glance to understand it all. He didn't have that kind of time, so he would have to depend on her to give him the highlights.

"I believe that others believe it to be true, Luca. Regardless of what is inside the trunk, the trunk itself is a relic and should be preserved. It could be empty, but it existed at that time for a reason. I never saw it in person. It was sent off the base before I arrived. I've only seen the images in the file."

"How do you have the file if you weren't in charge of the trunk?"

"It wasn't meant for my eyes, but I didn't know that then. I found it on a flash drive still in a computer on the base. I didn't know who the flash drive belonged to, but it was the only file on it. I may have transferred the file to my drive before I turned in the original."

"Why?"

"It intrigued me—The Lost Key of Honor. It drew me in and made me want to find it. I was intrigued by the question, where is it, and how could it even exist hundreds of years later?"

"It can't exist," he said with assuredness. "Not anymore. That country has been bombed and destroyed to the point no stone tablet from that time would ever be anything but dust."

"Unless it was protected somewhere," she said with a lift of one brow.

"Protected?"

After scrolling with the mouse several times, she pointed at the screen. "This picture shows the trunk with the half tablet in place. What do you notice?"

Once she enlarged the image so he could see it better, he stared for quite some time before pointing at a ridge. "There. Why would a ridge be in the center if it was one tablet? It's more like there are two separate tablets."

"Exactly," she said, a grin on her face. "Do you see the complicated notches on the side without the tablet?"

"All the indents?" he asked, and she nodded. "That's the key to opening it?"

"Best I can figure," she agreed. "The file indicates that several molds were made in an attempt to make a new key for it, but they all failed to open it."

"Strange. I'm surprised someone hasn't just busted the trunk apart by now. Why continue to search for something likely long gone?"

"Human nature? Spiritual beliefs? Fear?"

"Fear?" Lucas asked, holding her gaze, wholly engaged in the conversation even as he kept his ears open to the noises outside the motel. Cars speeding past on the highway. Tires at an even speed, not slowing or turning. No footsteps crunching across the snow. All was quiet.

"Fear of what might happen if they break the trunk to get it open. What does the other half of the tablet say? Is it a curse to open it without certain people present? That kind of thing. If people think this trunk holds the Holy Grail, they would never destroy it to get it open."

"Okay, I get that, but we both know that the other half of the tablet is long gone. Even if it's not, if the people of Iraq can't find it, how could we as foreigners?"

"I don't have the answer to that, only that they were trying."

"As a good faith mission for Iraq or...?"

"Again, I don't have the answer to that. I don't know who started this file or sanctioned the search. It's been six years. For all I know, the trunk has been returned and none of it matters now. I've been running for six years from some unknown enemy who wants me dead, and I don't know why! I just want to know what's going on!"

On instinct, he pulled her into him and held her

tightly. "It's okay," he promised, soothing her by rocking her gently. "I know you're stressed, scared and exhausted. You're not alone anymore, and we might not be able to solve this in one night, but you have help now."

Lucas fell silent, rubbing her back as he held her, letting her rest her chin over his shoulder, heavy with fatigue. It was time for her to get some sleep, but he would be selfish a bit longer and continue to languish in the feel of her wrapped around him. He'd missed her warmth and how she made him feel safe in an unsafe world. Now it was his turn to do that for her, and he would. First, she needed someone to take care of her. He was grateful to be the one to get that chance again.

"Come on," he said, hoisting her from the chair and helping her to the bed. "It's time to let your mind rest and your body recover. You're exhausted. You need to sleep in a bed where you can stretch out and recoup."

Lilah didn't argue. Instead, she lowered herself to the bed and let him remove her boots before she slid her legs under the covers. "You're safe here tonight," he promised, pulling her spectacles off her face and setting them on the nightstand. That was a blanket statement he shouldn't be promising, but he willed it to be true. "I'm going to contact the team and stand watch."

"Just a few hours," she murmured, her eyes drooping as he stroked her forehead. It was an old trick he used to use when she refused to sleep that summer, worried he'd do something terrible to himself while she did.

"I'll wake you in two hours," he promised, but he wouldn't. He'd let her sleep in the safety of another human being for as long as he could. While Lilah slept, he hoped Mina would find something they could use to move this investigation forward and get the target off her back. They'd already been shot at twice. As he lowered himself to the computer and minimized the file that might hold the answer to everything, the only thought running through his head was, the third time was the charm.

Chapter Thirteen

"Lilah, wake up." She opened her eyes to see Lucas looming over her. "Time to go."

Without question, she sat up and tied on her boots. "Did they find us already?" she asked, slipping her glasses onto her face again.

"Hard to know, but Cal reported that someone is sniffing around the vicinity of the medal. He wants us to move again to be on the safe side."

The room was dark as she stood from the bed and took in her surroundings. He'd packed up all the equipment, and the bags sat ready by the door. He handed her his Secure One parka, the sleeves already rolled up.

"Here, put this on. I know it's a bit too big, but it's snowing now, and if we go off the road, you need something warmer than the coat Mina gave you."

"What about you?" she asked, slipping her arms into the coat that was, in fact, a bit too big, but with the sleeves rolled up, it would be wearable and keep her legs warm, too.

He slid into his field coat and buttoned it up. "We might as well use it to our advantage, right?" His tone told her he needed her to agree.

"Right," she said, grabbing the front of it and planting a kiss on his cheek. "I'm proud of you, Luca."

His smile told her she'd given him the answer he needed. "Wait here. I'll take the bags to the van and see what I see."

After her nod, he turned to Haven, already dressed for the weather. "Rest, Haven. Stay with Lilah." As though the dog understood the assignment, he walked over and sat, his ears at attention. "Good boy."

Lilah wanted to reach down and scratch his ears, but she knew better than to touch any service dog while they were working. Instead, she motioned for Luca to go and stepped back so she wasn't visible when he opened the door. Watching through the window, he threw the bags where they could reach them quickly and then checked for anyone on the road before he pulled off the magnet on the side of the van and switched it out.

"Get ready, boy," she said to Haven. "It's going to be cold."

She pulled the hood up on the parka and was ready when he opened the door. "Haven, fall in." The dog headed straight for the open van door while Luca helped her out of the motel and into the passenger seat. "Buckle up," he said, shutting the door for her before he secured Haven and slammed the side door.

Once they were on the move, she glanced over at him. "Where are we headed?"

"Somewhere southwest. Mina says we're supposed to drive out of the snow quickly. I hope she's right. The conditions aren't great."

Lilah tried to see through the falling snow, but it was nearly impossible in the dark, even with the windshield wipers on high. "Try the conditions are terrible, and no plows will be out way up here."

"The only upside is we have the road to ourselves. If nothing else, it will be a white Christmas."

"I can't argue with you there." After a glance in the side mirror, she started to chuckle. "Larry's Computer Repair. If we can't fix it, it ain't broke," she read from the sign on the side of the van. "Really?"

Luca wore a grin when she glanced back at him. "What can I say? Cal has a sense of humor. It's not much in the way of camouflage, but it does say something different than the last one, which was pizza delivery. With a little snow packed on the license plate, no one will know it's us immediately."

"You said Cal has eyes on someone stalking the medal?" She hadn't wanted to ask the question, but at the same time, she wanted to know the answer.

"That's what his eyes in the sky say, but he's waiting it out to see if they're just in the area or specifically searching for something."

"Or someone. I can't believe you might be right about this," she said, chewing on her lip. "It never occurred to me, mostly because I can't believe they could be tracking me with something so small for so long."

"Technology has evolved, Lilah. They make trackers now that only use power when they're pinged. The rest of the time, they're off. These small military trackers only use solar power to charge them, so it wouldn't take much time out of your pocket each month to keep it charged. For instance, having it out on a dresser for a day would give it charge for months."

"But why?" she asked, her hand grasping the door

handle as the wheels slid toward the shoulder of the road. He got it under control again just before hitting the rumble strips, wherever they may be under the snow.

"I think we both know why," he said, tightly gripping the wheel. "They want to know where you are at all times. They may not know about the flash drive, but you exist, and you know things about what went down there."

Lilah fell silent as she watched the wipers clear the glass and the snow cover it again in a comforting pattern. She did know things. Things she wished she didn't and things she wished she knew about now that she was faced with people hunting her. She rubbed her chin absently as though that would make the jagged scar disappear. A thought struck her, and she gasped, the sound loud in the quiet van.

"What if I didn't even earn the medal and they just gave it to me to keep track of me?" To her ears, the sentence was incredulous but also wholly possible.

"No," Luca said, shaking his head as he steered the van around a sharp corner. They were doing barely twenty in a fifty-five, but until this snow quit, they were at its mercy. "Don't think like that. We don't even know if it is the medal. It's just a hypothesis right now."

"But you said Cal has seen activity around it."

"I also said he's waiting to see if it's approached, so just give him time to get back to me."

"What else did Mina say?"

"She's looking into the news archives about antiquities or tablets discovered or displayed over the last six years. She's also trying to get more information about the accusations against Major Burris."

"Something is fishy there," Lilah agreed. "The major

was always professional and was scarily knowledge-able about the laws and customs that applied in armed conflicts."

"Even knowledgeable men have a price, Lilah."

She fell silent for several more minutes as she thought about Burris. Was he the kind of man who willingly stole precious artifacts for money? Not the man she'd worked under, but then again, everyone has a face they show the world and a face that hides below. She had to wonder if the face Burris hid was one of corruption and theft. "I hope she finds something helpful. Tell me how you started working at Secure One," she said to change the subject.

Luca's chuckle was self-deprecating if she'd ever heard it. "When I left the training program with Haven, my first job was working security for Senator Dorian in Minneapolis. Secure One worked an on-site event for the senator's daughter during the Red River Slayer's reign. Do you remember that?"

"Of course," she said with a nod. "That was a terri-fying time for women around the country. It was hard to believe when the whole story came out."

"Truth. While Secure One was at the estate, I helped them protect the property's perimeter when the senator's daughter was at risk. Once the case was wrapped up and Secure One went home, Cal reached out and thanked me for helping them with everything. I replied that if there were ever any openings on his team, I would love to interview, with his understanding that it was two for the price of one," he explained, his gaze flicking to the rearview mirror to check on his dog. "He had me drive up within days, and I was hired on the spot. They had so much work coming in after being in the public eye so often over the previous years with high-profile cases that they were turning down jobs."

"That's fabulous to hear, Luca," she said, touching his arm as he drove. "I'm glad you took the chance and asked."

"I almost didn't," he admitted with a tip of his head. "High-stress situations were always difficult for me after we returned, but I'd worked for the senator for three years without problems. Not that it was high stress, other than Senator Dorian loved nothing more than to yell about everything that went on across the property, right or wrong. My therapy from the VA and training with Haven was put to the test during those few days that the property was locked down, and I was able to handle it without difficulty. That was the only reason I inquired about working at Secure One. Well, that and the fact that his core team was all ex-military and understood the ups and downs of PTSD."

"Mina indicated that was the case to me, too," she agreed. "Understanding helps, but so does having a brotherhood again, right?"

"At first, I thought that might work against me," he admitted, letting the van pick up speed a bit more now that the snow had turned to just flurries. "I was afraid the environment would remind me too much of my military years, but I quickly saw that wasn't how Cal ran the business. He was a participant in the company and not the boss. It all works, despite our different experiences and reactions to them."

"No, it works *because* of your different experiences and reactions to them," she clarified. "You all bring different perspectives and knowledge to the table about different aspects of the security world. That's what makes it work. You're an expert at weapons but need a sharpshooter like Efren to use your knowledge practically."

"You know Efren was a sharpshooter?" She noticed the quizzical look he wore when he asked the question.

"Mina gave me a bit of a rundown on everyone as I was changing clothes," she explained. "She didn't want me walking into a meeting completely uninformed."

"That sounds like Mina," Luca said with a chuckle. "She's always about keeping the playing field level, which is funny coming from her."

"Why?"

"Mina is the smartest person in the company, male or female, and we all know it. None of us can do what she can with a computer and a few hours on her side. Before Mina joined the team, from what they tell me, they were nothing more than glorified security camera installers. Cal was doing work on the side to fund the company."

"What kind of work on the side?"

Luca cleared his throat and kept his eyes straight ahead. "Let's just say he did many things he didn't want to do to help good people who were suffering."

Her military experience translated that statement quickly into one word. Mercenary. "Understood."

"Now that Mina is part of the team, the business has grown, so Cal is starting a cybersecurity division. Mina will be heading it up. I foresee it quickly overtaking the personal security aspect of the business."

"There will be no doubt," she said, noticing a sign pointing them back toward Whiplash, Minnesota. Secure One was located on the town's southern border, but they wouldn't go there again until her situation was cleared up. Then again, she'd probably never return to Secure One, no matter how much she wanted to. "I worked remotely for a company for three of the six years I was on the run. My job was to keep their server safe, build their website utilizing hidden pages and code everything into a box. If anyone tried to brick their system, mine would do it first, allowing me to unbrick it again once the hackers were caught."

He glanced at her quickly before putting his eyes back on the road. "You can do that?"

"I could, back then," she agreed. "It was difficult work but worth it. These days, those techniques may not work anymore."

"It couldn't have been that long ago, Lilah. You were only gone six years."

"I quit three years ago, and things change at lightning speed in the tech world."

"Why did you quit?"

"I didn't see any other choice when they found me for the fourth time in three years. My only hope was to go completely underground and stay off their radar. Little did I know I may have been carrying that radar with me. Anyway, I banked a lot of money during the years I worked, and since it was remote work, it didn't matter if I had to move to a different town. I saved every penny I could over the years by living in some disgusting places, but it paid off. I survived on what I had for years and only needed to do odd jobs here and there to keep myself fed and clothed. I've spent so long on the run, I'm not sure I know how to stay in one place anymore."

"It's easy," he said with his lips quirked. "You find someplace that feels like home and you stay there."

"Easy coming from your side of the van, yes," she agreed, leaning her head on the cool glass of the window. "Not so easy when where you feel at home is off-limits."

"Where do you feel at home?"

"I've only ever felt at home with you, Luca."

Chapter Fourteen

I've only ever felt at home with you, Luca.

Try as he might, he couldn't get those words out of his head. Her sweet voice telling him how she felt even when she couldn't tell him how she felt made him want to stop the van and drag her across the console to finish that kiss from the motel room. He knew better. Whatever had stopped her last time was still between them, and while he wished he knew what it was, all he could do was let her reveal it in her own time.

Those words had kept him alert and awake on a long drive through bad weather. He wanted to keep her safe, so he'd driven as long as he could before fatigue set in. They'd found another small motel and pulled over for the night, knowing if he didn't, they wouldn't see morning.

"Secure one, Whiskey," the voice said, and Lucas hit the microphone button to connect.

"Secure two, Lima."

Mina's face filled the screen, and she immediately assessed the room around them. "You're safe?"

"For now," he said with a nod. "We're in a new motel south of the Minnesota border. We didn't pick up any tails, and all's quiet on the western front."

"Do you have enough supplies?" Cal's voice asked from off in the distance. Mina zoomed the screen out and included the rest of the room in the shot. Cal and Roman were there with her.

"We stopped and picked up food at a small grocery on the way down the hill."

"Wearing Secure One gear?" Mina asked with her lips in a thin line.

"No, I, uh, actually wore my field coat. Found it in my duffel and thought it would be good cover." All three sets of brows went up, but they said nothing, so he cleared his throat. "Would you thank Sadie for dumping that giant bag of food in the back for Haven? It's less stressful when I don't worry about him."

"You know she's got her little dude," Mina said with a wink.

Lilah laughed, and he sat silently until the sound died away, soaking it up in case he never heard it again. "Have you learned anything since we last talked?"

"Yes," Cal and Mina said in unison, but Mina motioned for him to go first.

Cal spun his computer screen around to face the camera in the conference room. "We've been monitoring the house where I put the medal. It's an old abandoned place north of town and within a thirty-minute walk of the storage units."

"To make it look like I escaped and took shelter there?" Lilah asked.

"Exactly. I did it because you wouldn't stay there long if you were with us. They would need to move quickly to get another team there."

"Or there was already another team waiting."

Cal pointed at her and nodded. "I believe that's the case. As you'll see." He hit a button on the computer, and they watched as four men approached the house with their rifles raised.

"Are those AR-15s?" Lucas asked immediately.

"No, M4 Carbine EPRs," Cal answered.

"I thought M4 Carbines were for military only," Delilah said.

"These are law enforcement guns. The ERP stands for an enhanced patrol rifle. Better sights. Better stock. There's more room for mounting optics and accessories. The guys at the storage unit debacle had the same ones," Cal said, his face wearing a grim expression.

"That's odd because an AR-15 is much cheaper these days. If you're a gun for hire, you're carrying an AR-15, not an M4," Lucas said, confused by the whole thing.

"Unless someone is buying them for you," Lilah whispered. They all went silent as the four men left the house like ninjas in the night. "Do you think they found the medal?" she asked, gazing at the screen. Lucas could hear how much courage it took her to ask.

"No. It's inaccessible to them, but it will have to remain there for now," Cal said.

"Either way, they know we're on to them," Lucas said, reaching over and squeezing Lilah's hand. She held on for dear life, so he didn't let go. Instead, he ran his thumb over her hand to keep her calm.

"How did you even get that footage?" Lilah asked, her head cocked as though the thought just struck her.

"Drone in a tree," Cal explained. "Easier and faster than putting up a camera when your timeline is short."

"Okay, we know they're still looking for Lilah," Lucas

said, getting them back on track. "We also know some of them are ex-military or law enforcement. Mina, did you find out anything?"

"So many things," Mina said with laughter on her lips. It brought a smile to his, and he glanced at Lilah to see her wearing one, too. Leave it to Mina to keep the moment light.

"I did some digging into Major Burris. He was never tried for the war crimes he was accused of because, according to JAG, the case was weak, with little evidence. However, he was within a year of retirement, so he served it at a desk and was ushered out on his last day."

"I bet he was," Lilah murmured. "I would love to know who brought those charges against him. Burris was always professional and the person we could go to when we had an issue. It seems off for his level of command and his personality."

"War does funny things to people," Mina gently said. "Kindness to his people doesn't mean he was kind to the enemy."

"That's true, I know," Lilah agreed. "I would just like to find out who was at the heart of those charges."

"Burris is now living near Rochester, Minnesota. I'll see if I can dig deeper and find more information about his accusers," Mina said, making a note. "Colonel Swenson is still working but is now a general in Minneapolis."

"Not surprised," Lucas said. "I worked a few ops with him, and he was voted most likely to be in the army for his career. He lived for the accolades and back patting he got moving up the ranks. He went into a funk if someone didn't tell him how wonderful he was every day. We used to call him Major Payne and Captain Fantastic."

Cal snorted while biting back a smile, but Lucas saw it. There wasn't a guy who had served who didn't know someone like Swenson.

"You'll find a lot of that kind of guy in the military," Roman said, still chuckling. "I guess that's one of the reasons we have career army men. They thrive in that environment. Anything else, Mina?"

"Yes," she said, leaning in on the table to address Lucas personally. "I called about that trunk you asked me to check on. The museum doesn't have and never has had a trunk like you described."

"What?" Lilah asked in surprise. "I have documented paperwork that it went to them."

"Not according to the museum curator who I spoke with there. He said they are sometimes sent to a different museum during shipping because one may have more room. I haven't had time to call other museums, nor would I know where to start."

Lilah cut her gaze to Lucas for a moment, and he recognized the look. She wasn't convinced that Mina was right. "I'll take care of it," Lilah said before Mina could say more. "As long as I can use the Secure One computer for a little questionable hacking?"

"As long as you're only looking," Cal said with a brow raised.

"Look, but don't touch. Got it," Lilah said with a wink.

"We can split the list if you send me the information," Mina said, elbows on the table. "I'm at your disposal."

When Lilah shot a look Lucas's way, he read in it that she wanted no one else involved more than they had to be. "It's no problem. I can do the museums while you keep looking into Burris's accusers?"

"Sure," Mina said. "I'm just worried you're both running on little to no sleep."

"I got to sleep last night while Lucas drove. He can sleep while I work."

"No," Lucas said immediately and without hesitation. "Someone has to be on watch. We can assume the medal was their dowsing rod, but we can't be sure. We can't let our guard down."

"You also can't go without sleep," Cal said, his words pointed. "Everyone in this room knows what happens when we push ourselves past the brink of exhaustion."

"I can keep watch and do the work," Lilah said, emphasizing her sentence by squeezing his hand no one else knew she was holding. "We're a team, and I can carry my weight on it."

Cal pointed at the computer screen. "What she said. We'll let you get to it. It's 6:00 a.m. now. The next check-in will be at noon unless something imperative arises. If you need backup, you know how to reach us. I still have the van monitored, so I know your exact location. You should be good for the day as the snow is about to hit your area and no one will move anywhere until it passes."

"Tell me about it," Lucas muttered. "Driving down from the North Shore last night was one of the most dangerous things I've done, and I worked munitions."

"You don't mess with Mother Nature," Roman said. "Take advantage of the break. Hopefully, by the time the snow passes, Min and Delilah will have what you need to take the next step."

"Charlie, out," Cal said, and the screen went blank.

Lucas turned to Lilah and took her other hand. "Why wouldn't the museum have the trunk?"

"That's what I want to know, too," she agreed.

"Can it just happen that a shipment is diverted?"

"Not unless the museum it's going to has burned down and closed. Then it would just get returned to sender, essentially, and routed back to central shipping. All of these antiquities have well-documented shipping papers for a reason. We never want to be accused of stealing other countries' precious art or artifacts."

"Maybe it did get returned to sender and sent somewhere else? There would be no way for you to know once we left the base."

"Except that the trunk was shipped before I got to the base, remember? I have images of that trunk in a museum in The Lost Key of Honor file."

"Are you sure it's a museum?" he asked, his brow raised.

She paused and tipped her head, probably thinking about the pictures she'd seen. "No, I can't be sure. I'll go through the images and inspect them closer."

"If it was at a museum, how would you track it down? Mina is right. There are a lot of museums."

"I'm going to do it the easy way."

"The easy way? Only contacting the museums you know took in antiquities during that time of the war?"

"No," she said, turning to the computer and inserting the flash drive. "I'll start by looking for the first six I sent out when I arrived. I know those left the base."

"To what end?"

"It's a first step. I'll know if some of the artifacts made it to their destination or if none of them did. It's a place to start while you sleep."

"No. I'm not leaving you without protection."

"If you don't sleep, you'll be useless to me if we need to run, Luca. Cal is right. Exhaustion makes everything worse, and I need you to be able to think on your feet. Look, the snow has already started." She moved the curtain aside so he could see the flakes falling. "No one is going anywhere, including us."

His shoulders slumped in defeat. "Only a few hours. Wake me the moment you think you hear something. I mean it, Lilah. It's easier to be proactive in these situations than reactive."

"On my honor, I will wake you at the wisp of a worry that there's trouble."

She stood and held his hand as she walked him to the bed. The motel only had rooms with one queen, and they'd taken it, but he had seen how her eyes grew when they walked in. She was hiding something he was determined to figure out. Once he had laid down on the bed, boots on, she covered him with a blanket and turned off the light. It was early and the sun wasn't up yet, but the way the storm was howling, he doubted they'd see much daylight over the next twelve hours.

Lilah kissed his cheek and lingered as though she were fighting a war with herself before she walked back to the desk to sit. Lucas fell asleep to the backdrop of her keys clacking as she set about her work. He couldn't help but wonder if the secrets were really hidden within that file or if they had been hidden in her all along.

Chapter Fifteen

Confusion and frustration filled Lilah as she stared at the screen. She had been working her way down the list of the dozens of shipping logs for the antiquities she had on the flash drive. She was nine deep, and so far, none of them had found their way to where they were supposed to be. In fact, it was as though they had just disappeared into thin air.

Lilah started typing again, trying to cross match the item across museums in case the schedule got screwed up when the base fell. Maybe one didn't reach the intended place but went to the museum where a different artifact was scheduled. Her fingers paused on the keyboard. If that were the case, they would have been returned to central shipping. It didn't make sense. She had no other ideas, so she tried it anyway, just in case museums were told to keep the item rather than return it.

After another hour of digging, it was easy to see that the theory was also incorrect. How was it that all these items had gone poof into thin air? The antiquities she was searching for weren't even on the base when it fell, so there would be no reason to think they didn't get shipped correctly.

Her neck and back aching, she stood and stretched, her shirt pulling up to reveal what she was trying to hide from the man sleeping on the bed behind her. She quickly pulled her shirt down and tucked it back into her pants. She had been working for nearly five hours, meaning Lucas had been sleeping for as long. Everything was quiet, and she was confident they'd have until the snow stopped before they had to worry about being on guard. Then again, if the medal had been to blame for leading these guys to her door, it would be much more difficult for them to find her now.

The idea that they took something she had pride in and turned it against her made her sick to her stomach. Had she earned the medal or was it just how they decided to keep track of her? That was risky, considering she could have done what Lucas did and stored the medal. Her mind drifted back to some of her conversations with other soldiers. She had said more than once that if given a medal, she would carry it with her always as a reminder that she could do hard things. Someone could have easily overheard her and used that statement to their advantage.

Now, here she was, six years of her life gone. Six years she didn't get to spend with the man sleeping behind her because someone played her strength as her weakness. Ironic. None of it made sense, though. Why would the government want or need to track her?

"Hey," Lucas said, sitting up and stretching. "How long have I been out?"

"Almost five hours," she said, the room nearly dark even in the middle of the day. The snow was falling so hard it felt like night rather than morning. "Feel better?"

"Much," he admitted. "That drive wore me out last night. Everything quiet?"

"As a church mouse. No one is out in this. You can't see your hand in front of your face. Why don't you take a shower?"

"No," he said, shaking his head at the suggestion. "Vulnerability could get you killed."

Her sigh was heavy when she stood to face him. "I'm capable of taking care of myself, Lucas Porter. I took Haven outside to do his business while you were sleeping and look, we're both fine."

"You did what? Why didn't you wake me up? You shouldn't have gone out there!"

"I was trained by the United States Army and kept myself alive through attack after attack for the last six years. I have a gun and know how to use it. Stop acting like my bodyguard and start acting like my partner." She tapped his chest with each syllable to drive her point home.

She didn't miss his small step back as he raised his brows. "Your partner?"

"We always made great partners, Lucas. No matter what we were doing, we played to each other's strengths and weaknesses without the need to communicate them. It was that way from when you picked me up off the tarmac and we pushed that old golf cart out of our way. I know it's been years, but you can trust me to have your back."

The look in his eye told her he remembered when they were partners in crime *and* between the bedsheets. "I'll be out in a few. The rifle is by the door if you need it."

Her salute was jaunty, bringing a smile to his lips for

the first time since he woke up. "When you get out, I'll share what I learned while you slept."

After grabbing his bag and giving her a nod, he jogged into the small bathroom and closed the door. Lilah lowered herself to the chair and wondered if the Luca she used to know was still under those black fatigues or if he had become someone completely different since their summer on the island. Spending time with him the last few days told her that he was someone completely different from everyone but her. He had a hard edge to him now that he had never carried before, but maybe that was how he managed his emotions in the workplace and kept himself grounded during high-stress events. He was never sharp with her, and when their eyes met, it was as though the last six years had been stripped away. That was when she saw the same vulnerable, scared, resilient man before her.

Lifting her shirt, she ran her hand over her belly, the scarred ridges of puckered flesh under her fingers a reminder of how she had changed. When she stripped her clothes off, she was no longer the same woman he remembered. She was alive but dead inside, her heart only beating at the thought of, or the sight of, the man in the shower. Even though she knew she couldn't be with him again, a tiny piece of her heart wanted that chance. A second chance at a fleeting love of youthful innocence. It wasn't youthful innocence, though. It was a shared understanding of a shared experience that shaped who they would become. The love wasn't fleeting, either. It was still there. She could feel it every time they touched, but it was a different kind of love now. Instead of a roaring flame of desire, it was a barely-there ember that could remember what they had together but could never flare strong enough to start that fire again.

Lilah shook her head and sighed, rubbing her face while she tried to refocus on the things she learned during her search. She had sent Mina a message asking if she had more information about the charges against Burris, but she hadn't replied yet. It had only been a few hours, but she was anxious to make some part of this complicated, frustrated puzzle fit together. She had purposely not mentioned what she found to Mina, hoping that Lucas could help her understand it before relaying the information to the team.

When she heard Lucas rustling about in the bathroom to dress, she made him a cup of coffee from the single cup maker on the counter and handed it to him when he came out.

"Thanks," he said, lifting it in the air. "Did you track down the trunk?"

He lowered himself to the end of the bed to sit opposite her while they talked. She liked how he was always dialed in on her and was never distracted by outside factors. She could tell he had a firm handle on everything outside the motel, which was very quiet right now.

"I didn't track it down. It's nowhere to be found, but that's not all," Delilah said, spinning in her chair and showing him how she had made a spreadsheet as she cross-referenced all the items she couldn't find.

"Wait, all of them are missing?"

"Missing in the respect that I can't find any of them in the places I sent them or even as being checked into a museum. My original thought was maybe they got the wrong shipping labels put on, so I looked for each one at each of the six museums, but there was nothing."

"How is that possible?"

"That's what I've been asking myself for hours. I'll keep checking the remaining items, but I feel squishy inside."

"Squishy?" he asked, his head tipped to the side in confusion.

"That two plus two doesn't equal four in this case. Squishy in my gut, wondering if I blindly participated in something I shouldn't have."

"You were following orders, Lilah. Don't take whatever this is on your shoulders. Can you tell me first why these items needed to be protected and second why they would disappear?"

"No," she said with a shake of her head. "Well, I know they were being protected from theft or destruction from war. Why they'd disappear is anyone's guess. They may not have disappeared. They could be in a warehouse somewhere. All I can do is follow the paper trail that leads me nowhere."

"It's been six years. Maybe they were returned to their respective countries already?"

"I would say that's possible if there was any evidence that they had been checked into a museum and back out again. We don't have that evidence, and like anything in the military, it should be there with bells on."

"True," he agreed, his hands massaging her shoulders as he stood over her chair to read the screen. He worked at the knotted muscles that were the consequences of too much time hunched over the laptop, stress and too many years away. But with his hands on her again, she melted under the familiarity of his touch. "Did Mina find anything while I was asleep?"

"I messaged her but haven't heard back." An idea came to her, and she glanced up at him. "I just thought of something!"

Her fingers flew across the keyboard until a website popped up.

"The Smithsonian?" he asked, his hands pausing on her shoulders.

"They were going to host one of the full exhibits we sent over."

"Six years ago, darling," he said in that familiar drawl that sent her right back to the first time they met. He'd driven her to the cafeteria where they'd had lunch together. When it was time to part, he'd said, "If I never see you again, I want you to know I think you're darling. A bright spot in a place where there are few to go around and little is charming. I do hope to see you again, my darling Delilah." I guess that was the moment she'd become smitten with Warrant Officer Porter.

"Right, and I don't expect them to still have the exhibit open, but their archives are open to the public to search. Since I have the names of those exhibits on the flash drive, it's easy to see if they were ever on display at the museum."

She typed the name of one of the exhibits into the search box, changing spellings and the order of the words every way she could to get a hit, but nothing came up, no matter what she typed in. He continued to massage her shoulders, which relaxed her and keyed her up simultaneously. Being with this man again was hard enough, but having his hands on her and knowing she couldn't have him was torture.

"There's nothing here."

"I'm starting to share your squishy feeling," he said, gazing at the screen. "Something should have come up, right?"

"Many somethings," she agreed, facing him to break the connection between his hands and her body.

Delilah stood and started pacing, trying to think of other ways to search for these exhibits. There were so many museums they could have gone to if they'd been routed wrong, but after all these years, it was anyone's guess where.

"There you go, buddy," Lucas said, lowering himself to the bed again after he put food in Haven's bowl. "We slept through breakfast." The dog tucked into the bowl, crunching kibble as she continued to pace. "The question is, why were none of these things put on exhibit if that was why they were sent here?"

She tapped her chin and stared at the window, the ugly, brown floral curtains blocking the snow and the daylight from the room. She was wrapped in a cocoon of safety that she knew would dissipate when she stepped out those doors. Someone was still after her, and she needed to figure out why.

"No!" she exclaimed as her heart started to pound. "The question isn't why weren't they on exhibit."

Luca was leaning back on the bed, braced on both hands, when he glanced up at her. "Okay, what is the question then?"

"The question is and always has been, why do they keep trying to kill me?"

In one fluid motion, Lucas stood in front of her. "Kill you? I thought they were trying to take you against your will."

"In the beginning," she agreed, intimidated by his stance before her. As she gazed into his eyes, she accepted it wasn't intimidation. It was protection. He would take a bullet for her before he let her get hurt. She leaned into his chest with her fist and forearm, the memories of the last few days hitting her square in the chest. "You might remember that the last few attempts have been all bullets and no brawn."

Instinctively, he grasped the fist she had against his chest and held it there. "We haven't stopped moving long enough for me to consider that, but you're right. They weren't trying to take you hostage. They were trying to kill you."

"The last time they found me, right before I sent you the message, they came in guns blazing, too. I think they shot my neighbor." Her eyes closed, and her voice broke on the last word. "That's on me."

"No," he said, tenderly kissing her forehead. "That's on the guy with the gun and no one else. He didn't need to shoot your neighbor. He chose to shoot your neighbor. You can't blame yourself for anything that's happened over the years since we were discharged."

"I do, though. I made choices that had ripples of consequences both for me and the people around me without them even knowing."

"What dictated those choices?"

She leaned her head against his chest to avoid his gaze. "The people after me. The alerts that I'd been found. The fear that filled me all day, every day."

"The people after you. That's who is responsible for any fallout around us, Lilah. I think it's time to go back to the beginning if we want to sort this out."

"Back to the beginning?" she asked, lifting her head.

"To the first time you were attacked. I want to know everything day by day, year by year, until we met up again on that island."

"Luca, that would take all day."

His hands went out to his sides to motion around the room. "We have no place to be. In fact, we have nowhere to go until we come up with some reason why ex-military hitmen keep knocking on your door, so let's do our due diligence now in the hopes that a week from now, you'll have your life back."

She held his gaze, read his thoughts and understood his frustrations. There was more in those chocolate eyes than determination and frustration, though. There was desire. A heat she knew all too well. A need left unfulfilled for too long. Her reckoning was coming, but she had an ace in the hole that would squelch that desire and extinguish the ember once and for all. She just had to be strong enough to play it.

Chapter Sixteen

Lucas listened to Lilah walk him step-by-step through the horrifying events she'd lived through over the last six years. Delilah was stronger than anyone he'd ever known, and he let her slip through his fingers. The moment she didn't show up to visit at the hospital as promised, he should have checked himself out and gone after her before her trail went cold. Instead, he let his past abandonment issues with his mother color the situation. He let his pain and his pride prevent him from tearing apart the entire country to find her.

"Why did I allow this to happen to you?" he muttered when she turned from the makeshift whiteboard they'd made with paper on the motel wall.

"Luca, you didn't allow anything. You had no control over it."

"I had control over what I did the moment you didn't come back to visit me. I had control over the way I let my hurt and embarrassment at being discarded by another woman I loved consume me. I should have stopped to remember the Delilah Hartman I knew. That woman always kept her promises. If I had looked at it in the proper light, I would have realized that you didn't abandon me.

No, that's what I did to you!" he exclaimed, his finger jabbing himself in the chest.

Lilah laid the marker down on the desk and walked to him, slipping her arms around his waist to rest her head on his chest. The memories hit him from the early days, but when he gazed down at her, the reality of the situation was evident in the jagged scars across her chin.

"You have to stop, Luca. I would have thought the same if I had been in your shoes. This isn't about who did the right or the wrong thing. This situation is about circumstances neither of us controlled, okay?"

Rather than agree or disagree, he held her, his chin resting on her head as he swallowed every bit of her warmth and comfort. His gaze was pinned on the wall of information that she'd been writing down, searching for any pattern or clue as to who was terrorizing her and why.

"What does 'The Mask' mean?" he asked, looking at the four events she'd written the words next to, including one just a few weeks ago.

She stepped out of his arms, and while he mourned the loss of her heat, he had finally found a pattern. He walked to the board and pointed to the four dates. The first was the night she'd dropped him at the hospital. The second was several years later, the third was about ten months ago and the final one was the night her neighbor had been shot.

"Those are the times I was approached by the guy I call 'The Mask.' He wore one of those extremely cold weather military masks."

"The ones that cover the nose and mouth and only leave the eyes uncovered?"

"Creepy as all get-out up close on a dark street," she said, a shudder going through her. "He covered his eyes with reflective sunglasses or goggles, which made it more terrifying. You could see your reflection in the lenses. You were a witness to your own agony splashed across your face with the jab of his knife. All you could wonder was what sick pleasure he took in being anonymous while he hurt you."

Lucas walked to her and ran his finger down the scar on her chin. "He's responsible for this?" Her nod was short. "Tell me exactly what he said to you that night, Lilah."

"The other guy always did the talking, but The Mask, he came in hot with the knife, sliced me up and left me for the other two guys to acquire—"

"Who always failed to?"

"Oddly enough, yes," she said with a shrug. "I could always escape their grip and run, but I knew they'd be back."

"Could that have been on purpose?"

"Like, they let me go?" she asked, and he nodded, adding a half a head tilt to make it questionable. Another shudder went through her before she answered. "You think they were just playing with me?"

"I don't know what to think other than he had a chance to slit your throat that night and didn't," he said, pointing at her chin and neck. "Instead, he stopped just short of slicing your carotid. He could have ended you being a problem six years ago instead of 'hunting' you for all of them," he said, adding air quotes. "It doesn't make sense." The more he studied the map and the list of attacks, the less sense it made. "What happened in year three when he showed up?"

If she thought he missed the subtle way she crossed her arms over her belly, she was wrong. "Same type of situation. He came in, tortured me a little and left me for the other two." She held up her hand. "Except he whispered that time."

"What did he say?"

Her tender throat bobbed once as her eyes went closed. "That the next time would be our last visit together. As the pawn, I can only move forward, not backward or sideways, the way he could as the king. He said I was surrounded and he'd made sure I had nowhere to go but where he sent me. He also said no one could help me now and that he'd be back to collect his pawn when he needed her to win the game."

An expletive fell from Lucas's lips before he walked to her and wrapped her in his arms. "I'm so sorry, darling. He's playing a game that only he understands. He didn't attack you with a knife the last two times?"

"Oh, yes," she whispered, a shiver spiking through her until he rubbed it away with his warm hand against her back. "He definitely attacked with a knife. He took extreme pleasure in hurting me."

Lucas stepped back and eyed her. "Where?"

"It doesn't matter, Luca," she said, but he caught the spike of fear in her eyes. "What matters is now I can't stop thinking that those guys let me go each time at The Mask's orders."

"Where, Lilah?" he asked again as though he hadn't heard her last sentence. "Tell me where."

He waited and watched the war reflected in her eyes

until she shook her head. "I'm not showing you." Her swallow was so harsh it was audible, and he stepped toward her again. "I will say that when he found me ten months ago, it was so bad I shouldn't have been able to fight them off or escape, but I did. Why didn't I think of that? They never wanted to capture me. They wanted to toy with me."

"Why do you think that is?"

She walked to the wall and stood in front of it. "They wanted to keep me off balance? They wanted me to move?"

"They wanted you too scared to go to the authorities?" Lucas asked, coming up behind her.

"Or to think the police wouldn't help me if I did go to them," she agreed. "Not that I ever did or could. With my clearance level, walking into a police station was a sure way to put Delilah Hartman back on the map."

"I hadn't thought of that, but you're right," he agreed. "Then they'd ask why you were using a different name. When he attacked you ten months ago, the words he whispered were chilling. He would come and collect his pawn, 'when he needed her to win the game.' Is that what made you believe this had something to do with the flash drive of information?"

"I didn't know what else it could be about, Lucas. I was afraid they knew I had read The Lost Key of Honor file and had information I shouldn't have."

"If that were the case, killing you would have been the right answer. The fact that they didn't makes me think you know something—"

"Or they think I know something," she interrupted. "Something I don't know."

"That you think you don't know, but you don't know what it is, so there's no way to know if you know it or not."

Lilah burst out laughing, nearly doubling over as her shoulders shook. When she got herself under control, even he was grinning despite the grim circumstances. "That was the most convoluted but understandable sentence I've ever heard. Whether I know something or not is beside the point because they think I do. What are we going to do with this mess?" she asked, letting her hand flick at the wall until it fell to her side.

"We're going to contact Mina and see if she can find out where Major Burris was on the dates The Mask attacked you."

Rather than respond, she just stood in one place and stared at him open-mouthed. "Are you—have you lost it? Major Burris?"

Lucas took her shoulders and forced eye contact with her. "We know your medal was most likely what they used to track you. That indicates military involvement. We also know the guys who are tracking you are ex-military. We know that all those artifacts that are missing shouldn't be. It's not a stretch to think Burris is somehow involved in this."

"It wasn't him," she said, shaking her head. "I know it wasn't him behind that mask. I didn't recognize his voice."

"Maybe not, but it doesn't hurt to have Mina find out where he was, right?"

"It's not him, Lucas."

"Humor me?"

Lilah motioned at the phone on the table and sat on

the bed to watch him type. He kept his facial expression neutral despite the fire raging through his veins. He wanted to find the man tormenting her and give him a taste of his own medicine. Right or wrong. He would do anything to protect Lilah now that she was back in his life, but he couldn't protect her from the pain and fear she suffered in the past, and that filled him with rage. He snapped the phone down on the desk and stalked toward her. "Show me."

"Show you what?" she asked, her head cocked to the side in confusion.

"Where The Mask cut you."

"Absolutely not," she said between clenched teeth.

"What are you afraid of, Lilah?"

"I'm not afraid of anything, Luca. What happened in the past should stay in the past."

"If I had a million dollars, I would bet all of it that where he cut you is why you turned me down on the once-and-done request yesterday."

"Wow," she said, drawing out the last *w*. "You do think highly of yourself."

"Not at all," he said, taking another step closer. "But I know you—"

"No, you knew me. There's a difference, Luca. I'm not the same woman who left that hospital. That woman is gone."

"Maybe some of her is gone, but the woman I held on my lap with my lips on hers in an old motel was the same woman I held on my lap with my lips on hers on a beach in the middle of Lake Superior. At least until that woman remembered she had something to hide."

The phone beeped, and she let out a relieved breath. "You better get that. It's Mina."

"She's on it," he said, dropping the phone to the desk. "Said she'd get back to us, as she had just gotten into the files on Burris's trial."

"Good. Maybe we'll finally get the information to move forward and clear my name." She turned and walked to Haven, patting him on the top of his head where he slept. When she turned back around, Lucas grasped her arm.

"You can pretend the past doesn't matter if that makes you feel better, but one day, I will find out what that animal did to you and I will kiss every last scar."

He dropped his voice to the timbre he knew always made her melt inside. The timbre that said he meant every word and what he said could be trusted.

"Just in case the destruction of my face isn't enough for you," she said, righteous indignation filling her words, "let me make it incredibly clear that I'm your past, Lucas, and you should be glad I am!"

With her fingers shaking and tears in her eyes, she lifted her shirt to reveal what she'd been hiding all this time. Unable to process the scene before him, he stumbled backward onto the bed without a word.

Chapter Seventeen

Pain flooded Delilah as the look on his face transformed from caring to stunned to horrified. She hated that she had to destroy the memory of what she used to be to him, but it didn't matter. When this was over, they'd part ways and this moment of humiliation could be stored in the box where she kept all of her Lucas Porter memories.

She turned away and walked to the window, pulling back the curtain to see the snow still falling and the sky getting darker. The sun set early as Christmas approached, and she couldn't help but wonder if she'd live to see her thirty-fourth Christmas. It used to be her favorite season—not for the decorations, goodies or gifts, but for the sense of hope and renewal it ushered in. When she was a child, her father was the one who made Christmas merry. He loved everything about the season, from the carols to the candy to the tree and treats. After he died, her mom worked hard to keep joy in the holiday, but there was always something missing.

Then she joined the service and spent her first Christmas away from home. She had struggled to find joy that first year, so she was surprised it came so easily to her in the midst of war. Delilah had found joy in singing

Christmas carols around a tiny tree and sharing treats sent by caring family members simply by reminding herself that Christmas, no matter the place, was a time for family. The soldiers on the base were her family, and she took comfort in having them. During war, Christmas was a time of hope for peace, even if that hope was always short-lived. That hadn't changed since she left the service. The last six Christmases she had spent alone but always took a moment to find joy in the day, and hope that it would be her last Christmas under wraps. It was then she realized, one way or the other, this was the end.

Her heart pulsed hard, and she rubbed her chest, but it didn't relieve the pain. Luca was everything she had wanted in her past life, but now he could be nothing to her, even if she wished their lives could be different. This would be their first and last Christmas together, leaving her with nothing but memories for every Christmas season to come—if she made it out of this alive, that is.

"My God," he whispered, his breath whooshing out again. "How did you survive something like that, Lilah?"

"He made sure to slice me just deep enough that I was maimed but not deep enough to kill me. It took forty-four stitches the first time and seventy-seven the second time to put me back together. The hospitals forced me to file a police report, but it didn't matter. The woman who walked into that hospital ceased to exist the moment she left."

"This sick animal needs to be stopped," Lucas said between clenched teeth. "We've got you now," he said, walking to where she stood at the window. "I know you don't need protecting, but I'm going to be here to fight with you until we find him and end this game he's playing."

"I want to believe that, but we've been together for two days and are no further ahead than when you found me."

"You're wrong. We have pieces of the puzzle, but we're missing the one pivotal piece that will bring the picture into focus and reveal the artist behind the design. You've fought too long and worked too hard to give up now."

Delilah knew that to be the truth. "But I only did it for you, Luca. I wanted to protect you."

"Then let me protect you now, my darling Delilah."

His words were desperate, and she turned just as he pulled her into him and took her lips, reminding her of all the reasons she had to keep those memories of Lucas locked up in a box. Allowing herself to feel them was too painful. Her heart and body couldn't take more pain. Still, she kissed him back, unable to deny herself the feel of his lips and the way his hot tongue cuddled hers.

"Lucas, we can't," she said, her lips still pressed to his. "We can't do this. It's not fair to either of us."

"Do you know what's not fair?" he asked, walking her backward to the bed. "Thinking I desire you less than I did before because of superficial scars on your skin. It's unfair to yourself and me. It's as though you think I'm superficial and never really cared about you."

"I don't think that, Luca," she whispered as he set her down on the edge of the bed and hoisted her up to the pillows. "When I say it's unfair, I mean it's unfair to ourselves knowing we can never be together again."

"Never is a dangerous word, Delilah Hartman. I never

thought I'd see you again, but here you are, under my lips, reminding me why you never left my mind all these years. Why you were the last thought I had every day and the first every morning."

He lifted her shirt while he whispered sweet nothings, letting the cool air brush across her tender skin. She had a decision to make. Stop this now and continue to fight against the current trying to pull them under, or let herself have a moment of pleasure in a world full of pain.

His lips feathered a kiss across where her naval used to be before the ropy scar took over in a morbid smiley face. With a sharp intake of breath, her belly quivered as he moved his lips to the left and kissed her again, following the trail of the scar to her rib cage. His hands, so familiar against her skin, wrapped around her torso and pushed the shirt to her bra, making room for his lips as he traced another jagged scar to the right and down to her hip.

How was she supposed to fight against this when it felt so good? So right? His words came back to her. Once and done. It would never be done for her, but as he trailed his tongue across another scar, she decided once was better than none.

"Luca," she whispered, her breath heavy in her chest. When he lifted his head, his pupils were dilated and filled with heady need. "We don't have any protection."

A wicked smile lifted his lips as he rose and rifled through a bag beside the bed. He came up with a silver package in his hand. "Secure One has us covered," he promised, tossing it on the nightstand before he went back to kissing her belly, drawing a moan from her lips.

The sound was fuel to his flame, and he tossed her

glasses on the nightstand, stripped her of her shirt and, just as quickly, her bra. He leaned back on his knees, his gaze raking her breasts. "You're even more beautiful than the last time I made love to you. I didn't think that was possible. Softer. Sweeter," he whispered, his head dipping to tease a nipple with his tongue.

"The last six years haven't been kind to my body," she whispered, her hands sliding into his soft locks.

He lifted his head and took her lips for a hot ride through the past. "Darling, your body is my resting place. Always has been. That hasn't changed."

Rather than answer, she slid her hands under his shirt until he grasped the hem and pulled it over his head, letting it sail across the room. Her hands roamed over his muscles while he quickly did away with their boots and cargo pants. He loomed over her, his gaze filled with flames, and then, slowly and with the utmost tenderness, he lowered himself to rest gently across her body, their lips perfectly aligned.

He closed his eyes as his lips neared hers. "I have dreamed about this day for so long, Lilah. To cover you again and let your aura raise my soul from its resting place. To forget about everything for the moments that we're joined as one."

His honesty brought tears to her eyes, and she reached up to stroke his cheek before she grasped the package from the nightstand and tore it open. "Let's be one then and forget about anything but how we make each other feel."

Lucas dove in for a kiss while she deftly rolled the sheath over him, drawing a moan from deep in his throat. The room quieted for a single breath as he filled her before he swallowed her soft moan with his lips. Fire built in her belly, spiraling until her legs shook and her nails raked his back while she begged him to let her go. To let her fly into the sky and for him to be there with her, holding her hand as they soared.

"Patience, beautiful," he whispered, thrusting forward again as he nipped her earlobe. "We only get one second chance, and I'm going to cherish every last second of it."

With her head pressed into the pillow, she raised her hips, allowing him to slip a bit deeper to nestle in the place he loved the most. He told her that spot, that little piece of heaven, was his dwelling place.

"Lilah!" he exclaimed, his hips pressed tightly to hers. "I'm home." He whispered those two words into her ear as he thrust one more time and carried her over the threshold and into a second chance at life together.

"Secure one, Whiskey."

Lucas quickly moved to the desk and connected the computer. "Secure two, Lima." His gaze darted to Lilah, who was asleep on the bed. After they'd made love twice, she had showered and fallen into an exhausted slumber. He didn't want to wake her, so he addressed Mina quickly with a finger to his lips.

"She's exhausted," he said, without adding the part about how he was responsible for it.

"I can understand why. This is a nightmare of a dumpster fire, and none of us have an extinguisher."

Lucas couldn't help but chuckle. Leave it to Mina to sum it up so perfectly. "I couldn't agree more."

"I can't even imagine dealing with this alone the way

she has been for so many years. It's one twisted mess. I'm not sure we'll ever get to the bottom of it, but I'm not giving up. That said, dealing with the government is like entering the second level of hell whenever you need information."

"You're not wrong," he agreed, his gaze sliding to the bed again to check on Lilah. "Did you find anything?"

"I found some interesting tidbits, but still no trunk. It's like it never existed in the world, even though we know it did."

"Lilah searched a bunch of archives, too, but never found proof that it was in the possession of a history museum in the United States. There was also no history of it being returned to its rightful country."

"What's going on?" Lilah asked behind him, rubbing her face several times before climbing out from under the blanket he'd covered her with when she fell asleep. Thankfully, she had been fully dressed.

Lucas's cheeks heated, and his body stirred at the thought of holding her again, but he had to accept that their second chance had come and gone. Once she was free, the last place she'd want to be was confined within the walls of Secure One. Unfortunately for him, he needed those confines to feel safe. For a brief moment, while buried deep inside her, he wondered if he could be safe wherever she was, but he knew the truth. He was far more likely to hurt her when his world wasn't stable, and that was the last thing he wanted. She was happy with one and done, so he had no choice but to accept the same—even if it had been two and never done for him.

"I was just telling Lucas what a dumpster fire this mess is."

Lilah's laughter filled the room as she walked toward him until he could feel her heat wrap him up tightly again. "I wish I could say you're wrong, but I can't. It makes less and less sense the deeper we dig."

"Well, what I have to tell you also aligns with that."

"Oh, boy," Lucas said as he stood and offered Lilah the chair. "What did you find?"

"I'm glad you're sitting down," Mina said, her lips twisted into a grimaced smile. "When I got down to the paperwork regarding Burris's war crimes—" she put the words in quotations "—you're listed as a key witness to the events."

"I'm what now?" she asked, leaning in as though she hadn't heard her right. "I'm not sure I understand. The paperwork says I turned him in?"

"No, I can't see who turned him in. Just that you are listed as a key witness to the crimes."

"The crimes he didn't commit or go to jail for?"

Mina pointed at her with a nod. "Did you witness Major Burris commit any war crimes?"

"Seriously?" Lilah asked, her voice full of frustration and anger. "I worked with him only while I was in Germany. I was a computer geek. I had nothing to do with what was happening on the field."

"That's not true," Lucas said, leaning on the back of her chair with both hands to avoid touching her how he wanted to. Mina couldn't suspect there was more than friendship between them, or she'd insist that Cal replace him with someone who could be impartial about the situation. That wouldn't be necessary. As a soldier, he'd learned to separate his personal life from his professional, and he could do the same now, even if his personal life was at the heart of this professional situation. "You were tracking the ops and fielding any issues with the technology."

"Which," Mina said with a tip of her head, "if Burris was committing war crimes using the operations you were tracking, would make you a key witness."

"Even if I wasn't aware?"

"That is the question," Mina agreed. "You can be a witness to a crime without knowing, but that doesn't mean you can testify to those crimes in any way."

"The next question is, why wasn't I notified that I was considered a witness?" Lilah asked, her voice loud and clear now that the sleep and shock had disappeared. "And why wasn't I called to make a statement before they released him from the charges?"

"Those are also questions I can't answer other than…" She paused and shifted in her chair, obviously uncomfortable and not because of the pregnancy. She wasn't comfortable with what she had to say next.

"Other than?" Lilah asked. "Be straight with me, Mina. If this all comes down to something that happened in the service that I'm not aware of, I'd like to get it straightened out and get my life back before more years are stolen." Delilah tipped her head up to make eye contact with Lucas. He tried to keep his smile easy, when all he wanted to do was pull her into his arms and protect her from all of this.

"I wonder if the information I can see has been doctored."

"Whatever for?" Lilah asked. "Why would they need to doctor paperwork to make it look like I was a witness to something I wasn't a witness to?"

"As a reason to track you," Lucas said without hesitation.

Mina tipped her head in agreement. "That was my first thought, too."

"Tracking me is one thing. Attempted murder is something else entirely."

"I did warn you that this would make no sense," Mina said with a shrug. "As for Burris, he's living near Rochester now with his wife. He isn't working anywhere, but is heavily involved in several veteran organizations."

"Nothing else nefarious?" Lilah asked.

"On Burris? Not yet, but I will search property records, vehicles and bank situations. I came across something else that I thought was definitely concerning."

That got Lucas's attention, and he spun around a chair to straddle it. "How concerning?"

"Deadly," she said, her lips thinning for a moment. "It may be nothing, but I was hoping Delilah could shed some light on it."

"I'll do my best, but I've been out of touch with the world for years."

"While I was researching Burris," she said, shuffling papers around until she grabbed one from the pile, "I found the names of four other logistics officers listed as key witnesses to his war crimes."

"That's not surprising," Lilah said. "The supply chain in the military is massive. There were a lot of logistics officers."

"Agreed," Mina said, flicking her eyes to Lucas. The look she gave him said what came next was the surprising part. He put his arm around Lilah to ground her.

"When I searched those women, I discovered all four of them are dead."

The room was silent for two beats before Lilah spoke. "They're what now?"

"Dead," Mina repeated. "All victims of violent crimes."

"Did they involve knives?" Lilah asked, and Lucas heard her voice quiver on the last word.

"Three of the four," Mina answered. "This is the part that confuses me. All four of them were living under an alias like you. The first two women were found in an alley, as though it was a mugging gone wrong. Ultimately, their fingerprints were used to identify them since their identifications were poor fakes. Another woman was found naked in bed. It was staged to look like a BDSM scene gone wrong, but she had been strangled and moved to the bed. The final woman was pulled from a river. Whoever killed her made it look like she jumped, but the police have questions since she was obviously stabbed before she went into the river. That victim was also using a false name."

"I have questions," Lucas said, rubbing Lilah's back to keep her grounded. A shudder went through her, and he gently squeezed her neck to comfort her. As her anxiety built, Haven raised his head, assessed the situation and walked to Lilah, resting his head on her leg. Lucas noticed her stroke his head, and her shoulders relaxed as she did.

"The deaths of four women who did the same job I did is not a coincidence, Mina."

"You won't get an argument out of me. It is a dead end since the crimes were never solved. They remain open, but the last death was a year ago, so they're all cold cases now."

"Wait," Lucas said, leaning forward. "When did they find the first woman?"

Mina searched the paper and counted backward. "Almost five years ago. The next woman was found three years ago, the third was two years ago, and the river victim was last year."

"I was next," Lilah said, her voice surprisingly steady. "That's why The Mask showed up at the apartment building this time. It was my turn to die."

"The Mask?" Mina asked, glancing between them.

"That's what she called him," Lucas said before Lilah could. He didn't want her to have to explain it. "He did that to her chin and cut her several other places."

"I noticed the scars when you were dressing," Mina admitted, addressing Lilah now. "I'm so sorry that happened to you."

"Lucas pointed out that any of the three times he attacked me, he could have killed me." Mina nodded her agreement. "It was about ten months ago when he showed up and whispered in my ear. He said I was his pawn and he'd come for me when it was time for him to win the game."

"That's what finally spurred her to contact me," Lucas explained. "When he showed up a few weeks ago, she knew she was out of time."

"I was hoping to use the flash drive as a bargaining chip for my life," Lilah said, sarcastic laughter filling the room. "That was never going to happen."

"I'm curious as to why these other women were killed,

though," Mina said, flipping the camera to show the entire room since Cal and Eric had walked in.

"Is it possible you weren't the only one shipping artifacts back to the States?" Cal asked, sitting down at the table.

"I never considered it, but there had to be people on other bases also taking in antiquities to protect, right? There were other bases in other parts of those countries. You would think word would spread like wildfire throughout the curator community that we would keep their treasures safe. Do you have the real names of the women who were killed, Mina?"

Mina nodded and read off the women's names and ranks, but Delilah shook her head before she finished.

"I don't know any of them. Not that unusual, as I was working more cybersecurity than supply chain by that point in the war, but what is unusual is that they all died questionable deaths."

"And the timeline is scarily precise," Mina finished. "As though someone was checking off a box once something was completed."

"We just need to know what that something was and who was killing them," Lilah said with a groan. "Were there any other witnesses listed on the paperwork?"

"No, it was the five of you, and you're the only one left standing."

Lucas tipped his head to the side. "Mina, did any of those women get medals for their service?"

"Boy, I didn't dig that far. Do you think it's important?"

"I do," Cal said. "That's why we're here. Eric retrieved the medal from the abandoned house today."

"It was still there?" Lilah asked. "I figured if they were tracking me with it, they'd take it."

"They might have if they had time to search for it," Eric said, pulling out a chair. "But the medal was in the tree with the camera. I put it there to protect it. It would lead them to the house, but my gut said the tracker wasn't pinpoint accurate."

"Meaning it just gave them a general area she was in?" Lucas asked.

"Exactly," Eric agreed as he pulled it from his pocket. The medal was in two parts now as he laid them on the table. "I apologize that it's ruined," he said to Lilah, who shrugged as though she no longer cared. "When I broke it open, inside was the smallest GPS I've ever seen. Lucas, you were right. It was solar powered."

"You didn't bring it back to base with you, right?" Lucas asked, and Eric shook his head.

"No, that's why I did it in the field. I left the tracker in the tree. If they tag it again, it will get plenty of power to keep it active. I wasn't sure if we'd need it for evidence, so I didn't want to destroy it."

"All of that said, what's our next move?" Lucas asked.

The room fell silent until Lilah spoke. "I think it's time we pay my old major a little visit."

"No. Not happening," Lucas said, leaning over the chair and grasping her shoulders. "You're not going anywhere near him."

"Do you have a better idea?" Delilah asked, her gaze locked with his as though the rest of the team no longer existed in the conversation. "You know what they say. If you want the truth, get it straight from the horse's mouth."

"She's not wrong," Mina said from the computer.

"You're not helping, Mina," Lucas snapped.

"She is, though," Lilah reminded him. "That's why this has to end. I've gotten so many people involved in this nightmare, including you. It's my responsibility to get you back out of it alive and in one piece. I can't do that holed up in this motel room!"

"I don't like it," Lucas said, his hand fisted in his hair. "We don't have enough information to walk into a mission we don't understand and expect to come out unscathed."

"I don't like it, either," Mina and Cal said in unison, giving the moment a bit of levity. "But she's right," Mina finished. "There is no way to solve this from that motel room. Let us talk together as a team about options. We'll call you back?"

Lucas shook his head in defeat. "Fine, but I already know this is not smart."

"Maybe, but I'm not sure we have any other move on the board. Whiskey, out."

The screen went black, and the room went silent.

"Luca," Lilah finally said, her voice soft in the quiet of the room. "You know I'm right about this."

The answer he had to give was one she wouldn't like, so he said nothing while he shrugged on his field coat and grabbed Haven's lead. "We're going to check the perimeter. Lock the door behind me."

"Luca," she called as he opened the door and walked out into the blackness, but he let the night swallow anything else she had to say.

Chapter Eighteen

If Lucas was going to agree to this plan, Delilah needed to find a tidbit of information to prove that going to Burris was the only answer, even if she already knew it was the only answer. She didn't know how she knew, but something told her the only way to find the end was to start at the beginning.

That was her plan as she opened The Lost Key of Honor file again and started scrolling. She had read it so many times that nothing stuck out to her as applicable. There had to be something, though. Claiming five women were witnesses to something they couldn't back up with facts just to kill them didn't make sense otherwise. Then again, if Lucas was right, and the war crimes occurred during the ops, she'd be in charge of troubleshooting, so it was possible she had information and didn't know it. That honestly felt like the only answer as she scrolled down the rows, because the file revealed nothing it hadn't already. All this correspondence was nothing more than a back-and-forth sharing of buildings checked, people contacted and the next steps.

While she read, her mind wandered back to the time spent in bed with Lucas. They'd gone as slow as they could the first time they'd made love, but it was still too fast. The second time had been more about learning how they had changed and discovering how they had stayed the same. Their touch had been gentler, longer and more precise, leading to an intimacy they hadn't shared that first summer. She knew why, too. That summer, they thought they'd be together forever. This Christmas, they knew their time together was fleeting.

Someone in the room next door dropped something, and Delilah jumped, accidentally clicking the mouse on the file. That click brought up a box asking her if she wanted to go to the link provided. Did she? Yes. Could she? Her gaze tracked to the VPN that had her as a user based in Switzerland. There were ways to see a VPN, but she hoped the file no longer mattered or they would take it at face value if they noticed anyone on the link. Her laughter filled the room. No, they'd know immediately that Delilah Hartman had clicked the link, but Cal's stealth VPN was impossible to get around. It offered her a cloak of invisibility she never had before when online. If ever there was a time to take advantage of it, now was that time.

A click on the yes button took her to a chat website and into a private room. There was a chat transcript going back eight years, with the latest entries from someone named *Iamthatguy* being one month ago when he'd replied to someone called *Bigmanoncampus*.

Any luck this time?

None. I don't believe this tablet exists anymore. If it did, it surely would have been found by now.

I don't care what you believe. The tablet is out there.

Do you have any new leads? I sure as hell don't. It may be time to let it go, boss.

Don't tell me to let it go! We're a month from the big event and we still don't have the main attraction! I've got a new lead, but I'll need you to go back to where this started. The information will come in the usual manner. I'll be waiting to hear.

When *Iamthatguy* responded, he certainly didn't sound happy.

Back to the beginning? This is exhausting and I'm not getting any younger. I'll go one last time, but after that, I'm out.

You're out when I say you're out! *Bigmanoncampus* replied. Delilah could almost hear the venom dripping from his words. Get the job done, we're running out of time! If you don't, you'll be spending your Christmas in a very small box.

Delilah had no doubt they were talking about the tablet to open the trunk. Undeterred, she scrolled up to a feature where items could be pinned, curious about the files and why they would pin them there. She clicked open the first file and was surprised to see a map of a small village in Iraq. It had been methodically marked off with a red *x* through each building on the image. The following three files she opened were the same.

The fourth was a list of names with red lines drawn through each one.

"The snow has stopped, but with that fresh layer on the ground, it's cold," Lucas said, coming back inside with a snow-covered Haven. His return surprised her, and she glanced up to see him strip off his coat and pull off Haven's boots.

"How long have you been out there?"

"Too long," he answered, motioning for Haven to follow him to his food bowl. "But I cleared the van of snow so we can go."

"You agree that we need to find Burris?" she asked, her tone giving away her surprise.

"No, but we also can't stay here much longer." She could tell he was trying not to be short with her when all he wanted to do was shake her silly until she understood what a bad idea it was to show up on Burris's doorstep. She completely understood what a bad idea it was, but that didn't mean she had a choice. Lucas would end up on the run with her if they didn't do something soon. While she wouldn't mind that, something told her Cal and the other guys at Secure One would. No, it was time, once and for all, to find out what they wanted from her and give it to them. If they wanted her, she'd turn herself over to the US government and hope for the best. She couldn't continue to put other people at risk because she was afraid.

Her spine stiffened with the thought, and she turned back to the computer. There was one more file, and she clicked it open, but this time, page after page after page opened. "What is going on?" she muttered as Lucas came up behind her.

"What are you looking at?"

Without turning, she quickly flipped through the pages, stopping long enough to glance through each one. "I accidentally clicked inside the file for The Lost Key of Honor. It took me to this chat room–type website where *Iamthatguy* and *Bigmanoncampus* discuss their search for the missing tablet. This," she said, motioning at the screen, "has maps of villages in Iraq that were searched, and these," she tapped the open file on her screen, "are detailed dossiers on what I think are other artifacts they found during the search." She took a moment to read more of each file, a whistle escaping as she recognized several artifacts on the list she had been told to catalog. "What in the world?" The question was barely whispered as her hand froze on the mouse.

"What did you find?" he asked, kneeling beside her chair.

Her finger shaking, she pointed at the screen. "The trunk hasn't disappeared. Whoever these two guys are have it in their possession."

"They want access to it so when they find the tablet, they can open the trunk."

"Feels a little Indiana Jones in here, right?" Delilah asked, leaning back in the chair. "We all know that never ended well for the greedy treasure hunters."

Lucas stood and started to massage her shoulders again, almost like he knew she needed a calming hand at the helm. "It's not going to work out for these guys, either, once we find out who they are, that is. Is there a way to send these to Mina?"

"I can't download them," she said, checking the files' properties. "I could just send her the whole file." She bit her lip and stared at the screen. If she shared The Lost Key of Honor file with Mina, that made her a witness to anything illegal they found in the files and an accomplice to data theft. She didn't want to put that on Mina's or Secure One's back. Then again, considering what Mina did there, it wouldn't be her first rodeo with backdoor access to files.

"What are you thinking? Walk me through it," he encouraged, still massaging her shoulders.

"I could send Mina a digital copy of the entire flash drive. Then she'd have The Lost Key of Honor file and access to all of this and the full dossier on each artifact. The problem is that makes her a witness to any crimes we discover and an accomplice to any data we use to bring this to an end."

"Darling, if Mina was worried about being an accomplice to data theft, she wouldn't be doing what she's doing. Send her the file."

"Somehow, I knew you were going to say that." Laughter spilled from her lips, and it felt good amid all the angst that filled her.

Delilah enlarged the first open file and opened the snipping tool app.

"What are you doing? I thought you said you can't save the files."

"I can't, not in the traditional way, but I can take screenshots. There's a fifty-fifty chance that the chat room ceases to exist as soon as I close this tab."

"What now?" he asked, leaning on the desk, ankles crossed. "Why would it cease to exist?"

"There could be a failsafe on it, so if anyone but them login, it shuts itself down."

"Wouldn't that happen right away? It's letting you read it."

Delilah kept at her task as she talked, afraid he was right and the screen could go black any second. "I followed the link from the file, making the page think I was one of them, but I'm not taking any chances that Mina can't get back in to read this stuff." After a few more clicks of the mouse, she saved everything in a new file. While at it, she saved the chat in a sequence of screenshots and then highlighted the dates for Mina to see. "Okay, I think I have it all." She clicked out of the chat room and let out a sigh.

"Package that up and send it to Mina. Then, we're leaving."

"To go where?" she asked, adding the files to the flash drive and zipping the contents.

He held up his phone. "We're about to find out. Is that ready to go to her?" Delilah nodded, and Lucas hit the call button, holding the screen out for her to see. "Secure one, Lima," Luca said, waiting for a beat until they heard Mina's reply. When her face filled the screen, it was lined with fatigue. Delilah immediately felt guilty for putting this on their shoulders. What made her feel a little better was knowing this was almost over. They could all go back to their lives, even if she was lost to time forever.

THE VAN WAS unnaturally quiet. It was as though they were holding their breath, knowing something big was coming but unsure if they'd survive whatever it was. When the team called back, they sent them south, sticking to back roads and two-lane highways to avoid the freeway. Mina programmed the van's GPS with the location of Burris's house in Rochester. They'd head in that direction while she went through the files on the flash drive Lilah had sent.

He glanced at the woman in the seat next to him and fought back the wave of protectiveness that filled him. Hard as it was, he couldn't protect her from this. The only way out of it was through it. He feared the through part would leave them both shredded and bleeding. Four women were already dead. There was no way he would let her be the next one. What he was struggling to understand was, while a pet project wasn't unusual for the military, hiding other countries' treasures was immoral at best and illegal at worst. The US government would never sanction that. The only thing worse would be auctioning them off to the highest bidder. Lucas gasped.

Lilah glanced at him immediately. "What?" she asked. "Are you okay?"

"Fine, but I was just thinking. Do you think the two guys from the chat room plan to sell the artifacts on the black market?"

"Well, yeah. Going by the dates in the chat room, my bet is, they have an auction scheduled on Christmas Day. They want the tablet to complete the trunk, thereby making it the main attraction. It will surely bring a bidding war unlike any ever seen."

"Christmas Day?"

"He said the big event was in a month, counting forward that makes it Christmas Day. I see the allure of the ultrarich wanting a new trinket on that day."

"Okay, but how do you find buyers for stolen artifacts? It's not like you can use Sotheby's."

He couldn't help but smile when she laughed. He loved being the one to make her laugh now that they were together again. At least for however long they were together. This second chance of theirs could end quickly and without warning. That thought stole the smile from his lips.

"The black market is deep and dark, Luca. There are plenty of buyers for these artifacts who are all too happy to keep them locked away from the world forever. We can't let that happen."

"This *Bigmanoncampus* and *Iamthatguy*, do you think they're military?"

"I did get to the page via the file, so that would make the most sense."

"True." Lucas drove in silence for a few moments. "But what if the military is monitoring the page for intel?"

"Could be that, too," she agreed. "There's no way to know unless we can see who's behind the fake names, which I doubt even Mina can do. Not on the dark web like that."

"Wait, that was the dark web?"

"Uh, yeah," she said, biting her lip. "I thought you knew."

"I'm not a computer nerd, Lilah. I thought it was just a web page."

"Who you calling a computer nerd?" she asked haughtily before they both giggled.

It was several miles down the road before they got themselves together again. "Okay, this is serious business," Lucas said, but his smile defied that statement. He loved being with her again and refused to think about how boring life would be when she was gone.

"We already know these artifacts aren't in the museums," Lilah said, leaning back into the seat. "Which means they have to be somewhere else. They may not even be in the country at this point."

"I wish we knew if that chat room was being monitored by the military, created by them or owned by someone else entirely."

Lilah nodded, ready to speak, when the phone rang, making them both jump. Lucas hit the answer button on the dashboard. "Secure one, Lima."

"Secure two, Whiskey," Mina said.

"Did you find something?" Lilah asked, sitting forward in her seat to turn up the volume. Lucas scanned the road for somewhere to pull over and noticed an old rest stop ahead.

"Hang on, Mina, I'm going to pull over." He slowed, turned and pulled the van under overgrown trees before he doused the headlights. There was no sense in being a sitting target if someone was looking for them. "Go ahead."

"I haven't had time to go through all of the flash drive files yet, but I did get results for the property search on Burris."

Lilah glanced at Lucas quizzically. "I thought we knew that already. Isn't that why we're driving to Rochester?"

"Yes, he has a home in Rochester, but he also has hunting land southwest of the Rochester airport."

"There's hunting land all over that part of Minnesota. I'm not sure how that helps us," Lucas said, frustrated by the lack of answers at every turn.

"It may be nothing, but he applied for a building permit to put up a garage on that land. Said he was going to store his hunting equipment in it."

"That makes sense," Lucas said, a huff leaving his lips as he let out a long, frustrated breath. "We're in hunting country. You know that, Mina."

"I do," she agreed, "which is why I checked DNR records next. George Burris has never had a hunting license in his life."

Chapter Nineteen

Lilah's heart pounded hard at Mina's revelation. "You think he built the garage for other purposes?"

"I see no other reason than to store something," Mina agreed. "It could be innocent, but I'm starting to think it's not."

"Me, too," Luca agreed.

"Especially since we can't find evidence that any of those artifacts in your files ever made it to a museum."

"What is the working theory then, Mina?" Lucas asked, rubbing his hands on his thighs before he tapped out a rhythm in threes. He felt exposed sitting in such an isolated location and wanted to get out of there. Haven stuck his snout around the side of the seat to bop his arm. It was a reminder to breathe, so he inhaled to three and held it, counting to three while he waited for Mina to answer.

"I think we all know the answer to that question," Mina said.

"That Burris has somehow managed to funnel all these artifacts to a garage in Minnesota?" Lilah asked.

"With or without help from someone else," Mina agreed. "The how—I can't answer that. The why, well, the simple answer is money."

"Did you get into the chat room?" Lilah asked out of curiosity.

"No, you were right about it locking me out. I clicked around on the file, but it went nowhere."

"Let me give you the highlights," Lilah said. "I think they're planning an auction for Christmas Day and wanted the trunk complete to encourage a bidding war."

"We can't let that happen," Mina vehemently said. "If that's the case, we have three days to stop it."

"Are they onto us?" Luca asked, his gaze tracking the area around the van with caution.

"No, they're onto the fact that someone else was in the chat room. I assume they were notified. The dark web is tricky, as Lilah knows."

"That's why I took the screenshots," she said. "I was relatively sure that's what was going to happen."

"You told me it was a fifty-fifty chance," Luca said, turning to face her.

"I didn't want to freak you out," Lilah admitted to Mina's laughter.

"We still have no proof that Burris is behind this, though," Lilah said. "It's just a gut feeling on our part."

"I always go with the gut," Mina said. "It's rarely wrong."

"I'm feeling exposed out here without backup," Lucas said. "I don't want to approach this place alone."

"That's why the main team is getting ready to leave. They'll meet you at the Rochester airport at 0800 hours."

"We'll be in Rochester in an hour," Luca said, eyeing the clock that read 5:00 a.m.

"Head to the airport and wait for the rest of the team. Since the chat room won't let me in, I can't dig into who the two people are conversing on it. I'd bet my firstborn that one of them is Burris."

Luca's laughter filled the van. "Roman wouldn't be happy with you betting his little girl, but I agree."

"Me, too," Lilah said, a lead weight settling into her gut. "That would explain the tracker in the medal. If he'd been led to believe I was a witness, he'd be nervous since we worked so closely together on what I thought was preserving these artifacts. Instead, he was looting them to sell illegally and killing anyone who knew about it. I guess, in a way, that does make me culpable."

"No," Luca and Mina said together. "You were following orders," Mina said. "You had no way to know that the artifacts weren't going where you sent them. Someone was cutting them off at the pass. I aim to find that person, but so many years have passed that it may be impossible."

"I need to get back on the road," Lucas said, his nerves frayed. "We'll meet the team at 0800 hours unless we hear otherwise. If you need anything, you know how to reach us."

"Ten-four. Whiskey out."

Luca glanced at her. "With any luck, we'll find something useful at the property."

"And then what?" Lilah asked. "If we find proof of something, and I report it, they're going to accuse me of the crime since I have no proof that I didn't know the artifacts weren't being shipped properly."

"You've been on the run for six years!" Luca ground out. "Why else would you run?"

"On the run can mean a lot of things. They could say I was running from the law, not for my life."

"I think the scars covering your body would say otherwise, Lilah."

She sat nodding, trying to figure out what was bothering her. "Burris isn't The Mask, though. I know for sure he's not the guy coming after me."

"That doesn't mean he isn't involved," Luca responded, flipping on the headlights and putting the van back into Drive. "The Mask could be another hired thug."

"True, but it felt far too personal for any old thug. It's like the man behind the mask has a personal vendetta against me."

"Like he couldn't kill you yet, but he needed to keep you off-kilter and afraid."

"That," she said without thought. "It makes me wonder if that's why he came at me at regular intervals. He never wanted me to get comfortable with the idea that he was gone for good or that I wasn't being watched. Regardless, I could still get trapped in this, Luca. I could go to prison for all of this."

"That's where you're wrong. The information on that flash drive proves that you didn't know what was happening. It shows a straight chain of command. The items went to central shipping when they left your hands. Your major signed off on that. There was no way for you to know they didn't get to their next destination. Your responsibility ended when Burris signed off."

"When Burris signed off," she said slowly. "Burris had to sign off, which means he could have easily changed or deleted all of my shipping labels. He could have shipped them elsewhere or moved them out of the countries in other ways. That might be our proof that Burris is behind this. Regardless, I'm scared this will blow up in my face and I'll be left holding the bag. Worse yet, it blows back on you and Secure One."

"Let's take this one step at a time, okay?" he asked, reaching out to take her hand and squeeze it.

"What happens if we don't find anything at Burris's property?"

"I guess we wait for Mina to find us another lead."

"No," she said, her head shaking as she thought about the future. "I'm done running. If we don't find anything at the property, I'll confront Burris—alone."

"You are absolutely not doing that," Lucas said between clenched teeth. "Selina tried that and nearly died at the hands of the person after her. On the off chance Burris is The Mask, I refuse to let you take that risk. Backed into a corner, he might stop cutting and start killing."

Lilah bit her tongue to keep from arguing with him. He was wrong, but he was also right. She was stuck between a rock and a hard place that might only be solved by her sticking her neck out. Luca may not understand that, but as the final puzzle piece snapped into place, she did. Burris wasn't The Mask. With a sinking heart, she realized who it was.

"CAL IS NOT going to be happy about this," Lucas whispered for the third time, but Lilah wasn't listening. "We were supposed to wait for them."

"We are waiting," she answered. "He didn't say we couldn't approach Burris's other property."

"I'm rather sure he meant in general, Lilah," he said between clenched teeth. He'd been trying to get her to listen to him for the last hour, but she wasn't budging. She was keeping something from him, and he didn't know what it was, but ever since they left that rest stop, she'd been withdrawn and somber.

"Hold up a minute," he said, pulling her and Haven into a grove of trees near Burris's property line. The houses were spaced far apart, with at least an acre of land surrounded by woods that made for natural fencing. They would have to do it methodically if they approached the Burris home. The last thing he wanted was for someone to call the cops. "What is going on with you? Since Mina called about Burris's other property, you've been uncommunicative, combative and bossy."

She stood before him with stubbornness written across her features in a way that said she wanted to tell him the truth but was determined not to in order to protect him. Lucas wasn't having it. He wrapped his arms around her and pulled him into her, kissing her forehead before he leaned down near her ear. "I'm already involved in this, Lilah. I'm already involved with you. We can't deny that, but I can protect you. Just tell me what you're thinking. Have you even thought this through?" He paused and put his lips on hers, but sensing her hesitation and fear, he pulled back. "You haven't, but you know it needs to end, so you're willing to sacrifice yourself to protect me."

"You're right, I am!" she exclaimed, tapping him in the chest. "I need to stop dragging other people into this nightmare and stand ready to defend myself and my country. That's the oath I took in the army and the one I hold myself to today. You don't have to like that choice, but you do have to respect it." A tear tracked down her cheek, and he pulled off her glasses, wiping the tears with his thumb. "No more innocents can lose their lives because of me, Luca. Enough people have already died due to greed and corruption. It's on me to stop this now. I understand if you want no part of it. Take Haven, get in the van and go home. You can't save me now. I'll pay the piper, whatever the cost, so no one else has to. That's the only right and fair thing to do."

A tendril of anger worked its way from his gut into his throat. Anger for the men who started this mess and at her for thinking she had to go this alone. "For the longest time, I was mad at you, Delilah Hartman, but never as mad as I am now. I'm standing alongside you, ready to defend you or go down trying, but you want to play the hero and do it all yourself!"

"That's not what I'm doing! I'm giving you a damn out before things get real, Luca. This isn't your war to fight. It's mine. I won't ask you to walk back into battle for me again."

He grasped her face in his hands and brought her lips to his, drinking from her like a man who hadn't had water in days. When the kiss ended, he held her gaze, the sky lightening enough for him to see the look in her eyes that said he had to go all in if he wanted her to listen. "You're not asking me. I'm volunteering. I would walk into any battle with you, Delilah Hartman. I'd rather die by your side than live without you again. Do you understand what I'm saying?" Her nod was enough for him. "You haven't been able to trust anyone for a long time, and I understand that, but you could always trust me, right?"

"Always," she said, her words breathy on the cold morning air.

"Then trust me this time, the most important time

of your life, Lilah. Let us help you end this war. No one fights alone. You have special ops cops and a sharp-shooter headed here to fight with you. They wouldn't do that if they didn't think the fight was worth it. You can trust them for the simple reason that I trust them."

The silent morning stretched between them as smoky tendrils rose from the trees, warmed by the rising sun. Haven leaned into him, checking his handler for shaki-ness that wasn't there. Lucas was firm in his declaration to this woman, and he would wait however long it took for her to accept it and make the right decision.

"I'm terrified, Luca. Terrified that I'll die and terri-fied that you will. I don't know what the right answer is anymore."

He rubbed his thumb across her forehead and smiled. "I know you don't. That's understandable. You want this to be over, but you see no other way than to walk in guns blazing. Trust me when I say Secure One has your back."

When her shoulders deflated a hair, Lucas knew she'd made her decision. His heart nearly broke in two when she nodded, biting her lip to keep it from trembling. "Let's go meet the rest of the team and make a better plan. I'm not in the mood to die today."

The truth spoken, he leaned in and kissed her, gently this time, pouring all of his soothing care into her. No one needed it more than her after all these years alone. When the kiss ended, she smiled at him, her gloved hand patting his face. "Thank you for being my voice of rea-son in a world where nothing makes sense."

"I'll continue to be until this is over," he promised as they returned to the van. He secured Haven while she climbed in, then joined her and started the van. He cranked the heat up to warm them after being out in the cold.

"Secure one, Charlie." Cal's voice filled the van, and Lucas hit the answer button on the dashboard.

"Secure two, Lima."

"Why in the hell is my van outside George Burris's home? I will not have another team member go rogue on me!"

"It's my fault, sir," Lilah said without hesitation. "I thought I had to fight this battle alone, but Luca convinced me otherwise. Don't be upset with him."

"I was never going to let her go in there, boss."

"I didn't think you would, son."

"You don't sound like you're in the air yet," Lilah said, her head tipped as she listened to the background noise.

"We're not. Plans changed. I decided filing a flight plan might tip someone off to your presence there. Besides, bringing mobile command is easier when we don't know what we're up against. Roman, what's our ETA?"

"We'll hit Rochester proper in an hour and thirty-seven minutes. I need you to scout a location for us to circle the wagons and then send us the coordinates."

"We're headed in the direction of the airport now. You'll have the coordinates in forty-five minutes or less."

"Counting on you, brother," Cal said. "Charlie, out."

The line went dead as Lucas sucked in a breath of surprise.

"Are you okay?" Lilah asked. At the same time, Haven rose from sleep and put his head on his handler's shoulder.

"Wow," Lucas said with a shake of his head as he

pressed a fist to his chest. "That was the first time he called me brother instead of kid. I wasn't expecting it."

"I'm confused?"

Lucas reached back to stroke Haven's head while he processed the moment. Once he had, he turned to her with a smile. "The guys always called me son or kid, but it didn't bother me. I'm the youngest and the newest on the crew, so I accepted it as being under their wing and learning the ropes."

"Now you're equals."

He tipped his head in agreement as he put the van into Drive and let off the brake. "And I'm not going to let them, or you, down now."

"You won't let me down, Luca," she promised, squeezing his shoulder. "We're a team, but you're the leader. How do I help?"

"Watch our six," he answered, pulling onto the road again just as dawn finished breaking. "Let me know if we pick up company. I need to concentrate on finding a place to meet the team. One way or the other, this war ends today."

There was no greater feeling in the world than knowing he had found a brotherhood again, and that was what Cal had given him with one simple word. It was time to prove to the team that he'd earned it. Glancing at the woman beside him, with all her attention focused on the side mirror, made him wonder if they could be a team when this mission ended. The part of him who remembered their summer together said yes, but the other part of him, the part that needed Haven to live his life, reminded him that she deserved better than the life he could give her. He'd do well to remember that.

Chapter Twenty

The truth of the situation settled low in Delilah's belly when she lowered the binoculars. "There's not much for cover anywhere."

Cal grunted his agreement. "The forest on the western edge will help, but you still have to cross three acres to reach the garage from the woods, while the other three sides would remain unprotected."

When Luca found an abandoned gas station to use as a meeting place, they parked the van behind it and got busy gearing up while they waited for the rest of the team. Their first step was to check out the property, which they'd been doing for three hours, and there'd been no movement in or around it other than four-legged visitors. Unfortunately, their options were limited with their approach to the garage, something she suspected Burris had planned for.

"Anyone else wonder why he built a garage smack-dab in the middle of a field without easy accessibility?" Luca asked, lowering his binoculars, too.

"It crossed my mind," Cal agreed. "I'm starting to think we're barking up the wrong tree. If they're hiding priceless artifacts in that garage, there's no way to move them in and out without being seen. There's no power out here, so there can't be cameras or a security system unless it's solar powered."

"You could move them under the cover of darkness," Luca said, glancing up at the darkening sky as another snow shower approached. "Still not ideal for vehicle access or moving about unnoticed, though."

"Or it's the perfect situation," Lilah said slowly, bringing the binoculars back to her face. "All you need is a shotgun, boots and a camo jacket with an ATV parked outside the door. Not a soul pays attention to a hunter on their own land. Not in this part of the country."

"She's got a point," Roman agreed, setting his notebook down. "For right or wrong, we have to make a decision."

"We're going in," Delilah said without hesitation. "There's no choice. If we're correct, the auction will be in three days. We can't allow it to happen. If we can rule this place out, we know our next target is confronting Burris at home."

"Agreed," Luca said. She smiled, happy to have him on her side. "Chances are, it won't take long to clear the place, but if we're lucky, we find something that tells us where to go next. Cal, Roman, Lilah and I will go through the woods on the west side. Cal and Roman will hold coverage there while Lilah and I approach the building."

"What about the other three sides of the building?" Cal asked, a brow raised.

"Mack keeps mobile command secure and the communications running while Eric runs the drone overhead," Luca said. "Selina," he said, turning to the woman who had kept them all alive for years. "You and Efren take our van behind the property and find a place for him to set up his gun. You may have to trespass, but again, we have few options."

"We'll go through the forest on the west side and find a tree stand. Burris may not hunt, but I assure you, others do, so there's bound to be a few stands out there. That will give me a view from above that will cover the entire perimeter of the garage," Efren said, having thought it out already.

"Excellent," Lucas said with a thankful nod. "We'll give you a head start. If you see anything, alert Cal and Roman. It's not ideal, but again, we have few options in this situation."

"Agreed," Cal said with finality.

Selina and Efren were already getting their gear on. "We're heading out now. Give us twenty minutes of scout time, but we'll be on coms," Selina said, fitting one in her ear. "We'll let you know if we encounter anything that will change the current plan."

"Ten-four," Cal said as they exited the mobile command station and disappeared. He addressed Lucas again. "All of that said, you'll have to hold your own out there if someone approaches. We're easily—" he put the binoculars to his face and swung them back and forth between the woods and the garage "—five minutes out, and that's if we're not dodging bullets."

"Understood," Luca said. "I say we move soon. The snow will give us cover."

With everyone's jobs defined, they prepared their gear for the trip, including lights for Delilah's pistol and Luca's long gun. She didn't want to carry a rifle, fearing it would slow her down. Lucas was taller, stronger and better suited for carrying a gun that size through knee-deep snow. Besides, the garage was small, which made her think this was all a lesson in futility, but when it came to her life, she could leave no stone unturned.

"Ready?" she asked, checking that her pistol was easily accessible.

"I'm in the lead," Luca said, taking her hand and pulling her to the door where Haven waited. "I'll plow through the snow, and you follow in my footprints with Haven."

"We're on your rudder," Cal said as he and Roman lined up behind them.

With a nod, they exited mobile command and found their way into the woods. The walk would be long, but it was the only way to keep their vehicles away from Burris's land on the off chance it was being monitored, or he showed up.

Lucas moved quicker than expected, and she found it challenging to keep up with him, especially trying to keep clear of Haven. She bent over to catch her breath when they reached the forest's edge.

"I'm short, Luca," she said, puffing air from her lips. "Give me a second to catch up."

Luca hung back and waited for Cal and Roman to approach them. Once they were together, she stood, and Cal motioned to his right. "There's a thicker grouping of trees that will give us good cover about a hundred yards down. Give us a few to get set up before you head toward the garage. Tango and Sierra, are you in place?" He was addressing Efren and Selina now, as they'd been quiet throughout the walk.

"Ten-four," Efren whispered. "Just made it into a tree stand. Sierra is on the spotting scope. So far, it's still clear. Proceed with usual caution."

Cal nodded at them before he and Roman broke off and headed away. Luca clicked off their microphones before resting his forehead on hers. As the snow melted on her glasses, he shimmered before her like an angel come to save her. "No heroics, got it?"

"I don't see any reason why they'll be needed, but I'll say the same to you," she whispered. "I also want to say thank you. Thank you for stepping up and helping me when you didn't have to."

"Thank you for reminding me that I can do hard things."

She smiled then, her heart cracking open as he used her words in a way that held so much honesty and truth. "Let's do one more hard thing and find justice for our fallen soldiers. Right?"

"Right, but first..." He removed his glove and pulled a cloth from his pocket before gently removing her glasses. Carefully, he wiped them down with the cloth and slid them back on her face. "There's the pair of eyes I see in my dreams," he said with a wink before he stowed the cloth.

Her heart nearly melted into a pool of mush on the forest floor, knowing he had brought the cloth to keep her vision clear. Even with Cal's special coating applied to them, he knew the snow would be a problem for her. He still cared about her, which gave her hope that they could remain friends when this was over.

Once Luca was ready again, he grabbed her hand and pulled her to the edge of the trees. "On my lead." She nodded, and he took off, Haven tight by his side this time.

The closer she got to the building, the more fear and dread built in her belly. A garage in the middle of a field felt like hiding in plain sight, and she worried whatever they were hiding was going to get her killed.

Once they were through the open space, they stood tight to the side of the building and took a moment to catch their breath. Their earlier assessment had been correct. There were no cameras under the eave of the garage. There may not be power out here, but you could buy solar-powered camera units, so that was another red flag as far as she was concerned.

"I'm telling you, Lucas. Burris isn't dumb. There's no way he'd put anything here without cameras or more security. This is a futile endeavor."

"Maybe, but there may be something else in there that will help us sort this out. Old paperwork or equipment that we can jack the black box on," he answered. "Mina is still running down Burris's finances and doing another property search."

"I wish she could have gotten into that chat room," Lilah whispered. "If we knew who *Iamthatguy* and *Bigmanoncampus* are, then we'd know if we're on the right track." A little voice said she did know who they were. She just didn't want to admit it to herself.

"Unfortunately, that's lost to us for good, so all we can do is the legwork. Eventually, something will break. Keep your light off until we're inside and I've secured the door."

"Got it," she said, flipping her microphone back on as she crouched low and worked their way down the side of the garage.

Delilah stood behind Lucas while he inspected the side door, pulling his lock-picking kit from his vest. He glanced at her and checked the knob, a look of shock crossing his face when the door swung open. Haven was at his side as he swung his gun around the opening before stepping inside. Delilah followed from the rear and pushed the door closed.

"Door secure," she whispered, knowing the team could hear them, too. "Why wasn't it locked?" Before Lucas could answer, Haven growled low in his throat in a way she had never heard before. "What's wrong with him?"

"I don't know," Luca answered. "Haven, rest."

The dog didn't follow his handler's orders. Instead, he bolted to the right behind a pile of boxes.

"Haven. Return," Lucas hissed as he flicked on the gun's flashlight. She did the same with hers, illuminating a simple one-car garage filled with boxes.

"Do you smell the copper, too?" she asked, moving closer to where Haven had disappeared.

"Haven, return!" Luca said again as they walked around the boxes, but he stopped short. Lilah bumped into him before she could stop herself. "That explains the smell."

"What?" Cal asked through their earpiece. "Give me an update."

"Dead body," Lilah said, strangely detached. "Haven found him behind a pile of boxes."

"Him?"

"Definitely male," Luca said. "I haven't rolled him yet."

"There's no need," Lilah said, knowing who it was. "It's George Burris," she whispered, motioning at his left knee for Luca to see. "He had that knee brace made after he was hurt on a mission. He had to wear it all the time."

"Repeat. You've found Major George Burris dead?" Cal asked through their earpiece.

"Affirmative," Lilah said with her lips in a thin line.

"Looks like a round to the chest from the exit wound I can see on his back, as well as a round to his temple," Lucas reported.

"Where is his weapon?" Efren asked.

"Sidearm on his belt," Lilah answered.

"Rifle resting on a box five feet away," Lucas added. "Not staged as a suicide."

"He knew his attacker then and didn't feel threatened," Efren responded.

"You need to get out of there," Cal said. "I'm not ready to deal with the murder of an army major."

"We haven't had a chance to look around. Give us five?" Lilah asked.

"Negative. Get out while the snow is falling to cover your tracks. I do not want to deal with the police and the army."

"Not the army," Lilah said, motioning to Lucas to spread out and search. "He's been discharged, so he's a civilian now."

"All the same," Cal said, and she could picture him rolling his eyes. "We need to move out."

"No one wants to know why someone shot a former army major in his garage?" Efren asked, making Lilah snort internally. "Can you tell how long he's been down?"

"Not long. Maybe twelve hours," Lucas said. "Doubtful anyone would be worried yet."

Lilah was walking around the garage, which was big enough for a car or a boat but not much else. "These boxes are empty," she said, pushing on one until it fell to the ground. "There's nothing in this garage."

"Except for a dead army major and you two. Get out.

Now," Cal repeated, and they looked at each other, their brows raised.

"Ten-four," Luca said, shaking his head at Lilah and clicking his mic off. She did the same while he walked over to her. "We have two minutes. Go."

Lilah walked behind the boxes she dumped, shining her flashlight around the floor and the walls, looking for anything that shouldn't be there or didn't belong there, but the garage was filled with empty boxes and nothing else. Haven had his nose on the ground as he sniffed through the garage. His ears pointed to the ceiling as he went, and his concentration was undeterred by Luca's commands.

"Why didn't they pour a concrete pad for this building?" Lucas asked, bouncing on the floor a bit. "Plywood is going to rot in these conditions."

"It feels temporary to me," Lilah said, motioning at the walls that were nothing more than studs and particle board. "Like they had no intention of using it very long."

Haven growled again, the sound raising the hair on the back of her neck. "Luca, we need to get out of here. Haven is a mess."

Luca walked to his dog and crouched low. "Haven is a retired war dog, but he's acting like an active one now. He's reacting to the major's death."

Lilah walked up behind him, her boots thudding across the cheap plywood. It was her final step that made her pause. "Did you hear that?" She stepped back on her right foot just as there was a metallic snap. The floor bounced, and they jumped back, their eyes locking when the floor no longer sat flush.

"Trapdoor?" she mouthed to Luca, who nodded. He

motioned her to flip her mic back on as Cal demanded to know where they were.

"Secure one, Lima," he said, letting them know they were now in a situation that required rapt attention. "On our way out, Lilah tripped a trapdoor. Give us three to investigate it."

"Negative," Cal instructed. "Get out of there now. There's already one dead body in there. I don't want three."

"There's no one here, boss. I suspect whatever is below us is empty, but this is why we're here. It could be the answer we're looking for right below our feet."

They both heard Cal's heavy sigh on the other end of the mic. "Fine. Charlie and Romeo will approach."

"Affirmative," Luca said, flipping the mic off while motioning for Lilah to stand back. She stepped out of the way and grabbed the handle on Haven's vest to hold him back. She nodded, and he lifted the door, sweeping his gun across the opening. "Empty," he said, motioning for her to look down the hole. "Notice the stairs?"

"Well made." There were even handrails on each side of the staircase going down. "I was expecting a rung ladder."

"Me, too, but this tells a different story."

"A story of someone with a bad knee using them frequently?"

Luca nodded with his foot on the first step. "Haven, return." As soon as Lilah released the dog, he followed Lucas. They went down the stairs back-to-back so he could sweep the space on the way down as she kept her sidearm pointed at the top. It was possible Burris's killer might show up before Cal and Roman.

"These steps are better made than the floor above

them." He swung his flashlight around, assessing the situation. "Old shipping container," he said. "They must have buried it and built the garage above it."

Their feet hit the container floor and Lilah swung her flashlight along the wall, illuminating shelves that ran the entire length on both sides, all filled with relics of a different time and place.

"I believe it's time to call in the cavalry," she whispered, her heart sinking at the thought. Once again, her problem would become his and Secure One's by default, but it was too late to back out. All she could do was go forward and pray that of the two left who knew about these artifacts, she was the last one standing.

NONE OF THIS made sense. Lucas walked along the side of the wall in shock and horror to see so many treasures from other countries. "Someone has done all the provenance on these," Lilah said, pointing to documentation next to each treasure. "They're ready for an auction."

"That probably explains why Burris is upstairs dead," Lucas said, his gaze trained on two bronze chalices on a shelf. "Whoever he's working with double-crossed him." He stared at the cups on the shelf, willing his memory to recall where he'd seen them.

"Mack, we need to contact the local police, military police, homeland security and JAG. We must establish a chain of command and custody for these relics, not to mention, deal with the murder victim," he heard Lilah say. Still, his mind was off in a different time and place.

"Porter, let no one through these doors until we return."

"Yes, Colonel Swenson." He held the door for the

colonel and two other men that Swenson had simply introduced as "men of faith." Lucas could only assume they were local church leaders or priests who had information for the government, but that was above his pay grade. His job was to make sure the colonel didn't die on this social visit.

He climbed inside the Humvee and sat at the gun turret. He wasn't happy when he'd been assigned to take the colonel out alone, but Swenson had insisted they weren't in combat territory and the locals were their allies. Lucas didn't believe for a hot second that anyone in this hellhole of a country was their ally. He'd seen far too many of them blow up his friends. He trusted no one except his K-9, Hercules, who stood at attention by the door, his head swinging right and left as he scanned for enemies and listened for vehicles approaching.

As a munitions officer, it wasn't Lucas's job to be out using the ammunition. It was his job to make sure they had enough. He wasn't given a choice today when Colonel Swenson needed backup immediately and no one else was available.

"In and out, right, Hercules?" he asked the dog while they waited in the hot desert sun. Sweat dripped down his spine, running a shiver through him. Something was off. He swung the gun around, expecting an ambush, but finding nothing in any direction. "Come on," he hummed, glancing at the building door and praying it would open. His sixth sense was telling him to get out of there now. He pressed the button on his walkie-talkie. "Porter to Colonel Swenson. ETA?"

"Coming now," was the answer.

Lucas hopped down from the gun and opened the pas-

senger side door of the Humvee. He commanded Hercules to stand next to him. Swenson was the first to emerge, and then the two men, one carrying a large white bag.

Lucas didn't get a word out to the colonel before a barrage of bullets struck the stucco wall behind them. Lucas swung his gun around and sprayed the area, unsure where the enemy was. "Get in!" he yelled to the colonel, standing over the two men sprawled on the ground. "Get in, now!"

Swenson grabbed the white bag and jumped in the open passenger door. Hercules followed him in while Lucas sent another burst of gunfire and then slid into the driver's side. He threw it into gear and took off, sand and gravel flying from under the tires.

"I thought the locals were our allies!" Lucas yelled, angry that, once again, they'd been lied to. "Who were those guys?"

"Men of faith," Swenson said again. "They're the only two dead, which should tell you something."

"Why would anyone want men of faith dead?"

"I can't answer that, Porter. Just get us back to base in one piece."

"Yes, sir," Lucas answered between clenched teeth. He pretended not to notice the bag by the colonel's feet that had fallen open and revealed a bronze chalice...

"Luca?" He turned his head as reality filtered back in. Haven had his nose pressed hard into his thigh, so he took a minute to breathe in threes, noting his heart rate slowing as he stroked Haven's head. "Thanks, buddy. I'm fine."

"You look like you saw a ghost," Lilah said, still swinging her flashlight around the space. There were dark corners he didn't like. He was praying Cal arrived soon with backup.

"I may have," he said, motioning at the chalices. "I've seen these before."

"What? Where?"

"I'd been on the base about two weeks when Colonel Swenson wanted transport with two other men to a building in a small village. Everyone else was busy, so he demanded I take him."

"Alone?"

He nodded. "I told him it wasn't a good idea, but he wasn't budging."

"Which meant you couldn't ignore a direct order."

"Not without spending time in the brig. Four of us went out, but two came back, along with these chalices. Do you remember putting these through for shipping?"

Lilah shook her head, her lips in a thin line. "I recognize only about half of these items, Luca. I'm starting to think those dead women were doing the same thing for him as I was, but on different bases."

"Only they weren't going to museums. My logical mind had Burris building a personal collection, but with him upstairs dead, I'm starting to think he was the grunt man for someone much higher up."

"That memory you had is the answer."

"Colonel Swenson?"

Before she could nod, clapping started from the darkness. Lucas swung around, bringing his gun to his shoulder as a man stepped into the beam of his flashlight. Lucas felt his world tip when the man before him was indeed Colonel Swenson. "Aren't you smart?" he asked as Lilah's flashlight illuminated the item they'd been searching for all this time. Behind Swenson was the trunk—half a tablet present in the top.

"Colonel Swenson?"

"That's Major General to you, Porter," he spat. "And you," he said, addressing Lilah. "You have been a trial. I have to say, I'm glad this is over." He kept his gun at his shoulder but stretched his back. "Thank goodness you finally arrived. Do you know how uncomfortable the floor is in a storage container?"

"You knew we were coming?"

"The alert that someone accessed the chat room told me it was time to take care of some final business. I always knew you had the file, but as long as you didn't click on it, I could keep you alive. Now, I'm afraid that's no longer possible. Especially since you know of my involvement in this. Since I couldn't track you—you finally caught on to the medal. Good job," he said with a sarcastic smirk. "I hedged my bets that you'd end up looking for Burris once you decided he had the answers. Sad, but you know what they say, dead men don't speak."

"Just tell me why," Lilah said, stepping closer to Lucas as Swenson advanced on them. "Tell me why I was tracked and harassed for so long."

"You were a real pain in my back quarter, Hartman. You were tracked because you had all the information in your head about these little baubles," he said, swinging his arm out at the wall. "Not to mention, you saw The Lost Key of Honor file. I had to keep you quiet until the auction."

Lilah whistled, and a shiver ran down Lucas's spine.

"It's a shame that I saved all the information about these—what did you call them?—baubles to a flash drive before the base fell," Lilah said, doing exactly that. "It's already in the hands of the authorities. It would have been smarter to kill me, but you didn't. You took great pleasure in slicing me up, but why play the game with me when you killed the other four women?"

Lucas tried not to react to the information that Swenson was The Mask. He wondered if Delilah knew who was behind it before they even set foot in this basement and never told him. Haven leaned in hard against his leg, a steady low growl coming from his throat as he glared at the man before him.

Swenson raked Lilah lasciviously. "I have to say, I always wondered what my creations looked like once they healed. Your chin," he said, motioning at her face. "Not bad work there. I do hope your gut healed well."

"You son of a—"

Lilah cut Lucas off. "You didn't answer my question. Why didn't you just kill me like you did the other women?"

"We were still looking for one more artifact. On the off chance I needed to have a little chat with you about something you may have seen or heard, you had to be breathing."

"The Lost Key of Honor," Lilah said as Swenson smiled like an animated horror puppet.

"Such a powerful name, right?" he asked, almost giddy as he advanced on them. "I'm sure you can understand why it was important to keep you out of the picture until I could ascertain the piece and finish the auction."

"And did you?" Lucas asked. "Ascertain the piece, that is."

Swenson's smile dissipated, and he shook his head.

"Unfortunately, no, but the auction will still happen. I have too many people looking for these trinkets, and I can't disappoint them on Christmas morning. I still have a few days to decide what to do with the trunk. Our time together is over, though. I do wish I had my knife and an unlimited amount of time to turn you into beautiful artwork, but I don't, so a bullet to the head for each of you will have to do."

There was commotion overhead, and then Cal yelled, "Secure One, drop your weapon!"

Cal and Roman came barreling down the stairs, and Haven pounced at Swenson. A gunshot rang out, and Lucas stumbled backward into Cal, who lowered him to the ground. Lilah fired three times in quick succession.

"Haven!" Lucas screamed, afraid the dog was in the line of fire. "Haven! Return!"

The small space quickly became chaotic as it filled with team members yelling different things simultaneously. Lucas sat there, detached from the room and his body as he breathed in to three, held it for three and let it out to three.

"Luca!" Lilah said, dropping the gun and running to him. "Call an ambulance!" she yelled as Lucas watched Cal handcuff a raving Swenson. Lilah's bullets had found a home in his shoulder, arm and knee. None of them were life-threatening, but satisfying nonetheless to inflict a little pain on someone who had tortured her for years.

"You're going to be okay," she said, but the expression on her face said something else entirely. She stripped off her jacket and held it to his chest, pushing so hard it made him grunt with pain. "I know. I'm sorry to hurt you, but I need to keep pressure on this wound."

"Wound?" he asked, his voice holding disbelief.

"Swenson shot you," she explained. "If Haven hadn't pounced on his arm at the last second, the bullet would be in your head. You'd be dead."

"That rhymes," he said, laughing once before he started to cough, the taste of blood in his mouth.

"Don't talk, just conserve your energy," she ordered, so close he could kiss her.

"Don't leave me, Delilah Porter," he whispered, his words stuttering as he spoke. "I will follow you anywhere."

She brushed the hair back off his forehead and kissed him. "All the days since I left you, I've wished my name was Delilah Porter," she whispered. "I'm not going anywhere. Everything I've done for the last six years has been for you. To protect you. To keep you safe, but in the end, I couldn't do that. You can't die on me now, do you understand? You have to hang on. Hang on, Luca."

It wasn't lost on him that he had this woman back in his life because death came calling and he'd answered the phone. He'd been given the gift of a little more time, something others often weren't fortunate enough to get, and he hadn't wasted a moment of it. Lucas had brought closure to a situation he never thought he would, and for that, he was grateful. If death took him this time, he would accept that his work here was done. Then she pressed her lips to his, and he knew he'd die a very happy man.

Chapter Twenty-One

The old adage that no good deed goes unpunished had settled deep in Delilah's bones as soon as the military and homeland security arrived at the shipping container. The man she loved was hauled away by ambulance while she was forced into custody as a party to real war crimes. While she'd been treated well and was comfortable, she'd spent the last two days under lock and key while they tried to sort out who knew what in this bizarre case of unabashed greed.

Thankfully, she could use the flash drive and screenshots of the chat room to her advantage. It turned out that *Iamthatguy* was Burris and *Bigmanoncampus* was Swenson. She should have thought of that sooner, but honestly, she didn't have officers of the US Army stealing antiquities to sell on the black market on her bingo card. That was what they had planned to do, though.

The way Swenson told it, they started with good intentions, wanting to help the locals, but they quickly realized what the relics were worth on the black market and how easy it was to make them disappear. Sadly, the one thing she wasn't expecting was to learn that the base was attacked because of Swenson's and Burris's actions.

They had systematically gone out and killed every person who had turned in relics to the base. It was easy to make it look like they died in the war, but if there was no one left who knew where the relics went, there was no one to thwart their plan. No one but her, that is. The locals didn't believe that revenge was best served cold. They believed in immediate revenge in the most brutal of ways. A shudder went through her at the memory.

"Are you cold? I can turn the heat up," Mina said.

"No, I'm fine," she answered, staring out the window at the white fields stretching as far as the eye could see. "I was just thinking about what Swenson told the police. Evil on a level I never want to see again, Mina. How could I be so wrong about them? How did I not see the evil?"

"The true psychopaths in our midst never reveal themselves, Delilah. We've seen it so many times. Look at my situation with the FBI. No one would have seen that coming."

"True," she whispered, staring at her hands as they drove silently for a few miles. "The army offered me veteran benefits."

Mina lifted a brow as she steered the van around a curve. "Disability benefits?"

"Yep, as well as the Secretary of the Army Award for Valor along with the Purple Heart, neither of which I want."

"The Purple Heart is for those wounded in battle during active duty."

"True, but PTSD and a traumatic brain injury may not be visible but still qualify. Also, these are quite visible," she said, motioning at her chin. "The stabbings weren't while I was on active duty, but from what I understand, it came down from rather high up on the chain of command. The other four women will also be receiving them posthumously. I want to refuse them both."

"Unfortunately, that's not how it works, Delilah," Mina said with a chuckle. "When you're the pivotal person to help return priceless artwork and antiques to their respective home countries and paid heavily because of it, you get medals."

"And a whole lot of memories I'd rather not have."

"Now, that's a true story." She nodded. "Cal told us they offered you a job."

"Ha! Yeah, like I'm going to go back to work for the government. Hard pass."

Mina's lips tipped up. "Can't say that I blame you there. You've been through enough."

"How bad was it for Cal, Mina?"

"Secure One came out just fine, so don't worry. Don't forget that Cal is an army veteran. He was looking out for another, and we had plenty of paperwork to prove it. We were out of there within a day. I wish the same had been true for you."

"Me, too. I want to see Luca. How is he? I talked to him yesterday and he said he was feeling fine, but he hasn't responded to my text from this morning."

"He's only alive because Haven pounced on Swenson. He was using armor-piercing rounds in that gun. Lucas would be dead."

"I'm not sure a bullet to the chest is much better, but I'm glad that he's healing." She sighed, and it was heavily weighted with sadness. "When we talk now, it's awkward because I don't know what to say to the man who saved my life. I can't face him knowing he took two bullets for me in the span of a week."

Mina's laughter filled the van as she turned right and guided them down a narrow road. "Sweetheart, that man would take all the bullets for you. You'll know the right things to say when you see him again. Just trust your heart."

Sure, trust your heart, she says. That's hard to do when you aren't sure if it'll get stomped on. Would Luca stomp on her heart intentionally? No, but she was afraid of the unintentional consequences of this event, especially since she had no one else in her life but him and the team at Secure One.

When Delilah glanced out the car window, she was surprised. "Why are we at a cemetery? You said I had to talk to the Rochester Police about the incident."

"You do, but someone else will be taking you there. I'm officially off duty."

She barely heard a word Mina said as she stared through the windshield, the sun making it hard to see anything, but she did notice a man standing in front of a grave with a dog at his side. "Luca?"

"Go to him. You need each other right now."

"But, Mina, what do I say?" Her question was desperate as she turned to the woman she had come to count on as a friend and confidant.

"The truth." Mina reached into the back of the van and grabbed Delilah's winter coat, which she shrugged on, along with a hat, scarf and gloves.

Was she prolonging the inevitable? Maybe, but knowing it was time to face the man she had loved for six long years made her pause and search her heart for the words she'd need when she faced him again. She slung her purse around her shoulder and let out a sigh.

"Thanks for the ride and the advice, Mina. Merry Christmas," she said, throwing her arms around her friend. "Be careful on the drive home."

"Roman is waiting at the police station. I'll pick him up and head home while you ride with Lucas and Haven."

With a nod, Delilah pushed the van door open and climbed out, her eyes glued to the man just a few feet in front of her, his back turned as he stared at a gravestone.

"Hey, there, Lilah," he said, his back still to her.

"Luca," she said, but blinked twice when she realized he was wearing his dress uniform, his polished black shoes reflecting the sunlight as she glanced down at the grave marker. It read Tamara Porter. "Your mom's grave?"

"I thought since I was down here, I'd let her see me in my dress uniform on Christmas morning. Better late than never, right?"

Her heart wanted to burst at the implications of this moment. "Luca, I'm stunned."

"You shouldn't be. You were right, Lilah. I gave that bag way too much power, and it was time I stopped. It's time to change the way I think about what I did in the service, and that's already helped with my anxiety. You reminded me to stop feeling guilty about who I lost by remembering who I saved. It's still a work in progress, but now I wake up with less burden from the past and more hope for the future."

"I'm happy for you, Luca," she said, leaning into him. "Are you okay? I need to know that you aren't in pain."

He took her hand and brought it to his chest, pushing it against his skin. He didn't flinch. "No pain. It was a through and through, so a few stitches and a few weeks means it will be nothing more than a scar. We all have them, right?"

"Some of us more than others." That was when she saw it. "Luca," she whispered, glancing up at him. "Your medals." She ran her hand across the row of medals now attached to his uniform.

He shrugged but avoided her gaze. "If there was one thing my mother was proud of me for, it was my service. I wore them for her this morning."

"She was a proud army mom," she agreed with a smile. "Nice touch. I know wherever she is over the rainbow, she's never been prouder."

"One down then," he said, finally turning to her and taking her hands.

"One down then?" she asked, confusion filling her voice. "I don't understand."

"Being here in this uniform is a reminder that one woman I love is proud of me. Now I need to know if the other woman I love is proud of me, too."

"Me?" Delilah asked, and he nodded, smiling as she nearly melted into the snow with relief.

"I've loved you since the moment I picked you up off that tarmac, Delilah Hartman. I told myself that day I was going to marry you. I intend to keep that promise or die trying."

"You've nearly died trying enough times, Lucas Porter!" she exclaimed, watching a smile grow on his face. "You don't need to keep trying. I love you, Luca, and I'm overwhelmingly proud of what you've overcome to be standing in this uniform today. I sent you to that clinic alone six years ago because I loved you. I walked away from you that day and stayed away for the same reason. I would do anything to protect and keep you safe, even if it meant we could never be together."

"That's over now, my darling Delilah," he promised, lowering his head for a kiss that warmed her head to toe even on this cold Christmas morning. When he lifted his head, his eyes glowed with happiness in a way she had never seen. "I want to explore us," he said, holding her tightly. "I don't know how that will work since we live such different lives, but I know one thing. I'll follow you anywhere. I know you got a job offer from the army. If you want to take it, say the word. I'll be right behind you—"

Delilah put her finger to his lips. "Secure one, Delta."

Her smile grew when his brows went up. "What now?"

"Turns out, another job offer awaited me in the civilian sector. Cal offered me a position as a cybersecurity tech to work with Mina, building Secure Watch, the new division for Secure One. I accepted this morning. I want to be with you, Luca, through the good times and the bad. I know that sometimes our memories paint outside the lines of the present, but we'll face those together, too. How do you feel about that?" Her question held a tinge of nervousness as she waited for his answer.

"I think there's only one thing left to say, Delilah Hartman."

"Then say it, Lucas Porter."

"Secure two, Lima."

Then his lips were back on hers as they stood in the bright sunshine of a day that, for the first time in years, offered her true joy, hope and peace. They shared the first kiss of the rest of their lives, ready to focus on a future they could build together from a place of love, understanding and acceptance of their past that led them to this place in time. His tender kiss was a layer of comfort over the jagged scars in her soul, assuring her that he'd heal them completely with enough time.

"Happy?" he asked, lifting his lips from hers.

"Better than happy," she whispered.

"What's better than happy?"

"Being healed."

A smile lifted his lips as they neared hers again. "I couldn't agree more. Merry Christmas, my darling Delilah," he said, pulling her steamed-up glasses from her face.

"Merry Christmas, Luca," she whispered before they shared another kiss to the sound of Haven's joyful barking.

* * * * *

INTRIGUE

Seek thrills. Solve crimes. Justice served.

Available Next Month

Child In Jeopardy Delores Fossen
Mountain Captive Cindi Myers

....

Cold Case Discovery Nicole Helm
Shadowing Her Stalker Maggie Wells

....

Special Forces K-9 Julie Miller
Fugitive Harbour Cassie Miles

Subscribe and fall in love with a Mills & Boon series today!

You'll be among the first to read stories delivered to your door monthly and enjoy great savings.

WE SIMPLY LOVE ROMANCE